Beyond Summer Dreams

OTHER BOOKS AND BOOKS ON CASSETTE
BY JENNIE HANSEN:

All I Hold Dear

Chance Encounter

Coming Home

Journey Home

Macady

The River Path

Run Away Home

Some Sweet Day

When Tomorrow Comes

Beyond Summer Dreams

a novel

JENNIE HANSEN

Covenant Communications, Inc.

Covenant®

Cover photo © 2001 PhotoDisc, Inc.

Cover design copyrighted 2001 by Covenant Communications, Inc.

Published by Covenant Communications, Inc.
American Fork, Utah

Printed in the United States of America
First Printing: September 2001

08 07 06 05 04 03 02 01   10 9 8 7 6 5 4 3 2 1

ISBN 1-57734-889-3

Library of Congress Cataloging-in-Publication Data

Hansen, Jennie, 1943-
    Beyond Summer Dreams: a novel / Jennie Hansen.
      p. cm.
    ISBN 1-57734-889-3
    1. Young Women—Fiction. 2. Grandmothers—Fiction. 3.Veterinarians—Fiction. 4. Fathers and daughters—Fiction. 5. Idaho—Fiction.
    I. Title
PS3558.A51293B4 2001
813'.54--dc21   2001-037267
                                      CIP

Love and thanks go to
MarJean and Darrell, Ron and
ZoAnn, and again to Boyd.

CHAPTER 1

Taylor pressed the doorbell again, fearing the worst. What if Grandma Lilly had fallen or somehow injured herself? Maybe she'd run off and married old Mr. Darnell. No, of course not. That was just a silly threat, made to annoy Daddy.

With a sigh, Taylor set down her suitcase and turned to the path that led through a gate to the backyard. Following stepping-stones around the side of the house, she opened the gate and froze as a voice reached her ears.

"Cut that out!" The voice was familiar and followed by a girlish giggle. A loud guffaw in a voice several pitches lower rang through the summer air, and Taylor raised her eyes to the mammoth shade tree that grew between the garden and the spot where Grandpa had once cut and stacked firewood. A ladder stood under a sturdy bough, its top disappearing into the green cloud above.

"Hold still! I don't intend to chase you all over this whole blamed tree," the male voice spoke in a controlled whisper as though its owner was running out of patience. Once again a feminine giggle ensued from somewhere behind the leafy screen.

Taylor gasped. The woman in that tree was her grandmother! And from the sound of things, the dear old lady had slipped past senile to just plain crazy. Perhaps Daddy was right. Grandma really did need someone to look after her and keep her from doing something foolish, like climbing trees or carrying on with some old man she claimed she was thinking about marrying. Taylor dashed toward the tree, where she grasped the side of the ladder and gazed upward into the thick foliage. Far above her head, two slender, denim-clad legs ending in Reebok walking shoes dangled from a thick branch. Next a second pair of blue-jeaned legs, this time with western boots attached, popped into view mere inches from the walking shoes.

"Easy, girl. Come on now," the man's voice coaxed. "Come to Papa, or I promise you'll be real sorry."

"Now, Tom, you stay right where you are," Grandma's voice admonished, still with a hint of laughter.

Taylor's eyes grew rounder. What was going on in that tree?

"Grandma, I'm coming," Taylor shouted as she scrambled up the splintered rungs, ignoring the way the ancient wooden ladder wobbled as she climbed. A sudden silvery streak shot past her face. She jerked back, causing the ladder to tilt. She scrabbled for a hold on a nearby limb, and a second object whizzed past, striking her shoulder. Struggling to retain her balance, Taylor grasped the tree tightly with both arms and felt the ladder pitch to the side. With her arms wrapped around the tree limb, she could feel her feet lose their perch as the ladder crashed to the ground. Dazed, she clung to the tree and stared down in horror at the grass more than six feet beneath her dangling toes.

"Taylor, is that you?" Grandma's face poked through a thick cluster of leaves. "I didn't expect you until later this afternoon."

"Uh, I got . . . an early start," her voice came in short gasps as she struggled to maintain her precarious hold. "Are you all right?" she thought to ask.

"Well, of course, I'm all right. Why shouldn't I be? You're the one who fell off the ladder. You didn't hurt yourself, did you?" The older woman was all solicitous concern.

"No, I'm fine," she assured her grandmother then muttered under her breath, "But I'll probably break my neck when I let go of this branch, then I'll break Grandma's 'friend's' neck."

"Do you see Tom anywhere?" her grandmother called. "He's so naughty."

"T-Tom? Isn't he still up there with you?" Taylor called back.

"Oh, no. There's just Stewart and me up here now." As the older woman spoke, a second head appeared through the leafy canopy. This one was thin and male with decidedly gray hair and an exasperated air about him. Grandma went on, "When you shouted, Rambo flew away and Tom jumped after her. Look around and see if you can see them. If Tom catches Rambo, Clay is going to be really upset with me."

"He couldn't possibly be as upset as Daddy will be when he finds out both his mother and his daughter managed to get themselves stranded in a tree," Taylor muttered under her breath.

Looking down, Taylor saw nothing but the collapsed ladder and lots of green grass directly beneath her. The thick branches obscured her view of anything else. Unfortunately, the grass was farther away than she would have liked, and looking down made her slightly dizzy. She'd read somewhere that a person shouldn't look down when caught in a position anything like hers. Anyway, there was nothing to see; there certainly wasn't anyone who might be Tom. And whoever this Clay person might be, he wasn't around either, she thought.

Her arms were aching, and she suspected she wouldn't be able to hold on much longer. The rough bark of the tree was chafing her skin and snagging the sleeves of her jacket. She dreaded finding out how much damage her new suit had sustained.

She shouldn't have dressed up for the drive here, but she'd been so disappointed when Daddy had insisted he needed her more than Donovan Enterprises in San Francisco needed an assistant manager of acquisitions. Taylor had been hopeful that the position would develop into an exciting career, but her father wanted her to spend the summer with his mother. Taylor loved her grandmother and wanted to help her, but it was disappointing to postpone her own plans—again. She didn't know whether or not Donovan Enterprises would still be interested in her after this summer. She was afraid she'd have to start all over again, submitting her resumé and worrying about interviews.

It seemed that every time she made plans to travel or begin a life of her own, some family emergency arose. She'd woven dreams for years around moving to a large city and beginning an exciting career in the business world. Two years ago, after receiving her bachelor's degree, she'd almost accepted a position with a bank in Salt Lake City, but Daddy's secretary had taken an extended leave of absence to travel with her husband, and Andrew Jordan had needed his daughter to help in his office. He'd convinced her that she could fill in for his secretary and pursue an MBA at the same time, and she'd finally agreed.

Taylor lifted her chin at a firm angle. Her work experience, combined with her degrees, could only assist her in her career goals. She had her degree now, and nothing was going to stop her. This was just a little detour.

She'd endured four hours at the mall, carefully shopping for a few success-oriented clothes, and hadn't been able to resist showing off a little bit for her grandmother whom she hadn't seen much of while going to college and graduate school.

"Oh, well," she sighed with a mournful glance at her new suit; she'd better kick off her shoes and pray she wouldn't break an ankle when she dropped to the ground. If she didn't get the ladder back up and help the two elderly people, one or both of them might fall and be seriously injured.

With the toe of one shoe, she worked the other shoe free and gave a kick, sending her shoe flying. Ignoring the sound of tearing fabric as she twisted about, she began working on the other shoe. She had no intention of dropping six feet to the ground with high heels on; neither did she want to land on her shoes when she hit the ground. Dodging the ladder would be challenge enough. She let the second shoe fly.

"What the . . . ? Of all the stupid . . . !" An angry male voice exploded in half-finished sentences from somewhere nearby. Startled Taylor glanced down just as two large hands settled around her ankles, and she found herself staring down into two light brown eyes dotted with flecks of gold. Thick black lashes surrounded eyes set in a face that was all sharp angles and planes. She had a quick impression of dark wavy hair before her eyes settled on a mouth drawn tight in a straight, angry line. The mouth moved, but no words registered in her stunned mind. He was the most gorgeous man she'd ever seen, and for a moment she forgot to breathe. But then the words he was shouting slowly began to penetrate.

"Anyone with a lick of sense should know better than to throw a dangerous object without looking first!" Taylor winced at the volume of his explosion, then noticed the trickle of blood on his cheek and one of her shoes at his feet. She must have kicked her shoe right in his face just as he ducked beneath the tree's sagging branches. The realization brought a pang of guilty remorse. She hadn't even looked down after her first search for the elusive Tom. She was about to apologize when she heard him continue in a muttered tone she was apparently not meant to hear.

"Of course if you had a lick of sense you wouldn't be climbing a ladder in spike heels in the first place." The derogatory accusation canceled her intended apology, leaving her grappling for some means of defending herself. She latched onto the first thought that entered her mind.

"They're not spike heels!" she shouted back, her own temper beginning to mount as she wondered why she'd picked the most inane portion of his accusation to defend. If he'd been watching where he was going, he wouldn't have walked into her flying shoe! Still, Taylor admitted, he probably hadn't seen her dangling from the tree branch as he'd approached the tree, and by the time he had, it was too late.

"If you'd said something to alert me to your presence, I wouldn't have kicked off my shoes," she told him a little too sweetly in her struggle to hang on to her temper. If he'd let go of her ankles, she'd probably kick him. Spike heels indeed! Her shoes, designed for a busy career woman, were sensible and professional.

"Women!" he muttered in a voice she suspected wasn't meant to carry to her ears, then in a louder voice, he said, "Come on. I haven't got all day."

"Let go of me!" she shouted back and tried to wiggle clear of his grasp.

"Hold still!" he ordered. "I'll be happy to release you as soon as you let go of that tree you're trying to strangle."

"If I let go, I'll fall. But I suppose that's what you're hoping!" She knew her words were childish even as they left her mouth, but something about him left her feeling defensive, and she chose not to excuse his dictatorial attitude just because she'd hit him in the face with one of her shoes. He shouldn't have been standing so close without warning her of his presence!

"Look, lady, you're not going to fall. I don't have all day to hang around here rescuing some silly woman from her own folly. Either let go, or I'll walk away, and you can wait for the fire department to get you out of that blasted tree!"

It was tempting to let him walk away, but a downward glance reminded her that it was a pretty long drop to the ground. It could be hours before anyone else noticed her plight and called the fire department. In the meantime poor Grandma might fall from her perch several limbs higher up the tree. With that thought, she let go.

For a second time, a bright streak flashed before her eyes. The obnoxious stranger's hands flew from her ankles to her waist, and both of them fell to the ground. Taylor was aware of two things happening almost simultaneously; just as she slammed her face against a hard chest, a streak of fur leaped over their tangled forms. Abruptly the hands at her waist lifted her and set her away with a resounding thud on the grass. Her breath whooshed out of her body, her posterior smarted, and tears stung her eyes.

When she caught her breath, she scrambled to her feet and bit her tongue to keep from venting her fury over the stranger's cavalier treatment of her. She still had to rescue her grandmother, and that was her first priority. Lifting her eyes to the tree, she realized the feet were no longer dangling from the high branch where she'd seen them earlier. Quickly scanning the area where she'd fallen, she saw no one, but a short distance away she discovered the exasperating man standing with his feet wide apart and his hands on his hips, staring up into the tree. Glaring was more like it!

If that man helped Grandma Lilly the way he'd helped her, the poor old lady's bones would shatter. Taylor took a step forward and reached for the fallen ladder.

"I'm coming, Grandma," she called.

"No, you don't!" the man snarled, and Taylor promptly dropped the end of the ladder she'd started to raise on his foot.

"Ow!" the man yelped but didn't change his stance.

The big baby! The ladder barely grazed him!

"Get down here. Now!" He didn't exactly shout, but there was no doubt he expected instant obedience. How dare he? That was no way to talk to her grandmother. Grandma Lilly couldn't possibly get down without the ladder, and though climbing a tree was certainly a foolish thing for a woman her age to do, it still wasn't right to shout at her. And Taylor would tell him so!

Settling her fists against her hips, she marched toward the man. She'd give him a piece of her mind and send him on his way. She'd take care of rescuing Grandma herself.

"Don't talk to—" she started to inform him. Once more a streak flashed before her eyes, and she forgot what she was going to say as a brilliantly white cockatoo landed on the man's shoulder. The bird preened its feathers for a few seconds, showing off the bright salmon-hued underside of its wings, then cocking its head to one side, seemed to examine the man's disapproving face. It bent its neck a little further and pecked him on the cheek like a spoiled child delivering a conciliatory kiss to distract an indulgent parent from some form of intended punishment.

"Taylor!" Grandma Lilly called. Confused, Taylor glanced up into the tree, then at the woman emerging from behind the wide tree trunk. A tall, thin man who looked to be about Grandma's age, dressed in boots, jeans, and a chambray shirt with pearl buttons followed her, holding a huge yellow cat. The cat's tail switched back and forth as its round yellow eyes zeroed in on the bird perched on the stranger's shoulder.

The next thing Taylor knew she was being smothered in one of Grandma's enthusiastic hugs. "It's so good to see you." Lilly beamed at her granddaughter. "It seems like forever since the last time Andrew let you come for the whole summer." Taylor stifled a protest that she was an adult and didn't need her father's permission to spend the summer with her grandmother, but since she really was here at her father's instigation, her protest wouldn't be entirely honest.

"Taylor, dear, why ever did you climb that rickety ladder?" her grandmother asked, stepping back to take a good look at her granddaughter, just as she had always done at the beginning of each summer, when a younger Taylor had come to spend her summer vacations with her grandparents.

"I was going to . . . to help you down." Taylor felt as though her head was spinning. How had her grandmother come down from the tree so quickly and in one piece?

"To help me? But I wouldn't set foot on that ladder without a strong man to hold it for me." She glanced appreciatively first toward the old man beside her, then at the stranger. "It's only out here because the elders quorum president used it to check my roof, and he must have forgot to put it back in the garage. We used the tree house steps on the other side of the tree."

Taylor grimaced. The steps! How stupid! She'd forgotten all about the tree house stairs. Of course, she had been only eight years old the one time she'd gotten up the courage to visit the tree house. She'd had to sneak behind her father's back to climb to the hidden platform, but of course, Daddy had found her there and been extremely angry; he'd forbidden her to climb the narrow steps ever again. They were too dangerous, he'd said, and warned her that if she fell, she might die. She didn't want to be dead like her mother, so she'd heeded her father's warning.

Grandpa had scoffed at Daddy's concern, telling him there was no harm in a child playing in the tree house and reminded her father that he'd played there as a child himself. But even after Grandpa added a rail to the stairs, Daddy had still forbidden her to climb up there, and she had never disobeyed. In all the excitement of discovering her elderly grandmother in the tree, Taylor had forgotten the steps even existed.

"Grandma, you shouldn't be climbing trees!" Taylor protested, even though her grandmother's climb had certainly been a lot safer than her own.

"Well, I don't usually," Grandma Lilly explained. "But when Rambo escaped her cage and Tom took off after her, I had to stop him from catching that silly bird." *That explains who Tom is,* Taylor thought, eyeing the large cat still confined in the arms of Grandma's friend.

"But you might have been hurt!" Taylor continued to protest her grandmother's action.

"Nonsense, dear. I wasn't in any danger," Lilly dismissed Taylor's concern. "Now let me introduce you to these two gentlemen. This—" she linked her arm with the older man's, "—is Stewart Darnell. I don't know whether or not you remember him from when you used to spend summers here." Taylor shook her head.

"The good-looking young man who saved you is Clay Curtis," her grandmother went on. Something in her voice alerted Taylor that Grandma Lilly was up to something. It occurred to Taylor to wonder why the older woman, who had been in a perfect position from above to see the whole thing, hadn't said a word while Clay had "rescued" her. Beaming as she made the introductions, as if they automatically made everyone friends, Lilly continued in an innocent voice, "Clay and Blaine Gardner were missionary companions a few years ago, and he's the new vet here in Fairfield."

"Nice to meet you," she acknowledged the introductions as graciously as she could manage. She didn't remember the older man at all, but she did vaguely remember Blaine Gardner, a boy in Grandma's ward who was a few years older than herself. Grandma obviously liked both men, and Taylor had been taught to be forgiving and gracious. Guiltily she acknowledged to herself she really hadn't behaved well—although neither had he. She attempted a smile.

"Always a pleasure to meet a beautiful lady." Stewart's eyes twinkled. His arm slipped around Grandma's shoulders, and he gave her a gentle hug as he continued, "You look just like your grandma."

Taylor groaned inwardly. The old man was obviously trying to butter up her grandmother, or he thought he was paying Taylor a compliment. The only resemblance between grandmother and granddaughter was their green eyes. Lilly's white hair had once been as dark, curly, and unmanageable as Taylor's, but those were the only similarities. Besides, what twenty-three-year-old woman wants to be compared to her seventy-eight-year-old grandmother?

She caught a quick nod from Clay Curtis in acknowledgment of her grandmother's introduction. He didn't appear any more enthused about making her acquaintance than she was about making his. His smile was as fake as her own, she decided. She tried to think of something polite to say, but before she could think of anything, he thrust the cockatoo into Grandma Lilly's hands, saying, "Keep her in her cage, and it wouldn't hurt to keep Tom locked up, too. I'm on my way back out to the Wilsons', and it will probably be late when I finish." He strode around the corner of the house and was gone.

"I don't know how she got out," Grandma Lilly mused, apparently talking about the bird she held as she addressed Taylor. "I'm sure the cage was latched. I checked it just before I came out to pick a few flowers for your room."

"The catch on that door is kind of flimsy. Rambo probably figured out how to open it, or Tom might have bumped it," Stewart offered a couple of theories.

Taylor was only half listening to them as she watched long strides carry the veterinarian across the lawn until he disappeared around the side of the house. She was tempted to follow the man and tell him what he could do with his orders, but a more reasonable part of her mind told her the man wasn't really rude so much as busy. She glanced toward her grandmother, who didn't appear the least upset by the man's abruptness. Having always been a little leery of animals, Taylor eyed the large parrot-like bird suspiciously. Daddy considered animals dirty and dangerous, and her early attempts to befriend puppies and kittens had proved him right. The bird stared back at her, and it definitely didn't look friendly.

Rambo. It figured. Clay Curtis was obviously the kind of man who would name his unruly pet Rambo, even if the trouble-making bird was a female. The cockatoo continued to glare back, making it clear she wasn't too impressed with Taylor either.

Taylor sighed. She wasn't really such a judgmental person. Deep inside, she knew she wasn't as upset with Clay Curtis as she was embarrassed to have met him under such unfortunate circumstances. Circumstances that had come about because of her own failure to think the situation through properly. Her father didn't consider her capable of managing her own life, and during her first hour in Fairfield, it seemed she'd proved him right. If this was an example of how she handled problems, how was she ever going to carry out Daddy's instructions to persuade her grandmother to give up her house and move to the new senior complex being built a few blocks from her father's house?

"Come, dear," Grandma urged as she began walking toward the house. For a moment Taylor wasn't certain whether Grandma meant her, Stewart Darnell, or the bird. In any case, she followed her grandmother to the back door of the house, stopping with one foot across the threshold of the enclosed back porch her family had always called a sunroom.

It had certainly changed since her last visit to her grandmother's house! A huge desk piled with clutter dominated one end of the space. Several large boxes sporting the names of top-of-the-line computer equipment companies sat on the floor under a stack of magazines. File cabinets with half-open drawers and more papers piled on top than in them stood in a row behind the desk. A telephone with a series of blinking red lights sat on the desk beside a spindle, stacked with messages, and a Rolodex. An open telephone directory occupied the office chair, and a small refrigerator hummed away in one corner. It was the most awful excuse for an office Taylor had ever seen.

She slowly turned in the opposite direction, and her eyes rested on a huge birdcage into which her grandmother was depositing Rambo. The beautiful cut-glass water and feed dishes, sparkling like crystal, contrasted sharply with the sturdy prison-like metal bars that formed the cage. A row of smaller wire cages lined the wall across from the windows. Some of the cages looked empty, but others held various small creatures ranging from a brown rabbit to two small guinea pigs.

As Taylor looked around in stunned silence, Mr. Darnell walked over to the kitchen door, which connected the sunroom to the rest of the house. Thrusting the big tomcat into the house and closing the door, he walked over to the cage to examine the latch. After a moment's careful thought, he rummaged on top of the desk until he found a large paper clip, which he straightened and used to wire the small door closed.

"Grandma, what is going on? What is all this?" Taylor had never known her grandmother to collect clutter or pets. She needed to get to the bottom of this and quickly. Obviously her father didn't know anything about this, and it would fall to her to let him know.

"It's temporary, dear, just until Clay gets his office built," her grandmother answered airily as though there was nothing at all to be explained.

"That contractor he hired is as slow as a January thaw," Stewart Darnell added. "Young Curtis is probably paying him by the hour."

"You mean that man is using your house for a veterinary clinic?" Taylor nearly choked. This would never do. She'd call her father, and he'd put a stop to it. In fact, he would probably even decide not to wait until fall to move his mother. Grandma Lilly wouldn't be happy about leaving her house, but Daddy was right. It would be for her own good. That thought eased Taylor's conscience a little. She'd been feeling guilty ever since agreeing to Daddy's plan, since her own motivation had more to do with distracting her father's attention from her plans than with concern for her grandmother's well-being.

"Oh, no. Not a clinic," her grandmother hastened to assure her. "Clay's just using the sunroom for his office until his clinic is finished. He has a few pens for horses and a kennel for the dogs he boards, but no office space or a place to keep small animals. It was my suggestion that he use the sunroom until his clinic is ready."

"But why your sunroom? Couldn't he rent space closer to his clinic?"

Mr. Darnell answered for her grandmother. "This is as close as it gets. The boy bought the Meyer place next door. He's got big plans for fixing it up."

She remembered the acreage beyond Grandma's side gate. Her father had called it an eyesore as long as she could remember, but she'd loved the large empty field with a creek near one end. She used to play there among the trees and splash in the shallow water. Daddy hadn't approved of her playing there, but Grandma had insisted that Andrew and his sister, Linda, had both been just fine playing there when they were children, and Taylor would be, too. A quick glance through the sunporch window revealed what looked like a foundation with the bare beginnings of framing and a long, low cinder-block kennel. The trees obscured the hill where she remembered picnics with her dolls. A sense of having lost something special saddened her. Some of the happiest times of her childhood had been spent playing in that field, and now it belonged to someone else!

Shaking off childhood memories, Taylor glanced back and forth between the two elderly people. She couldn't believe it! Neither one seemed the least upset by the prospect of a veterinary clinic moving next door. She wrinkled her nose, imagining the smells and noise. Her grandmother's smaller lot wouldn't be the same without the adjoining open space. Fortunately her grandmother wouldn't still be living here when Clay Curtis got his clinic finished.

CHAPTER 2

Pushing the plunger on the syringe, Clay withdrew the needle from the cow's thick hide and tossed it into a small box he kept for discarded needles. With the back of his forearm, he wiped sweat from his brow and stepped back to allow John Wilson to turn his cow loose. That was the last one. All 420 milch cows had now been inoculated, as were the 70 young heifers the dairy farmer expected would soon begin dropping calves.

"Well, that does it," Wilson removed his cap and slapped it against his leg a couple of times before shoving it back on his head. "Carol has started the afternoon milking, so I better go give her a hand. Those two new guys I hired aren't catching on as quickly as I'd hoped, so she'll be needing my help. Send me a bill, and I'll settle up the first of the month." He turned and with long, ambling strides disappeared in the direction of the milk parlor.

Send him a bill? Clay was already two months behind in his billing, and if the fat letter from the bank he'd noticed sitting on his desk earlier this morning was what he suspected, he was facing cash flow problems now, too. If he didn't get his office straightened out soon, he'd lose his practice, not from a shortage of patients, but because he couldn't find time to handle the business end of it. He hated to ask, but perhaps Lilly Jordan could spare a few hours to help him catch up on his paperwork.

On second thought, she probably wouldn't have any time now that her granddaughter had arrived. He imagined Taylor as he had last seen her—dark curls gleaming in the bright sunlight as they tumbled around her shoulders, green eyes flashing indignantly, and full lips parted as though she were about to give him a piece of her mind. The granddaughter was pretty—no, make that gorgeous—but unfortunately he knew her kind. He'd certainly met his share of beautiful, but basically useless women, none more so than his former fiancée, Jessica Winslow. Lilly would be too busy shopping with her granddaughter and trying to keep her entertained to help with his books. He just hoped Taylor wouldn't run up bills her grandmother couldn't afford to pay. Unlike his mother, Lilly didn't have a fortune to squander. He hoped, too, for Lilly's sake, the girl wasn't planning to stay long.

He was being unfair, he thought, feeling faintly guilty. He didn't even know Taylor Jordan, but their encounter that morning hadn't been encouraging. From her expensive clothes to her snooty attitude, she didn't belong in the remote, small town he'd adopted as his own. He'd concede she hadn't deliberately thrown her shoe at him, but that hadn't made the impact or the gash to his forehead any less painful. Neither was it her fault he was exhausted from working fourteen-hour shifts for the past two weeks to protect cattle on the surrounding ranches from a fast-spreading range disease that was particularly threatening this spring.

All right, he thought. As long as he was being honest, he'd admit Taylor Jordan was too attractive for his peace of mind. Not even Jessica had left him feeling clumsy and unable to form a coherent sentence the way Taylor had. And that scared him. He'd learned the hard way not to trust beautiful women like his former fiancée and her friends. Ever since he'd joined the Church, he'd wanted a home and family of his own someday and to marry in the temple. Experience had taught him that Jessica and women like her were more interested in money and glamour than in the man behind the image the New York City society pages had painted Clay to be. As the great-grandson of one of the country's fabled financiers and possessing a face that didn't come even close to cracking mirrors, he'd become cynical about the reasons beautiful, glamorous women sought him out. They had their sights on his mother's fortune or they wanted bragging rights to the kind of immoral adventures he was determined to avoid.

He stooped to pick up the box of used syringes and the other supplies he'd spread out where they'd be handy and carried them to his truck. His legs and shoulders were cramped and tired, making him wish he could head straight home to a hot shower. Unfortunately, he had two more stops before he could call it a day.

He'd been running nonstop since four this morning. The few minutes between appointments he'd hoped to spend eating lunch had instead involved a chase after Jessica's spoiled cockatoo. Their engagement was off, so Clay couldn't quite figure out how he'd become saddled with Rambo. Surely one of her friends back in New York could have kept Rambo, or even one of her cousins. Despite their recent differences, Jessica and her three cousins had been raised together and should want to help each other. Jacob was busy running their grandfather's empire, but Ben and Seth didn't have a whole lot to do.

Clay's next stop didn't take long. He'd delivered a foal at the Friedrickson ranch the day before and had promised to stop by to check on the mare and her baby today. Everett Friedrickson met him at the barn door with a handshake before leading the way inside the barn. As Clay stroked the foal's silky coat, he heard a sound behind him and turned to see two blond, blue-eyed little girls streaking toward their father. A woman followed. She too was blond with a smattering of freckles on her turned-up nose and a hint of laughter in her sparkling eyes. For a moment the freckles on Taylor's nose and cheekbones came to mind. Quickly brushing aside the memory, he watched Peggy Friedrickson and the girls greet Everett before turning to say hello to him. Their obvious closeness as a family sent a stab of longing through him for a wife and family of his own.

His mother was still living, but his family had never been close. His parents had always seemed to be at odds with each other, but he hadn't realized what he was missing until he'd joined the Church in his teens. He'd become acquainted with the families of some of his friends, then served a mission where he'd seen up close the love and commitment many families shared, and his own lacked. As he'd become involved in the elders quorum of this rural farming community, he'd been impressed by the partnerships he saw between couples like his friend Blaine Gardner and his wife, Andrea, and the Friedricksons. Unfortunately, in this rural Idaho town, women like Peggy Friedrickson and Andrea Gardner were already married.

"Did everything go all right at the doctor's?" Everett asked his wife as he bent to give her a quick kiss.

"Yes, Dr. Tarrington said Cindy's doing so well he expects she'll be able to drop down to monthly checkups by the end of the summer." Clay smiled, enjoying the good news, too. The Friedricksons' five-year-old daughter, Cindy, had had heart surgery right after he'd moved here six months ago, and he'd quickly come to respect the family for their unfaltering faith through the ordeal they'd faced.

Turning to Cindy, Clay asked, "What are you going to name this baby?"

"Daddy said her name is Melisandra's Dream, but it's okay if we call her Sandee." The five-year-old's words were enunciated with solemn care. He noted that her blond hair was pulled back as though Peggy had tried to plait the fragile, thin hair. Pale strands wisped around her face, unlike the thick braids of her younger sister, Gina.

"Okay, Sandee, you and your mommy look just fine to me." He patted both animals before reaching for his bag and preparing to leave their enclosure. He closed the stall and was surprised when a little hand slipped into his.

"Thank you for taking care of Miss Molly and her baby," Cindy's four-year-old sister, Gina, lisped in the same careful way her sister had spoken.

"My pleasure." He grinned at the small girl whose mouth curved in an impish smile. Something melted in his heart, and he found himself wishing he had a little girl just like this one to go home to every night.

Since the mare's delivery had been a difficult one, he gave Everett instructions on what he should watch for in case an infection should develop, said his good-byes, then climbed in his truck once more to head toward the Carlson place, the last scheduled stop for the day— barring any emergencies.

The sun was going down and the shadows were long when he turned onto the dusty lane leading to the Carlson farm. Absently he noted that the white board fences on either side of the lane needed a coat of paint, as did the barn. The hay was past ready to cut, but there was no sign of machinery in the fields. The Carlson farm must have once been a prosperous place, but it now looked shabby and run-down.

He pulled to a stop in front of the barn and stepped out of his truck. He stretched to release the kink in his shoulder and looked around A couple of dogs began barking, and a woman's voice yelled at them to be quiet. He looked toward the house in time to see Wendy Carlson, in bright red shorts and a white tank top two sizes too small, step onto the porch and begin a calculated saunter down the steps. A white, long-haired kitten, wearing a huge purple bow around its neck, perched on her shoulder. He swallowed a groan. He was much too tired to deal with Wendy Carlson.

Wendy wasn't a bad kid, and she certainly didn't lack anything in the looks department, but she was everything he'd left New York to avoid. She could be Jessica's twin if she had been twenty-six rather than eighteen. He knew the elaborate moussed curls cascading from a top knot on Wendy's head had taken hours to style, and the vivid purple polish on her fingernails and the toes he could see peeking through her open sandals accounted for another chunk of the young woman's day. One look at her face made him want to drop her in the nearest horse trough. A girl with her looks certainly didn't need the paint she'd doubtless spent at least an hour applying.

"If Wendy wants to paint so much, Paul ought to start her on the fence or the barn," he muttered under his breath.

"Hi!" she breathed in what Clay knew was meant to be a seductive whisper. He wished she'd find someone her own age to practice on or go away to school like all her classmates had done the moment they'd graduated from high school. He felt a moment's twinge of guilt for his lack of sympathy for the girl. He, too, had found being single in a small, remote town difficult. He hadn't had a date since he'd arrived in Fairfield six months ago. At first that was because he'd been engaged, but Jessica had given him back his ring and broken their engagement when she found she couldn't persuade him to give up his plans to set up his veterinary practice in rural Idaho. Since then he hadn't met anyone he cared to date.

"Hello, Wendy," Clay responded to the girl's greeting. "Is your father in the barn?"

"No . . ." She batted her eyes. "There's no one here but you and me."

Uh oh. He took an involuntary step backward. The last thing he wanted was to be alone with Wendy Carlson.

"There was a message on my answering machine to stop by . . ." He let his voice trail off.

"Oh, that was me," she said. "I was just calling to let you know I can start tomorrow."

"Start?" He seemed to have lost the thread of conversation.

"Your ad in the paper." She set the kitten on top of a fence post and moved closer until her shoulder brushed his chest. Her long purple nails lightly skimmed up his arms. The dogs came running to sit adoringly at her feet.

He glanced down at her and frowned. His ad for an office manager had been in the paper so long he'd almost forgotten about it. He'd certainly given up hope of finding anyone in Fairfield willing and qualified to keep his accounts and appointments straight.

"Can you type?" Why was he even asking? Even if she was the most qualified office manager in the whole state, he didn't want her in his office.

"Of course I can type," she purred as she wrapped her arm through his. "And answer the telephone and do all those other things."

Somehow he doubted her assertion. He'd have to discourage her, but how? He didn't want to hurt her feelings. He knew she was lonely and had only developed a crush on him because all the males her age had gone away to school or were serving missions. Tommy Beredsford liked her, but he was still in high school, and she made no secret of her view that he was too young for her. That left only Palmer Gunder, the only other single male over eighteen and under forty in the valley, besides himself, but Palmer was as wide as he was tall and had no ambition beyond sitting behind the counter at his dad's service station. It was too bad her parents insisted she stay home until she married instead of encouraging her to go to school, but it wasn't any of his concern.

"Wendy, I don't think you'd like working for me," he began, taking a step back. "Sometimes my assistant has to help me in surgery."

"I can do that." He doubted her assertion.

"Some of my patients are pretty dirty, and you might have to help me hold them. Sick animals can be messy."

"Okay." She still sounded confident as she closed the gap between them again. He looked at the kitten, then back at the dogs. He knew she had her own horse as well, so maybe she really did want to work in a veterinary office.

"And be in the office by eight every morning," he added, feeling confident that stipulation would discourage her.

"Oh, I knew you'd say yes!" She stood on her toes and kissed his cheek.

"I didn't say . . ." He didn't finish the sentence but beat a hasty retreat to his truck. The crazy girl looked like she was about to throw her arms around him. That's all he needed—to have her plastered to him about the time Paul and Joyce returned to the farm. Joyce had been finding excuses to throw him and her daughter together ever since he arrived in town, and Paul had advised Clay in a fatherly tone that a man in his profession needed a wife. Paul had gone so far as to remind him that some General Authority had said any young man who reached thirty without marrying wasn't living his religion. And Wendy never missed an opportunity to touch him.

Dust clouds billowed behind the truck as he dodged potholes on his way back to the county highway. Turning on his headlights, he headed toward town. He didn't know whether to be angry or amused. Finally he settled for a kind of discouragement. He needed an office manager, and it seemed he now had one. Even Wendy had to be better than his present situation. He just hoped neither she nor her parents interpreted Wendy's presence in his office as more than a professional relationship. The last thing he wanted was to find himself drifting into a personal relationship with the girl.

A short time ago he'd been looking forward to getting married. In fact he'd imagined himself a husband before finishing school and sharing a cramped married student housing apartment with his bride. He'd thought it would be kind of fun, but Jessica had wanted to wait until he had his degree. She hadn't found the prospect of a tiny apartment or living on a budget the least bit appealing. He'd also discovered belatedly, she was having too much fun playing around to want to settle down too soon.

Was it his fault he hadn't met the right woman yet? His friend Blaine said he was too fussy and apparently agreed with Paul Carlson that he somehow wasn't living his religion to still be single. He smacked one fist against the steering wheel. He wasn't that old. He'd only turned twenty-eight in March, so if thirty was some magical cut-off age, he still had nearly two years. He was getting tired of people pushing him toward marriage or speculating about his reasons for still being single. He'd even read between the lines of a few carefully worded questions and knew some people were wondering whether or not he was even attracted to women. Well, he liked women just fine. Unfortunately he'd fallen for the wrong woman instead of one who fit into his chosen lifestyle. That experience had taught him that no matter how much he wanted to be part of a couple and have a family, he couldn't marry someone who wasn't right for him.

His thoughts continued as he turned onto the highway leading into town. It was too bad Fairfield's selection of single women consisted of Wendy Carlson and Betty Glendowski. Wendy, though pretty, was a mental lightweight and much too young for him, plus they had nothing in common. Tall and muscular, Betty outweighed Clay by at least fifty pounds and pursued him a bit too relentlessly. A picture of Taylor formed in his mind, but he quickly dismissed it. Taylor was only here for a short visit; besides, he'd promised himself he'd never again get involved with another woman like Jessica. As much as he appreciated an attractive woman, he wanted someone whose beauty went beyond face, figure, and sleek packaging.

Jessica hadn't always been obsessed with money, Clay remembered sadly. When she and her cousins were children, Clay had played with them during frequent visits to their grandfather's Long Island estate and at the nearby mansion belonging to his mother's family. Clay and Jessica had become close friends, and money had never been a part of their friendship, but everything had changed after old Mr. Winslow's two sons and their wives had been killed in a private plane accident. Jessica and her three cousins had gone to live with their grandfather, and he had spoiled Jessica outrageously, disciplined Jacob and sent him to Harvard Business School, and ignored Ben and Seth, the two younger brothers. In all ways he had made it clear that Jessica and Jacob were his favorites. Clay had foolishly thought that once he and Jessica were married and away from her grandfather's influence, she'd become the old Jessica again, but after the old man's death, she'd become even more obsessed with the fortune she'd inherited. Eventually Clay had been forced to realize that a marriage between the two of them would never work out.

Clay shook his head in disgust. He didn't know what had gotten into him or why he was spending so much time thinking about Jessica. He was over her. He supposed it was seeing Wendy Carlson, who looked a great deal like a younger Jessica, that had started this train of thought, along with a sense of loneliness he'd experienced lately while driving between remote ranches, but it was time to stop it. It was time to think about the future. That was part of the problem he realized; he *was* thinking about the future. He'd like to start dating again, but his time was so limited and the prospects so unappealing, he felt discouraged.

He turned the wheel sharply and pulled into the space beside his partially completed clinic. Not much had been accomplished that day, he noted. Again. If the contractor hadn't been the only one in town, Clay would have already fired him by now. The young vet didn't have time to agonize over every detail with the man, and yet if he didn't, nothing got done.

After checking the two dogs in the kennel, Clay threw some feed to the horses, then lifted a hoof and examined the mare's fetlock. Satisfied she was doing fine, he locked the gate to the cinder-block enclosure, and stepped back outside. The thought of the paperwork awaiting him brought a slump to his shoulders. He really didn't enjoy that part of his job. With a sigh of resignation, he headed for the gap in the hedge between his clinic and the house next door. He'd take just a minute to check his messages, then take a hot shower, and go to bed. He'd tackle billing and his checkbook in the morning.

* * *

Taylor examined her skirt critically. Grandma had helped her re-stitch the seam that had ripped, and it really wasn't noticeable anymore, but both the skirt and jacket were wrinkled. They needed to be steamed. Slipping the suit onto a hanger, she hung it behind the bathroom door. It would smooth out while she showered.

Humming to herself, she lined the bathtub shelf with shampoo, conditioner, and her favorite shower gel. She looked around for a place for her bath powder and cosmetics, finally deciding to make the small drawer in the vanity her own. Grandma Lilly used the downstairs bathroom, so she wouldn't mind if Taylor used the drawer. When she pulled it out, she found the drawer was surprisingly cluttered, but it didn't take long to transfer its contents to a plastic bag which she tucked under the sink in the small cabinet where her grandmother kept cleaning supplies and extra toilet paper.

She turned back to the tub, adjusted the shower nozzle, draped her robe over the sink, and stepped into the shower. It was pure bliss. She could almost feel the pressure and frustration slipping away. She sighed and leaned against the tile wall. The three-hour drive hadn't been bad—she liked to drive—but the fiasco in her grandmother's backyard had been emotionally and physically exhausting. She'd begun to think Grandma's friend would never leave when he suddenly rose to his feet and announced his departure right after dinner. Grandma had looked surprised but had walked him to the door, and in Taylor's opinion, took a little too long telling him good-bye. An uneasy thought crossed her mind. There had been a decidedly masculine array of toiletries in the drawer she'd cleaned out. Surely they didn't belong to old Mr. Darnell! No, the very thought was absurd.

Taylor gingerly rubbed the spot where she'd fallen, and a picture of her supposed rescuer came to mind. She hoped she'd never have the misfortune of meeting him again, even if he was the best-looking man she'd ever met. She'd be glad when this summer was over, and she could head for San Francisco. There were probably plenty of handsome men there with much better manners. But then, she wasn't going to San Francisco to meet men; it was the career opportunities that fascinated her and drew her there. Corporate finance, organizational techniques, managing the mega-businesses that ran the world—these challenges were the magnet that drew her to a city that was a force to be reckoned with in world commerce. Her banking internship, the time spent managing a major portion of Senator Maxwell's successful campaign, and even her experience working in her father's busy office had only served to whet her appetite for the business world. Glowing recommendations from the senator, the bank president, and several of her professors had garnered her the job offer with Donovan Enterprises, which she had had to turn down. If only Daddy could have spared the time to come to Fairfield himself! He could have explained the move to

Grandma Lilly and helped her pack and dispose of the house and furniture she would no longer need.

Thinking of her father reminded Taylor that she should call him as soon as she finished her shower. She dreaded telling him about Grandma Lilly turning her sunporch over to a veterinarian, and when he heard about the tree incident, he would say that was proof he was right about his mother needing someone to look after her. The prospect of Daddy moving Grandma Lilly to Pocatello sooner than anticipated—thus freeing Taylor to be on her way sooner—should have lifted her spirits, but it didn't. Somehow it made her feel like a traitor. It wasn't really Grandma's fault. It was the veterinarian's!

At last she rinsed the conditioner from her hair and shut off the water before pushing back the curtain and stepping into the steamy room. Quickly she toweled off, then taking a second towel from the rack, she swiped at the mirror, but it did little good. Shrugging, she wrapped one towel turban-style around her wet hair, pulled on her thick pile robe, and buttoned it from neck to ankle before unscrewing a cap and smearing a thick layer of freckle cream on her nose and the tops of her cheeks.

Taking a deep breath, she congratulated herself. Yes, she definitely felt much better, and tomorrow she'd have a long talk with her grandmother and tell her of the darling apartment her father had picked out for her. Then she'd tackle removing the obnoxious veterinarian's pets and junk from the sunporch. She yawned. But that could wait until morning. Right now she could barely keep her eyes open.

Tucking a damp strand of hair beneath her towel turban, she flung the other towel over her shoulder. Tomorrow morning she'd do a load of laundry for her grandmother. Right now, all she wanted was her bed. Opening the bathroom door, she took one step and walked straight into Clayton Harriman Curtis, IV, D.V.M.

CHAPTER 3

"You!" They spoke simultaneously. His hands gripped her shoulders, steadying her, he assured himself, though she glared at him as though he had taken some kind of indecent liberty. He hadn't anticipated seeing Lilly's granddaughter again this soon, but he should have, the way his luck had been running.

"What are you doing here?" she demanded in that superior way she had. He didn't doubt she could outdo Jessica when it came to looking down her nose at the snooty maître d' at the Four Seasons.

"Just headed for the shower." He held up his hands in a surrendering motion and took a step backward.

"Here?" Her voice was filled with incredulity and had him glancing at his shoes to see if he'd stepped in something.

"Of course here," he found himself snapping back.

"Why?" She seemed truly mystified, and for just a moment he felt a grin trying to break free. Something told him she wasn't going to like his answer.

"I live here, that's why." He brushed past her to enter the bathroom, closing the door soundly behind him. Then he did grin. He could imagine her shocked expression, the wide green eyes, a smattering of freckles standing out through the goop she'd smeared on her face, and that absurd towel unraveling to allow a strand of dark hair to slide down one cheek. The grin slipped from his face. He liked the face he imagined and all that went with it a little too much. And he wasn't really too proud of himself for the way he'd baited her.

He'd nearly had a coronary when he'd spotted her dangling from a tree earlier—just before one of her shoes smacked him between the eyes. He'd found her attractive earlier, but even in a bulky robe, with her hair in a towel and her face decorated with some kind of thick white cream, she was still gorgeous.

As he prepared to step into the shower his gloom deepened. Both times he'd seen Taylor, she had been at less than what she would naturally consider her best, but he had no trouble imagining her in designer clothes such as an elegant evening gown, leaning toward her tuxedo-clad dinner partner at the Carlyle. The outfit she'd been wearing earlier hadn't been designed for climbing trees and hadn't withstood the rigors of chasing Rambo any too well, but it obviously hadn't come from a discount store. Just like its owner, it shouted first-class all the way.

So why was he attracted to the kind of woman who looked as though she'd just stepped off the pages of one of those slick women's magazines? he asked himself with a touch of irritation, especially when his head told him repeatedly that the packaging wasn't nearly as important as the contents. He wondered if the old adage was true that men chose their mates based on appearances because the male of the species could see better than he could think.

Slowly he became aware of his surroundings. The bathroom smelled like gardenias and steam hid the mirror. There was something about the thick, seductive scent of gardenias that enticed and hinted. He was beginning to hope Taylor's visit would be really short. He gave the faucet handle a quick twist.

"Yi-i-i," he yelped as a blast of cold water struck him full force. Frantically he scrambled to increase the hot water and shut off the cold. It took only seconds to realize there was no hot water. Taylor had used it all!

If he were a swearing man, this would be the time. As it was, he clenched his teeth together to stop their chattering and doused his head under the frigid spray. His hand fumbled for the shampoo, and as he dumped gardenia shampoo on his head, his temperature rose a notch. He couldn't even scrub out the smell with soap because his deodorant bar was gone, and in its place was some floral-scented gel. Angrily he shut off the water and reached for a towel only to find the towel rack empty.

Lilly had placed two clean towels on that rack every morning since he'd moved in. He suspected she hadn't forgotten today;

someone else had usurped his towels. The memory of one lock of hair straying beneath one of *his* towels increased the steam level in the tiny bathroom. He knew there were more towels in the linen closet, and Lilly wouldn't mind if he helped himself, but with the linen closet outside the bathroom and down the hall, the towels might as well be in China. He certainly wasn't going to open the door and prance halfway down the hall in his birthday suit! His gaze settled on Taylor's blue suit hanging on the back of the bathroom door. He was tempted, but no—

His mood darkened as he reached for the little hand towel beside the sink and found it already damp. The only recourse left was his own robe. He wished it were one of those thick terrycloth numbers instead of the sleek, stylish, near-useless fashion statement his mother had given him last Christmas.

By the time he found his hairbrush, along with all of his other personal toiletries in a bag under the sink, he was ready to have it out with a certain young lady. If she thought she could move in here and push him out, she could think again. He didn't care if she was about the most beautiful woman he'd ever seen; she was just plain trouble.

Jessica was beautiful, too, and she'd taught him an important lesson. She'd put off their wedding, but had kept him dangling until all risk of living with a student's limited time and finances was past. She'd also angled for him to be hired as an executive for a major pet food corporation when she knew—because he had told her plenty of times—that he wanted to work directly with farm and ranch animals. While he'd been naively dreaming of the open spaces of the West, she'd taken an option on an upscale New York City condo.

He'd learned the hard way not to trust a beautiful woman. Between Jessica and his mother, he'd had the best teachers! He'd known since his early teens that his mother had never been faithful to his father, and in that last stormy blowup between Jessica and himself, she had thrown her amorous adventures in his face. He hated the fact that he'd been as gullible as his father had been; both had fallen for women who believed looks and money were all that mattered. But Clay was through letting himself be manipulated by selfish women who thought only of what they wanted and never gave his preferences a moment's consideration.

He thought of how two months before graduation he'd received a letter from an old missionary companion in Idaho with the exciting news that a veterinarian was needed in his hometown and that a two-acre parcel of land on the edge of town was available and perfect for a clinic. Clay had traveled to Fairfield and met with the manager of the small bank there who had helped him arrange financing and close the deal.

He'd called Jessica with his thrilling news—only she hadn't been thrilled. He could choose his open spaces and backward small town, or he could choose the condo, a high-paying job, jet-setting friends, and her. He'd chosen Fairfield. Jessica had flown out at once to try to change his mind. Beautiful and glamorous, she'd kept his heart racing, but she'd despised his plans for living above the clinic until he could arrange to have a house built and ridiculed the small, dusty town, nearly fainting when she discovered the closest mall was two hours away and was definitely not in a class with the Trump Tower.

The clinic was the only thing Clay had ever wanted half as much as he'd wanted to marry Jessica. He'd almost capitulated, but some sane voice in the back of his head warned him that if he sacrificed his dream now, he'd spend the rest of his life and possibly eternity as well, sacrificing his dreams to satisfy hers. He'd had a sudden vision of himself, growing old and disappointed like his father. Reluctantly he'd concluded he didn't love Jessica that much. He'd known he had made the right decision when he discovered he didn't miss her half as much as he'd expected. It was the dream he missed.

Opening the bathroom door, he took several long strides down the darkened hallway and stopped before the room he knew Lilly had prepared for her granddaughter. He raised his fist to knock, then paused. Telling Taylor what he thought of her selfish disregard for others might make him feel better, but it would distress Lilly Jordan. Lilly had been kind to him, renting him a room and office space, feeding him far more often than their agreement called for, and taking messages for his business while he searched for an office manager. He wouldn't repay her by fighting with her granddaughter. Besides he had a hunch Taylor would take one look at him standing there with his hairy, bare legs sticking out beneath his damp, too-short satin robe and burst out laughing.

Turning on his heel, he crossed the hall and entered his own room. Uncertain whether he'd wimped out or allowed reason to prevail, he decided he'd just have to tolerate cold showers and stay away from the Jordan home as much as possible until Taylor left. And maybe he ought to take another look at Betty Glendowski. At least she was a country girl through and through.

* * *

Taylor slept late the following morning. When she stumbled into the bathroom, she felt a flush of guilt. Every surface gleamed and fresh towels hung beside the tub. She'd meant to return to the bathroom and straighten it, but running into Clay and discovering he was actually living in her grandmother's house had driven every other thought from her mind. She certainly hadn't expected Grandma Lilly to clean up after her.

She washed her face and opened the small vanity drawer, expecting to find her brush and makeup. Instead her hand settled on a can of shaving cream. Seconds later she discovered her toiletries stuffed in a plastic bag under the sink. Fuming, she dumped her things back in the drawer and once more assigned Clay's to the plastic bag. She tossed the bag as far under the sink as it would go.

In the kitchen she found her grandmother pinching the edges of a pie crust. Behind her a drain rack sparkled with freshly washed dishes, too many dishes for just one person, Taylor noted.

"Sit down, dear. It will only take a minute to pour a little batter on the griddle and poach an egg the way you like." Lilly bustled toward her with a glass of orange juice.

"Grandma, sit down. I can fix my own breakfast." She moved toward the stove.

"Well, if you're sure." Her grandmother looked hesitant, then smiled brightly. "I'll just finish these pies while you eat."

"Four pies?" Taylor looked askance at the pies lined up along the countertop.

"I hate to just make one pie," her grandmother smiled innocently. "It's such a waste of effort. Besides, Sister Davies is coming home from the hospital today with a new baby, and I thought I'd just run one over for their supper. And Kerrie Morris looked a little down at church Sunday. A pie might cheer her up a bit. Clay and Stewart won't have any trouble helping us finish off the other two."

"Grandma . . ." Taylor had to word this just right. She didn't want to hurt her grandmother's feelings, but she couldn't allow her to be taken advantage of either. "Are you allowing that veterinarian to sleep in your house and cooking meals for him as well as letting him use your sunporch?"

"His name is Clay, dear, and he's such a joy to have around, but he works much too hard. I don't think he takes time out to eat lunch most days, and he never knows what time he'll finish up at night, so I try to keep a bit of cake or pie handy, just in case he gets a moment between calls to run home."

"He's not your responsibility." Taylor turned to face the older woman. "He's taking advantage of your kind nature."

"Oh no, Clay would never do that. Goodness, he insists on paying me a hundred dollars a month for your dad's old room that was just sitting there empty, and every time he has to go to town he brings back more groceries than I know what to do with."

"For you to cook!"

"Well, of course for me to cook. A busy young man like Clay doesn't have time to cook decent meals. Besides I enjoy cooking for a man with a healthy appetite. It gets boring fixing meals for just me." Grandma Lilly calmly opened the oven door and slid two of the pies inside. Obviously the entire women's movement had skipped Lilly Jordan.

"Do you think it's wise to allow a stranger the use of your home?" Taylor tried to reason with the older woman.

"Oh, he's not really a stranger. He and the Gardner boy were missionary companions," Grandma explained.

"Taking in a boarder and his menagerie of animals is unfair to you. I'm afraid you'll get overtired and be ill," Taylor pointed out.

"You sound like your father, dear," Grandma continued blithely. "He's such a worrywart." Taylor frowned. She loved her father, but she didn't like being compared to him, though "worrywart" wasn't the term she'd heard Daddy's secretary use to describe him. She'd called him "a control freak," and though Taylor thought the term unkind, it had stuck in her mind with a certain ring of truth.

"Clay is no bother at all," Lilly continued, "and now that Wendy's come to look after his office, I won't even get to write down his messages."

"Wendy?"

"Wendy Carlson. She's Clay's new office manager. She's kind of young, and I don't think she's had much training, but I'm sure she can answer the phone just fine." She looked thoughtful. "You don't suppose she just came to work for Clay because she wants to get married, and Clay's the best prospect in these parts?"

Taylor barely suppressed a shudder. If Clay Curtis was the best prospect in Fairfield, then the little town certainly didn't have anything to boast about in the romantic opportunities field.

"Do you think she'd like a bowl of homemade chicken noodle soup for lunch?" Her grandmother's question stopped Taylor's musing.

"Does Clay Curtis expect you to feed his secretary, too?"

"Oh, no. We didn't discuss it, but I'd feel guilty eating nice hot soup while she's in the next room eating some dreadful sack lunch."

"What about Mr. Darnell? Are you cooking for him, too?" Taylor didn't mean to be sarcastic, but somehow her grandmother needed to be made to see that she was surrounded by men who were asking too much of a woman her age.

"That man!" Grandma's eyes sparkled with mock annoyance. "I'd like to set him down to a real dinner every day. He needs a little fattening up. His daughter-in-law invited him to take his meals with her family, but he thinks it would be imposing to show up for dinner more than once a week, and every time he eats here he thinks he has to take me to the café the next night. I don't mind eating café food once in a while, but most of the time I prefer my own cooking."

"Grandma, you're working too hard."

"Pooh! You sound more and more like your father every time you open your mouth. That's what comes of spending so much time alone, just the two of you. It's time you got out more, found a husband, and had a passel of little ones. I swear Andrew has forgotten how to have fun." Grandma Lilly bustled about the kitchen, wiping counters and scrubbing an invisible spot on the refrigerator.

"Daddy works hard, and he has a lot of responsibility," Taylor defended her father as she cleared her dishes from the table and took them to the sink to wash. "He worries about you living all the way up here alone. He thinks you'd be happier living closer to the family."

"I'm not the one who moved away."

"Grandma, you know he couldn't make a living here. There isn't one CPA firm in Fairfield."

"I might not be alone much longer anyway." Lilly's eyes glinted with a hint of laughter, and she looked as though she might burst from holding back a secret.

"Oh, Grandma, don't tease. You can't be serious about marrying Mr. Darnell."

"You don't like Stewart?" Her grandmother appeared hurt.

"I'm sure he's a nice man, and I'm glad—we're both glad—you have a congenial friend, but you can't be serious about getting married." A hint of exasperation tinged Taylor's words.

"Because I'm too old?" Something flashed in the back of the older woman's eyes, and Taylor felt regret that she'd reminded her beloved grandmother of her advancing years. Placing the dish towel she held on the cupboard, she stepped closer to her grandmother and wrapped her arms around her.

"I love you," she whispered. "As do Daddy and Aunt Linda and all of the family. We want you to be happy and live a long, long time. You nursed Grandpa while he was ill, and we don't want to see you go through that again. You've earned the right to rest and take it easy."

Lilly looked surprised. "Why, Taylor, I never regretted a minute I spent looking after Frank. Besides there's nothing wrong with Stewart except being skinny as a scarecrow. A few months of my cooking will take care of that. And as far as taking it easy and laying around doing nothing, that would drive me crazy. Then I would feel old!" She turned away from Taylor and headed toward the laundry room.

Suspecting she'd hurt her grandmother's feelings, Taylor started to follow her so she could apologize then thought better of it. She didn't want to hurt her feelings, but everything she'd said was true, and if there was any possibility Grandma would think about Taylor's words and become more reasonable, then she had to keep reminding the older woman of the realities of aging.

By noon Taylor was feeling restless and bored. Grandma's house was spotless, which meant there was no housework to help with. That left mowing the lawn or weeding the garden. She supposed she could do that after lunch. The tantalizing smell of the soup that had been simmering all morning mixed with the aroma of freshly baked apple pies. She'd have to be careful this summer or she'd put on weight. She knew she didn't have the willpower to refuse her grandmother's cooking, so she'd have to concentrate on exercising.

A loud blast of rock music struck her ears, and she hurried to finish setting the table. She didn't know how Clay's new office manager could work with the radio turned up so loud. Fortunately the door between the kitchen and the sunporch had been kept closed all morning, but several times her grandmother had made quick trips to her garden, and each time she'd passed through the door Taylor had winced. This time the door remained open longer, and Taylor assumed Lilly had gone to invite the new office manager to share their lunch. Looking up, she saw her grandmother entering the kitchen alone.

"Where's the office manager?" she asked.

"She said she planned to eat at the café."

"That's probably best," Taylor remarked.

"Eating out every day is expensive. I'm sure Clay doesn't pay that girl a big salary, and she should be saving every penny she makes to go to school." Grandma shook her head as she reached for the soup ladle.

"Perhaps her high school courses are all she needs to run Dr. Curtis's office." Speaking of Dr. Curtis, she wondered where the man could be. She'd expected to see him making his way through the hedge separating the two properties promptly at noon.

Pausing with the spoon in midair, Grandma went on, "I don't think she learned much in high school. Near as I can tell, all she did in high school was chase boys. I know her grades were never very high, and she wouldn't have graduated with her class if her father wasn't on the school board. Will you say the blessing, dear?"

Taylor bowed her head and offered a quick prayer before returning to her grandmother's remarks. "She doesn't need much— just a little typing and good telephone manners. Dr. Curtis doesn't seem to be too busy. I haven't seen one patient arrive at his clinic this morning." She dismissed the veterinarian's business as too small to merit professional skills.

"Goodness, child, Clay wouldn't sit at his clinic waiting for patients even if it was near enough to completion to be used. Few of his patients are pets. In this part of the country, a veterinarian looks after ranch stock, traveling hundreds of miles most days to see his patients."

"But the cockatoo and Tom . . ."

Grandma Lilly laughed. "That silly bird belongs to Clay's former girlfriend. She just sent it to him because she's planning to spend the summer in Europe. Anyway, that was what she said. I really think it was just her way of trying to get him to pay attention to her again."

Taylor found the mention of a former girlfriend, who might want Clay back, a little unsettling, though why it should bother her made no sense. To avoid giving her reaction too much credence, she reminded herself that she and her grandmother were discussing pets, not the doctor's love life. "And Tom?" she asked.

"Tom belongs to me."

"You? Grandma, I thought you didn't like pets in your house," Taylor voiced her astonishment.

"Well, I never did until Tom," Lilly admitted. "He was a stray that just showed up at the door one day last winter. He looked so thin and cold, I started feeding him. First thing I knew he'd moved right in. I enjoy his company, though I'm not sure whether he decided to stay after the weather turned warmer because of any fondness for me or because he spotted Rambo and decided to make it his life's work to catch her."

"What if he succeeds in catching Rambo? Cockatoos are expensive, and she's someone's pet." Taylor stared in horror at the fat cat busily sniffing the bottom of the sunroom door.

"If I were a betting person, I'd place my money on Rambo," Lilly declared. "That's the sneakiest, orneriest critter I've ever met. She's a lot like her owner."

"You know her owner?" For some reason that surprised Taylor. She'd gotten the impression Clay was a stranger to Fairfield.

"Jessica and Clay were engaged—they're both from New York—and she came all the way here to see him once." Lilly frowned. "I invited her to use one of the upstairs bedrooms, but I could tell she was disappointed there wasn't a nice hotel in town. Her stay lasted less than a day. They had some kind of disagreement, and she gave him back the huge diamond she wore. And he had to make that two-hour drive to Boise and back again twice in one day."

"They aren't engaged anymore, but his former fiancée still sent her bird to him to care for while she's gone?" Taylor wasn't surprised that the woman had decided against marrying the veterinarian, but she must be having second thoughts, or surely she would have found some place closer to her home in New York to board her pet. Again, the thought that another woman was interested in Clay disturbed Taylor momentarily, but she refused to consider it further. Placing a forkful of pie in her mouth, Taylor closed her eyes savoring the rich fruity, cinnamon taste. No one else in the whole world could make an apple pie like Grandma Lilly.

A persistent ringing interrupted her enjoyment.

"I guess I'd better answer that." Grandma started to rise to her feet.

"No, stay where you are. I'll get it." Taylor jumped up and turned toward the telephone on the wall. As she reached for it, she realized it wasn't the kitchen phone that was ringing.

"That's the vet's phone." She turned back toward her grandmother who was getting to her feet.

"Yes, but Wendy's out, and it might be important." Lilly looked with concern toward the sunporch office.

Taylor hurried past her grandmother. She supposed she'd have to answer it since her grandmother seemed to think someone ought to. Personally she had no desire to help the man or to set one foot inside his cluttered office. Before reaching for the telephone, she unplugged the boom box resting on one corner of the desk, bringing a welcome silence to the house.

"Dr. Clay Curtis's office," she spoke in her most businesslike voice.

"This is Bob at Walco International in Twin Falls. Would you let Dr. Curtis know his shipment has arrived?" a voice stated his business without preamble.

"Shipment?"

"Yes, his order is here. Thanks." The line went dead.

Searching around for a pen and paper, she frowned when the only notepad she found was covered with doodles of hearts and flowers. Tearing a page off, she turned it over and wrote on the back, then searched for a spot to leave the message. The desk was so cluttered it would probably get lost there. Uncovering a tape dispenser, she tore off a piece of tape and stuck the message to the side of the closest file cabinet.

When she returned to the kitchen, she discovered the dishes were done. She peeked in the front room to see her grandmother sitting in a chair with her feet propped on a stool and Tom curled in a mound on her lap. The television was on, but Grandma didn't seem to be watching it. Taylor suspected she was asleep. Leaving the room quietly, she made her way outside to the garden.

Taylor had helped her grandmother weed her garden in the past, before getting caught up in her own summer activities and then going to college, so she knew what to do. There weren't a lot of weeds, thanks to her grandmother's diligent care, but it took a little more than an hour to work her way through the rows. The garden was another of those things her father said was too much for his mother. He complained that she nearly killed herself raising enough vegetables to feed the whole town.

The sun felt good on Taylor's back, and she felt a twinge of regret for the older woman, who she knew derived a great deal of pleasure from gardening and sharing the fruits of her labor with her neighbors. When Taylor finished weeding, she stretched aching muscles, brushed dirt from her knees, and removed her shoes. She clapped them together smartly to shake off the mud, then left them on the back step before entering the house.

A cloud of depression settled on her shoulders. How was she going to survive the summer? The house was spotless, the garden was weed free, and someone had mowed the lawn before she got up this morning, so what was she going to do for the next three months? She'd had summer jobs ever since she'd turned sixteen, and sitting around watching television held no appeal. She adored her grandmother, but she needed something to do. She'd loved her summers here when she was a little girl and had never run out of things to do then, but she wasn't a little girl anymore. Surely it wouldn't take all summer to carry out her father's instructions to persuade Grandma Lilly to leave all this hard work behind.

CHAPTER 4

Stepping inside the sunporch, she glanced toward the office end and nearly groaned. Here she was barefoot, dressed in faded cutoffs, and with her hands and knees caked with garden dirt while before her sat the aggravating vet's office manager. She was beautiful and groomed to perfection with shining moussed curls cascading over her shoulders. She looked awfully young, and her outfit wasn't quite what Taylor considered proper office attire, but it certainly looked good on her—what there was of it. Now she was being catty, she caught herself. There was no reason to react negatively to the girl.

"Hello! I'm Taylor Jordan," she introduced herself to the young woman.

"Hi! I'm Wendy." The girl glanced up from the magazine she was reading just as the telephone rang. She cracked her gum once then went back to studying a perfume ad.

"Aren't you going to answer that?" Taylor asked when the phone continued to ring and the girl made no move to answer it. *And get rid of that gum before you do*, she wanted to add but didn't.

"Can't. My polish isn't dry. She waved one hand in front of the magazine, revealing long, tapered nails shellacked a deep pumpkin orange. *Obviously the girl wasn't hired for her keyboard skills.*

Taylor reached for the phone. "Dr. Clay Curtis's office."

"Let me talk to the doc," a gruff male voice barked in her ear.

"He's not here at the moment. Could I take a message?"

"Get on the horn and let him know Bertha's in labor. I need him out here right away."

"If I can reach him, who should I say called?"

"Oh! Sorry, miss. Thought you was Lilly. Tell 'im to get out to Buzz's place." With that, the man ended the call.

"Do you have a way to get a message to Dr. Curtis?" Taylor turned back to Wendy, who was still absorbed in her magazine.

"No, he said he'd call in, but he hasn't." Wendy didn't seem concerned, so why should she be? Taylor wondered.

"How about his appointment calendar. Won't it tell you where he is?" She didn't know why, but something told her the message from Buzz was important.

"What's an appointment calendar?" The blond looked bored. "His ad didn't say anything about any calendar."

"Do you mind if I look?" Taylor started around the desk.

"Go ahead, if you want to." Wendy shifted her feet from one of the boxes to a wastepaper basket to allow Taylor to pass behind the desk. From this side of the desk, it was impossible not to notice how short Wendy's skirt was; it went way beyond mini—more like micro. *It's none of your concern,* Taylor reminded herself and plunged into the mess stacked on the desk.

Starting at one end, Taylor swiftly sorted mail into one stack, loose papers into another, and assigned journals to a pile on the floor. "Here it is!" she exclaimed triumphantly as she unearthed a large calendar taped to the wooden surface at the opposite end of the desk. Her triumph turned to disappointment when she noticed the squares were all empty except for a few hearts and flowers.

"Oh, that thing." Wendy leaned forward to see what Taylor was studying.

"That thing is an appointment calendar," Taylor's voice held an edge of sharpness. "It should be filled with Dr. Curtis's appointments. Aren't you keeping any record of who he is supposed to see? How does he know who is expecting him?"

"I don't know. He took a handful of pink papers off that wire thing when he left this morning." She pointed to a message spindle. Taylor groaned. She'd never seen a less organized office—or a more indifferent office manager. Obviously the vet had hired Wendy for her physical attributes and not for either her brains or skill. The mail she'd stacked had the appearance of both checks and bills, none of which had been opened. Lab reports were mixed with junk mail, and several patient files sported a trail of orange enamel dots across them. Of course, it wasn't any of her business. If the country bumpkin vet went out of business before he even got his clinic built, why should she care?

But somehow she did care. She'd spent years taking business and management classes. Her summers and after-school time had been used filling in for her dad's secretary, then later, she had interned as assistant manager at the largest bank in Pocatello. After graduating, she had temped as an administrator for the office of Tate, Tate & Lowendecker while waiting for final word on the position at Donovan Enterprises. She'd even volunteered at the Bannock County medical clinic to manage the fund drive for acquiring updated dialysis equipment, and had also begun as a volunteer in Senator Brock's campaign. Before the campaign ended, she was running his eastern Idaho office and supervising a staff of fourteen. Her experience had given her an abhorrence of sloppy business practices, and this make-shift office cried out for organization. She decided to ignore the cry, but after looking around the cluttered office once more, she found she couldn't.

Scooping up a stack of junk mail and advertising fliers, she flung them toward the waste basket. Wendy yelped and knocked the basket over as she swung her feet out of the way, sending the basket and its contents rolling across the floor.

"I'm sorry," Taylor hastened to apologize. "It's just that I can't stand clutter, and I forgot you were using the trash can." She knelt to clear up the mess. Wendy stood over her with wide, confused eyes. *It didn't seem to occur to the airhead that she could help pick up the mess,* Taylor grumbled to herself. She reached for the last piece, and as she held the large wad of paper in her hands, something clicked in her head. As she carefully smoothed it out on the desktop, her suspicions were confirmed. She glanced at the date at the top of the page, then at the one on the desktop calendar. The one she'd just smoothed out was June; the one on the desk pad was August. Lifting a corner of the crumpled page she saw July.

"Wendy, this is June. Why did you throw away June and July?" Taylor turned to the young woman, who had returned to the swivel chair behind the desk. Absently she noticed that the girl's skirt was leather, what there was of it.

"Somebody scribbled all over them, then I spilled a teensy bit of polish, so I threw them away before something stuck to them." Wendy's voice was a mite defensive. "Are they important or something?"

"Yes, Wendy, these pages are important." Taylor continued to smooth the papers with her hand while reminding herself not to lose her temper. Wendy was young and lacked training. It wasn't her fault the vet had assumed that because she was female, she could automatically run an office. If Wendy was willing, perhaps Taylor could give her a few pointers. It might even help to pass the time if she took the younger girl under her wing.

"See these little squares." Taylor pointed to the date boxes. "Each one is for a different day. Your boss has written in each one where he plans to be for that day. Today's box has four names in the P.M. section. It's mid-afternoon so he must be almost through these appointments. Start with the last name and start calling. Keep calling until you locate him."

Wendy appeared doubtful for a few seconds, then her face brightened. She turned around to snatch the telephone directory off a pile of books, scanned a page quickly, and began dialing.

"Mrs. Ross, this is Wendy Carlson. Is Clay there at your ranch?" She paused to listen, then appeared annoyed. "You know perfectly well who I mean. The new vet." There was silence for a few moments, then Wendy said, "No, this is not a frivolous call. I work for Clay, and I have an important message for him . . . Yes . . . No . . . I don't know if it's an emergency, but it's important. Is he there or not?" More silence.

"I don't know why you can't tell me!"

Taylor took the telephone from Wendy's hand, and in her most efficient, no-nonsense voice began to speak. "Mrs. Ross, this is Dr. Curtis's office. We have a situation here that requires the doctor's attention. We don't have time for games. Has the doctor arrived at your ranch?"

"I see. You expect him within a quarter hour. Please have him call his office immediately. Thank you." She hung up and turned to look at the younger woman. "He called from his last appointment to let the Rosses know he'd be late."

"Why didn't she tell me that?" Wendy let her pique show. "I'm his office manager." Something in the girl's hurt expression touched Taylor in an unexpected way. The girl wasn't as indifferent as she'd thought. She was really overwhelmed and feeling insecure.

"Wendy," Taylor tried to explain tactfully. "Even if you and Dr. Curtis are good friends, when you call from his office, you should use his title and let the person you're calling know the call is business."

"I've known Mrs. Ross all my life. She's an old snoop and she never has liked me," Wendy complained. She sat down in the office chair just as the phone rang again.

"Be professional," Taylor whispered as the girl reached for the instrument. "Just say, 'Dr. Curtis's office, may I help you?'"

Their eyes met and they both grinned as Wendy repeated the words into the mouthpiece.

"Clay!" Wendy squealed after a brief pause. "I had the hardest time finding you. When are you coming back?"

"No, that isn't why I called. Buzz Morgan called. He said Bertha is in labor and you should go right over." Wendy delivered the message, then frowned as she listened to Clay's response.

"What? Won't I even see you? I thought we—" Clay must have interrupted her, because she didn't finish her sentence. She listened again, then sounded reluctant as she responded.

"Oh, okay. Bye." She hung up the phone and drummed her fingertips on the desktop. When she looked up, she had tears in her eyes.

"Did he hurt your feelings?" Taylor asked sympathetically.

"I don't think he meant to—I mean, he never said he'd take me to dinner after we finished tonight. I just kind of hoped."

"Are you and Clay dating?" It really wasn't any of Taylor's business, but if they were, perhaps it would explain why he'd hired someone who knew so little about managing an office. Besides she was curious.

"Not really," Wendy admitted. "But he's so good-looking. I keep hoping he'll ask me out. I thought if I worked here and we were together everyday, he'd start to like me. When he finds out I don't really know anything about being an office manager, he'll probably be mad at me. You seem to know a lot about running an office. Could you show me what to do?"

She looked so pathetic, Taylor's heart twisted. Other than his looks, she couldn't see what Wendy saw in the overbearing vet, but if he was the man the girl wanted, who was she to judge? Besides she'd heard often enough that there was no explanation for love. If learning to be a good office manager would help the girl, she'd teach her. She might as well. Her grandmother's apartment wouldn't be ready until fall, and Taylor didn't have anything else to do this summer.

* * *

Fortunately the Morgans were only ten miles from the Ross ranch. The old dog probably would have done fine on her own, but Buzz was a nervous wreck. She'd been the last puppy Buzz's child-hood dog had given birth to, and he'd always been a little disap-pointed that he'd never been able to breed her. He'd been elated when she finally began to show signs of imminent motherhood, but he worried since Bertha was at an age when most dogs stop producing offspring.

When Clay's truck stopped near the barn, Buzz came running to usher the vet to the stall where the old dog had chosen to give birth. Clay hid a chuckle when he saw the dog lying on a thick, soft, hand-made quilt, no doubt straight off Buzz's own bed. Mary Louise would probably shoot her husband when she discovered her quilt's fate.

Easing down beside the panting dog, Clay gave her a quick exam-ination. She seemed to be doing fine. Over the next half hour her puppies arrived one by one, and Bertha behaved like a pro, nuzzling and licking each one in turn, while Buzz paced and twisted his hands, seeming to suffer far more than the dog.

"Did you ever see such beautiful pups?" Buzz finally asked.

Clay glanced at the older man to see if he was serious. The look of rapture on his face said he was. Clay glanced back at the puppies. They certainly didn't have the grace and coloring of their pedigreed mama. In fact they appeared to be a conglomeration of colors and breeds that hadn't blended to any artistic degree. He had a hunch they were mutts through and through. He shrugged his shoulders. Pedigreed or not, Buzz thought they were beautiful. Clay had person-ally never seen an ugly puppy, but these came close.

When Clay climbed into his truck to leave the Morgan ranch, he left Buzz sitting in the straw staring at the four odd-colored pups in awe, an obvious case of love at first sight. Somehow the picture he carried away with him lifted his spirits, and he whistled as he drove back to his last scheduled appointment.

Pulling into the lane that led to the Ross ranch, Clay couldn't help a grin as a stubby-tailed mongrel, looking as though he'd rubbed up against a newly whitewashed fence and an old red barn, challenged his right to be there. Unless he missed his guess, the Rosses' mixed-breed cattle dog had accomplished what all of the fancy breeding kennels Buzz had hauled Bertha to over the years had failed to bring about.

Two hours later he returned his equipment to his truck and headed back to town. On arriving in Fairfield, he parked beside the foundation that would one day be his clinic. It looked just the way it had the day before, and the day before that. At this rate, he'd be ready to retire before his clinic was ready to move into. He took time to check the animals in the old stable on the property and feed them before turning toward his office. It hadn't been a bad day, and it was only eight o'clock. He was glad Wendy had tracked him down to tell him about Buzz's dog, he thought as he opened the back door. His being there for the birth of the puppies had been important to Buzz. He looked around and was pleasantly surprised to see she had straightened his desk. He sat down and rifled through his mail, finding it a welcome change to have a cleared space on which to work, and to be spared the task of weeding out the junk mail. He frowned when he saw how wrinkled and blotched his appointment calendar had become and wondered at the strips of clear tape holding it in place. He stared curiously at the small blotches of orange on the paper, then shrugged his shoulders. Accidents happen. All in all, Wendy had done much better than he had expected. Hiring her might prove to be a smart move after all.

His step was lighter as he stepped into the kitchen and found the plate Lilly always left next to the microwave. While the food heated, he found himself nibbling at the huge wedge of apple pie she'd cut for him. No two ways about it, Lilly Jordan made the best pie he'd ever eaten. He was halfway through his dinner before his senses registered that he wasn't the only one in the house still up. Lilly was always in bed by nine so that left her granddaughter. He resigned himself to another shower minus hot water. He just hoped he'd be fortunate enough to avoid running into her tonight.

He finished his dinner and rinsed his dishes in the sink before starting up the stairs. From halfway up the stairs he caught a flicker of movement off to his left. Turning he saw Taylor, the telephone pressed to her ear, pacing back and forth across the living room carpet. He couldn't hear her side of the conversation, but it appeared she was unhappy with someone. Probably her boyfriend. Somehow that thought pleased him. He hoped her love life was just as miserable as his!

He watched a few seconds more, enjoying the swing of thick dark curls across her back. He hadn't realized she had so much hair. The first time he'd seen her, it had been fastened in some kind of knot at the back of her head, and the next time he'd seen her, all but one stray lock had been caught up in a towel atop her head. Good grief, the thick curly mass reached almost to her waist! She'd been a knockout in severe navy blue; in the soft, clingy, flowered dress that just brushed her knees, she was sensational.

Catching himself staring, he resumed his trek up the stairs, his good mood gone. He wasn't going to waste his time staring at Taylor Jordan. That was one woman who had dollar signs written all over her. He knew her type. She had her sights set on city lights and big bucks just like Jessica and Wendy did. All he wanted was a simple country girl.

He found himself slightly disappointed when he turned on the shower and found plenty of hot water. His soap and shampoo were on the window ledge instead of in the shower caddy and a thick clean towel was right where it should be. He wondered if Taylor had placed them there or if Lilly had. Of course it was Lilly! There was no reason for a picture of Taylor to keep coming to mind. Instead of seeing that thick cloud of hair and slender waist, he needed to remember his vow to stay clear of her. It would be easier to keep his distance from Taylor if he could stay angry with her. Finding his deodorant and razor back in the bag under the sink helped some.

Whistling cheerfully, he upended the bag onto the counter and pulled out the small vanity drawer. It was a tight squeeze, but he got all of the drawer's contents in the bag.

* * *

Taylor glared at the can of shaving cream and the array of masculine toiletries neatly lined up in her drawer just as she had done every day for a week. That man! He made her so mad! She wished he'd go away and get out of her life. She reached under the sink for the plastic bag, and as she'd done every morning all week, she consigned his things to the bag and placed her toiletries back in the drawer. She hoped he'd soon give up trying to take over her grandmother's house. Her cosmetics were getting a little battered from their daily drawer-to-bag-and-back trips.

Wandering downstairs, she found her grandmother in the kitchen preparing breakfast. At least that obnoxious man didn't hang around to eat with them each morning. Actually he spent little time at the house. In the past week she'd only caught a couple of quick glimpses of him. For a moment she felt almost disappointed. No, of course she wasn't disappointed. The less she saw of Clay Curtis the better!

"Good morning, Grandma." She kissed the older woman's cheek and noticed she seemed a little distracted. Her attention seemed to be on something other than breakfast and it looked as though the pancakes might be in danger of burning. Reaching to take the spatula from her grandmother's hand, she deftly turned them.

"Thank you, dear." Her grandmother smiled and turned back to the packages and cartons covering one section of the countertop.

Taylor watched her carefully place half a dozen deviled eggs in a small plastic container, then turn to cut thick pink slices from last night's ham. Noticing a large wicker basket sitting at the end of the counter, she asked, "Are you planning a picnic?"

Grandma Lilly actually blushed as she answered. "Stewart invited me to go fishing with him today, and I offered to take a lunch. He should be here any minute." She hesitated a moment then asked, "Would you like to come with us? I'm sure Stewart wouldn't mind."

Memories of trailing her grandfather along some clear mountain stream came abruptly to mind. She could hear the wind soughing in the treetops, the water gurgling nearby, and feel the sun on her face. She'd loved those fishing trips. Daddy had tried to discourage her from going, but Grandpa hadn't paid any attention to his worries about mosquitoes and sunburn, or even the possibility of a rattler or some other wild creature. She hadn't gone fishing since Grandpa died, she realized a little sadly. But she'd been too old by then anyway to tramp through mud and weeds, getting sunburned and bitten by mosquitoes. At least that was what Daddy had told her when she'd tried to talk him into taking time from work for a fishing trip together. Now she wondered if she'd given up too easily.

Carefully she considered the invitation. She hadn't been fishing for years and something about the prospect drew her. Maybe it was just the boredom; she'd found little to do since she'd arrived. Besides, she could watch her grandmother better, make sure she didn't get hurt or do anything foolish, if she went along with the two elderly people.

On the other hand, she sensed the invitation had been offered more from courtesy than from any real desire to have her accompany the older couple. From the way Grandma Lilly was acting, she clearly considered the fishing trip a date, which really was absurd. Seventy-eight-year-old grandmothers didn't date. She supposed that was all the more reason she should go along. She could see to it that nothing happened to Lilly, and her father would certainly consider it her responsibility to make certain her grandmother didn't become over-tired. He wouldn't like the idea of only an eighty-year-old man looking after his mother, especially one who seemed to be romantically interested in her.

She opened her mouth to say yes at the same time her grand-mother spoke with some irritation in her voice. "Why doesn't that girl answer the phone?" With the words, Taylor realized the vet's phone had been ringing for some time.

"I don't suppose she's here yet," Grandma went on as she headed for the sunporch. "I swear she arrives later every day."

"I'll get it," Taylor called. She was closer anyway. Hurriedly she opened the door and reached for the ringing telephone sitting on the edge of the desk.

"Dr. Clay Curtis's office," she said in her best professional voice. Silence met her words, so she repeated the greeting.

"What are you doing in my office?" The words were loaded with suspicion. Obviously the friendly local vet wasn't thrilled to hear her voice. "Where's Wendy?"

"She hasn't arrived yet." Taylor informed him.

"Let me speak to Lilly." It was more demand than request.

"She's busy," Taylor informed him curtly. There was a heavy sigh at the other end of the telephone.

"This is important," Clay returned. She could tell he was struggling with his temper. "I'm going to be beyond cell phone reach for several hours, and I'm expecting a call. I need to be sure Wendy has the right information to give the pharmacy. Now put Lilly on the phone."

"We're leaving, dear." Grandma Lilly's voice came from the other side of the house, followed by the closing of the front door. Taylor had been so busy arguing with Clay, she hadn't even heard Mr. Darnell arrive. At least she didn't have to choose between accompanying them as her father would insist she should do or following her own instinct that said three would be a crowd.

"You're too late," she came close to taking delight in informing Clay. "She and Mr. Darnell have gone fishing." Silence met her announcement.

As the silence lengthened, Taylor felt a stab of guilt. She might take a perverse kind of satisfaction out of annoying the vet, but she certainly didn't wish to damage his business, only encourage him to move it elsewhere. And it really wasn't his fault Wendy was late this morning.

"I can write, you know." She broke the silence. "Give me the information, and I'll leave a note where Wendy can't miss it."

"Are you sure you don't mind?" Clay sounded hesitant.

Biting back a smart remark, she assured Clay she didn't mind. Silently she questioned her own sanity in offering the vet any assistance, no matter how minor. He still sounded uncertain as he dictated the information the pharmacy would need. She couldn't help grinning as he carefully spelled the names of several drugs and asked her to repeat back each quantity. Either he'd learned the hard way that Wendy's spelling was atrocious, or he had a pretty low opinion of Taylor's ability. She couldn't fault him for being cautious. Pharmaceutical exactness was just as critical in treating animals as in treating people, and he had nothing by which to gauge her competency.

After she hung up the phone, she grinned. She had a pretty good idea how hard it had been for Clay Curtis to trust her with the message. In a week's time the only communication between the two had been the silent tug-of-war for the small drawer in the upstairs bathroom. She looked around the small office for a good place to leave the note, finally deciding on the top of the daily calendar next to the telephone. Surely Wendy would notice it there.

As she set the note down, she discovered another note written in broad slashing strokes on a sticky note attached to the calendar pad. It looked like a list of tasks Clay expected Wendy to accomplish. She paused, noticing the list was several days old. Slowly she read through the tasks Clay had given Wendy. Catch up billing, prepare bank deposit, make account/patient folders and file notes, enter patient data in computer files.

Taylor settled back in Wendy's chair and gazed thoughtfully at the overflowing wire baskets piled on top of the metal file cabinets. It didn't appear anything had been filed. She had a sneaky suspicion Wendy didn't understand the simple basics of office filing. Several times since she'd arrived, she'd toyed with the idea of training Wendy. In fact she'd halfway promised to help the girl. But wouldn't helping Wendy be helping Clay? And if she helped Clay, wouldn't he be just that more determined to continue living in her grandmother's house and running his business from her back porch?

A loud squawk emanated from Rambo's corner. She jumped, then glared at the bird. There was something about that bird she didn't like. It glared back, making its animosity toward her clear. It was probably her imagination. No, it was *definitely* imagination. The bird couldn't know what she was thinking, which made her the one imagining things to think the bird had taken a dislike to her.

She turned her back on the bird and considered. If she took on the task of training Wendy, she'd have something to keep her busy and an excuse to sharpen her office skills. It would annoy Clay half to death if he ever found out. That was a plus! And she'd see what she could do about getting that bird shipped back to New York.

CHAPTER 5

Curiously she turned on the computer and began a search for patient records. The first name she recognized was Buzz Morgan. Clicking on his name she brought up his file. The last entry was dated two months ago, not last week. Yet she felt certain that was the name the man on the phone had given her last week when she'd helped locate Clay for him. Frowning, she reached for one of the baskets. She thumbed through the papers and notes until she found what she was looking for. A yellow sheet of paper told her Clay had delivered four puppies to a dog named Bertha belonging to Buzz Morgan the day after she'd arrived in Fairfield.

Most of the papers in the metal basket were yellow sheets just like the one she held in her hand. Obviously Clay carried some kind of record book with him. He probably gave each farmer or rancher the original when he finished caring for their stock and kept a copy for his files. A wave of annoyance kept Taylor frowning. Why hadn't Wendy entered the information from all of these forms in the computer, then tucked each one in its own file jacket inside the file cabinets? Without updating the files on a daily basis, it would be impossible to bill Clay's accounts accurately.

The telephone at her elbow shrilled, and she automatically reached for it. She listened for a moment, then penciled in an appointment on the large appointment calendar, thanked the caller, and hung up.

Since she already had the Morgan file open in the computer, she entered the information from the yellow paper in the file, then turned to the file cabinet to search for a folder to place it in. She turned at the sound of the porch door opening. A wave of guilt swept over her. She shouldn't be snooping in Clay's files without his or Wendy's knowledge or permission, even if her intent was to help Wendy.

"Hi!" Wendy called as she slipped inside the room, appearing completely undisturbed at finding Taylor in her chair with the office computer on. She tossed her oversized handbag on the floor and went straight to Rambo's cage, where she cooed a greeting to the bird, who preened and acted delighted to see her. She added a handful of seeds to the bird's dish, then turned to Taylor.

"It's so hot out there!" Wendy vigorously fanned her face with one hand.

"Hi, yourself," Taylor smiled back at the girl, noticing her shorts and bare midriff. Wendy saw the direction her eyes took and preened a bit, looking smug.

"I drove into Ketchum last night and found this shirt in the cutest little boutique. Mom says everything in those stores is over-priced and meant for tourists who have nothing better to do with their time and money than to spend it on junk. But I just couldn't resist. It's so cute and I just know Clay will love it."

"It's cute all right," Taylor tried to be diplomatic. "But don't you think Clay would prefer you dress a little more businesslike for the office?"

"Oh, he's not stuffy or anything like that." She popped her gum, then rushed on. "Besides, it's too hot to wear a suit. Not that I even own one. Mom wanted to buy me one for graduation, but Daddy said I could wear whatever I wanted, and since it would be covered by my graduation gown, it didn't matter what I wore. He was right, too. I got this really awesome little leather skirt and nobody even saw it until the party at the twins' house afterward." She giggled. "Their mom about had a heart attack."

"You're a veterinarian's office manager, not a banker's secretary, so I don't think a suit is necessary, but don't you think you would be able to help Clay better if he needs your help with some of the animals, and make a better impression on his clients, too, if you wore slacks and a more conservative blouse?" Taylor cautiously tried to reason with the girl.

"Oh, pooh, you're as bad as Mom. She says Clay is a returned missionary, so he probably likes girls to dress like they've already been to the temple. That's silly. I saw that girl he was engaged to, and she sure didn't dress like she had anything to hide." Wendy glared at her fingernails, then opened a drawer and reached for a file and a bottle of nail polish.

Wendy's flippant words bothered Taylor. "Wendy," she said, "I don't think women who have been to the temple think of their style of dress as 'hiding something.' It's true the cap sleeves and legs on temple garments would show if a woman wasn't careful about her choice of fashions, but I think most of those women would choose to wear modest clothing anyway."

"Only the fuddy-duddies." Wendy dismissed the whole subject airily. "I'm going to wear what I want, even after I get married."

"You're not planning to marry in the temple?" Taylor asked. She knew the girl was a member of the Church because Grandma Lilly had mentioned that Wendy had finished Young Women and should be attending Relief Society now, but Lilly hadn't seen Wendy there yet.

"I'll probably have to get married in the temple." Wendy leaned forward to blow on her freshly polished nail. "Mom knows Blaine Gardner's mom really well. Blaine was one of Clay's missionary companions. She said Clay and Blaine promised each other they'd never marry anywhere else. But I'm not going to wear icky garments after we're married."

"But that's one of the promises people make when they go to the temple." Taylor was horrified at Wendy's casual reference to something she'd always envisioned as a symbol of sacred promises, promises she'd been considering making, even though she wasn't married. In fact, she had already decided she wanted to go through the temple before she left home for San Francisco. At twenty-three, she wasn't sure she would ever marry, and even if she did, it wouldn't be for a long time.

"Lots of people take them off when they're a nuisance," Wendy went on. "Even Daddy doesn't wear the hot old things when he's working outside in the summer. He wears them on Sundays because people are mean and they'd talk if they couldn't see them through his white shirt at church. Do you think Lilly has a fan someplace we could plug in?"

"I'll look," Taylor promised. She felt a little sick, but it wasn't from the heat. Perhaps she was as old-fashioned as her grandmother or as strict as her father, but she couldn't help feeling there was something dishonest about Wendy's plans. She hesitated before going to search for the fan. She wasn't sure it was any of her business, but she couldn't hold back the words that came tumbling out of her mouth.

"Wendy, I know many people feel wearing temple garments somehow cramps their style and limits which fashions they can wear, but if you feel that way, it might be because you're not ready to go to the temple. I don't think I'd want to make promises to God I had no intention of keeping." Taylor couldn't resist saying this much to the other girl. She had strong feelings about making commitments and keeping promises. She couldn't keep quiet on a subject that mattered deeply to her.

"Well, I'm not going to," Wendy stubbornly insisted. "I don't think God cares what I wear. My mom is always harping about me dressing modestly, but I've seen pictures of her when she was my age, and she didn't worry about stuff like that then either. She's just like those sour-faced old pioneer ladies who thought up garments because they were jealous and didn't want their husbands to marry pretty, younger women."

"Oh, Wendy," Taylor laughed. "I don't think you know a whole lot about the purpose of temple garments or modesty. My grandmother has a book on preparing to go to the temple. It also explains the seriousness of the promises made there. She and Grandpa used to teach a temple preparation class. I'll see if she'll loan it to you when she gets back."

"You mean someone wrote a book about all that temple stuff?" Wendy looked astonished. "I thought it was supposed to be a secret."

"Grandma told me a long time ago that the things that happen in the temple and the promises people make there are not secrets the way we usually think of secrets. A temple is a sacred place and everything that happens there has deep spiritual meaning. Heavenly Father has told us not to talk about those spiritual happenings outside of the temple because to do so reduces the reverence we feel for them," Taylor tried to explain.

"You know about lots of things," Wendy sighed, and there was something wistful in her voice. "I wish I was smart like you."

"You are smart," Taylor told Wendy.

"Smart enough to know I'm too hot," Wendy shot back, picking up a stack of papers to fan herself.

"I'll go look for that fan right now," Taylor promised. "Besides I'm keeping you from getting any work done, and I can see Clay left you a long list of things you need to do." She started toward the door, then stopped as the phone rang. "There's a list of pharmaceuticals beside the phone that your boss wants you to order if that's the veterinary supplier in Twin Falls."

"Dr. Curtis's office," she heard Wendy chirp into the phone as she left the room. When she reached the basement stairs, she wedged the door open and turned on the light before starting down the steep steps. A slight shudder shook her shoulders as she descended the stairs. After all these years, she was still afraid of the roughly finished basement. Steeling herself against the edginess she always felt in tight spaces, she began her search for the fan. She was pretty certain she'd seen one when she'd come down here one day last week to get some pint jars for her grandmother who had needed them for strawberry jam. As she searched the shelves and eyed the rows of bright jam, she sighed ruefully. She wasn't doing too well when it came to convincing Grandma to slow down. Last night when she talked to Daddy, he'd been pretty annoyed that she'd been at her grandmother's house more than a week and she hadn't yet found the right opportunity to tell her about the apartment.

The rows of brightly colored jars bothered her for another reason, too. Coupled with Wendy's remarks, she wondered about her own adherence to gospel standards. The fruit jars were a vivid symbol of homemaking, and all her life she'd listened to teachers and speakers proclaim a woman's role in the Church as that of wife, mother, and homemaker. But Taylor didn't want that kind of life. Did that make her a hypocrite after what she'd told Wendy? She loved Grandma Lilly and Aunt Linda, but she didn't want to spend her life doing the things they did, like bottling jam and baking pies when she could be organizing an ad campaign or negotiating multimillion-dollar contracts. She really didn't want to live alone all her life, but she would never consider marrying out of the temple, and the kind of man who could take her to the temple would expect her to do all the Mormon mother/homemaker things instead of having a career.

Spotting the fan, she pulled it off the shelf and carried it upstairs to find Tom waiting in front of the door separating the kitchen from Clay's office. He was crouched on the floor with his tail switching back and forth.

"Forget it, Tom!" She bent over to stroke the cat's ruffled fur. "You're never going to catch that bird, and even if you did, something tells me you'd regret it." With one foot she gently scooted the cat back from the door before opening it and swiftly slipping through it, then with care closing it equally swiftly behind her.

"Here's the fan," she announced, waving it triumphantly. Wendy didn't show the enthusiasm Taylor expected. In fact, she looked about to cry.

"Wendy, what's wrong?" Taylor set the fan on the desk and went to the young woman.

"He was just so rude!" she whispered.

"Who? Was Clay rude to you?" She felt herself bristle. Wendy was the kind of girl that back in high school Taylor would have called an airhead, but there was something about her that Taylor liked anyway.

"Clay?" Wendy looked puzzled. "I haven't talked to Clay this morning. It was that man on the phone. He said mean things. He called me stupid, and he said Clay stole something that belongs to him."

"Are you saying someone just called on the telephone and said Clay stole something?" Taylor asked incredulously.

"Not exactly," Wendy's big eyes filled with tears. "I answered the phone, and I did it the way you said I should. I said, 'Dr. Clay Curtis's office, may I help you?' No one said anything, so I said it again. Then this man said, 'Get Curtis.' I told him Clay wasn't here, but if he needed an appointment, I could write it down for him."

"Didn't he believe you when you said Dr. Curtis was out?" Taylor prompted the younger woman to go on with her story.

"I don't think so. He started swearing, and he said I was lying and stupid and a bunch of other things. I know sometimes people are disappointed because Clay can't come the minute they call, but he didn't have to be so mean." Tears spilled down Wendy's cheeks, and Taylor placed an arm around her.

"He had no right to be rude to you," Taylor assured Wendy. "When Clay returns you tell him about it, and he should make the man apologize to you."

"I don't know his name," Wendy wailed. "He wouldn't tell me. I asked if he'd like to leave a message, and he said, 'Yeah, I have a message for that—' he said a word you'd get mad if I repeated—

'I know where they are, and I'll get them back. They're mine. And if he tries to stop me, there'll be more than one neck wrung.'"

"And you've no idea who he was or what he wanted?" Taylor tried to remain calm and give Wendy the assurance the young woman needed, but the words sent a chill down her back. To her they sounded like more than rudeness; the man, whoever he was, was threatening Clay. "Wendy, I think you should write down exactly what that man said. It might be important."

Wendy looked doubtful but began searching for a pencil and paper.

"Wouldn't it be faster to use the computer?" Taylor asked as she watched the other woman begin to write.

"I don't know how," Wendy admitted reluctantly. "Clay's computer isn't anything like the ones we had at school."

"Is that why you haven't done the billing?" Taylor asked. When the girl gripped her pen tighter and didn't answer, Taylor sighed. It wasn't only in office procedure and etiquette Wendy lacked training; she didn't have any technical skills either. It didn't say much for Clay Curtis's business acumen to have picked an assistant who knew absolutely nothing about running an office. From what Taylor had observed, she'd already figured out that Wendy wasn't really Clay's girlfriend either although the girl wanted to be.

"Wendy," Taylor asked. "Did you take any business classes in school?"

Wendy ducked her head, looking embarrassed. "Not really. Everyone had to take a keyboard class one year."

"But you didn't study accounting or bookkeeping, office machines, or any secretarial classes?" Taylor knew the answer before Wendy shook her head.

"And you haven't had any office experience either?" Taylor continued. Again the other woman shook her head. "Does Clay know you don't know anything about managing his office?"

"No, I said I could do it," Wendy admitted. "I didn't know it would be so hard or that he'd never be here." She looked resentful.

"He didn't ask for references or check to see what training you'd had, did he?" Taylor was appalled at the carelessness Clay had exhibited in hiring Wendy.

"I sort of tricked him," Wendy mumbled. "I never thought about what he'd want me to do," she went on in a contrite voice. "I just wanted to be with him. I thought we'd go to lunch together and ride around in his truck every day to see all the animals."

Taylor didn't know what to say. Wendy hadn't been honest with Clay about her qualifications. Remembering their earlier discussion, she knew Wendy was willing to be less than honest with the Lord, too. She had a hunch the other woman didn't consider herself dishonest, but no matter how she justified her actions, she'd certainly misrepresented herself.

She shook her head at Wendy's naiveté. There was something sad about being so young and inexperienced that the girl thought being in love justified whatever means it took to be with her beloved—even if he didn't return her devotion. But what did she know about love? It was an emotion Taylor had never experienced herself. She'd dated a few men she'd met in her college classes, but she had never fancied herself in love with any of them.

"Wendy," Taylor began tentatively. "I don't think you're being fair to Clay. He's paying you a salary to do certain things, and if you don't do them, he shouldn't pay you." A picture of the plastic bag full of Clay's toiletries flashed in her mind, and suddenly she wondered about her own justification of the petty feud she had been perpetuating with her grandmother's boarder.

"It's like stealing," Wendy responded glumly and Taylor realized the girl was more aware of the ethics of her situation than she had given her credit for. Wendy's words added to her own sense of shame that she, too, had only thought of what she wanted, ignoring Clay's arrangement with Grandma Lilly.

"If you really want to fulfill your end of your bargain with Clay, I'll help you learn how to run Dr. Curtis's office," Taylor offered, making up her mind, then promptly wondering if she'd lost it. She didn't want to help Clay; she wanted him to leave her grandmother's house. If Wendy continued the way she was, Clay would soon be out of business and would have to leave. On the other hand, she didn't want Clay to lose his business. She just wanted him gone and she really did want to help Wendy. Besides she didn't want to spend an entire summer letting her own office skills go dormant. The argument continued to wage in her mind as she reached for the first of the wire baskets.

* * *

A cloud of dust billowed behind Clay's truck as he drove up the winding road into the hills. The Morrow ranch was the most remote ranch he'd been called to since he began practicing in Idaho. Amy Morrow wasn't really a rancher; she was an actress, according to Lilly. He never found time to watch much television, but Lilly had filled him in on Ms. Morrow's career as a daytime soap heroine and the community's most illustrious celebrity. It was rumored that she planned to build a ski resort on the property in the scenic mountainous area north of Fairfield that she'd purchased two years ago. So far she'd had a beautiful log home built and a state-of-the-art stable for the dozen or so horses she kept. There was also a landing strip for her and her friends' private planes.

He'd been surprised when Ms. Morrow's foreman, Joe Terrence, had contacted him through another rancher, requesting that he check one of the horses at the ranch. Ms. Morrow didn't patronize any of the local businesses as a rule; she usually flew in supplies for her ranch, including a vet who specialized in equine medicine when any of her horses needed care. According to Terrence, one of Ms. Morrow's horses needed immediate attention, and their regular veterinarian was unavailable for a few days.

It was a beautiful day and the higher he drove, the more beautiful the scenery became. He passed several small lakes and saw meadows dotted with cattle give way to thick pine forests. A stream ran close to the road, filled with tantalizing spots that made him itch to stop and dig out his fishing gear. The day would be perfect—except for Taylor Jordan. Just thinking about her brought a frown to his face. He wondered if she really would pass on the message he'd left for Wendy, and if she did, would she get it right?

Fleetingly he wondered why Wendy was late this morning. He hadn't expected much from the girl, but he'd been pleasantly surprised at the way she'd arranged his office and set up his computer. She took messages well, too. Her efficiency amazed him, seeming way out of character for the girl he thought he knew, but to borrow one of Lilly's phrases, it didn't pay to look a gift horse in the mouth. He hoped she soon found time to bill clients; his bank account was getting close to rock bottom. He also hoped Lilly's granddaughter wasn't hanging around, distracting Wendy from her work.

The thought of Taylor Jordan messing around in his office and answering his phone made him uneasy. She'd taken an instant dislike to him, and there was no telling what kind of mischief she might get up to if Wendy wasn't around to look out for his interests. His feelings toward Taylor weren't very charitable, he reminded himself. He wasn't prone to making rash judgments based on first impressions, but there was just something about the woman that got under his skin.

Rounding a curve, Clay saw the Morrow ranch spread before him. It was breathtakingly beautiful. The main house was built of logs and set back against a sheer rock face. It was flanked on either side by a grove of pine trees. He planned to use pine trees the same way to offset the house he envisioned building on his own property one day. The stable and a smaller house, probably where the foreman and his wife lived, sat a short distance away from the main house. Clay's property was smaller than Ms. Morrow's and didn't have quite the same dramatic mountain backdrop, but for a moment he could see the picture repeating itself on the acreage between the creek and his clinic.

As he drew nearer the ranch buildings, he spotted a roan mare cantering toward him, completing the perfect picture. A slender woman sat astride the horse, swaying rhythmically with the animal's motion. Her long curly hair bounced against her back, and Clay did a double take. Taylor Jordan! No, it couldn't be.

He braked sharply and rubbed his eyes. As the woman drew closer, he could see she wasn't Taylor and felt chagrined that he'd imagined for a moment she was. This woman was older and taller, her hair lighter, and her eyes a definite blue. Darn Taylor! It wasn't enough that she'd invaded the house where he lived, especially the bathroom and his office. Now he was even seeing her where she'd never been!

"Hello," the rider called. "I'm Amy Morrow, and I'm glad you could come on such short notice." She slid from the horse's back and held out her hand with a smile as Clay climbed down from his truck.

"Nice to meet you," Clay responded, taking her hand and returning the smile. "What's the problem?"

Ms. Morrow released his hand slowly and began walking toward the stable, leading her mare. Clay walked beside her.

"One of the colts got out sometime last night or early this morning," she told him. "When we found him, it looked like he had tangled with a big cat. Joe cleaned him up, and I called the vet who usually checks my horses, but he's dealing with an emergency and suggested I call you."

Joe Terrence met them at the stable door. Clay entered and was surprised to see that the stable was larger than it had looked from the outside and that it was built to hold close to two dozen horses, though he could see there weren't that many in the stable or grazing in the nearby pasture. Together they approached the box stall where the colt was nervously pacing. Joe held the young horse steady while Clay checked the deep lacerations in its shoulder.

"He was lucky," Clay said, turning to speak to the other two. "The scratches are deep, but not dangerously so. I think the cat who jumped him was quite young. A full-grown mountain lion's claw marks would have been spaced a little further apart and would have slashed much deeper. I doubt he would have survived an attack by an adult cat." He applied disinfectant, then with a local anesthetic, stitched the deepest cut. When he finished, he injected an antibiotic.

"I think he'll be fine," he said to Ms. Morrow. "I'll stop by in a couple of days to check on him, and you can call my office if there are any problems or questions."

They spoke briefly before shaking hands again, and Clay returned to his truck. As he drove away from the ranch, he looked back for one last glimpse of the picturesque setting. In his mind's eye, once more he saw Taylor Jordan flying across the meadow on the back of the roan. Was it disappointment he'd felt when the rider turned out to be Amy Morrow? He was irritated with himself because the picture haunted his mind with firmer tenacity than the unexpected reality of a famous actress riding toward him and touching his hand. He turned back to the road and pressed a little harder on the gas pedal.

CHAPTER 6

Clay glanced at the small wicker basket on the countertop. At first he didn't grasp its significance, but when he opened the vanity drawer and saw his razor and shaving cream neatly lined up with all of his other personal toiletries, he understood. Instead of grinning with triumph, he felt a twinge of disappointment. He'd won—the drawer was his, but suddenly the battle felt petty and the triumph small. Belatedly he recognized the tug-of-war had never been about winning. He wasn't too sure what it had been about, but stuffing Taylor's brush and cosmetics in a bag and tossing them under the sink every morning had been a lot more satisfying than claiming the drawer as his own could ever be. And seeing her things staring him in the face from the little basket that had become their home would be a nagging reminder of their silent tug-of-war. Viewing his toiletries in the drawer felt more like losing than winning.

He'd managed to make avoiding Taylor an art form, yet he'd gotten some perverse kick out of their silent struggle over the little drawer. He left the house before she was up each morning, and in the evening he went fishing or retired to his room to avoid her. While passing behind her on his way to the stairs, he occasionally caught a glimpse of her dark hair swaying against her back as she paced the floor and talked with her father on the telephone. Clay had learned from Lilly that the telephone calls were a nightly ritual.

For the past two weeks, his only contact with Taylor had been the drawer. He'd been called out on an emergency last Sunday, so he'd even managed to avoid bumping into her at church.

Picking up the can of shaving cream, he sprayed a liberal amount on his hands, then patted it on his face before reaching for his razor. He stared into the glass, but it was Taylor's face, smeared with freckle cream, that he saw. He'd handled the tube of cream enough over the past two weeks to know she covered her nose and cheeks with it every night in a vain attempt to fade away the little sun kisses he found so intriguing. No, they weren't intriguing; they were just unusual for a grown woman.

"Ouch!" He winced as a speck of red appeared on his chin. Grabbing a piece of tissue paper to stick on the tiny nick, he determined to keep his mind on the task at hand. But after a few seconds, it started to drift again.

Deliberately turning his thoughts away from the exasperating Taylor, he let his thoughts travel to the pleasant surprise Wendy had turned out to be these past two weeks. The sunporch had actually become an organized office. Files and invoices were in their correct places in the file drawers, bills were paid, and payments deposited in the bank. His printer/fax had been unpacked and set up, and each night when he sat down at his desk, he found a neatly typed list of phone messages and appointments for the following day. Other than an occasional splotch of nail enamel on various papers and an unending series of suggestions that he return to the office early enough to take her to dinner, Wendy was doing a much better job than he had anticipated.

Guiltily he recognized he'd been avoiding Wendy, too, which was probably unfair considering all she'd done to make his work run more smoothly. He considered taking her out to dinner as a kind of reward for all her efforts, then talked himself out of the gesture. He'd never believed it was a good idea to see an employee socially.

Showering in record time, he was dressed and ready for church in minutes. He intended to be out of the house and on his way long before Taylor set out, but he couldn't resist a quick glance toward her door as he hurried toward the stairs. He breathed a little easier seeing it was still tightly closed.

He could hear the shower running in the first floor bathroom as he tiptoed down the stairs and wasn't surprised that Lilly was already up. In the kitchen he found a plate of warm rolls on the counter beside a basket of fruit. He helped himself, then opened the door to the sunporch. He'd feed Rambo and the gerbils before going outside. He was only boarding two dogs currently, and feeding them wouldn't take long. He could see that they had food and water without messing up his suit. He gave an appreciative glance at the office end of the porch before heading toward the bags of feed.

He whistled softly as he scooped feed into the gerbils' food dish and slid a generous portion of nuts and seeds into Rambo's cage. He smiled, seeing the elastic hair clip, something like a small bungee cord; it looked like Wendy had substituted it for the wire fastener Stewart had devised for keeping the cage door secured. But it was frayed and probably wouldn't last much longer, so he'd have to think of a more permanent solution. Gathering up water dishes, he returned to the kitchen to fill them.

Back on the porch, he set down the gerbils' water on the corner of his desk and turned to Rambo. With one hand he opened the cage door and blocked the bird's usual effort to exit the cage before he could close it. Noise erupted behind him, and Clay turned to see Tom launch himself toward the cage. With his hands full of water dishes, he'd forgotten to close the kitchen door. Rambo seized the moment to swoop past his face, and the chase was on.

"Tom!" he shouted as he lunged toward the cat, sending a small cage flying. Tom leaped from the birdcage to the top of the gerbils' cage and onto Clay's desk. Rambo squawked as she landed on the computer monitor, then fluttered to the top of the file cabinet with Tom right behind her. The gerbils' water spilled across his desk calendar as Clay tried to snatch the cat back from achieving his goal.

Tom yowled as he landed on the file cabinet, and Rambo streaked toward the open kitchen door. Papers flew and cages tipped as Clay pursued the cat, determined to catch him before he could follow the bird into the house. Giving a mighty lunge, Clay went sprawling, but his fingers closed satisfyingly around the tip of the cat's long, furry tail. Tom shrieked and turned to sink his teeth into his captor's hand.

"Ouch! Stop that!" He struggled to get a better grasp on the animal and catch his breath at the same time.

"What is going on!?" The kitchen door slammed shut as though punctuating her words. Ten pink toes stopped inches in front of his face. It was all he could do to prevent a groan from escaping. It would be Taylor, not Lilly, who caught him in such an undignified position. At least, the pesky girl had enough sense to close the door so Tom couldn't follow Rambo into the house. Taking care not to release the cat, he made an undignified scramble to his feet.

"Oh, here!" She took Tom from him, and the nasty-tempered beast cuddled comfortably in her arms like a satisfied kitten. With what looked to Clay like a taunting smirk, Tom rubbed his head contentedly against the soft fleece of Taylor's robe.

"Stupid cat!" Clay growled as he searched for something with which to staunch the blood dripping from the back of his hand.

"Most people learn by the time they're two not to catch a cat by its tail." Taylor accompanied her words with a tissue. Grudgingly he accepted it, slapping it immediately across his bleeding hand.

"I wasn't trying to catch him by his tail; I was merely trying to keep him from following Rambo into the house," he attempted to defend himself.

"There's antiseptic and bandages in the upstairs bathroom medicine cabinet," she pointed out. He noticed there wasn't a lot of sympathy in her tone of voice.

"I know." He should; he put them there.

"Look what I found!" Lilly spoke as she opened the door and stepped onto the sunporch with Rambo perched on her shoulder. She was carrying a flexible metal chain with a simple sturdy fastener, the kind often used to string keys together.

"Hold onto that cat!" Clay shouted a second too late. Tom launched himself toward the bird, who at once swooped toward his cage. Leaping forward, Clay slammed the door shut before Tom could follow. Appropriating Lilly's chain, he wrapped it around a spoke of the cage then around a thick wire in the door before joining the two ends together.

"Bad kitty!" Lilly picked up the disappointed cat and headed toward the kitchen. "You two better hurry, or we'll be late for church," she called over her shoulder before disappearing from sight.

Clay turned around slowly, taking in the mess left behind by his mad scramble to keep the two animals apart. His desk was a wreck. Water dripped slowly over the edge from the spilled water dish. Papers littered the floor. Cages lay on their sides. From one, the two gerbils could be seen cowering in a corner. Beside the desk stood Taylor, and there was no mistaking the disapproval on her face.

"Go on! Go take care of that bite," she told him.

"I'll just straighten up—"

"First aid first. I can take care of this," she cut him off.

"I still need to give Rambo some water and feed the dogs," he argued as he bent to pick up a handful of the scattered papers. "Besides you don't know where—"

"I'll figure it out." She took the papers from him.

"All right," he agreed reluctantly. He didn't intend to stay and argue with her. He'd spray some antiseptic on his wound, see about the dogs, and return to clean up his office once Taylor went back upstairs to dress for church.

As he washed the small wound and applied the antiseptic, he noticed a red smear across the front of his white shirt. He pulled the shirt off and threw it in the sink. He'd have to leave it soaking in cold water until he got back from church. With a sigh, he slapped on a bandage and returned to his room to begin searching for a clean shirt. Failing to find another white one, he decided pale blue would have to do. It had been too long since he'd taken time to do his laundry. Lilly had offered to do his washing, but he'd refused. She already did more than their bargain called for. Swiftly buttoning the fresh shirt, he began tucking it into his slacks.

"Darn!" His pants hadn't escaped this morning's debacle unscathed. The darker fabric had hidden the stains better, but they were there. Now he'd have to find time to drop his suit off at the cleaners this week when he made the nearly two-hour trip to Twin Falls to pick up supplies. There was nothing for it but to find another pair of pants. That took longer than the search for a shirt. He'd have to wear Dockers to church. It might be a good idea to call his mother sometime today and ask her to send out more of his clothes.

He was standing with one leg in his Dockers when his phone rang. He automatically reached for it, stumbling a little as he scooped up the extension he'd had installed at the same time as his office phone.

"Clay Curtis," he tried to sound dignified which he found hard to do while stumbling around with his pants trailing from one ankle. He heard a small click before Betty Glendowski's voice boomed over the line.

"Doc, Pa's got a little problem. Said I should call you. One of them llamas he got from that doctor in Buhl is acting funny. He wondered if you could come over."

"Llamas?" He'd never treated a llama. His training had been in livestock, farm animals, pets, creatures like that. He'd left wildlife and exotic animals pretty much to others. He'd heard of a few ranchers raising llamas for pack animals, but he hadn't expected to see any around Fairfield, Idaho.

"I didn't know your pa was raising llamas," he hedged while he tried to recall the little he knew about the South American beasts of burden.

"Oh, he's not raising them serious-like. They just sort of intrigued him so he bought a couple to stick in that pasture behind the feed store," she told him.

"Okay, I'll be there in a few minutes," he promised and hung up the phone. He finished dressing, then dashed down the stairs and out the front door. It might be cowardly, but he didn't want to tangle with Taylor again. He just hoped nothing important had been damaged in Tom and Rambo's early morning escapade and that Taylor wouldn't make a worse mess of things. Without taking time to open the gate between his property and Lilly's, he vaulted the fence and rushed to the kennel, where he quickly fed the two dogs before climbing into his truck. He was glad he'd left his bag in the truck last night.

* * *

Taylor grabbed a couple of kitchen towels to sop up the spilled water, then looked around in dismay. The room was a wreck. Picking up the scattered papers and righting the overturned cages didn't take long, but she'd be late for church if she took time to file the papers or print a new desk calendar. Dropping the papers in the wire basket on top of the file cabinet, she refilled the spilled water dishes. Rambo's water dish was surprisingly heavy. It occurred to her that it might be crystal rather than the cut glass she'd assumed it to be. *What kind of nut uses a crystal bowl for a pet's water dish?* she asked herself, shaking her head in disdain before hurrying upstairs to dress for church. From her bedroom window, she saw Clay's truck back out of the drive next door and pull onto the street.

"Impossible man!" she fumed. He should know that even an animal doctor should keep animals out of his business office. The two just didn't mix. And what did he plan to do once summer was over?

The sunporch wasn't insulated well enough for a tropical bird during an Idaho winter. He was supposedly building a clinic next door, but nothing much had been accomplished that she could see since she'd arrived. Occasionally someone showed up to putter around a bit, and some man who claimed to be the contractor had called Wendy a couple of times and left messages for Clay, which he didn't seem to respond to. Perhaps if she let the usurping veterinarian know he'd have to move whether his clinic was ready or not this fall when Grandma Lilly moved into her new apartment, he'd do something about getting the construction moving.

Stewart showed up to drive her grandmother to church and insisted Taylor accompany them. When they reached the small chapel, he helped both of them out of his car, then offered them each an arm as they made their way up the sidewalk. When they reached the door, it opened as if by magic.

"Thank you." Stewart smiled at the tall, broad-shouldered man who stood beside the door. "I was wondering how I was going to manage the door without letting go of the two best-looking women in Idaho."

"Some people have all the luck." The man laughed back in a booming voice that matched his large size. "I saw your problem right off, and I figured that if I helped you out, you just might introduce me to this young lady." He looked at Taylor and winked broadly. Startled, Taylor returned a hesitant smile. The man was old enough to be her father, but she got a definite impression he was flirting with her!

"This is Lilly's granddaughter, Taylor," Stewart announced. Then completing the introduction he added, "Taylor, this reprobate is Gar Glendowski. He owns the feed store over on Main Street. You might have met his daughter, Betty." A vague impression of meeting a large, blond woman just a little older than herself at church last Sunday came to mind.

"Nice to meet you, Brother Glendowski," she murmured politely and extended her hand, which turned out to be a mistake. The big man took it in a firm hold and showed no signs of returning it anytime soon.

"Gar will do just fine," he told her. "Obviously takes after her grandma," he said in an aside to Stewart. "Not a bit like ol' Andy."

He grinned, then still holding her hand, he started toward the chapel and Taylor soon found herself wedged between Stewart and Gar on a wooden bench with her grandmother on the other side of Stewart.

When she attempted to withdraw her hand, Gar seemed reluctant to let it go, but she persisted and he slowly released his grip. He opened the hymn book and she had little choice but to share it with him. Concentrating on the words of the hymn was difficult with the large man beside her a little too close for comfort, and she found her attention wandering around the room as though searching for an escape route. Her eyes met her grandmother's, and she read a warning there. She wasn't certain whether her grandmother was warning her not to make a fuss or to steer clear of the man who seemed enamored of her.

She wasn't in the habit of making a fuss in church, and she certainly wasn't interested in the middle-aged Romeo beside her, so Grandma Lilly had nothing to worry about! His casual reference to "Andy" confirmed her suspicion that he was a former classmate of her father's, though no one called Andrew Jordan "Andy" anymore. She couldn't imagine a time when anyone had. If the big clown followed her to the Gospel Doctrine class, she'd detour to the nursery. She'd met one of the nursery leaders last week, a pretty young woman with two blond little girls in tow, and she had offered to help anytime she was needed. She had a hunch Peggy Friedrickson just might need her today.

A rustling sound in the aisle caught her attention. Turning, she could see the young woman she thought was Gar Glendowsky's daughter leading Clay down the aisle. Her arm was tightly wrapped around his, and she was beaming as though she'd captured the prize of the century. There was a wet splotch on Clay's shoulder and he didn't look nearly as happy as his companion did. That cheered Taylor up some, until they crowded onto the same bench where she and her grandmother sat with Stewart and Gar.

Gar slid his hand over to cover Taylor's fingers where she held the hymnal. She released her hold on the book, and while Gar scrambled to keep it from dropping, she tucked her hands in her lap. Feeling eyes watching her, she glanced from under her lashes to see a grin of amusement on Clay's face. The grin disappeared when his companion slipped her arm through his again and snuggled against his side. It was Taylor's turn to grin. The girl with Clay was nearly as tall as he was and she probably outweighed him. On closer observation she noticed a distinct resemblance between the woman and Gar. Both were big boned with broad faces and were heavier than was healthy. Father and daughter, she surmised, and felt a moment's pity for Clay.

The song ended and Taylor felt a stab of guilt. She'd paid no attention at all to the opening hymn. She couldn't even remember which hymn had just been sung. As she bowed her head for the opening prayer, a figure dashed up the aisle and sat down on Clay's other side. Forcing herself to listen to the prayer being said, she kept her eyes closed, but the moment "amen" was spoken, she darted a glance toward the end of the bench and wasn't surprised in the least to see Wendy.

Hearing a soft snort beside her, she turned in time to catch Stewart attempting to hide a smile. Suddenly she felt a swell of giggles arising in her throat. Their whole bench was ludicrous. Grandma and Stewart were carrying on an octogenarian romance, she was attempting to politely discourage a man who probably graduated from high school with her father, and Clay was practically being smothered by a female barracuda on one side and a teenage vamp on the other. To make matters worse, she caught sight of a skinny young man with glasses glaring at Clay and Wendy from behind the sacrament table.

Clapping one hand over her mouth, she fumbled for her scriptures with the other. This was sacrament meeting, not a sanitarium for Cupid's mistakes! She had to get her mind on the service, she reprimanded herself.

It was the longest sacrament meeting Taylor had ever sat through, and when it finally ended, Stewart won a multitude of brownie points in her book by adroitly insinuating himself between her and Gar, and cheerfully sending him on his way to teach a Sunday School class. Thankfully, not the same one she and her grandmother would be attending. The young man with the glasses propelled Wendy toward one class, and the large-boned blond relinquished her grip on Clay since it seemed she had a Primary class to teach. Clay wandered off to sit with Blaine Gardner, his former missionary companion, who appeared happy to see him. Clay looked equally happy to have escaped the barracuda.

Sunday School class went well, and several times Taylor found herself impressed by the insightful answers Clay gave to several of the teacher's questions. She also noted the respectful way the teacher and class turned to Stewart for clarification on points of doctrine. Perhaps he wasn't quite the doddering old man she'd assumed him to be. Actually, he seemed to be a very nice man. If he just didn't fancy himself in love with Grandma, she could quite like him.

After Sunday School she turned toward the Relief Society room and saw Wendy heading purposefully toward a side door. Following a hunch that the girl planned to skip Relief Society, Taylor went after her. "Wendy, wait a minute," she called softly and was pleased when the other girl stopped. "Aren't you coming to Relief Society?" she asked as she stopped beside her.

"Relief Society is for old ladies." Wendy pulled a face.

"Thanks!" Taylor pretended to be offended.

"Oh, I didn't mean you," Wendy hastened to clarify. Underneath the scatterbrain persona she showed the world, she really was a caring person, Taylor reflected.

"I'm glad," she laughed as she defended the women's organization. "Actually Relief Society isn't just for older women anymore. I enjoyed Relief Society all the way through college."

"But you probably weren't the only young woman there," Wendy huffed. "Here, everyone is older and married. I can't go back to Young Women's, and I feel dumb going to Relief Society."

"You could sit with me, then there would be two of us," Taylor coaxed. Wendy seemed to consider, then something she saw over Taylor's shoulder helped her make up her mind.

"We better hurry!" Wendy grabbed Taylor's arm and rushed her toward the Relief Society room doors. Just as they ducked through the door, Taylor caught a glimpse of Gar making a beeline in her direction.

"Thanks," she whispered as the two women took their seats.

"Gar Glendowsky thinks he's a real stud," Wendy whispered. "He was a big shot in high school ages ago, and all the girls chased him—even my mom. He and his girlfriend eloped two weeks before high school graduation. She died six years ago, and he's gone right back to thinking he's God's gift to women."

Taylor stared at Wendy, appalled. She wanted to avoid the man, but she really hadn't wanted to be the recipient of quite so much information. Trying to change the subject, she whispered, "Who was the good-looking guy who walked you to Sunday School class?"

"Oh, that was just Tommy Beredsford," Wendy answered nonchalantly. "He thinks he's in love with me, but he's still in high school."

"If a guy is a little bit younger than a girl, it doesn't really matter once they're both adults," Taylor pointed out. "I dated a guy for a while at the University who was two years younger than me."

"It's not just that," Wendy seemed to squirm. "He's just so serious. He's planning to go on a mission, then to college. Even if I liked him, which I don't, I'm not waiting that long. I just can't live at home for six more years!"

"You don't have to get married to leave home," Taylor whispered back as the prelude music began. "You could go to school or even get a job in another place."

"Try telling my parents that," Wendy retorted. "Anyway, with my grades I'd never get into college."

"You're an adult now, you don't have to settle for what your parents think your future should be. You can be anything you want, if you're willing to work for it," Taylor whispered back. As the words left her mouth, she wondered if she really believed them. Wasn't she just like Wendy, letting her dad keep her from the career she'd chosen?

* * *

Clay hung around after priesthood meeting, hoping Betty would leave before he reached the foyer. She might be a country girl, but she certainly wasn't what he had in mind.

"Good lesson, Blaine," he complimented his friend as he reached for a picture Blaine had used to illustrate a point in the lesson.

"I don't know," Blaine sighed. "Sometimes I think I'm just talking to the walls."

"That's not true. You were well-prepared and brought out some aspects of Joseph F. Smith's life I found interesting," Clay tried to reassure his friend.

"Interesting isn't what I'm trying to accomplish," Blaine was suddenly earnest. "Before I started teaching this course of study, I don't think I really knew much about Joseph F. Smith. He seemed to be so overshadowed by Joseph Smith, Brigham Young, and today's prophets, I never gave him much thought. But the more I study his speeches and the way he conducted his life, the more convinced I am that he set a pattern for dealing with today's problems. I don't think I'm supposed to be teaching an interesting history lesson; the real purpose is to help the elders in this class use his insights to be better husbands, fathers, and priesthood leaders."

"That's what made you such a great missionary. You could always see beyond the concept to the application," Clay said. "But I know what you mean. In some ways it was almost easier teaching gospel concepts to nonmembers and watching them catch fire as they accepted their truthfulness than it is to get those who have been members of the Church all of their lives to actually live what they know."

"That's the point I'm trying to make. Somehow I've got to get beyond talking about what a great guy Joseph F. Smith was and start helping the elders in our quorum change their lives by putting the things he stood for into their lives." Blaine ran his hand through his sandy hair, lightening it further with a liberal application of chalk dust.

Clay laughed. "You sound like a certain mission president I remember well. 'Knowing isn't enough! It's doing that counts!'"

"He was right," Blaine grinned sheepishly. "I guess I've adopted his soapbox. And speaking of doing, what are you doing coming to church with Betty Glendowski and flirting with Wendy Carlson? I know I've been pushing you to settle down and get married, but I don't think either of them are what you're looking for. I'd think that granddaughter of Lilly Jordan's would be more your type."

"I didn't plan to come to church with Betty. I got a call this morning to look at her dad's llamas. Afterward it seemed rude not to offer her a ride. And I wasn't flirting with Wendy," he defended himself.

"Uh huh," Blaine agreed in a disbelieving tone. "I suppose the llamas were terribly ill."

"Well, no," Clay conceded, and Blaine's grin widened.

"And you gave Wendy a job and saved her a seat this morning because you feel sorry for her," Blaine deadpanned.

"Oh, come on. She's just a kid," Clay protested. "And I didn't save her a seat. I can't help it if she chose to come sit beside me."

"Some kid!" Blaine smirked.

"I'm not sure how she came to be working for me, but I have to give her credit." Clay was determined to be fair. "She's doing a good job. My office was in complete chaos and now it's organized." He didn't mention the chaos he'd left behind that morning. Besides that mess wasn't Wendy's fault, and it was only temporary.

"You're kidding, right?" Blaine laughed. "My younger brother was in her class in school. He said she barely missed flunking out of school and that her only goal in life was to get married."

"Maybe she's done a little growing up," Clay defended his assistant. He wasn't about to admit to Blaine that that had been his impression of the girl, too, until he'd seen the way she'd taken over his office, nor would he share the nagging feeling he had about the situation being too good to be true.

"You're not letting the scenery interfere with good sense, are you?" There was a worried note in Blaine's voice.

"I'll admit the scenery is fine, more than fine, but I'm not interested," Clay told his friend before jabbing him in the ribs. "By the way, what are you doing looking at the scenery? You're a married man."

"Marriage doesn't cause blindness," Blaine shot back. "It just encourages a man to not look too long or too hard. But what about you? Is temporary blindness your excuse for not noticing Lilly's granddaughter? Or could it be she turned you down, so Betty and Wendy are your means of letting her know there are other fish in the sea? It won't work. She'll see right through a juvenile tactic like that."

"I'm not interested in Taylor Jordan," Clay informed his friend a bit too emphatically. "There's not a minute's difference between Taylor and Jessica, and I'm not letting myself in for that again."

"No difference between Taylor and Jessica?" Blaine looked startled, then resumed gathering up his teaching materials. His jaw tightened and he seemed about to speak, then changed his mind. Finally he shut off the light and stepped into the hall. Clay followed him, wondering what his friend had wanted to say but didn't.

Ahead Clay noticed Betty Glendowski waiting near the front door. Near her stood Blaine's wife and Peggy Friedrickson. They were talking animatedly while their little girls played around them. A pang of envy struck him, and he almost missed hearing Blaine mutter something about needing his head checked as well as his eyes.

CHAPTER 7

As soon as Clay returned to Lilly's house he hurried to his room, partly to avoid Taylor and partly because he'd used calling his mother as an excuse to avoid having dinner with Betty. He dialed the number and waited for his mother to pick up the call in her New York apartment.

"Clay, darling," Samantha Curtis gushed as soon as she heard her son's voice. "I've been trying all morning to reach you. You simply must come home. Someone broke into Jessica's apartment, and she's so upset."

"I thought she was in Europe," he muttered.

"No, she changed her mind and came back a few days ago," his mother spoke with a tinge of sadness which he knew from experience was supposed to make him feel guilty. "She couldn't enjoy herself while you were angry with her."

"She wasn't hurt in the break-in, was she?" He refused to comment on his mother's reference to his former relationship with Jessica.

"No, she wasn't home when the apartment was burglarized," his mother told him.

"Good, then all she needs to do is call her insurance agent, and he'll take care of everything." He knew his mother would think him callous, but he knew Jessica. She had plenty of money, little or no sentimental attachment to any of the expensive gadgets and pieces of furniture in her apartment, and she loved to shop. It would be no hardship for her to replace a television or stereo.

"Nothing was taken except that cute little address Rolodex she keeps on her desk." Samantha Curtis was clearly annoyed with her son's obtuseness. "But they made a terrible mess—they tore up a lot of papers, and cut holes in cushions and pillows, and even ripped the clothes hanging in her closet. She needs someone to comfort her."

"Tell her to call Jacob," Clay told his mother, then went on. "Speaking of clothes, that's why I called. Could you send me a couple suits and half a dozen shirts? I left a lot of things in my closet there in your apartment, thinking I wouldn't need them here, but I find I don't have time to do my laundry as often as I thought I would."

"Jessica doesn't need her cousin," his mother wailed. "She needs you."

"About those shirts, Mother," Clay ignored her plea. "I've put on a little weight, so send the larger ones."

"Clay–"

"I've got to go," he interrupted. "Thanks, Mother." He hung up the phone.

A short time later he sat across from Taylor at Lilly's dinner table and knew that contrary to Blaine's accusation, there was absolutely nothing wrong with his eyes. She was beautiful, gorgeous, stunning, et cetera. And the most aggravating female he'd ever met, next to Jessica, of course. She was up to something, but what, he couldn't quite figure out. She'd started out by asking him how soon his clinic and office would be completed. All she had to do was look out the window to see it was going nowhere fast.

"Bib Jones isn't much of a self-starter," Stewart joined in the conversation. "He does good work, but he needs someone to give him a push or two to get him started most days."

"He's got detailed plans, and I've arranged for credit at the building supply store," Clay pointed out in exasperation. "I don't have time to hold his hand."

"Perhaps you could have your office manager check on him each morning and encourage him along. I'm sure Wendy wouldn't mind." Lilly spoke to him, but she gave Taylor an odd look that seemed to suggest her granddaughter might have some influence with Wendy or the contractor.

Taylor scarcely seemed aware of the conversation going on around her, but then she spoke up, as if she'd been paying more attention than she'd appeared to be doing. "You know, Grandma," she said, "just two blocks from our house in Pocatello, there are some apartments under construction. I've been watching their development since they were just a hole in the ground. They'll be finished in late August or early September. They're really cute and the people who live in them can bring their own furniture or rent them already furnished. They have big sunny windows and clever little garden balconies. I've been thinking of going home for the Fourth of July. Why don't you go with me for a little visit, and I'll show them to you?"

"I don't know," Lilly sounded reluctant. "Stewart and I have been talking about going to Hailey for the parade."

Clay looked from Taylor to her grandmother. There was more behind Taylor's invitation than appeared on the surface. They had been talking about his clinic, and suddenly Taylor was bringing up some construction project she'd been watching. Suddenly it hit him. Taylor thought that just because she'd watched the construction of an apartment complex, she was qualified to supervise the construction of his clinic! *No way,* he thought. He'd better have a talk with Wendy first thing tomorrow morning.

He excused himself from the table and started toward his office. He'd check on how much needed to be done to finish cleaning up this morning's mess, then if he didn't get any emergency calls, he'd settle down with a good book for a while. He might even retreat to the tree house, out of reach of his mother—if she tried to call back—and well away from Taylor.

He paused to stroke Tom's fur as he passed the sleeping cat on his way up to his room to collect his book. He'd never tell Taylor so, but he really hadn't meant to pull the poor old cat's tail. He was actually rather fond of the old opportunist. Tom didn't open his eyes or as much as twitch his whiskers. So much for Clay's peace gesture.

Taylor gathered up the dishes and shooed her grandmother out of the kitchen. She could wash the dishes while the older lady relaxed in the front room with Stewart. It amazed her how much two old people found to talk about.

She scraped the last of the chicken gravy into Tom's dish and looked around, wondering why the silly cat didn't come running. He usually made such a nuisance of himself at mealtime that he had to be put outside, and if any scraps were put in his dish, he was there so fast one would think he had radar.

"Here, kitty," she called but Tom didn't come running. She knew he was in the front room. She'd seen Clay stop beside the chair where the cat lay curled in sleep to stroke his fur before going up the stairs. She shrugged off Tom's uncharacteristic behavior. This morning's activity must have worn him out. He'd come when he got hungry.

Finishing the dishes, she glanced toward the sunporch door. Most of the mess in Clay's office still needed to be taken care of, but today was Sunday. She should leave it until tomorrow morning. Besides if she didn't call Daddy pretty soon, he'd call her and be upset because she'd kept him waiting. She looked toward the telephone and sighed. Perhaps it would be all right just to check that nothing had been ruined by the spilled water before she called Daddy.

A gust of wind caught the door as she turned the knob, slamming it against the wall. A flurry of papers flew toward the outside door, which was standing open. Immobilized by shock, she took in the overturned cages, the tipped file cabinets with their empty open drawers, the debris heaped on the desk and floor.

Regaining her usual presence of mind, she closed the back door to keep the loose papers from flying through it. She noticed that the latch appeared to be broken, which explained why the door wouldn't stay closed. She'd have to find something to fasten it with. Turning around, she saw the gaping birdcage door. Rambo's cage was empty! Her gasp came out more like a scream.

A shrill screech reached Clay's ears, and he rushed back downstairs. Lilly and Stewart crowded the door to his office as he reached it. He didn't see Taylor until he got close enough to look over Lilly's head. She seemed to be perfectly all right, but his office was a worse shambles than it had been earlier this morning. He knew at once that not even Taylor could have made this big of a mess. His eyes went immediately to the small refrigerator where he kept the drugs he needed in his practice. It didn't appear to be damaged.

"Are you all right, dear?" Lilly squeezed past Stewart to reach her granddaughter. Her arms went around the girl's shaking shoulders. That's when Clay noticed one long white feather in her hand.

"Where's Rambo?" He pushed past Stewart to enter the room. One glance around the room told its own story. The cage was open, as was the back door. The little chain he'd used to secure the birdcage door was on the floor.

"I—I don't know," Taylor stammered, straightening from her grandmother's grasp. "He isn't here. And . . . and Tom didn't come when I called him for lunch."

"Did Tom . . ." Lilly began, a look of abject horror on her face.

"Now, Lilly." Stewart stepped to her side. "That blamed bird must've flown away. Tom tries, but he doesn't ever get close."

"I don't think Tom did this," Taylor protested. She appeared more calm as she went on, "If Tom had caught Rambo, there would be more feathers—and blood or bones. He couldn't swallow a bird that size whole!"

"Of course, Tom didn't do this," Clay thundered. "That cat is still asleep in the front room. He can't open doors anyway. Whoever was in here last must have left the door open." He glanced pointedly toward Taylor.

"I never even opened the back door this morning. And for your information, the latch is broken," Taylor snapped back. "Obviously someone didn't close the cage door all of the way."

"Children, let's not fight." Stewart's voice was saved from severity by a slight chuckle. Clay flushed at the older man's gentle chiding. He noted Taylor's face took on a crimson blush.

"Do you suppose some of the neighbor children came in while we were at church and let Rambo loose?" Lilly asked.

"That's probably what happened," Stewart concurred and Clay groaned. When he'd first arrived, the careless way Lilly left her doors unlocked had bothered him, but as he'd later discovered, it was pretty much standard operating procedure in the community, and he'd stopped worrying about it. He should have known better. No place was safe from theft or vandalism. And even small rural towns had drug problems.

"Rambo's probably hiding in the apple tree again," Lilly sighed. "I suppose we'd better all change into jeans and go after her."

"It would take a pretty large child to knock over filing cabinets or open the fastener on that chain. It's so stiff, I could barely open it when I put water in Rambo's cage this morning," Taylor grumbled as she reached for a stack of files and began shuffling them into order.

"Jessica will kill me," Clay muttered as he headed out the open door and started toward the tree. Since he wasn't wearing dress pants anyway, there wasn't any reason for him to change before going after Rambo. Taylor's words caught up to him as he stood beneath the canopy of leaves, searching their depths for his former fiancée's pet. "It must have been teenagers," he mused. "But why would teenage vandals steal a bird and ransack my office instead of trashing the whole house or stealing drugs? At least you'd think they would steal my computer or Wendy's boom box. And Fairfield doesn't have a huge teen population. The few kids I know are so busy herding cattle, milking, or mowing hay, they don't have time to do something like this."

"So Rambo belongs to Jessica," Taylor fumed as she deftly straightened files and gathered up the scattered papers. She'd heard the name mentioned enough to know Jessica was Clay's former girl-friend. Her hands automatically sorted papers and straightened office equipment. Suddenly her hands stilled. What was it Wendy had said about Clay taking something that didn't belong to him? Might Clay have taken the bird to make Jessica worry or come after her? That thought irritated Taylor, but she didn't stop to wonder why. Wendy had said it was a man who called. Could he be Jessica's father—or perhaps a new boyfriend?

"Clay!" Grandma Lilly rushed past Taylor. The big, long-haired cat hung limply in her arms, his yellow fur swaying in the slight breeze, the only sign of movement. Stewart hurried after her, and Taylor dropped the papers she was holding to follow.

"Something is wrong with Tom," Lilly gasped as she slid to a stop beside Clay. "He won't wake up."

"What do you mean he won't wake up?" Clay took the cat and gently laid him on the grass. Kneeling beside the cat, he checked his vitals and ran his fingers through the thick yellow fur. His fingers seemed to pause near the cat's shoulder, and a frown sketched two deep furrows between his eyes before he shook his head and continued his examination.

"You don't think he caught your bird and passed out from eating too much?" Stewart ventured a guess, not even he seemed prepared to take seriously.

"No, I don't think so," Clay murmured in a distracted voice.

"Was he poisoned?" Lilly's face took on a militant frown. "Some of the farmers still put out poison for rodents, and Amanda Bronson has been threatening to poison the birds that get in her cherry tree."

Clay's hand stilled and a look of disbelief crossed his features. "I think Tom was sedated," he muttered.

"You mean like a shot to put him to sleep? But why would someone do that?" Lilly grew indignant, then worried. "He will wake up, won't he?"

"I think so," Clay assured her. "He doesn't seem stressed at all."

"That doesn't make sense," Stewart protested. "That cat sleeps most of the time anyway. He only wakes up to eat and to see if he can catch that blasted bird; why would anyone go to the bother of putting him to sleep?"

"Maybe Rambo didn't escape because someone was careless," Taylor ventured. "What if someone took her?" She gave Clay a dark look. "And maybe that someone sedated Tom to keep him from getting in the way and creating a fuss."

"What if someone tried to sedate Rambo, and Tom got in the way?" Lilly worried.

"Who would want that fool bird badly enough to steal her?" Stewart scoffed.

"Whoever she belongs to might want her back," Taylor spoke a little too sweetly.

"I wish!" Clay growled as he stood with Tom in his arms. "I've written to Jessica twice, asking her to make other arrangements for Rambo. Since she hasn't bothered to answer, I assumed she was still in Europe. My mother just informed me she came back early."

"Pardon me," Taylor stepped to Clay's side feeling a little confused. "But if Rambo belongs to your former fiancée, why do you have her?" It probably wasn't polite to ask, but if her theory of how Clay had acquired Rambo was about to be shot down, and she had a hunch it was, she would appreciate a few more facts.

"Oh, Rambo arrived by plane one day a few weeks ago," Lilly provided the explanation. "Someone called from that little airfield in Hayley one day and said there was a bird there for Dr. Curtis, and would someone please come pick it up. I had no idea where Clay was that day, so I drove on down there and got her. She was in a box with little round holes cut in the sides, sort of like the farmers used to get their baby chicks in each spring. Jessica had sent a bag of feed and those fancy little dishes, but Rambo hardly ate or drank a thing for almost a week. She looked so pathetic and sad."

"Hmpff!" Stewart grunted. "Until she caught sight of old Tom. It's been war ever since," he finished the story.

"Oh look, Tom's waking up," Lilly observed. Sure enough, the cat's eyes were open to a narrow slit, and he flicked his tail as if experimenting to see if it still worked.

"I think he's going to be okay," Clay attempted to reassure Lilly as he settled the cat on the thick cushion of a nearby lawn chair. "You stay by him and look after him. Call me if he seems to have any problem. I've got to start searching for Rambo."

Taylor followed Clay back to the tree. She stared upward into the gnarled old limbs, but all she could see was one corner of the old tree house. But she didn't really expect to see anything. Someone had stolen the bird. She was convinced of that, but it seemed she was the only one giving her theory any credence. The message Wendy had repeated to her persisted in her mind. The specific words the caller had used had been "more than one neck wrung."

Her father had told her that was how roosters destined for dinner had been killed when he was a boy—by wringing their necks. She shuddered. As far as she knew, birds were the only animals that were killed by "wringing their necks." The caller had to have been referring to Rambo, though why anyone would want to wring Rambo's neck she couldn't begin to guess. Well, maybe she could. But surely that was merely a figurative expression. She'd assumed the threat was for Clay and wondered how serious the threat was, but she hadn't once thought seriously of Rambo being threatened.

"Clay," she began hesitantly. "Did Wendy tell you about a threatening call she received a few days ago?"

"Threatening?" Clay sounded more curious than upset. "No, what kind of threat did she get?"

"Wendy wasn't exactly the one threatened," Taylor admitted as she craned her neck for a better view of a white speck she'd glimpsed through the thick foliage. She repeated the threat as Wendy had explained it to her. "I thought it was just one of those dumb things people say when they're mad and don't know how to express their anger. You know, like 'I'll kick his butt, 'Someone ought to shoot him,' or 'I could wring his neck.'"

Clay didn't respond immediately, and she glanced over at him to see him staring back at the lawn chairs where he'd left Tom and Lilly. Taylor's mouth fell open. Rambo was strolling in his own lurching gait toward the chair where Tom slept. Obviously neither Lilly nor Stewart had seen her yet. But Tom had! She saw him tense for the leap. Before she could scream a warning, the cat launched himself toward the bird, only to collapse in an ignominious heap on the lawn several feet short of his goal. He made several stumbling lurches toward the bird, who merely hopped backward a couple of steps. In seconds Clay held Rambo firmly in his grasp.

Well, so much for my theory, Taylor thought as she trailed Clay back to his office. Lilly and Stewart followed with Tom.

"Naughty, kitty," Lilly scolded as she hugged Tom and carried him through to the kitchen. Stewart carefully closed the door between the kitchen and Clay's office, leaving Taylor on the office side of the door with Clay. She watched as Clay placed Rambo in his cage and securely closed the door. He didn't say anything and Taylor considered excusing herself to go into the main part of the house. Instead it was Clay who turned and exited out the back door.

Okay, she'd let her imagination carry her away, Taylor acknowledged. Rambo was an unusual bird, and she'd simply escaped. It wasn't like she'd never escaped before. Taylor absently pushed the file cabinet upright, then stooped to gather the rest of the scattered papers. Mindlessly she began stuffing them into folders, then inserted the folders into the file cabinet. Dropping a handful of pens and pencils into a holder on the desk, she smoothed out the battered desk calendar. Anyone could have left the back door open or not noticed the latch was broken. And Tom? Why had she assumed Tom's sleeping bout was necessarily connected to Rambo's escape?

Through the wide porch windows she saw Clay returning with a toolbox in his hand. Doubtless he thought her some kind of hysterical nut. Before he could laugh at her dramatic interpretation of events, she opened the kitchen door and beat a hasty retreat to her room. At least the day hadn't been a complete disaster. She had brought up the subject of the apartment complex where her grandmother would soon be living, and she'd come up with an excellent plan to speed up Clay's removal from Grandma Lilly's house. She glanced through the window to the construction site next door and smiled.

* * *

Taylor awoke the next morning to the sound of Clay's pickup truck leaving the driveway. She rolled over and looked at her watch. *Six o'clock!* He was certainly getting an early start. She flopped back on her pillow, intending to go back to sleep but found herself maddeningly awake. After a few minutes she sat up and reached for her robe. She might as well get a head start on straightening Clay's office for Wendy. She had a hunch the task would overwhelm the girl if it was left for her to do alone.

She noticed two things the minute she walked into the office: a padlock on Rambo's cage and a dead bolt on the back door. Oddly enough the sight of the two locks was more disturbing than reassuring. They seemed to give credence to yesterday's wild imaginings.

She found a note, obviously intended for Wendy, on the desk, held in place by a piece of tape. Taylor had no qualms about reading it. It wasn't in an envelope or even specifically addressed to Wendy. It was an apology for the office's condition, a request that she call him if the pharmacy in Twin Falls tried to reach him, and it mentioned keys to the deadbolt and Rambo's cage left in Lilly's kitchen for her.

When she finished grouping files and straightening the big desk, she looked at the boxes still stacked in one corner. She already knew they contained books. At least the top one did. She might as well arrange them in the bookcase, but first she'd have to put the bookcase together. She'd noticed it before, too. It was a simple precut four-shelf unit that required assembly. She had assembled her desk and bookshelves back home in her own room, so it shouldn't be too hard.

Taking a paper knife from the desk drawer, she slit open the box and spread the pieces on the floor. She was hard at work when she heard her grandmother call her name.

"Breakfast is ready, Taylor." She looked up to see Grandma Lilly standing in the doorway to the kitchen with a puzzled expression on her face. "Goodness, child, what are you building?" She looked around at the various boards scattered on the floor.

"A bookcase," Taylor laughed, "but I need an extra pair of hands. Do you think you could hold a few pieces steady for me after we eat?"

"I don't know," Lilly looked skeptical. "I always left the building to your grandpa. I can wield a pretty mean paintbrush, but hammers and nails are beyond me."

"No hammers, I promise." Taylor jumped to her feet and ushered her grandmother back into the house. "All I need is someone to steady a few boards while I screw them together."

"Is that what Clay was doing this morning? I heard something that sounded like a power drill last night, then this morning he was trying so hard to be quiet, I pretended I didn't hear a thing." Lilly looked worried as she went on. "He might not like it if you try to finish his project."

"No, the bookcase is my project. You must have heard Clay installing the new locks last night. He was probably just picking up his schedule this morning." She deliberately made herself sound calm, but she promised herself she'd take a look at that lock from the outside as soon as she found a quiet moment.

Picking up the pan of hash browns from the stove top before her grandmother could lift the heavy skillet, Taylor carried it to the table, where she deftly divided the pan's contents into two servings. Lilly followed behind her with a platter of eggs.

"New locks?" Lilly wandered back to the doorway to peek at the locks. "Why do you suppose he did that? No one ever locks their doors around here."

"Grandma," Taylor spoke gently. "No place is completely free of crime. Admittedly he should have asked first before installing one on your door, but the only way Rambo could have gotten out yesterday is if someone turned her loose. Clay's a veterinarian, and even animal doctors need to keep a few drugs on hand. That little refrigerator out there is not for soft drinks. I know he keeps it locked, but what if a child should come inside and somehow find it open? I don't think he wants to take that chance." Taylor was surprised to find herself defending Clay.

"You mean I'll have to go out the front door to tend to my garden?" Lilly obviously didn't like that possibility.

"No." Spotting several bright new keys sitting on one end of the counter, she picked them up to show Lilly. "He left keys for you and Wendy."

"Well, all right." The older woman took the key from Taylor and tucked it in her apron pocket. "But it seems to me like a lot of bother."

The two women sat down to breakfast, and Taylor noticed Tom snoozing under the table. He lifted one eye to stare at her expectantly, and she slipped a sliver of ham beneath the table. The cat swallowed it in one gulp. Whatever had happened the day before, it hadn't left any lingering side effects. Tom was apparently back to normal.

After the breakfast dishes were washed and put away, Taylor returned to Clay's office. Using the key he had left for Wendy, she opened the door and inspected the lock from the outside. Scratches in the shiny new metal brought goose bumps to her skin. Just as she'd suspected, it hadn't been Clay trying to be quiet at the back door early this morning.

She had barely resumed working on her bookcase project when she heard footsteps crossing the kitchen floor. She looked up expecting to see Grandma Lilly or Wendy. Instead it was Stewart who joined her in the sunporch office.

"Lilly tells me you need a little help." The man grinned in anticipation as he stooped down beside her. He studied the project she'd undertaken for a moment then spoke again sounding slightly disappointed. "Looks to me like you're about done."

"The screws need to be tightened," she offered, "and I can't stand it up by myself." She wasn't surprised when he took the screwdriver from her hand to finish settling the screws. Stewart Darnell really was a nice man, she decided, even though he seemed to consider assembling a bookcase to be a masculine project. Together they stood the bookcase upright, and Taylor busied herself with setting the shelf brackets in place.

"Who the thunder is that?"

Taylor straightened and followed the direction the old man was pointing in time to see two heads duck behind the back hedge.

"I don't know." She continued to stare at the spot where the heads had disappeared.

Striding to the door, Stewart twisted the new lock and stormed down the back steps.

"Wait, Mr. Darnell," she called, but when it became obvious he wasn't going to wait, she ran after him, her heart pounding. Those heads hadn't looked like kids to her. If they were the burglars, they might hurt the old man.

By the time they reached the hedge, there was no sign of the two, but the pasture grass next to the fence looked trampled to Taylor's inexperienced eye.

"Do you think we should call the police?" She turned to Stewart.

"What good would that do? There's no law against looking over fences." Stewart sounded frustrated. "Folks can look anywhere they're of a mind to—'cept in windows—even if they're city slickers."

"What makes you think they were city slickers?" Taylor wondered aloud.

"Suits. Folks around here don't wear suits on a Monday morning 'less'n there's a funeral." He turned to march back to the house. His ramrod-straight back said he was angry, and it took her a moment to realize why. He was angry with himself, with old age for slowing him down too much to catch the curious strangers. For some reason that saddened her. She didn't know what she might have done if the men had still been in sight when Stewart reached the fence and if he'd gone running after them.

Returning to the office, she hurried inside where she and Stewart quickly inserted the shelves in the bookcase and moved it to a spot within easy reach of the swivel desk chair. Lilly came out to inspect their work and was lavish in her praise. Stewart's chest seemed to swell with each word of praise she uttered.

"Thank you for your help," Taylor told Stewart and meant it. Even though she could have finished the bookcase herself, his help had made the task easier. And helping her complete the project had seemed important to the elderly man.

After Stewart and Grandma Lilly returned to the main part of the house, Taylor began unpacking books and placing them on the new shelves. At first she had difficulty concentrating. Her mind kept returning to the scratched lock and the two heads she'd glimpsed peeking over the fence. She would have to talk to Clay about the strange happenings, but she doubted he'd take her seriously. He seemed to think she was silly and not too bright.

She sighed, wishing the vet was more like her grandmother's elderly friend. She couldn't help thinking what a nice man Stewart Darnell appeared to be. She'd come to her grandmother's house with a picture of him as a problem. He was nothing like she'd expected, and in some ways that made him an even bigger problem. She could certainly see why Grandma liked him. He was a good friend to her, and she would miss him when she moved to Pocatello at the end of the summer. For the first time Taylor felt a twinge of guilt for what her father planned to do. Living closer to her family would be fine for Grandma Lilly, but what about Brother Darnell? Would he be terribly lonely without Grandma? She had a strong suspicion the two elderly people would miss each other a great deal.

Taylor finished the first box and started on the second. She paused seeing a roll of papers tucked in one corner of the box. Opening them up, she found a blueprint—but for what? With curiosity getting the better of her, she spread the roll out on the floor. It didn't take long to see that the blueprint was a plan for the clinic Clay was building next door. It included a waiting room, a large office and a smaller private office, examination rooms, and an operating theater. There was boarding space, too, for small animals and horses. She was pleased to notice that the plan called for a small apartment over the office, consisting of a combined sitting room and kitchen, a bedroom, and a bathroom.

The second sheet of paper looked like plans for a house. As she examined it she found that the roomy open spaces appealed to her. It had ample bedrooms and baths for a large family and two rooms designated as offices—his and hers? A picture of the house sitting on the elevation a little behind where an old house had once stood came to mind with the stand of mature trees and the small stream that bordered the large lot behind it enhancing the picture. She could imagine the wide windows and open spaces inviting the panoramic view practically inside the house. It would be a lovely place to raise a family. That thought made her uncomfortable, and she immediately rolled up the papers and shoved them back in their cylinders.

"The apartment must be temporary quarters until the house is built," she concluded aloud. "After that it might come in handy if the vet has an assistant. It's small, but I'm sure it will do for a bachelor until he gets the house built."

The ringing telephone interrupted her thoughts. Scrambling to her feet, she answered as she'd taught Wendy. It only took a moment to make an appointment for Clay to stop by the Morgan ranch the following morning. Listening to Buzz Morgan explain his dog and her puppies' needs, Taylor caught a glimpse of how many miles Clay put on his truck running from ranch to ranch because he'd didn't have a facility for boarding animals that needed daily attention or where their owners could bring them to be checked. There was no way for him to set clinic hours where animals could be brought to him because he didn't have a clinic—yet. Her mind drifted to the clutter of construction supplies next door.

As she made the notation on Clay's calendar, she checked her watch and noticed it was almost noon and Wendy still hadn't arrived. Sitting in the big swivel chair, she tapped the end of a pencil against her lower teeth and continued to stare out the window at the deserted construction project next door. Obviously the building crew set their own hours just the way Wendy did. She'd talk to Wendy, try to impress on her the importance of keeping regular office hours. But she wondered just how effective it would be to have Wendy talk to the construction foreman. Perhaps if she just showed her what needed to be done . . . Or what if she said something to Clay? No. If her plan was going to work, she'd just have to take charge herself!

A light tapping at the back door distracted her. When she looked up, she saw Wendy framed in the screen door.

"Hi!" Wendy laughed, tugging on the door. "It seems to be stuck."

"No, it's not stuck." Taylor crossed to the door to open it. "Clay installed a lock." She explained about the lock and took Wendy inside to retrieve her key.

Wendy looked around nervously as she bounced the key from one hand to the other before dropping it in a cup on the desk. "Do you really think a robber broke in here and stole Rambo?"

"We don't know what happened. It was probably kids playing some kind of prank, but Clay thinks we shouldn't take the chance someone might try again. Rambo has been a pet all her life, and she wouldn't survive long in the wild." Taylor attempted to downplay her own concern.

"Poor Rambo." Wendy walked over to the cage where the bird appeared to be sulking. She stuck two fingers through the bars and stroked the bird's wing. "Was somebody mean to you? Did they scare you, pretty baby?"

Taylor stared in astonishment as the bird scooted closer to the girl, who continued to croon to it. The bird tilted its head to one side as though considering a weighty matter, then she leaned closer to Wendy and gently pecked her cheek. Wendy made kissy noises back, and the bird preened with pleasure.

"I didn't think that bird liked anyone, but she obviously likes you," Taylor laughed as she spoke. Rambo minded Clay to a limited extent and seemed to tolerate Grandma Lilly but was totally disdainful of her. Taylor had a sneaky suspicion that if she stuck a finger anywhere near Rambo, she'd lose it, or at least get a thoroughly nasty pinch.

"Oh, she's a pretty darling," Wendy assured Taylor. "If that ornery tomcat wasn't always eyeing her like she was dinner, she'd be no problem at all."

"If you say so," Taylor agreed halfheartedly.

The ringing of the telephone drew their attention back to Clay's office and as Taylor listened to Wendy make several appointments over the next couple of hours and sort the mail with a minimum of questions about what she should do with various pieces, she felt optimistic about Wendy's progress—until Taylor realized that she was the one posting all of the payments which had arrived in the mail and preparing the bank deposit. Wendy had become an adequate receptionist, but Taylor had somehow assumed responsibility for managing what was actually a small business.

CHAPTER 8

"Are you sure that's a word?" Taylor looked up to see Wendy poised over the phone pad, her ear against the telephone receiver.

"I don't know which one," the girl said before beginning to write something, then stopped with a shrug of her shoulders. "I'll tell him," she muttered, then hung up the phone. She sat glaring at the paper in front of her.

"Wendy, that wasn't another call like the one you got before when that man was rude to you, was it?" Taylor didn't mean to pry, but the call had upset Wendy in some way. The week had been quiet, and Taylor had almost dismissed from her mind the troubling questions about the strange events which had occurred the previous weekend.

"No, he wasn't rude. I just don't know what he meant. He said some big words I've never heard of, and asked me which ones Clay wants. How should I know?" Wendy shrugged her shoulders again.

"Was that the veterinary supply store in Twin Falls?" Taylor straightened. "A few days ago I heard Clay say he needed to order some more prescription drugs. He wrote them down on a paper for you." She hid a private smile. Clay obviously hadn't wanted to risk dictating his pharmaceutical list a second time.

"I don't remember . . ." Her voice trailed off as she picked up the note Clay had left beside the telephone.

"You'll have to call them back," Taylor pointed out.

"But I can't pronounce these words," Wendy wailed. She stared at the paper for several seconds, then passed it to Taylor. "You do it. Please."

With a sigh, Taylor reached for the phone. When she finished straightening out the pharmacy order, she made a couple of notations on Clay's calendar, then made an entry in the computer. Finally she turned to Wendy. "Clay's order will be ready by ten tomorrow morning. His calendar looks pretty clear for tomorrow afternoon, so don't book any more appointments until Monday. It looks like you'll only need to call Everett Friedrickson," Taylor pointed to the name and number on the appointment schedule, "and move his appointment from afternoon to early morning. Clay has to go right by their ranch on his way to Twin Falls."

"Okay." Wendy cheerfully made the call, staying on the line to chat with Peggy a few minutes. When she hung up, she looked pleased. "Cindy—that's Everett and Peggy's little girl—was born with some kind of heart defect. She had surgery a few months ago, and since then Peggy has had to take her to Boise for checkups every week. Cindy's specialist said she's well enough now that she only needs to see her family doctor in Hailey every other week, starting tomorrow. Isn't that great news?"

Taylor nodded, picturing the two pretty, little girls playing in the sunshine in front of the church last Sunday. She'd had no idea that the cheerful young nursery leader who had befriended her had been through such an ordeal.

"Everett will be away, helping his brother move some cattle to another range, when Clay gets there tomorrow morning, but Peggy said she and the girls will be there. Everett wants Clay to check on the mare who just had a colt. She'll be in the barn," Wendy chattered on in her friendly way.

"You'd better leave Clay a note telling him all that," Taylor advised.

"Couldn't you just tell him?" Wendy suggested.

"I don't work for him," Taylor reminded her.

"I know, but you live in the same house, and you know a lot more about his work than I do." Wendy was busy gathering up her purse and checking her appearance in the small glass she'd mounted on one side of a file cabinet. "It's almost three already, and Clay said I should make a bank deposit today. After that I have an appointment to get my hair done. There's a dance in Sun Valley tomorrow night, and I'm hoping Clay will take me. Bye, luv." She pursed her lips and blew Rambo a kiss before whirling out the back door.

Taylor watched the door slam behind Wendy and sat stunned for several minutes. So much for speaking to Wendy about keeping office hours! With a disgruntled click, she turned off the computer. She wasn't Clay's secretary or office manager or whatever. And if Wendy didn't appreciate being taught how to do her job, then she could just make a mess of it. She didn't care! She was through trying to help.

As she stood, her eye caught a movement next door. She paused for a better look. Someone was wandering around the construction site, and parked in Clay's parking spot was a truck with Jones Construction blazoned on the door. Grabbing up a clipboard, Taylor charged out the door. If she didn't accomplish one other thing today, she would at least make a start on making certain Clay's clinic was finished so he and his office manager could move out of Grandma Lilly's house by September—if not sooner!

* * *

"Mother, I don't know what you expect me to do. I can't just leave here and go back to New York because someone broke into Jessica's apartment," Clay attempted to reason with his mother while holding the phone between his shoulder and ear and changing his clothes for the trip to Twin Falls. Had the world gone crazy, he wondered as he listened to his mother tell him about Jessica's break-in once more? He decided not to tell her about what he'd begun to think of as Sunday's break-in right here in Fairfield.

"Now, Clay, just because you two had some silly tiff is no reason to act this way. Jessica has always counted on you," his mother reminded him.

"Jessica is no longer my fiancée. She lives in New York where she has a life and friends. I'm building a business and a life in Idaho. Our relationship is over," he explained patiently for the zillionth time. Patience didn't come easily to him, especially when it came to dealing with his mother. He really did need to be on his way to Twin Falls to pick up the veterinary supplies he'd ordered. He'd expected them a week ago, and his supplies were low.

"Jessica is willing to forgive you. It's just that after you'd gone on that mission and then to school across the country, she thought you were ready to settle down. She went ahead and signed the lease for the condo, but she said she wouldn't push you. She'll just go on waiting until you're ready to come home." His mother went on speaking in that irritating manner that had annoyed him for as long as he could remember and made him wonder if he were invisible.

He supposed he couldn't blame his mother for thinking this was just another of the many breakups he and Jessica had gone through. Jessica had broken their engagement so many times he'd lost count during the years he'd been on his mission, going to college, then to veterinary school. Neither she nor his mother seemed to understand that this time was different. He wasn't rushing back to be with her when she stopped sulking and invented some crisis to bring him running.

"Mother, I'm not going back to New York anymore, except to see you," he tried to intervene.

"Well, of course you'll come see me. But it's Jessica who needs you right now. My goodness, she is so upset. Imagine coming all the way back from Paris to find your whole apartment ransacked. All of her lovely things were all over the floor. I mean everything, from her ice trays to her bath salts, were dumped out. And the cushions from her sofa were cut in shreds, her mattress, too. The poor girl was shattered, and of course, she couldn't stay there."

Clay switched the phone from one ear to the other, tucked in his shirt, and dived into his closet for a pair of shoes. "If I know Jessica, she won't mind replacing everything. She lives to shop and she probably brought so many clothes back from Paris, she would have thrown all her old ones out anyway." He and Jessica had never seen eye to eye on spending. Her wealthy grandfather had spoiled her until the age of twenty-four, then died, leaving her with a lifetime trust that easily perpetuated her affluent lifestyle and freed her of any responsibility to support herself.

"Clay, that remark is beneath you. I don't think living in that place is good for you. You used to be such a sweet, understanding boy." Clay grimaced at his mother's words.

"Look, I'm sorry Jessica's apartment was vandalized, but if she's paying for a condo, why doesn't she just move in there?" Clay was losing patience.

"You know she's saving that for when the two of you are married," his mother protested.

"I'm not marrying Jessica," Clay spoke bluntly.

"Darling, it's not like you to sulk. You're twenty-eight years old and it's time to stop this cowboys and Indians in the 'wild West' nonsense and come back home where you belong." Her voice caught as though she were struggling to hold back a sob. Clay rolled his eyes. His mother's mini-sob was a classic maneuver she'd used with great success on both him and his father as long as he could remember.

"It won't work, Mother," he drawled in the best mimicry of a western accent he could summon. "Jessica is a big girl. She's perfectly capable of moving into a hotel by herself, and if she needs any help, I'm sure she has any number of well-muscled friends who will be happy to help her. Her cousins would cheerfully help her if she'd care to join them on Long Island for a few months. Jacob didn't ask her to move out when he inherited the mansion. He's allowing Seth and Ben to live there, and there's plenty of room for Jessica, too. She doesn't need me, and I certainly don't need her."

"Of course, she isn't going to a hotel," his mother sputtered. "And you know perfectly well she can't live in her grandfather's house as long as Seth and Ben are living there. She isn't speaking to them. They didn't behave well at all about their grandfather's will."

"She could go to Jacob's home."

"Don't be absurd. Jacob's snooty wife would never let her stay in their condo." That was probably true, Clay admitted silently. Jacob's wife, Katherine, made no secret of her dislike for her husband's brothers or for Jessica. A busy attorney, Katherine had no time or patience for her husbands "useless" brothers and cousin.

"Don't tell me," he groaned. "You didn't let her move in with you?"

"I certainly did." His mother defended her action. "This is where she should be until you come for her."

"It looks like you have a permanent guest then," Clay responded wryly. "I have to go now," he said after a moment's pause. "I have an appointment—"

"Clayton Harriman Curtis the Fourth, you listen to me," his mother interrupted. "Jessica is frightened and she's worried about that bird of hers. She wants you to bring it home."

"I'll be happy to stick it in a box and airfreight it to her." He couldn't keep the sarcasm out of his voice. "Just like she sent the bird to me."

"Don't you dare! Jessica is afraid something might happen to that bird. She thinks Rambo is the reason someone broke into her apartment."

"That's absurd," Clay laughed. "Got to go! Talk to you later." He hung up the phone, but before he could shove his wallet in his back pocket and exit the room, it rang again. He hesitated only a moment, then walked out the door, and whistled all the way down the stairs. Seeing her son married to a Winslow had been his mother's goal as long as he could remember. He'd once thought that was his greatest dream, too, especially when Jessica had been baptized just before he left on his mission. At first she'd protested his leaving as strenuously as his mother had, then she'd suddenly capitulated and claimed she wanted to be baptized. He'd been thrilled, then disappointed, when she never attended church once while he was gone.

Recently the cynical thought had come to him that Jessica's baptism had only been a ploy to keep him from becoming interested in a young woman who shared his faith and who could go to the temple with him. It was even possible that his mother had engineered the plan. He sighed. Jessica didn't matter to him anymore except as someone who had shared his childhood. His mother would have to accept that truth eventually.

When he reached the kitchen, he stopped, his eyes going to Taylor, who sat across from her grandmother. He hadn't expected to find her in the kitchen this early. She looked fresh and crisp in a pale blue sundress. Her dark curls glistened in the early morning light with a faint reddish glow, and her eyes looked more green than Tom's. He wasn't certain whether she was wearing makeup or not. She had to be. No woman's natural lashes were as long and dark as that. And her skin was too flawless to be natural. It looked more like one of his mother's porcelain dolls. She grinned, and to his mortification he realized she'd caught him staring.

"'Morning, ladies," he greeted them breezily, hoping he could grab a roll or muffin or whatever smelled so good and be on his way before he got into another round with his landlady's guest.

"Would you like some breakfast?" Lilly asked with a cheerful smile. Not waiting for an answer, she rose to her feet and reached for another plate.

"I need to be on my way," he demurred, then sniffing the air, added, "but I wouldn't say no to one of those muffins."

"Sit down, son. It won't take a minute longer to eat a real breakfast than to wolf down a couple of muffins." She set a plate heaped with hash browns and eggs on the table before bustling back to the cupboard for a glass and utensils.

"You might as well," Taylor dryly interpreted his hesitant look correctly. "You know you're going to give in. No matter how convinced you may be that bacon and eggs are too high in cholesterol or how much of a hurry you might be in, there isn't enough willpower in the whole world to resist one of Grandma Lilly's breakfasts. You'll be perfectly safe; I don't bite this early in the morning."

Clay grinned wryly, took the vacant chair beside the heaping plate of food, and began buttering a muffin. For several minutes he concentrated on eating his breakfast, then Taylor surprised him with a question about plumbing of all things.

"Is a floor sink better than a cabinet sink for grooming animals?" she asked while calmly lifting a forkful of potatoes to her mouth.

"I plan to have both," he answered, surprised by her question. "Cabinet sinks are fine for small animals, but larger dogs and injured farm animals are easier to clean up in a floor sink."

"What about floor drains? Do you think one is necessary outside if an area is cemented?" she asked next.

"It makes cleanup easier for large animals like horses . . ." He stopped, sensing she was up to something he wouldn't like. "Why are you suddenly interested in plumbing?" he asked suspiciously.

Before he could get an answer out of her, the phone rang. "I'll get it, Grandma," she offered a little too eagerly, jumping to her feet and rushing across the room.

"Hello, Jordan residence," she said. She listened for a moment and her cheery expression faded. "Are you all right?" she asked. Clay and Lilly both paused, blatantly eavesdropping. Taylor listened for a longer period of time. Several times she seemed about to say something but was cut off before she could complete a word. Finally she managed a quick question, "Would you like to tell him yourself? He's right here."

Clay promptly rose to his feet and stepped across the room. Reaching for the phone, he expected Taylor to hand it to him. Instead she hung it back on the wall with a puzzled look on her face.

"What was that all about?" he asked, annoyed that she hadn't surrendered the phone as he'd expected when she realized the call was for him.

"That was the strangest thing." Taylor shook her head. "Wendy left here yesterday with plans to stop at the bank, then get her hair done. She said she looked at her watch and realized the bank deposit wouldn't be credited until today anyway, and she was already late for her hair appointment, so she skipped going to the bank. She stopped there this morning on her way over here, but as she got out of her car in that little lot behind the bank, someone hit her over the head from behind and stole her purse."

"My goodness, was she hurt?" Lilly gasped.

"No, she's fine, but her hairstyle is ruined." Taylor turned to her grandmother. "She's quite indignant about that because she just had it done yesterday and it cost her sixty dollars."

She turned back to Clay. "She said to tell you she won't be in today because Doris offered to do her hair over for free. I guess Doris is the local hairstylist."

"Oh, yes. Doris does almost everyone's hair around here, though there are a few ladies who drive all the way to Hayley or even to Twin Falls to get their hair done," Lilly assured her granddaughter.

Clay felt like pounding on something. He was glad Wendy was safe, but he hoped Taylor would get around to telling him what had become of the bank deposit, presumably his, that Wendy had been carrying.

"I assume the thief made off with my money," he muttered.

"No, that's the strange part," Taylor continued with Wendy's tale. "She said she was sitting on the ground, leaning back against her car, when she saw the man who snatched her purse stop, and another man jumped out from behind the next building. The two of them dumped everything out of her purse onto the ground and pawed through it for a couple of minutes, then one ran back toward her. She cringed and closed her eyes, but the guy reached right over her and stole her car keys out of the ignition. He didn't touch the deposit bag."

"What!" Clay exploded. "The thief took her keys, but not her car?"

"They left your money, too," Taylor told him, "which makes sense since it was all in checks, and maybe they were only looking for cash. She said not to worry because she has another set of keys at home, so she'll still be able to pick you up at eight."

"Was her car key the only key on her key chain?" he asked, wondering if he was becoming paranoid to even consider that the thief might have been after the key to his office. But why else would anyone steal car keys, but not the car they fit? One look at Taylor's face convinced him he wasn't the only one who was thinking of the new lock on the back door. He wished he'd awakened a little earlier; he probably should have warned Lilly that he'd heard sounds early Monday morning that might have been someone trying to open the back door. Suddenly the rest of Taylor's words sank in.

"Pick me up? What for?" he questioned aloud to anyone who might have a clue to what Wendy had meant.

"Actually there was one other key on her key chain," Taylor ignored the second question and answered the first, causing Clay's heart to sink. "Don't worry, it wasn't a house key. No one locks their doors around here. And it wasn't the new key you gave Wendy. That key is sitting in a cup of paperclips, pencils, and such on your desk. It seems the key to Wendy's diary is missing, and she's quite upset over losing it. She can't imagine who would steal it because she only got the diary for graduation a few weeks ago and hasn't written anything interesting in it yet."

"Someone stole the key to Wendy's diary?" he asked incredulously.

"And the one to her car," Taylor added solemnly, then began to giggle. The mere thought of anyone hitting Wendy over the head to get a peek at her diary was too absurd. The reason she was chasing Clay was because there was nothing happening in her life. Not that Clay wasn't good-looking and all that, but Wendy would chase any man she thought might be her ticket out of Fairfield and away from her father's farm. Even if she had been interested in keeping a journal, she didn't have much to write about. Of course, she might have made up some juicy entries.

"Why would someone want to steal Wendy's diary?" Grandma Lilly asked, obviously puzzled.

"I don't think the thief was after Wendy's diary," Clay answered. His eyes met Taylor's and she knew they were both thinking of the new locks on the sunroom doors. There was something exhilarating about this strange affinity of thought flowing between himself and Taylor.

"Finish your breakfast," Grandma reminded them both, suddenly all business, making it clear she didn't wish to discuss the matter any further. "Everything always looks better on a full stomach, and you'll be late getting back from Twin Falls, Clay, if you don't hurry."

"Why does it matter what time I get back?" Clay turned to Lilly with every appearance of being thoroughly bewildered.

"The dance starts at nine, and if you're late, Wendy will drive too fast," Lilly responded matter-of-factly.

"Oh," Taylor inserted, suddenly remembering the message Wendy asked her to give Clay the day before. "Mr. Friedrickson wants you to stop at his place on your way to Twin Falls to check a mare he's leaving in his stable. Wendy said Brother Friedrickson won't be there, but you should stop anyway."

"Okay, it will only take about five minutes." He checked his watch and forked up his last bite of breakfast before stating quite emphatically that he had no plans to attend a dance that night.

"Of course you're going, dear." Lilly patted his arm affectionately as she rose to her feet and began carrying dishes to the sink. "All the young people are going. You and Taylor should go, too."

"Me?" Taylor's voice hit a high note, and she shook her head in denial. "I'm not going to a dance tonight."

Clay suddenly felt angry. Taylor obviously thought herself too good to attend a dance with a bunch of farmers. It would serve her right if he made sure she couldn't get out of it! He wasn't sure how he would do it, but he would somehow! Pushing back his chair, he rose to his feet.

"Taylor, why don't you go to Twin Falls with Clay?" Lilly suggested and Clay snapped his head around at this. Surely she wasn't serious!

"I don't think . . ." Taylor began. *Good,* Clay breathed a sigh of relief. *She didn't want to go.*

"You haven't been anywhere since you arrived," Lilly went on. "It will give Clay someone to talk to on the long drive, and you could pick up some fresh fruit and that shampoo you couldn't find at our little corner market."

"I don't need—"

Once more her grandmother cut her off. "You've done nothing but work since you got here. You could go somewhere nice for dinner, even take in a movie. You'll have plenty of time before the dance, and it would be good for the both of you. You'd like the company, wouldn't you?" She turned to Clay and he found himself powerless to say no.

"Yes, sure. That would be fine." He practically stammered his approval when he wanted to shout, *NO WAY.*

"Good," she beamed. "Now you go feed that squawking bird, while Taylor runs upstairs to get her sweater. It might be cool when you come back. Don't worry abut these dishes." She took the plates from Taylor's hands. "It will only take me a minute to wash them. By that time Stewart will be here. We'll just dig a few worms from the garden and be on our way."

"You're going fishing again?" Taylor's voice held a note of uncertainty, and Clay experienced a moment's brilliant insight. The old couple wanted a little time alone, and with Taylor constantly underfoot, their moments alone were few and far between. He supposed he could help them out by taking Taylor off her grandmother's hands for the day. Lilly had done him more than one favor. In fact, he owed her.

"Your grandmother is right," he switched sides to encourage Taylor to accompany him. He could tell she wanted to protest further and she certainly didn't look thrilled at the prospect of spending the day in his company. For some reason that rankled. "Meet you at the truck in five minutes," he called to Taylor's retreating back when she finally turned toward the stairs. He grinned at Lilly and hurried out the door to feed Rambo. He'd keep Taylor busy all day if it killed him. And it just might, he thought with a groan as he scooped up bird feed, which didn't lessen his determination to make certain she went to that dance tonight!

CHAPTER 9

Clay was shifting items from the front of his pickup to the back when Taylor emerged from the house. He locked the shell that enclosed the back of the truck, then held the door for her to climb into the passenger seat. She looked dubiously at the high seat. How had she let Grandma Lilly talk her into this? Tossing her purse and her sweater ahead of her, she grasped the hand grip and pulled herself inside, wishing she'd worn pants. The big Ford 250 hadn't been designed for women in skirts—or maybe it had, she changed her mind, catching sight of the grin on Clay's face.

She wasn't sure she'd ever seen him smile before. She'd noticed he was good-looking, but that smile made him downright dangerous to any female around. Unfortunately, she was no exception even if, as she suspected, the smile was at her expense.

He didn't say anything when he stepped inside the truck or as he drove toward the Friedrickson ranch, and she resigned herself to a long, boring drive. But when he stopped near the rancher's stable, he turned toward her.

"Would you like to go inside the barn with me?" he asked. "The mare I'm checking on gave birth to a beautiful colt a couple of weeks ago."

"Sure," she agreed. He'd asked her nicely enough, and even though he may have been hoping she'd say no, she decided to take the invitation at face value. Not waiting for him to open her door, she opened it herself and slid to the ground. She wasn't too sure he would have opened it for her anyway.

Children's voices came from the back of a long, low ranch house, and before she and Clay reached the barn, Peggy and her two little girls hurried around the corner of the house and came toward them.

"Good morning," Peggy called.

"Good morning," Clay and Taylor both responded.

"Did you come to see my baby horse?" the younger girl asked Clay. She looked so cute in her pink denim overalls and with her long hair in thick braids, Taylor felt an uncharacteristic urge to hug the little girl. The reaction caught her by surprise since she didn't usually spend much time around children and seldom gave them a thought.

The older child held out her hand to Taylor. "I'll show you Sandee," she offered. Taking the child's hand, Taylor followed her into the barn. Inside, the light was dim, but her eyes quickly adjusted as they followed Clay down a wide aisle. When he stopped to pat the long nose of a beautiful chestnut mare, she spied the colt nursing at its mother's side.

"That's Melisandra's Dream," the fragile-looking girl in floral patterned jeans climbed the board fence to point out. "I call her Sandee because her name's too big for a little horse," the child solemnly explained.

"I like that." Taylor smiled down at the girl and felt an unexpected catch in her heart.

The filly raised her head and on long spindly legs minced toward the wooden panel that separated them. When she got close enough, Taylor reached between the panels to touch her silky coat. The young horse shied back a step, then curiosity propelled her forward again. This time she allowed Taylor to stroke the side of her neck and run her fingers through the tuft of hair growing between her ears.

"Come on, girls," Peggy motioned to her daughters after a few minutes. "We have chores to do and baths to take before we go see Dr. Stevens."

"I don't want to go." Gina stuck out her lip.

"Daddy isn't here, so you have to come, too." Peggy took her younger daughter's hand. Gina still looked rebellious, but she followed her mother, who called a cheerful farewell to Clay and Taylor. After they left, Taylor turned her attention back to the colt.

"You're a cutie," she crooned then glanced at Clay, feeling embarrassed. He was inside the stall and didn't seem to be paying attention to her, so she continued to stroke the little filly's shiny coat and whisper soft endearments to her.

Under her lashes, Taylor stole occasional peeks at Clay. She watched him slide his hand down the mare's rump and was amazed at how gentle his touch appeared. His hands were large, she'd noticed that before, but she hadn't noticed his long tapering fingers and how much they looked like the hands of a musician. From the contented way the mare accepted his touch, he might as well be playing music, Taylor thought, suddenly feeling a twinge of annoyance—or was it jealousy? Mentally she winced. She didn't know where that thought had come from. There was no way she could be jealous of a horse!

"All through." Clay left the mare to amble over toward her and the colt with a loose-limbed swagger reminiscent of some big-screen cowboy. He patted the filly and ran one of those big hands down the colt's legs. Taylor shivered unexpectedly and drew back from the wooden panel. "Mother and daughter are doing fine," he pronounced before shifting the wooden panel and joining Taylor in the aisle. His eyes met hers, and she felt little jolts of awareness slither down her spine. His eyes widened and the little specks of brown in his irises seemed to glow like a cat's eyes, a great big predatory cat. She nervously glanced away, but like a magnet she was drawn right back to his eyes, but in that second everything had changed. His eyes were just eyes, and he was looking at her with a slightly puzzled expression on his face.

"Shall we be on our way?" he asked.

She nodded and walked beside him to his truck, feeling slightly off balance. Why did she feel something momentous had happened back there in the barn? Nothing had happened. Clay had checked a patient and she had petted a colt. That was all. She was human and had excellent eyesight. She wouldn't be normal if she hadn't noticed the way Clay's shirt had tightened across his shoulders when he bent over the mare or the way his hair curled against the back of his neck. And his hands . . . They were just hands, bigger than most, but just hands. He was good-looking; she'd never denied that, but looks alone didn't impress her.

They rode in silence until a silver glint in the distance caught her attention. "Is that a lake?" she asked. She didn't remember seeing a lake before in this stretch of dry brush-covered desert.

"It's called Magic Reservoir," Clay told her. "It's a small man-made lake formed by Camas Creek and the Wood River. From the road it's scarcely visible unless the sun is shining just right."

"Grandpa Jordan used to fish on the Wood River, but he usually took me further north where there are smaller streams and pine trees," she remembered aloud. "I never liked fishing without any shade, and he said the river was filling up with silt so badly that it wasn't much more than a swamp."

"Do you like to fish?" Clay sounded surprised.

"I used to," she admitted. "When I was small, I spent a lot of time in Fairfield with my grandparents, and I enjoyed fishing with Grandpa." A wave of sadness swept over her as she remembered the big man who had been infinitely patient with a little girl who adored him and everything about the mountains and streams he loved.

"I've done a little stream fishing since I arrived here, and Blaine Gardner has been teaching me to fly fish on some of the beaver ponds and small reservoirs on the mountain side of town," Clay spoke with an enthusiasm that surprised Taylor. Fishing took a great deal of patience, and she hadn't thought of the vet as a patient man. Her thoughts went back to the slow, gentle glide of his hand down the mare's sleek hide, and for no good reason she felt a blush climb her neck and burn her cheeks.

"I once asked Grandpa why he didn't fish on the Wood River," she hurried to cover thoughts of Clay's hands. "He said the fishing wasn't any good anymore because the environmentalists had 'improved' the river so much it was too clogged with weeds to be any good for fishing or watering stock."

"Blaine said pretty much the same thing," Clay agreed. "Though there's a spot pretty close to where we are now that looks like it might be a good place to fish. There's an old cable bridge there that spans the river."

"I remember that spot." Taylor felt happy memories bubble to the surface. "I used to go there with Grandpa, too. The cable bridge is an old sheep bridge."

"Sheep bridge?" Clay sounded puzzled.

"Ranchers used to bring their sheep up here to graze in the summer. They built that narrow bridge, suspended on cables, as a shortcut to get their herds across the river," she explained.

After a few minutes they lapsed into silence again, but Taylor found the silence wasn't uncomfortable as it had been before. The fact that they had actually carried on a conversation without poking at each other was amazing, she thought. Seeing that Clay was in such a good mood, this might not be such a long trip after all.

"Grandma Lilly said you were from New York. I've never even seen New York City, but I've always dreamed of going there," she told him, hoping he would talk about the city. "I considered going there this summer, but the prospects look better for me in San Francisco. But I'll go there eventually."

"Once you've done all the tourist things, New York isn't much different from any other city," Clay told her.

"How can you say that?" Taylor was shocked at his easy dismissal of the fabulous city she longed to see. "It's the heart of the business world. Just think, the New York Stock Exchange, Wall Street, the World Trade Center, and most of the great banks and insurance companies are based there. Publishing, advertising, fashion, art, theater, and so many other industries reach their pinnacle in New York. There's the United Nations and—"

"Whoa, I didn't mean New York isn't one of the great cities in the world, maybe the greatest, but living there isn't as glamorous as you think. And I'm not talking about slums or muggings or anything like that," Clay told her. "If you're not into the night club or party circuit, and only attend an occasional Broadway show, your nightlife is about the same there as anywhere else, only there's a lot more nuisance involved in getting where you want to go. You can't just jump in the car and go wherever you want. You have to call a cab or take public transportation. Housing is expensive, and most people who work in those businesses you named usually live a great distance from their jobs and can spend hours each day commuting. Or they can only afford to live in old, cramped apartments."

"You didn't like living in New York?" Taylor sounded as though she couldn't quite fathom his lack of enthusiasm for the city she'd dreamed of most of her life.

"Not really," he admitted. "When I was small we lived on Long Island in a large house that belonged to my mother's family. There I could play on the beach with my dog, but when I got a little older we moved to one of the city suburbs, and I seldom saw my dad after that. He caught a commuter train before I awoke most mornings and arrived home about the time I went to bed. My mother hated being so far from her friends."

"What about you? Did you hate it, too?" Taylor asked.

"No, actually I liked it quite a bit. I made friends and started going to church with some of them. Mother thought my desire to be baptized was some harmless teenage whim I would eventually outgrow, so she didn't object. Dad even attended church with me a few times. I think he would have been baptized, too, if Mother had been the least bit encouraging."

"You didn't grow up in the Church, then?"

"No, I was fourteen when I joined. I lived in a good ward and have always been grateful for the people who included me and made me welcome there. I missed them a lot after Dad died, and Mother and I moved into the apartment her parents left her near Central Park."

"You went on a mission, so you must have stayed active in the Church," Taylor stated what she considered the obvious.

"I was a senior in high school by then, and a couple of my friends were planning to go to BYU for a year before going on missions. I applied for admission along with them. Mother didn't want me to go so far away, but Jessica's grandfather convinced her to let me go. He wanted Jessica to attend Vassar, and he thought it would be best if we didn't attend schools that were too close to each other."

"He didn't approve of you?" Taylor asked, surprise in her voice.

"Oh, he approved of me. He claimed he'd handpicked me for his Jessica. He just wanted her to finish school and have some fun before she settled down. He wanted me to be a doctor, but he didn't want Jessica tied down to a medical student for all those years." He laughed, but she had the feeling he wasn't really amused.

"So you came west. Did you find it awfully different?" Taylor asked in a quiet voice. As Clay talked, she'd begun to realize that he'd come from a pretty privileged background. She was also amazed at how quickly and easily they had moved into a rather personal conversation.

"Yes, it was different, but I liked it," he answered her earlier question. "I felt truly happy in a way I never had before. At first I thought it was just that everything seemed so much bigger and grander out here, but there was more to it than that. I already had a testimony of the truthfulness of the gospel, but at the Y my faith seemed to grow—maybe *intensify* is the word I should use. At home I had to be careful not to let my beliefs intrude on my mother's life or to offend Jessica and her family. I made some decisions that year about how I wanted to live my life."

"Why do I get the feeling those decisions didn't please your mother or Jessica's family?" Taylor was surprised at her own boldness, but Clay didn't take offense.

"You're right," he chuckled and shook his head. "Mother was horrified when she discovered I had changed my undergraduate major from human biology to animal science. Jessica was appalled to see my wardrobe change from jackets and ties to hiking boots and jeans. Her grandfather began inviting some of his firm's younger executives home for dinner and started talking about marriage being a stabilizing factor in a young man's life."

"Oh dear," Taylor suddenly laughed. "And I suppose it was at that point you announced your intention of going on a mission."

Looking sheepish, he admitted it was. "Jessica's cousin Jacob was the only one who approved of my mission, but then he and his brothers had always considered me a threat to their future control of Winslow Enterprises. I think he hoped I might get eaten by cannibals and never return!"

Taylor laughed and Clay's deep chuckle joined in. She was surprised by how much she was enjoying herself and how interested she'd become in learning more about Clay.

"Okay, we're halfway to Twin, and all we've talked about is me. It's your turn," Clay turned his head to smile at her. Her heart gave an annoying little flutter and she couldn't think of a thing to say. Outside the window she could see that the miles of sagebrush desert were indeed giving way to green fields, and ahead a cluster of trees hinted at the presence of the small town of Shoshone.

"Come on," Clay teased. "Your grandmother mentioned you live in Pocatello. I've never been there, so tell me all about it."

"It's not very big," she began. "It's mostly a college town, and it borders the Fort Hall Indian Reservation. It's hot in the summer and cold in the winter. The scenery isn't spectacular and when the wind is just right—and there is nearly always wind—there's a terrible smell from the phosphate plant."

Clay laughed. "The local Chamber of Commerce must love you."

She flushed. "It's like most small towns that just keep growing, but never lose that small town look or feel. There aren't any high-rise office towers, elegant hotels, or five-star restaurants. It was a railroad town, and though trains are still part of it, railroads no longer play the dominant role they once did. The university is an excellent school and the campus is a lovely oasis in a desert area; the reservation is largely under cultivation and from what I've heard about reservations, it's one of the more attractive and prosperous ones. Some of the businesses in the center of town haven't been able to keep pace with the newer malls and businesses on the outskirts of town and look rather bedraggled."

"What was it like growing up there?" Clay asked.

She shrugged. "It was okay. My mother died when I was seven, and I spent most of my summers in Fairfield until I was twelve and Dad decided I was old enough to not need someone to watch me every day. During my teens I went to my father's office after school and helped around there through summer vacations. Between summer school, day camps, and classes sponsored by the University, I graduated from high school early and started college just before I turned seventeen."

"What about boyfriends? Is there a special one, or do you just drive them all crazy?" Clay asked with a mischievous grin.

"I haven't really dated much," Taylor admitted with a hint of reluctance. "I'm much more interested in starting a career than in socializing." That didn't come out the way she meant it to, but how could she explain to a casual acquaintance how reluctant she felt to marry or have children, even though that was what Church teachings seemed to suggest she should want most? The business world held far more interest for her. Besides, getting close to a man who might expect the relationship to become serious didn't seem quite honest.

"Your choice, I don't doubt. Or are the men in Pocatello singularly blind?" He sounded a little disbelieving. "Are you trying to tell me you'd rather type letters and answer telephones than have a husband? A woman who looks like you?"

"I'm not trying to tell you anything," she snapped back. Something in his manner implied he didn't think she was smart

enough to be anything more than a decorative, entry-level receptionist or a bored housewife.

"Sorry," he raised his hands briefly from the wheel in a surrendering gesture. "I was just surprised. I didn't have you pegged as the
career-woman type."

"You and every other man! And that's why I don't date much. I'm
not a type! Men assume that if a woman doesn't look like the aftermath of a volcanic eruption, she isn't capable of thinking beyond
admiring some man's muscles! I don't plan to waste my life catering to
some man's ideal of the perfect Mormon wife!" Taylor retorted. "I
plan to be recognized for my own skills and accomplishments. I'll
make an impact in the business world, and possibly in politics, too."
Already regretting her outburst, she leaned back in her seat,
wondering whatever happened to the efficient way she usually dealt
with difficult people.

"Whoa! I didn't mean to imply all that," Clay attempted to
defend himself. "I didn't say you weren't smart."

"You didn't say it, but you were thinking it." Taylor refused to be
appeased.

"I'm sure there are lots of things you can do if you really want a
career," Clay sounded apologetic, but she still heard something
patronizing in his voice. "If you're really set on going to San
Francisco, or even New York, I know people who could help you get a
job. My mother could even get you auditions with several different
modeling agencies."

She turned away without answering to stare out the window,
feeling a cloud of depression weighing her down. They had been
getting along so well ever since they left the Friedrickson ranch. Why
did it hurt so much to discover Clay's low opinion of her? He'd hinted
he thought she was attractive, but he had just made it clear that he
couldn't see beyond her face and figure.

She'd heard it all before: the sly innuendoes that she'd somehow
used her appearance to gain her position on the senator's campaign
staff, that she didn't have to work as hard as everyone else to get A's in
her classes, that her promotions weren't the hard-earned result of how
well she did her work. Sometimes she thought her looks were a curse,
although at the same time she had no desire to be ugly. She just

wanted someone to see the real person beneath the skin and hair she'd acquired through no effort of her own, but simply by some quirk of genetic fate.

Clay had no idea what he'd said to upset Taylor, but he was pretty sure that whatever had blackened her mood was his fault. He'd never known a beautiful woman who didn't want to be told she was beautiful. As for brains, he really didn't think Taylor was stupid, just a little naive. Her big-city dreams were going to disappoint her. Without a lot of education and cutthroat drive, few people made it to the top in the city he'd so willingly left behind. He admired her spunk, but success in business or politics took more than eager determination. He thought of the few times she'd answered the telephone when he'd called his office to speak to Wendy and conceded she had handled the calls and messages well, but nice telephone manners were not nearly enough.

"I'm sorry, Taylor," he attempted to mollify her. "I really didn't mean any insult. True, I assumed you'd want marriage and a family, but not just because you're a woman, or because I think you can't do anything else. It's what I want, and it seems to be what most single adults are looking for, especially those who belong to the Church. I shouldn't have generalized that you would want that, too."

"Marriage just seems so constrictive," Taylor offered lamely. She could be magnanimous in accepting Clay's apology. She wasn't going to sulk and refuse to speak to him; instead she would try to explain her point of view. "It seems to me that it pretty well eliminates personal ambition for a woman."

"I was lonely growing up without any siblings, and my parents' marriage wasn't the greatest, so I guess I don't see family the same way you do. And being a man, I never considered that I couldn't have a career and a family, too. My career is really important to me, but I like the idea of someone knowing and caring where I am as well. Ever since I joined the Church and saw some of my friends' families, I've wanted a marriage which includes children, pets, church activity, and the whole typical Mormon matrimonial scene."

"Including a full-time wife!" Taylor jeered.

"Sure, a full-time wife," Clay shot back. "But I don't expect my wife to be a full-time housekeeper. Come on, Taylor, this is the twenty-first century, and I accept that many women, within as well as outside of the Church, have careers."

"And leave their children in day-care centers! No thanks—been there, done that! And I didn't like it!" The vehemence in her voice startled them both. She'd never before, even to herself, admitted how miserable she'd been while forced to spend her after school hours at a day-care facility rather than in her own home. There had been no one to share the events of her day with, no access to her own toys, or even privacy to curl up with a book.

"Some women think children are worth postponing or inter-rupting their careers," Clay reminded her.

Taylor turned to look at him. "I don't want children. I had a lonely childhood, too, but it hasn't made me idealize marriage or parenthood. My parents had a great marriage as far as I know, but Daddy never got over my mother's death—maybe I didn't either. I don't want to have to worry about someone I love dying, or have someone else's life ruined if I should die early like my mother did. I don't think of marriage or children as a way to escape loneliness."

"I wouldn't marry just to escape loneliness either, but it would be a nice sidebar," Clay admitted and Taylor didn't miss the slight wist-fulness in his voice.

"If you really want to get married, why don't you?" Taylor asked. "I know a couple of women who would be happy to hear a proposal from you."

Clay grimaced. "I'll pass. I don't want to get married so badly that I'll settle for just whoever is available."

"Mmmm, I'm sure your problem isn't a lack of opportunity," Taylor smiled wickedly, seeing her opportunity to turn his earlier words back on him. "You have looks, an education, and a business of your own. Judging by what you've told me about your family, you probably have buckets of money stashed in some New York bank, too. Add to that you're a returned missionary, and ninety percent of the single Mormon women I know would be happy to become Mrs. Clayton Harriman Curtis the Fourth."

"For your information, I don't have buckets of money stashed anywhere!" To her amusement, he responded as defensively as she had. "My mother has money she inherited from her parents, but it's tied up in a trust fund. She couldn't give it to me if she wanted to. Grandpa knew she didn't have a lick of business sense, and he never approved of my father who brought nothing to their marriage but an illustrious old name. He made sure she would always be well taken care of, but Dad wouldn't get any of the family money or property. My grandparents died before I was born, so I didn't get anything either. The condo on Fifth Avenue and a half-share of the Long Island house are Mother's during her lifetime. She has a generous allowance, but the property all reverts to her brother after her death. Dad's insurance policy supplemented my own earnings to put me through school, and I saved the money myself for my mission."

"You don't owe me an explanation," Taylor gasped. "Your finances are none of my business."

"I know I don't have to explain, but it's part of what makes me feel the way I do about getting married." Clay went on. "I want a wife who loves me and cares about the things that are important to me, like the gospel, a home, and our family. And she needs to be happy and comfortable living in the kind of rural community where my professional skills are needed. I want to be able to support my family well, but I don't want to find myself married to someone who sees dollar signs when she looks at me."

"I doubt it's dollar signs women see when they look at you," Taylor commented with a certain amount of drollery.

"And that's another thing," Clay flushed and stared straight ahead, his fingers tight on the steering wheel. "I can't help the way I look."

"I couldn't have said it better myself," Taylor muttered under her breath, but Clay heard her, and she felt slightly vindicated when he flushed guiltily. Aloud she couldn't resist teasing him. "Been proposed to a lot by total strangers?"

Clay turned a deeper shade of red. "Some woman came up to me as I was getting off a plane once and offered me $50,000 to spend the weekend with her."

"That's a proposition, not a proposal." Taylor giggled and Clay glared back at her.

"Oh, look." She pointed ahead, ignoring his discomfort. "There's the Perrine Memorial Bridge. Once we cross the Snake River, we'll be in Twin Falls."

CHAPTER 10

It didn't take long to pick up the veterinarian supplies Clay had ordered. After stowing the pharmaceuticals in a cooler in the back of his truck, he turned to Taylor. "Where to?" he asked.

"Oh, any supermarket will do," she told him. "I think there's an Albertson's on Addison Avenue."

"Supermarket? Surely that isn't the only shopping you want to do?" He knew women better than that, and he'd noticed a new mall right after they'd crossed the bridge. It wasn't Bergdorf Goodman, but he doubted many women could resist it. He glanced at his watch. He could give her a couple of hours.

She looked at him strangely when he parked the truck, but climbed out and looked around before saying, "From here, the other side of the river looks close, yet we can't see the water because the Snake River canyon is so deep. Sometimes it's hard to believe such a large river exists in the middle of a desert."

"Blaine has been encouraging me to take a day or two to go down in the canyon and do a little exploring," Clay told her as he ushered her toward the mall.

"You should do it," she seconded his friend's suggestion. "In some ways it's like an entirely different place down there in the canyon. There are magnificent waterfalls, orchards, fish hatcheries, boating, and picnicking. The trees and grass, and of course, the best melons in the world, are nothing like the dry, treeless desert here above the canyon." By tacit agreement they left any kind of personal discussion behind.

As his eyes adjusted to the cool, artificial light of the mall, Clay pointed in the direction of the largest department store. "I could use another dress shirt. Why don't we meet here in an hour?"

"Okay," she agreed, glancing at her watch. "We'll meet back here at noon."

Clay hid his smile until she turned away. He didn't expect to see her for at least two hours, but if he'd suggested two hours, she'd keep him waiting four. At least she hadn't demanded that he accompany her, as Jessica would have done.

Taylor wandered down the wide corridor, occasionally stopping to look at a display, but nothing held her attention seriously enough to warrant a trip inside the shop until she came to a small bookstore. Inside she browsed the short aisles, looking for her favorite authors. Spotting a romantic suspense by an LDS author she particularly liked and another by a new author she hadn't read before, she picked them up. She didn't particularly enjoy television, and she'd read all of her grandmother's magazines twice. Grandma Lilly had a great selection of doctrinal books, but not much fiction. Then seeing a selection of software, Taylor stopped to look at a few that caught her eye. Picking a colorful box, she read the back and grinned as she added it to her book selections.

A few minutes later with her purchases paid for, she left the store to wander toward the bench where Clay said they should meet. She glanced at her watch and nearly groaned. Only thirty-five minutes had passed.

When she reached the place where they had agreed to meet, she noticed Clay was already there. He sat sprawled on the bench with a paper bag beside him. His eyes were closed and he looked as though he were asleep. She stood watching him for several minutes, taking in the way a damp curl almost brushed his eye and his thick dark lashes formed half-moons against his cheeks. A tiny spot on his neck told her he'd nicked himself shaving that morning. Relaxed he looked different, not so strong and arrogant. He didn't exactly look soft, but certainly more touchable. She wondered what it would be like to trace his face with her fingers, feel the smooth ridge of his high cheek-bone give way to the slight scratchiness of his jaw. Catching where her thoughts were leading her, she drew in her breath sharply. She must have made some sound, because he opened his eyes. At first she saw a softness there, which changed to surprise, or perhaps wariness.

Speaking quickly to hide her own flustered sense of awareness, she asked, "Did you find what you wanted? Are you through shopping?"

"This is all for me." He held up the bag. "But I'm not in a hurry if you want to do more shopping."

"I really don't need anything. You know I only came because Grandma practically pushed me out the door." Taylor laughed, feeling strangely self-conscious.

"And why do you think she did that?" Clay couldn't resist grinning as he stood and began walking toward the mall exit with Taylor beside him.

"Because three's a crowd and she had a date to go fishing with Stewart," Taylor responded.

Good, he thought. *She understands that the two elderly people are romantically involved, although she doesn't look too thrilled about it. At least she hasn't tried to interfere.* He didn't say anything more as they crossed the parking lot to his truck, but he kept thinking about her answer.

"Does that bother you?" he asked as he helped her into the truck.

"Does what bother me?" she asked as though her thoughts had gone on to something else.

"Lilly and Stewart seeing each other," he reminded her of the question he'd asked only minutes before.

She didn't answer immediately, so he walked around and climbed into the driver's seat, then instead of starting the engine, he sat still, watching her.

"Yes. And no," she finally answered his question. "They're good friends, and I'm glad they enjoy one another's company, but they're too old to be in love and thinking about marriage."

"Is that what they're doing? Talking about marriage?" He almost whistled. He'd been amused and secretly pleased to watch two people he liked a great deal grow so close, but he hadn't considered they might go so far as to marry. But why not? Stewart was getting past the age when he should be driving ten miles each way to see his sweetheart every day. Besides they seemed so comfortable together and everyone thought of them as a couple, perhaps they ought to make it official.

"What does age have to do with love?" he baited Taylor.

"Don't be silly," she brushed off his question.

"So they're talking marriage?" He whistled a few bars of the wedding march.

"'Fraid so," Taylor sounded concerned, and he realized she really was worried. For some reason that annoyed him.

"Maybe that's for the best," Clay suggested, half expecting Taylor to blow up. "They're good company for each other. You should be glad they're not like some senior couples who just live together to avoid messing up retirement benefits or to avoid inheritance hassles. If they want to spend what's left of their lives together, marriage really is the best solution."

"Grandma would never just live with Stewart," Taylor told him. "Her moral standards are too high for that, but they can't get married." She was silent, then she surprised him by adding, "Daddy would never allow it."

"Lilly is a competent adult. She doesn't need her son's permission to get married," Clay protested.

"You don't know Daddy," Taylor shot back.

"Are you against their getting married?" Clay asked, then the corners of his mouth turned down. "Of course you are. You're the lady who's against marriage."

"That's not true," Taylor protested. "I'm not opposed to marriage. I just don't want to be the one getting married. As for Grandma, at first I didn't want her to marry Stewart, but he's such a nice man, and they both seem younger than their years when they're together. I can't forget, though, that Stewart is eighty years old. After the long difficult illness Grandpa went through, I can't help worrying about Grandma going through that again with Stewart if she marries him. Caring for Grandpa was really hard on her, and we worried that we might lose her, too. I don't want that, but I just don't know what to think anymore. Daddy is convinced that her desire to get married again is a sign she's getting senile, but I know that's not true."

"Darn right, it's not true." Clay shoved the truck into gear. "If Lilly's senile, more of us ought to be that way. You shouldn't try to keep them apart."

"I don't. Not really, even though Daddy expects me to discourage any romantic entanglement." She sighed. "I don't want to come between them, but being together so much is just going to make it harder for them."

"Why is that? Neither one is ill, are they?" Clay demanded to know.

"No, at least I don't think they are. It's just that Daddy has already made arrangements for Grandma to come live near him this winter. He's even signed the lease. Grandma will have plenty of people her own age around her, and Daddy will be able to check on her every day. I'm sure she'll be happy, but I worry about Stewart being left behind."

"Let's forget about Stewart for a minute and talk about your grandmother." Clay sounded angry. "It sounds like you're talking about one of those senior care facilities. What makes you think she'd be happy there?"

"Why wouldn't she?" Taylor wasn't sure why Clay was angry, but she felt her own temper rising to match his. Lilly was her grandmother, not Clay's, and it was her father's responsibility to see that his mother was well cared for. It really wasn't any of Clay's concern.

"Lilly loves that big old rambling house and her garden. Fairfield has been her home since your grandfather took her there nearly sixty years ago. She'll be miserable in some little city apartment." The truck's tires squealed against the pavement as Clay made an abrupt merge into traffic.

"Daddy says she works too hard, and it's not wise for someone her age to be an hour and a half from the closest hospital. In the winter, it can take even longer to reach medical help. At nearly eighty, she needs to be closer to family and a doctor." Taylor ignored Clay's driving and continued on, "She'll have her own apartment, not just a room in a nursing home."

"And no friends! No garden! She probably won't even be able to keep old Tom." Clay glared at a red sports car that cut him off as he turned onto Addison Avenue. "That's why you're here, isn't it? You came to railroad her into a retirement home. Were you planning to deed her house over to the state in exchange for her care, or are you selling her house to finance your big splash in the city!?"

"You don't want her to sell her house because when she does, you'll lose your place to stay, your office, and someone to wait on you!" Taylor stormed back.

"That's so absurd!" Clay snorted as he swung the wheel and pulled into the supermarket parking lot. He slammed on his brakes so hard Taylor had to thrust a hand against the dashboard to catch herself. Giving him a black glare, she reached for the door handle and scooted out of the truck.

Slamming their doors with simultaneous force, they marched into the store without speaking. She grabbed a shopping cart, and he wrested it away from her. She placed apples and bananas in the cart; he added strawberries and a melon. She picked up gardenia-scented shampoo and he reached for VO5. At the checkout counter she opened her checkbook, and he quickly handed the clerk cash.

Still not speaking, they added the produce to the cooler in the back of the truck and arranged their other purchases around the cooler. As Clay locked the camper shell, the small phone he wore clipped to his belt rang.

Lifting it to his ear, he identified himself, then listened quietly for several minutes. His face drained of anger and took on an expression of concern. Taylor knew she should get in the truck and allow Clay some privacy, but she couldn't move. Finally he asked, "You're sure you're all right? And Stewart is staying with you until we get there?" He paused to listen, then said, "Yes, we'll be there as soon as we can."

"Grandma! Has something happened to my grandmother?" Taylor instinctively reached for Clay's phone. He turned partially away from her, blocking her access to it.

"No, we didn't have any plans to go to dinner. And you're not spoiling anything. We'll just grab a hamburger somewhere and head back." He paused a minute, then added. "Don't worry, I won't drive too fast. Taylor's fine, and I'll give her your message. Bye."

"What happened?" Taylor cried. "Was there an accident?"

"No accident," Clay spoke slowly as though he were thinking something through. "Your grandmother is fine. She called to tell me that a rain squall came up while she and Stewart were fishing, so they returned to the house. They arrived to find someone had cut the sunporch screen, broken the glass, and gotten inside. She doesn't think the intruders found what they were looking for in my office because the kitchen door was forced, too. The upstairs bedrooms were ransacked, but the main floor was hardly touched other than my office. Stewart thinks whoever broke in heard them coming and escaped out your bedroom window to the sunporch roof and got away."

"Rambo and Tom? Are they all right?" She remembered her earlier suspicions.

"They're fine. Lilly said Wendy stopped by the house on her way to the beauty salon to pick up Rambo. It seems Doris had expressed some interest in seeing the bird, and Wendy decided to take her to the beauty shop, then keep her until Lilly and Stewart returned from their fishing trip. Tom's been outside all morning. He showed up wanting to go back in the house as soon as Lilly and Stewart pulled into the driveway."

"And you're sure Grandma is safe?" Taylor asked.

"She sounded fine," he paused a minute. "Can you drive a standard shift?"

"Yes, but . . ."

"Good! You drive and I'll make a few phone calls." He swiftly ushered her into the truck and raced around to the passenger side. She had the engine started by the time he slid in beside her. Their earlier quarrel was forgotten as they both focused on getting back to Fairfield as quickly as possible.

Driving Clay's truck wasn't much different from driving her Dad's SUV, and she'd done that any number of times. The foot pedals weren't as comfortable and took some getting used to, but she didn't hesitate to drive as fast as the speed limit allowed. Traffic was heavy on Bluelakes Boulevard and required all of her concentration, leaving her unable to hear more than snatches of Clay's side of the conversation he was carrying on with someone on his cell phone. She heard enough to suspect he was talking to his mother, then arguing with someone else.

Once they left the bridge behind, she increased her speed. Farmland flew past the windows unnoticed as she worried about her grandmother and Stewart. It must have been a terrible shock to return to her home and find it had been vandalized. What if the shock had brought on a heart attack for either of the elderly people? And why had only Clay's things and hers been searched? Was it because the trespassers ran out of time? She noticed Clay was no longer talking on the phone and asked aloud the question that was nagging at her mind.

"Do you think this break-in is connected to the one last Sunday?"

"Yes," he admitted slowly. "All the strange things that have happened the past two weeks must be connected some way."

"What strange things . . . oh, you mean the attack on Wendy. You think that was connected, too?" She frowned in concentration. "Stewart saw two strangers peeping over Grandma's fence one day, and there was the telephone call that upset Wendy . . ." Her voice trailed off.

"I heard strange noises at the back door during the night a couple of times, and the dogs I'm boarding have gone crazy every night this week. Then there's Rambo and Tom. Rambo's smart, but not smart enough to get out of that cage by herself, and Tom . . ." He paused to glance sideways at Taylor.

"Someone sedated a cat that sleeps most of the time anyway," Taylor finished flatly.

"I found the needle mark," Clay admitted. "What I don't understand is why. Whatever is going on seems to be directed at me."

"Do you think Grandma Lilly is in any danger?" Taylor couldn't hide the tremor in her voice.

"No, but I can't say for sure. Even Wendy wasn't really hurt, but if whoever is doing this doesn't get what they want, they might turn violent." Clay sounded troubled and he was quiet for a few minutes before going on. "It might be best if I move out."

Shocked, Taylor took her eyes off the road to give him a quick look. He slouched in the passenger seat taking up a good portion of the truck cab. His large hands toyed with the cell phone he still held. There was something about him. The word "substantial" came to mind, but it was something more than his size. Since the day she arrived, getting Clay to move out had been her goal, but now she wasn't sure that was what she really wanted.

"I'm not sure that would be a good idea," she voiced her thoughts hesitantly.

"I thought you'd be cheering if I moved out," he wryly acknowledged their silent tug-of-war and their earlier not-so-silent argument.

"We can't be sure you are the reason someone is breaking in," she told him. "If you leave, someone might still break in and hurt Grandma Lilly. Though I would certainly try, realistically I'm not sure I could defend her against a man determined to do her harm. And if there were two men . . . Anyway, I'm sure that's the way Stewart will reason. If you leave, I'm afraid he'll move in to protect us, and I'll worry about protecting two elderly people. I think our intruder will be more cautious if he knows a strong, young man is sleeping in the house . . ."

"You may be right," he acknowledged with a shake of his head. "I'll have to think about it."

A moment later he pointed ahead. "There's Shoshone. Right on the main road there's a fast food place. Pull in there and we can get hamburgers."

"I'm not really hungry," Taylor protested.

"I'm not either, but it might be the only chance we get for some time. Besides I think you should call Lilly just to make certain they're all right." When he put it that way, she had to agree.

In a few minutes Lilly was on the phone assuring her grand-daughter that she was all right and there was no reason for Taylor and Clay to hurry too much. The burglar was gone and getting there quickly wouldn't make any difference. A deputy had already come and gone, but there wasn't much even he could do, though he promised to check around town to see if anyone had seen anything unusual.

When they pulled out of Shoshone a few minutes later, Clay was driving again. He rolled down the window and rested one arm on the window sill. The temperature had cooled somewhat and the air coming in the open window had the refreshing tang of the desert following a summer rain. Somewhat reassured by her conversation with her grandmother, Taylor rolled down her window, too, and watched the miles of sagebrush go by. Suddenly out of the silence, Clay spoke.

"Jessica lied to me."

"What?" Taylor lifted her head to stare at the man beside her. Clay didn't take his eyes from the road, and she had no clue why he was suddenly bringing up his former girlfriend.

"Jessica was lying. I know she was," he repeated. "She knows more than she will admit to knowing."

"What does she have to do with all this?" Taylor asked, both puzzled and annoyed by the intrusion of Jessica into her concern for her grandmother.

"That was Jessica I talked to before we got out of Twin Falls," Clay answered impatiently as if she should already be aware of that fact. "I asked her if there was any reason why someone would want to steal Rambo. She said Rambo was a valuable bird, but I know she's not valuable enough that anyone would risk stealing her. But something didn't ring true in the way she denied it."

"How do you know she was lying?" Taylor puzzled.

"I've known Jessica a long time. I know when she's trying to hide something." His voice was grim, and Taylor couldn't help wondering about his strange relationship with his former fiancée. He had called his mother and found a past girlfriend there? That seemed more than a little odd to her.

"But why would she lie to you?" She almost added, *And why did you call Jessica in New York about a burglary in Idaho? Why did you call Jessica for any reason?*

"I don't know why she would lie. I also don't know why she sent Rambo to me months after we broke up, nor why, now that she's back in New York, she wants me to personally deliver the bird back to New York."

"You're going to New York?"

"No, I don't have time right now. I offered to ship Rambo back to her and she became hysterical." Clay grimaced. "The last thing I want to do is travel all the way to New York with that pack of trouble!"

"Why doesn't she just come get her pet?" Taylor asked what seemed to him a perfectly logical question, one he'd asked his mother, only to be told Jessica couldn't leave New York until she settled with the insurance company, which sounded like a lame excuse to him.

"Her apartment was broken into and ransacked. She said she can't leave New York until the insurance company settles her claim, but I think that's just an excuse to try to persuade me to be the one to travel across the country with that bad-tempered little beast," he told her.

"Her apartment was broken into, too?" Taylor focused on one part of his explanation and ignored the rest. "And you think that is connected to our problems here?"

"I don't know, but if Rambo is what our burglar is after, it's just possible. Our first break-in occurred a day after hers, and the only thing she's missing is an address book. Even gold plated, it's not valuable enough to pass up all the expensive trinkets lying around her apartment to take only that. I think Jessica's burglar was looking for something specific, and when he found the address book decided I must have whatever he's looking for." Clay swung the wheel to leave the highway for Route 20. "Perhaps we ought to call Wendy and warn her to be careful when she returns Rambo."

"Wendy doesn't have Rambo anymore. She already brought her back," Taylor informed him. "Grandma said she arrived and put Rambo in her cage right after she called you earlier."

"Good, she probably has my office straightened up by now, too." A smile briefly lit his face, and Taylor hoped he didn't see the face she pulled.

"Don't count on it," Taylor said aloud. "Grandma said the sheriff sent a deputy out to take a look, and he said not to touch anything until you and I have a chance to see if anything is missing from our rooms or your office."

"Wendy would know better than I about the office," Clay pointed out and Taylor rolled her eyes. "I had my reservations about her at first, but she is doing a great job. You wouldn't believe what a mess my business files were in before she took over."

That's what you think, Taylor muttered to herself.

"Perhaps she could give you some pointers," he went on. "If you're really set on looking for a job with one of the big corporations, a little practical experience might be helpful."

Taylor ducked her head, not knowing whether to laugh or cry. *If you only knew.* She found herself stifling a giggle. Once she was certain she could control her features, she looked up to watch the long, sweeping hills as the truck moved steadily toward Fairfield.

Through the windshield, she noticed the river was high for early July. It ran close to the road for a little way, though enough lower than the road that there was no danger of the road flooding. The runoff was usually finished by July, but spring had been late this year. Flash floods in the mountains sometimes raised the water level, too, and this summer had been wetter than normal. From the puddles still filling the low spots in the road, the rainstorm must have lasted a while, she surmised.

"Stupid fool!" Clay swerved to the right as an oncoming car in the other lane passed the slower-moving vehicle in front of it, cutting sharply in front of the slower car, then passing Clay's truck in a blur. As the driver of the slower car braked to avoid rear-ending the car that had just cut in front of it, the car hydroplaned on the wet road, sending the vehicle careening out of control. Frantically Clay hauled on the steering wheel to avoid a collision. The other car continued to spin until it teetered off the embankment and into the water below.

Taylor screamed and grabbed for the door handle as Clay brought the truck to a stop. Before the sound of the engine died away, they were both running toward the bank where the car had disappeared. At the edge of the water, Clay held out an arm to stop Taylor's momentum. From where they stood, they could see that the car had sunk rapidly, and only inches of its white roof showed above the water. The car appeared to be lodged against one of the large boulders that showed through the water in several places, causing whitecaps and swirling currents where it broke around them.

"The driver will drown!" she screamed as she struggled to escape Clay's grasp.

"Go back to the truck," he yelled. "Call for help on my cell phone. Camas County emergency services are programmed star seven."

She hesitated less than a second, seeing the swift, dirty water break against the roof of the car and fall away, trailing a stream of white foam. With her heart pounding, she dashed back to the truck to grab the small phone. Punching in the code, she ran back to the creek bank while she waited for a voice to respond. When a woman's voice came on the line, she explained that a car had gone off the road into the water. As she struggled to clarify their position she scanned the bank for Clay and the driver of the car. She saw no one.

CHAPTER 11

After what seemed an eternity, Clay's head popped above the surface, then immediately disappeared beneath the water again. Flinging the phone aside she waded into the stream, finding herself going quickly from knee deep to shoulder depth. The cold water was a shock, even though she knew the creek carried water from the melting snow higher up. She debated kicking off her canvas tennis shoes, then decided they would be some protection against the slippery stones.

Losing her footing in spite of the rubber soles, she slipped below the water's surface and fought her way back to the top. She was only a few feet from the submerged car now, and the swift current tugged at her, drawing her downstream.

Fighting the current, she drew abreast of the car just as Clay broke the surface a few feet away. In his arms was a child, her long blond hair trailing in the water. Clay glanced at the shore, then frantically back to the car before he spotted Taylor.

The child's mother must still be in the car! Without uttering a word, Taylor swooped toward Clay and reached for the child. He didn't hesitate. The moment she grasped his small burden, he released the little girl to dive back beneath the water's surface.

With the added burden of the child, Taylor swam toward the bank, trying to keep the child face up. Letting the current partially carry her and using her legs to propel her toward the bank, she traveled only a short distance before her foot struck a rock and she pulled herself upright. Swinging the child into her arms, she began to wade toward shore. She refused to think about whether or not the limp bundle was still alive.

Stumbling up the bank, she heard a deep gasp, and felt the small body squirm. Relief in the form of tears streamed down her face. The child was alive!

"Mama!" came the faint cry and the child increased her struggle.

"It's okay," Taylor tried to quiet the little girl's cries and run toward the truck at the same time. She twisted the girl to one side, resting her against one hip, as she tore at the truck door.

"Mama! Mama!" the child screamed.

"She's coming," Taylor gasped, hoping she was telling the truth. "You stay right here, and I'll go help her."

"No!" The child fought her. "I want my mama and Cindy." The name rang an alarm deep inside Taylor's mind. Two little golden-haired girls playing in the barn beside a new colt. This child was one of the Friedrickson girls! Cindy was still out there, and she was the one with a heart condition! She and their mother, Peggy, were still inside that submerged car.

"Gina," she said as she shook the child gently. "Listen to me. This is Dr. Clay's truck. He's with Cindy and your mama. You have to wait right here for him to bring them to you." Spotting her sweater, she wrapped it around Gina's shaking shoulders, closed the truck door, and sprinted back to the water.

At once she saw Clay staggering toward the bank with Peggy Friedrickson in his arms. She appeared to be unconscious. Blood streamed from a gash across her face and dripped down Clay's shirt. His hands were cut and bleeding, too, but Taylor didn't pause to ask questions. Her attention focused on the car, which seemed to have slipped lower in the water. Another little girl was still in that car!

The water reached her thighs as she waded past Clay. Briefly their eyes met and she whispered one word, "Cindy?"

"She's still in the car," he croaked. Taylor lunged forward in a powerful breaststroke without another word.

When Taylor reached the car, she took a deep breath. Praying silently, she ducked beneath the surface and began groping with her hands. It didn't take long to find the smashed window on the driver's side. Wiggling her way through it, she searched with her hands through the silt-laden water for the child. She wasn't in the booster seat behind the driver. With rising terror she extended her search across the backseat. Could she have washed out of the car? Could she even now be floating dead or unconscious down the river?

Taylor's lungs ached. She had to get out of the car and back to the surface. She had to breathe! Her head bumped the roof of the car, and she discovered the small pocket of air beneath the not quite fully submerged top of the car. Drawing in a shallow breath, she felt a movement against her cheek and reached her hand toward the spot. Her hand clasped a tiny tennis shoe. Following the shoe to a thin leg, she felt like weeping in gratitude. *Thank you, Father.* In her mind, she acknowledged His divine assistance then went on to plead, *Please let her be alive.* Taylor sought the child's thin chest, then lifted her hand to cover the small face.

Taking one last gulp of the nearly depleted air, she sank toward the broken window. The child resisted for a split second, or was it her imagination? Did she want the child to be alive so badly that she imagined the slight resistance?

Dragging herself and Cindy through the window presented a dilemma. How could she push the child through without releasing her grip on the small nose and mouth? The opening wasn't big enough for them to pass through together, but if she released her hold on the child's air passages, Cindy might inhale water into her lungs. Whether it was the coldness or the murkiness of the water, she felt her sense of direction slipping away. She thrust a hand toward where she thought the opening should be and met glass. With her lungs burning, she tried to locate anything identifiable. Her hand brushed what she hoped was the steering wheel and once more she felt for the broken window. To her relief, she felt another hand grip hers, a large hand she knew to be Clay's, reaching through the window from the outside of the car. Communication without words passed between them as he reached for the child she held. Taylor released her hold when she felt his hand replace hers over the child's face, then he pulled Cindy smoothly through the opening.

Taylor wiggled through the window, attempting to follow and feeling as though her lungs were exploding. The rush of water caught her and sent her tumbling, and before she could reach the surface she felt blackness moving in. She was going to die, and she didn't even know if the little girl was alive. Her arms ached and she was so tired.

For a moment she thought she still held a child, and she only had to let her go to be free. No, she couldn't let go. The child mattered too much, more than anything. Fireworks seemed to explode before her eyes. And in the brilliant flashes she saw her mother's face, only to be replaced by her father's sad and lonely eyes.

Several more seconds passed before the current slammed her against the bank. She saw a familiar face laughing at her, telling her she was weak and selfish. Anger roused her nearly extinct survival instinct. She wanted to deny Clay's accusation, to tell him he didn't know anything about her. Fighting the encroaching blackness, she flung out her arms frantically searching for something, anything to hold onto. Her hands closed around a protruding root and her head bobbed above the swirling water. She held on to the root, gasping and sobbing as she filled her lungs with life-giving air.

It seemed forever before she regained enough strength to pull herself out of the water. Trembling and shaking, she cast off the lingering blackness. Instead of taking time to clear her head and regain her balance, she began running, half stumbling, her way back upstream to where she could see Clay kneeling in the grass.

Falling to her knees beside him, she saw that Cindy was pale and unconscious, but her small chest was slowly rising and falling. Peggy was conscious and retching violently into the grass. Pale and shivering, she struggled to rise and Taylor crawled to her side.

"Peggy," she whispered. "You're safe now. Please try to rest. The paramedics will soon be here."

"My girls? Where are my babies?" The young mother moaned and struggled to raise her head.

"They're here." Taylor found it difficult to get the words out. How could she comfort this woman? Gina was fine, but Cindy . . .

"I've got to go to them. They'll be frightened." Peggy once more tried to raise herself. She gave a little moan and slid back to the ground.

Shock! Peggy Friedrickson had to be suffering tremendous shock. She'd read somewhere that shock patients should be kept warm. She'd given her sweater to Gina. She didn't have anything she could use to cover Peggy. Instinctively she turned toward Clay but decided she couldn't interrupt him. He was bending over Cindy, holding what looked like a stethoscope to her chest. Beside him sat a black case much like a physician's case. Of course! Clay was a doctor! His patients were generally the four-legged variety, but animals suffered injuries, too, so of course he would have medical supplies. She felt a wave of hope. Clay would save Cindy if anyone could. She didn't question why she felt so much faith in his abilities.

"Is she . . . ?" Taylor whispered.

"She's breathing, but she needs to be in a hospital. What about Peggy? Has the bleeding stopped?"

"I think she's unconscious," Taylor whispered back from where she knelt beside the unconscious woman.

"We need to get them warm. Rummage around in the back of my truck and see if you can find anything to cover them." Clay turned his attention back to the little girl.

Taylor ran toward the truck, but hearing the sound of an approaching truck engine, she stopped. Coming toward her was a large RV. Taylor began to wave her arms, screaming for the driver to stop. The gray-haired driver seemed to hesitate, then slowly brought the lumbering vehicle to a stop behind Clay's truck. Sliding open the window beside him, he called to her, "Something wrong, miss?"

"Yes," she ran toward the vehicle, shouting. "A car ran off the road into the river. A woman and two little girls are injured. We need blankets."

"My goodness." A woman with a plump face and gray curls stuck her head out another window. "We've got plenty of blankets." In less than a minute she burst from the vehicle with her arms full of quilts. The man followed with more quilts and a stack of towels.

Taylor pointed toward Clay before continuing on to Clay's truck. She opened the door, and Gina, tears streaming down her flushed cheeks, tumbled into her arms. Guiltily Taylor hugged the girl to her. Even with the windows down the truck had become an oven, and the little girl was as hot now as she'd been cold before.

"Let's go sit by your mommy," she whispered in the child's ear. It would be best if Gina didn't have to see her mother and sister in the condition they were in, but she couldn't be left in the truck any longer. Besides it might comfort her to know her mother and sister were out of the water.

The sturdy four-year-old taxed Taylor's strength to carry, yet there was something in her small arms clasped around Taylor's neck that provided her with comfort, too, chasing away the black fear that still hovered at the edge of her mind. She brushed aside the strange illusion she'd experienced earlier of holding her own child just this way. There wasn't time now to examine the emotions she'd felt while fighting for her own life earlier.

At last she set the child on her feet and took her hand. Taylor had to hurry to keep up with Gina, whose anxious steps carried her rapidly toward her mother. When they reached the riverbank, Clay was just finishing wrapping the blankets around his two patients. The gray-haired man sat with Peggy's head resting on his thigh while he held one of the towels against the cut on her face. He was speaking in soothing whispers to her, but when he saw Taylor and Gina, he beckoned them closer.

"Mama!" Gina ran to her mother, throwing herself on the ground beside her.

"Gina," the woman breathed her daughter's name and held out her hand as though needing the physical assurance that the child was truly alive. Taylor was glad to see Peggy was conscious again.

"I was scared." Gina's lip quivered as she grasped her mother's extended hand.

"I was, too," Peggy whispered back and tried to smile. The gray-haired man settled the little girl on his lap and encouraged her to continue talking to her mother.

Taylor turned her attention to the other little girl, lying so still on the rough, stubbly grass. Cocooned in a thick blanket, her eyes were closed and her breath came in a harsh, ragged rhythm, but at least she was breathing. The gray-haired woman sat beside the child, softly rubbing her hair with a towel and singing a song Taylor barely remembered from her Primary days.

Clay stood a little way off with the cell phone in his hand. Evidently he'd found it where she'd dropped it. Moving closer, she heard him say, "Everett, take it easy. An ambulance is on the way. I've talked to the hospital in Ketchum, where they'll be taking Peggy and Gina. They're both going to be fine. Peggy has a broken arm and some lacerations on her face. She probably has a mild concussion, too. The car slammed pretty hard against some boulders in the water. Otherwise, I'm sure she'd have gotten the girls out herself."

He listened a few seconds, then went on in that soothing voice. "Cindy was in the water longer. I was able to release her from her car seat so she could float to the top where there was a good-sized air bubble, so she wasn't deprived of oxygen long. Taylor got her out, and your daughter's breathing on her own, but she's unconscious. The hospital called for an air-ambulance to take her to Boise."

Once more he paused before going on. "They'll be on their way before you can get here. I'll take care of it. I have consecrated oil in my truck, and I'm pretty certain a tourist who stopped to help can assist. I think Peggy would want you to meet Cindy in Boise at St. Luke's; you can get there about the same time as the life flight if you leave now. Don't worry about Peggy and Gina. They're going to be fine, and I'll stay with them as long as they need me."

In the distance Taylor heard the wail of a siren, but it was still almost five minutes before an ambulance drew to a stop beside the motor home. In that few minutes Clay and the gray-haired man placed their hands on Peggy's head to give her a blessing, then did the same for Cindy. Stillness filled the air, and the words the two men spoke touched a spot deep in Taylor's heart. Peace and hope replaced fear. She felt a small hand slip inside hers, and she gave Gina's hand a reassuring squeeze. It was strange, she thought, that the child was reassuring her.

A sheriff's car rolled to a stop behind the ambulance and a muscular young deputy sprinted toward the two forms lying in the grass. Taylor stood back, watching, and keeping Gina out of the way, as one of the uniformed paramedics started an IV drip in Peggy's arm and placed a backboard beneath her. With the deputy's help, the paramedic carefully positioned the young woman on a stretcher and placed her inside the ambulance. Gina didn't cry, but her eyes were wide and frightened as she bit down on her own small fist, and her small body trembled.

Minutes later Clay knelt beside the child. "Gina, the ambulance is going to take your mother to the hospital in Ketchum. Would you like to ride with her?" Slowly the blond head nodded.

"When you get there, a doctor will check you, too, to make sure you don't still have any river water in you." He smiled his encouragement.

"I spitted it all out," she told him solemnly.

"That's good." He gave her a hug. "Your mom will be happier knowing you're with her."

"And Cindy?" she looked up at him with huge, worried eyes. "Can Cindy come, too?"

"No, honey. Cindy's going to go to a different hospital, the one in Boise where they fixed her heart. Dr. Tarrington is waiting for her there, and your daddy is going to meet her there, too, so it will be just you to look after your mother. Do you think you can do that?"

She nodded her head again.

"One of the paramedics will sit by your mother the whole way, so that if she needs anything he can help her. You can ride in the front with the other paramedic." He turned to Taylor. "Make sure she has her seat belt on and if there's an air bag disconnect it." He turned away, and Taylor caught the sound of an approaching helicopter.

The helicopter sat down on the highway a short distance from the other emergency vehicles. It didn't take long to load Cindy on the chopper, and in minutes both it and the ambulance disappeared from sight. The deputy assured the older couple they could leave and asked for an address where the blankets could be returned. The elderly man shook hands with both Clay and Taylor, and his wife gave them each a hug before climbing back into their motor home. Taylor waved until the vehicle was out of sight. She remembered something her grandmother had told her a long time ago. *God doesn't often send angels to answer our prayers; he usually sends ordinary people and lets them be angels for a bit.*

The deputy wandered down to the edge of the water, and Taylor's gaze went beyond him to the spot where Peggy Friedrickson's car had landed. It was gone! While they had worked to warm the accident victims and send them to hospitals, the car had slipped completely beneath the surface. A deep shudder rippled through her, and she found herself shivering in spite of the hot July sun. After a moment she felt something touch her still damp shoulders and looked up to see Clay snugging one of the forgotten quilts around her. He didn't release her when the quilt draped around her shoulders, instead his arms tightened. Slowly she leaned her head against his chest and let her arms slip around his waist. He lifted the quilt and enfolded her in his arms beneath its sheltering warmth.

CHAPTER 12

"We'd better get back to Fairfield and check on your grand-mother," Clay broke the silence.

"Yes, she'll be worried." Taylor straightened, strangely reluctant to leave the comforting warmth that enveloped her. Somehow she knew it wasn't the quilt alone giving her a sense of shelter and security.

"Before you leave, I'll need a statement." The officer walked toward them, the sun glinting on the small gold name badge that identified him as Deputy Rick Donaldson. "It's a shame about the woman and little girls. Did you see what happened?"

Clay explained about the speeding car, and the officer frowned as he made notations in a small book.

"Did you get a plate number, make and model, color—anything like that?"

"Not much," Clay answered. "It was dark—black I think—and midsized. It was traveling too fast to get a plate number."

"It was a Pontiac Sunfire, 2000 model, with Ada County plates," Taylor broke in. Both men turned to stare at her. The officer's face showed flattering appreciation, but she suspected his appreciation wasn't for the information she'd just given him. The disbelief on Clay's face was just a bit too obvious for her liking.

"You're sure?" the officer asked skeptically and glanced toward Clay, who half shrugged his shoulders, and Taylor had to restrain herself to keep from hitting him.

Instead she gritted her teeth. "Of course I'm sure. I rented four just like it last summer for Senator Maxwell. I only caught the 1A part of the plate."

"You work for the senator?" The officer straightened his shoulders and sucked in his stomach. Ordinarily Taylor would have grinned, but she was still smarting from Clay's obvious dismissal of her powers of observation.

"I don't work for the senator now," she answered a bit too politely. "I managed his eastern Idaho campaign office last summer and fall. Renting equipment was part of my job, and cars were considered equipment. Now if you don't mind, I need to get back to Fairfield and check on my grandmother."

"Sure, Miss Jordan." The deputy all but saluted before escorting her to Clay's waiting truck. "You go ahead. I'll just wait here for the salvage truck. I'll call you if I have any more questions."

Clay suspected the deputy would call her all right, and soon, but the only information he'd be looking for would be whether or not she'd go out with him. He resisted the urge to elbow the other man aside when he saw the deputy open the truck door for her, then place his hands on Taylor's waist to boost her into the truck. Cop or not, Donaldson didn't need to manhandle her, Clay groused to himself as a cloud of doom settled on his shoulders.

It was just letdown, he assured himself as he climbed in his side of the truck. All that adrenalin pumping so long had to take some kind of toll. He wasn't jealous, and he didn't feel possessive in the least where Taylor Jordan was concerned. Actually it might be a good thing if the deputy did come calling. Both his life and Lilly's were bound to run more smoothly without Taylor underfoot so much of the time. Unfortunately, he had a sneaky suspicion he was lying to himself. Clay shifted into gear, and the tires spit gravel as he drove the truck back onto the oiled road surface.

It didn't take long to reach Fairfield, and when Clay pulled into his parking space across the hedge from Lilly's house, Taylor was out the door and halfway to the house before he could shut off the engine.

"Grandma," she rushed toward the two figures sitting in lawn chairs on the front porch. Lilly rose to her feet and the two women hugged each other. Stewart, who was standing now, too, reached over to pat Taylor's shoulder.

"I was getting worried. Did you have a flat tire or something?" Lilly looked past Taylor to question Clay.

"Uh . . . no," Clay responded hesitantly. "We stopped to help someone."

"You might have called," she turned to scold her granddaughter. "Clay carries that little phone everywhere with him." She paused to give Taylor a careful once over, taking in Taylor's matted hair and the clothes that had dried to a stiff mass of wrinkles. "My goodness, what happened to you? You look like you went for a swim!"

"Doesn't look like she went swimming alone," Stewart observed dryly as he surveyed Clay.

Lilly looked from one to the other, then laughed. "That must have been some water fight."

"Leastways they weren't skinny dippin'," the older man added with a chuckle.

"There was an accident, a car slid off the road into the river, and we got wet helping the people out of the water," Taylor rushed to clarify their appearance. "I'll tell you all about it later, but right now I think we need to take a look at what happened here."

"You're right, dear," Lilly agreed. Clay and Taylor followed her to the back door. Taking the key from her pocket, Lilly unlocked the door and stepped inside. As she turned toward the shambles that had once been an orderly office, Clay caught a fleeting look of sadness on the woman's face. This house had been her refuge, a place of peace and love for sixty years. The vandals who had done this had hurt Lilly far more than they had him, no matter what they might have taken or destroyed. Until the vandals were caught and possibly even after, she'd no longer feel secure leaving her home unlocked.

After silently staring at the overturned and rifled files for several minutes, Clay and Taylor followed Lilly up the stairs. Clay reached for his bedroom door, then stared aghast at the mess. This wasn't simple vandalizing, or the aftermath of a fast search. The damage and destruction suggested extreme anger or revenge. His clothes had not only been flung about the room, but they were ripped and slashed. Dresser drawers hung open, their contents scattered on the floor, and not one item remained in his closet. Holes had been punched through the wallboard, soles ripped from his shoes, the mattress had been shredded and tossed about the room, and even the lovely hand-made quilt that had adorned his bed was reduced to bright ribbons of color scattered throughout the heaps of trash his belongings had become. Glints of glass spoke of the framed pictures that had graced the room's walls. Even the mopboards had been pried from the wall.

"No!" Taylor's voice penetrated the fog of shock that absorbed him. He hadn't noticed the others had moved on to her room until he heard her cry. He tore down the hall to where she stood in the doorway of her bedroom. Her belongings had met a similar fate to his, except only a few long gashes had been slashed through her mattress and a framed portrait of a couple he suspected were her parents still hung on the wall, albeit at a crazy slant. A scrap of lace dangled from one upended drawer. The open window suggested the burglar's exit route.

All four of them stood in the doorway surveying the vandalized rooms for several long minutes. Finally Stewart took a deep breath and volunteered to help clean up.

"Best get to it," he encouraged the others to begin. "Lilly, you help Taylor, and I'll see what I can do to give Clay a hand."

"There's something I'd better do first," Clay roused himself to think beyond the devastation of his and Taylor's rooms. He turned to Lilly and Stewart. "The people we stopped to help on our way here were Peggy Friedrickson and her girls. Her car went off the road into the river, trapping them inside. We got them out, and they're all three alive, but Peggy and the little girls were taken to hospitals in Ketchum and Boise. Everett left to meet Cindy in Boise, so I'd better go see about his chores."

"Goodness." Lilly's hand went to her chest. "Were they badly injured?"

"Gina seems to be fine, but Peggy was knocked out. She has a broken arm, and she swallowed quite a bit of water," Clay answered. "Little Cindy was still unconscious when the life-flight helicopter picked her up."

"You'd best let the bishop know, and I'll give Lorna—she's the Relief Society president—a call." Lilly wiped a tear from her cheek. "That poor family has been through so much."

"Give Blaine a call," Stewart told him. "He lives close to the Friedricksons, and he might be able to run over and take care of Everett's chores."

"I can do it," Clay protested.

"Yes, but you've got enough to do here and Blaine's his home teacher." Stewart said. "He'll be hurt if you don't give him this chance to do something for Everett and his family."

"I suppose you're right." Clay sighed as he gave his room one more look. "I'll call Blaine."

"Do the Friedricksons have family around here?" Taylor asked. "I don't think the hospital will keep Gina overnight. If she has grandparents . . ."

"Everett's parents are on a mission, and he's an only child. He has an uncle he visits in a nursing home in Gooding," Stewart responded. "I think Peggy has quite a bit of family, but they're in Utah."

"Oh dear! It'll take them a while to get here. I'd better give Lorna a call right now." Lilly started to walk away, then stopped as though she'd just remembered something. "How did the accident happen? Surely Peggy wasn't speeding!"

"No, the accident wasn't her fault," Taylor assured her grand-mother. "A black Pontiac Sunbird cut in front of her, and when she braked to avoid hitting it, she lost control and went off the road into the river."

"A black Pontiac?" Stewart repeated, a question in his voice. "I wonder if it was the same one Gloria over at the café told the deputy about."

"What about it?" Clay asked.

"Oh just that a couple of men, overly dressed for around here, have been in there a lot lately for meals and that she noticed they drove a black Pontiac," Stewart explained.

"The men fit the description of the two that stole Wendy's keys, too," Lilly added.

Taylor and Clay exchanged a look.

"I'd better make those calls." Clay turned toward the stairs.

* * *

Several hours later Taylor viewed the pile of rags on her carpet with resignation and reached for another large trash bag. The dress she'd worn last Sunday, two pairs of jeans, a single cotton knit shirt, and a few mismatched unmentionables were the only clothing she'd managed to salvage. The rest, along with the books, tapes, and shoes she'd brought with her from Pocatello were history. Grandma had used a curved needle she called a carpet needle to close the holes in her mattress and had found fresh bedding for Taylor. It was a good thing the burglars had been interrupted before they'd had time to destroy the rest of the house, she thought gloomily. At least she'd have a place to sleep tonight.

She was tired and she thought about going to bed, but a check of her watch showed it was still early, just seven-thirty. Perhaps Clay needed some help cleaning his room; if so, she should volunteer to help. She hadn't heard him and Stewart moving about for some time. He might be finished, her optimistic side suggested. Stifling a yawn, she walked down the hall. Clay's door was standing open, but the room was dark.

"Clay?" she called, wondering if he'd gone to bed. Then she remembered his bed was wrecked. When there was no answer, she switched on the light. The room was empty, and the broken bed and bureau, reduced to odd-sized boards, were neatly stacked against one wall. The mattress, clothing, and boxes were gone. Even the carpet had been pulled up, revealing a bare wood floor.

The emptiness gave her a strange feeling, reminding her she'd wanted Clay and all his belongings out of her grandmother's house. *But not like this!* A protest rose from somewhere deep inside her. There was no satisfaction here.

Wondering where he'd gone, she wandered down the stairs. She didn't understand the small catch in her throat when she saw him sitting at the kitchen table, wearing a bathrobe she recognized as once belonging to her grandfather. The vet was sorting through a box heaped with papers and miscellaneous small items. She watched him for a minute, then stepped closer and pulled out a chair across from him.

"Is anything missing?" she asked.

"A small amount of cash, my dress watch, a tie pin that had belonged to Jessica's grandfather, and my father's ring," he cataloged the missing items.

"Was the jewelry terribly expensive?" she asked.

He paused a moment as though thinking. "I guess that depends on what you consider expensive. The watch was a gift and I suppose it cost a few hundred dollars. Both the tie pin and Dad's ring have nice diamonds and are certainly worth stealing, but not so much that a jewel thief would specifically target either one."

"Do you think the burglars were jewel thieves?" The concept of jewel thieves in Fairfield, Idaho, seemed pretty far-fetched to Taylor. Miss Morrow, twenty miles up the mountain road was the only resident she could think of who might own any valuable jewelry. Most of the married women's wedding and engagement sets were probably the extent of their real jewels.

"How about you? Are you missing anything?" Clay asked without looking up from the papers he was scanning.

"I'm not sure. I have a nice opal ring with two small diamonds. It's not terribly valuable, but it means a lot to me. It belonged to my mother. I'm not certain whether it was taken or if I even brought it with me." It wasn't in the same league as Clay's missing ring and pin she felt certain. The opal wasn't large and the diamonds were so small they didn't quite qualify to be called chips. She leaned her elbows against the table and rested her chin in her cupped hands. "I'll have Daddy check my jewelry box when I call him."

"You haven't called your father yet?" Clay sounded surprised.

She shook her head. If she hadn't been so tired she might take offense at the implication that she ran to her father over every little thing. Actually the vandalism of Grandma Lilly's house wasn't such a little thing, but she felt reluctant to talk to her father. He'd get upset and demand that she take her grandmother to Pocatello immediately.

"Where are Grandma and Stewart?" she attempted to change the subject.

"Lilly insisted on washing and drying my clothes so I would have something to wear to that dance in Sun Valley," he told her with a lack of enthusiasm in his voice.

"I forgot about that." Taylor sighed. "We don't really have to go, do we?"

"I'm afraid so." Clay looked up from his sorting. "Your grandmother is quite insistent. She seems to think we need to relax with other young people and forget everything else that has happened today. She and Stewart have arranged for Stewart's son and his wife to come over to play board games with them while we're gone, so we can't use

worrying about your grandmother as an excuse. Every single person in
the ward, eighteen and older, will be arriving any minute so we can
drive together." The ringing of the doorbell punctuated his words.

"I'll get it," Lilly called.

"That's our cue to get dressed." Clay grimaced as he rose to his feet.

When Taylor entered the living room ten minutes later, she saw Clay
had gotten there first. He sat on the sofa, wearing the clothes he'd worn
all day. They'd been washed and mended, probably by her grandmother.
He appeared crushed between one arm of the sofa and Betty Glendowski.
Wendy stood near the door, glaring at Betty. Tommy Beredsford occupied the recliner chair, and he looked none too thrilled either.

In minutes she was sharing the back seat of Wendy's father's car
with Tommy and Betty while Clay rode in the front with Wendy.
Before they'd traveled five miles, Taylor was asleep.

She awoke when Tommy shook her shoulder outside a pretty A-
frame church in Sun Valley. At a glance she noticed Clay, too, must
have fallen asleep. He looked as groggy and confused as she felt as
they climbed out of the car.

Music and muted laughter met them as they stepped inside the
cultural hall. Betty immediately pounced on Clay and dragged him onto
the dance floor. While Wendy sputtered her objections, Tommy closed his
arms around her and lightly swept her away, leaving Taylor standing alone.

She wasn't alone long. "Miss Jordan!" She glanced up to see a tall,
dark-haired man smiling at her. It took just a moment before she
recognized Deputy Donaldson. He was almost as good-looking in
slacks and a sports coat as he'd been in his uniform.

"May I have this dance?" He smiled and she accepted. He was a
surprisingly good dancer for a man who appeared so stiff and correct,
and though he wasn't the most exciting conversationalist she'd ever
spent time with, she was grateful he'd rescued her from being a wall-
flower. As they passed Clay and Betty she stifled a smile. Betty held
onto Clay with a viselike grip, and the vet looked thoroughly miserable.

Minutes later the deputy swung her past Tommy and Wendy.
Tommy looked frustrated and Wendy was clearly pouting. Taylor
wondered for the hundredth time how she'd managed to get dragged
into such a disastrous evening. But at least the deputy was attractive
and seemed to enjoy being with her.

Two dances later, she longed for another partner. She was so tired and her partner so boring, she feared she might fall asleep in the middle of the dance floor. Another swing past Clay and Betty convinced her he was even more unhappy than she was. She remembered he'd said he'd like to get married. After his heroic actions this afternoon, her groggy mind told her he deserved someone special. Clearly Betty wasn't the right girl for him and she didn't think Wendy interested him either. She started studying the young women seated near the dance floor. Too short. Too thin. Too much makeup. Too flamboyant. In desperation she decided to enlist the deputy's help.

"Rick," she whispered. "Who is the prettiest girl here?"

He looked startled, then grinned as he answered, "You."

"No, not me," she dismissed his answer with a flash of annoyance. "You met Dr. Curtis this afternoon. He's here at this dance tonight, too, and he's sort of stuck with a partner he doesn't want to be with. Will you help me find him a partner he might really like?"

The deputy's jaw dropped and he looked as though he didn't quite understand her simple request. After a moment's reflection, he asked cautiously, "He isn't interested in you?"

"No, not at all," she assured him. He was quiet for several more minutes, then he started to chuckle.

"Watch that girl with the long, red ponytail," he said. "Do you think she will do?"

Taylor looked in the direction Rick indicated and gasped. The woman was gorgeous. She was about the same height and weight as she was, her face was flawless, and her smile breathtaking. Oh yes, she would definitely do!

"We used to go together," Rick whispered conspiratorially, "until Gary Powers, that's the jerk dancing with her, came to Ketchum. I owe him one. Okay, this is what we'll do: I'll introduce you to them, then suggest we switch partners, then I'll switch again with the vet. You'll be with Gary, and when you see I've got the girl from the feed store, you suggest another switch to ol' Gary. That'll put us back together and leave Gary with Betty!"

It worked like a charm, and she struggled to keep a straight face as Gary twirled away with Betty in his arms. She came down to earth with a sickening thud when she saw the redhead lay her head on Clay's shoulder and she felt Rick pull her closer. She should be cheering over how well her plan succeeded; instead she felt like crying.

Rick suddenly stopped and she found herself dancing with Betty's father. Wasn't Gar a little old for dances like this she wondered as she stumbled, trying to follow his lead. Gar pulled her close in a suffocating bear hug, and she wondered where all the chaperones were. When she'd attended stake dances as a teenager, there had always been someone who kept the dancers from clinches like this! A few more minutes and she'd probably pass out and not have to worry about it anymore.

Suddenly a new dancer stepped in and she whirled away, feeling as light as dandelion fluff. She didn't have to open her eyes to know it was Clay who had rescued her. She blinked and smiled tentatively. "Thank you," she whispered.

There was laughter in his eyes as he whispered back, "One good deed deserves another."

Taylor felt as though she were floating as they swayed to the music and the silent laughter bounced back and forth between them. When the music stopped, Clay kept his arm around her while he looked around for the rest of their group.

"Let's find the others and see if we can persuade them to call it a night. If you're half as tired as I am, I think it's time to make our way back home." He smiled at her and tightened his hold, then slowly let her go.

CHAPTER 13

"Grandma is probably asleep by now," Taylor whispered and Clay nodded his head in agreement but seemed preoccupied. Taylor and Clay had returned from the dance to find Stewart and his son and daughter-in-law playing board games with Lilly. When the Darnells had left, Taylor had offered to lock up, and her grandmother had readily agreed.

After locking up the house, Taylor watched as Clay took a seat at the table where he'd sat earlier, sorting papers and placing them in piles. He frowned as he turned a paper one way then another. His shirt pulled tightly across his shoulders, and she remembered how it had felt beneath her hand as they'd danced.

He looked up and caught her staring at him.

"Have you heard any more about the Friedricksons?" she asked, hoping he couldn't read her thoughts.

"Stewart said Bishop Beredsford called a little while ago to say he'd talked to Everett. Cindy is awake and alert, but her doctor wants to keep her in the hospital for a few days to monitor her heart just to be on the safe side," he told her. "Peggy's arm has been set, and her face required a few stitches, but she'll probably be released tomorrow afternoon."

"That's good." Taylor smiled her relief, ending with a yawn. "I suppose you'll have to sleep on the sofa tonight."

"Lilly said there was plenty of bedding in the linen closet upstairs." He pushed his chair back and rose to his feet. "I'll go get it."

As Taylor started toward the stairs leading to her room, she passed the chair where Clay had been sitting and noticed the papers piled in neat piles. Looking closer, she could see they were from his office.

Invoices were in one pile, patient records in another, and so on. A notebook lay open and as she skimmed it, she discovered Clay was trying to reconstruct his appointment schedule. Shaking her head, she opened the door to his office.

At first the papers and books flung about the room appeared too daunting and she almost backed right out again. A squawk from the dark changed her mind. Grabbing up a handful of towels, she picked her way to Rambo's cage.

"Hush up!" she warned the bird as she draped the towels over her cage. "I don't know how or why, but I suspect this whole mess is your fault!"

"Squawk!"

"Don't deny it," she muttered before picking her way back to the light switch. She turned the light on, then remembering Tom, hastily closed the door leading to the kitchen.

It took her a few minutes to locate all the right cords and plug them into the right places. When she did, she was gratified to hear the whir of the PC unit warming up. Thank goodness, the computer had survived the rough treatment it had been given. At the prompt she entered the password, and in seconds the appointment schedule she'd prepared for the week flashed onto the screen. It took several minutes to locate a few sheets of undamaged paper to put in the printer, but it took only a moment to print out the schedule. When she finished, she shut off the machine and placed the schedule on the kitchen table for Clay to find in the morning.

* * *

Clay groaned when the first stream of light hit his face coming through the front window. He could scarcely believe it was morning. He made his way to his office, where he picked up books and sorted papers in an attempt to straighten his office. He noted almost absently that the two guinea pigs looked none the worse for wear, in spite of having their cage upended the day before. He saw the list of appointments on the table and found the discovery troubling. Taylor was the only one who could have put it there. The computer was back where it belonged and plugged in. She was the only one who could have done that. How did she know he needed that list? And how did she figure out how to print it for him? Something didn't add up.

Mulling the questions over in his mind, he stumbled up the stairs and headed for the bathroom. As he shaved he looked at himself in the mirror and felt the first pangs of discouragement. He should stick around today and finish removing the ruined carpet and furniture from his room and make some kind of arrangements to replace it. Since he appeared to be the target of the attack, refurnishing his room should be his responsibility.

Every piece of paper in his office needed to be filed; some papers needed to be reprinted, then filed. Many of his books needed to be mended, and he had no idea what the status of his accounts—receivable or payable—might be or even if it would be possible to reconstruct the records. Leaving the task for Wendy to sort out seemed like a rotten way to repay all the hard work she'd put into his office over the past month. If he didn't have so many critical appointments . . .

He thought of Taylor rescuing him the night before. No one had said anything about the partner shuffle she'd instigated, but he knew she was behind it. He dressed in the clothes he'd worn the night before and wished he had time to do a little shopping. He wondered if Taylor would spend the day replacing her damaged clothing. At least she was free to go shopping today and replace essential items if she wanted to. He thought of the scrap of lace dangling from a broken drawer and quickly reached for a bottle of aftershave lotion. The sting of the astringent diverted his thoughts, but not for long.

As he drove down dirt roads from patient to patient, he kept seeing Taylor—Taylor sitting beside him in the truck; Taylor whispering endearments to the colt; Taylor with her chin in the air, grabbing items from the grocery store shelf; Taylor with her knuckles white on the steering wheel; Taylor smiling up at him beneath the muted lights of the Sun Valley Ward cultural hall; and Taylor sinking beneath the churning surface of the storm-clogged river to rescue a child. He saw her in a sky-blue sundress with her curls caught up on top of her head, and he saw her with her wet hair plastered to her scalp, her dress ripped and muddy, holding a frightened child in her arms. And he saw the list of appointments, neatly typed, clipped to his dashboard. And somehow he had a sinking sensation he wasn't seeing Taylor at all, that he never had.

* * *

Taylor awoke early. She lay still, listening to the old house, waiting. Then she heard it, the sound of Clay's truck starting, followed by the crunch of gravel as he left the driveway. Pushing a thick tangle of hair back from her face, she sat up and looked around seeing a sad emptiness. She might as well get up. There would certainly be plenty to do today.

She paused on her way downstairs to look at Clay's nearly empty room again. Her room had made her feel sad, but his made her angry. That room had been her father's while he was growing up and had been the room where he slept when they had visited her grandparents all her life. The pictures and the furniture that had been destroyed had been his. Yet it wasn't her father's loss or even her grandmother's that angered her. Someone had done this to Clay!

She whirled about to open the doors leading to two seldom-used bedrooms. The first, Aunt Linda's room, had been taken over a long time ago by her grandmother as a sewing room, though it still contained a daybed and could be used as a bedroom in a pinch. The second was furnished with a child's small bed, a crib, a toy box, and children's books. Neither room appeared to have been disturbed by yesterday's vandals. She'd slept and played in this room as a little girl until she'd become too big for the little bed and the toys. Her cousins, Jack and Eddie, had shared the room during their infrequent visits as well. Running a finger over a toy shelf where Jack had scratched his initials a long time ago, she wondered why her grandmother still kept the room ready for a child.

Was Grandma Lilly waiting for a great-grandchild? Something about that thought disturbed her. Jack had just received his mission call. Eddie was set to start high school in Phoenix this fall. And Taylor didn't have any desire to marry and have children. Grandma would be waiting a long time for another child to sleep in this room. The remembered weight of a frightened four-year-old in her arms seemed to mock her, and she quickly turned away, closing the door behind her.

Descending the stairs she found a pile of neatly folded bedding on the end of the sofa, and her grandmother's closed bedroom door indicated she wasn't awake yet. Slowly she drifted through the house, stopping to stroke Tom where he still snoozed in Grandpa's old chair, and as though a magnet drew her, she made her way to Clay's office.

She could see he had made a start on cleaning up the mess. Without consciously planning to do so, she began sorting papers into folders, tucking them in the file cabinet as she went. When the desk was clear, she turned on the computer and printed a new appointment calendar. She was glad she'd put the calendar in the computer. As often as Wendy spilled nail polish on it, it had seemed like a good idea. She reprinted several other papers that had been seriously damaged, then turned to mending and smoothing the rest.

As she worked, she knew she was postponing the inevitable. She had to call her father. Why she dreaded calling she didn't know. In spite of his strong personality, they had always been close. He'd probably insist she return home and bring Grandma with her. She hadn't wanted to come to Fairfield, but now she didn't feel ready to leave and she didn't know why. Maybe it was her stubborn streak; she'd never been one to leave a task unfinished. And there was so much that she didn't feel was finished yet.

Picking up the phone, she dialed. Her father answered on the second ring.

"Hi, Daddy." She made a point to make her voice sound cheerful. After exchanging a few pleasantries, she got up the courage to tell him someone had broken in to the house. Just as she'd expected, he demanded she return home immediately and bring her grandmother with her.

"We're fine, Daddy," she insisted. "Clay—you remember I told you about Grandma's boarder—installed dead bolts on the doors." She didn't tell him Clay had installed the dead bolts before the break-in.

"That's another thing," her father stormed. "I don't like you and my mother there alone with some stranger."

"He's not exactly a stranger," she protested. "George Reynolds over at the bank investigated him thoroughly before advancing him the money to build his clinic. Bishop Beredsford thinks highly of him, and he was Blaine Gardner's missionary companion. He's well liked by the farmers and ranchers around here." She surprised herself by once more coming to Clay's defense.

"I think it's time I make a trip up there myself to meet the man. If he's as reputable as you say, we might be able to work out a deal with him to rent that old house when we bring Mother here."

His words left Taylor speechless. She'd never considered the possibility that Clay might rent Grandma's house. On the surface it sounded like a great solution, but it brought troubling pictures to her mind. Clay would marry someday; he said he was looking for a wife. The sudden picture of his redheaded partner at the dance taking charge of Grandma's kitchen gave Taylor a queasy feeling in the bottom of her stomach.

"He has plans to build his own house," she informed her father.

"He has to live somewhere while it's being built, and if he has old Bib build his house, it might take ten years," he dismissed her attempt to dissuade him from his plan. "I can't make it next weekend, but I'll be up the one after." He ended the phone call and left Taylor staring at the instrument, feeling far from satisfied with their conversation. Why did her father think he always knew what was best for everyone? At least, she'd managed to change his mind about her immediate return to Pocatello, but she couldn't put off any longer talking to Grandma about the apartment in Pocatello. Daddy would come prepared to move Grandma, and she couldn't allow her to discover his plan that way.

At a soft rap on the door, she looked up to see Bib Jones peering through the screen door.

"Hi!" she called and went to open the door.

"Miss Jordan?" The contractor seemed relieved to see her. "I hate to bother you, but I wondered if you found out about those drains. Like I told you before, the plumbing has to be in before we can go any further."

"Oh, yes," she smiled at him. "Come inside a minute and I'll pull up the information on the computer so you can see how they're supposed to look."

He stood looking over her shoulder as she loaded the software she'd purchased in Twin Falls the day before. In minutes she brought up the images she wanted him to see. He watched as she displayed several pictures of dogs being groomed, then switched to grooming shots of a first-class equestrian barn. Finally she brought up the blue-print of Clay's stable she'd scanned in when she'd first gotten the idea to speed up the construction of Clay's clinic. With the enhancements from the new software, she had realistic views of the proposed surgery and grooming areas.

"Well I'll be . . ." the big man boomed. "I don't know how you did that, but it sure enough answers most of my questions."

"Would you like prints, Mr. Jones?" Taylor turned to look up at him.

"You mean copies of them pictures?" He grinned.

She nodded and he stuck one big thumb in the air in a celebratory salute. With a chuckle, she pressed the print button.

"Here you go, Mr. Jones," she said minutes later as she handed him a sheaf of papers.

"My friends call me Bib." He smiled as he headed toward the door.

"And I'm Taylor." She grinned back as he closed the door and ambled out of sight.

"Did I hear voices?" Grandma Lilly poked her head into the office to ask. "Oh my," she exclaimed as she looked around. "You've gotten a lot done."

"Clay did most of it." She gave him credit as she rose to her feet and stretched. She glanced at her watch and was surprised to see so much time had passed. "I'm sorry," she apologized as she walked toward her grand-mother. "I meant to have breakfast ready for you when you woke up."

"I don't need anyone fixing breakfast for me." Her grandmother patted her arm. "You're the one who needs a little fussing over, you and Clay. Now you just come in and sit down."

"In just a minute," Taylor smiled, reaching for the disk in the computer. Unsure where to put it, she slipped it back in its box and returned the box to the sack with her other purchases. As she did, she noticed the department store bag Clay must have picked up with hers and brought into the house the previous night. Peeking inside she found a plain white shirt. "Well, that's something," she smiled. "He'll have one clean shirt to change into." Closing the bag, she followed her grandmother to the kitchen.

Stewart arrived halfway through breakfast. He'd already been in touch with Bishop Beredsford and reported on the progress of the Friedrickson family.

"Andrea Gardner drove into Hailey last night and brought Gina home with her. Gina's used to playing with Blaine and Andrea's girls, so that worked out." He reached for a piece of toast, and while slathering homemade strawberry jam on it, he went on, "The Morgans are going to bring Peggy home this afternoon. Her mother's coming to help and should get here about the same time. She'll still need someone to do chores, so I offered to go over tonight and my boy'll go over in the morning."

Taylor smiled to hear Stewart refer to his son as his "boy." John was well past forty and had a son of his own serving a mission in South America. He was on the stake high council and his wife, Cricket, was a counselor in the Fairfield Ward's Relief Society presidency.

"Cricket told me to ask if you'd like to bake some cookies for Peggy and her little girl." Stewart was still talking to her grandmother. "She said she knows Peggy will be disappointed not to get one of your pies, but she's afraid pie might be too hard for her to handle with her arm in a cast."

"Of course," Grandma agreed. She was silent for a moment, apparently deep in thought. "I know," she suddenly beamed. "Tarts! They're almost as good as pie, and I still have those blackberries . . ." She stood, her face wreathed in smiles as she hurried toward the cupboard.

Memories of warm blackberry tarts made Taylor's mouth water. They were a lot of work but . . . She remembered her father's stern admonition to keep Grandma Lilly from working so hard. He'd given her a detailed list of instructions on the phone earlier for taking care of Grandma and making certain she didn't suffer any ill effects from yesterday's burglary. *She doesn't need to take food to everyone in Fairfield who sneezes,* her father had insisted. She looked at her grandmother again. Should she intervene? Then she remembered Grandma Lilly's sadness last night and the worry she'd tried to hide. She'd gone to bed early, looking older than Taylor remembered her ever looking before. Now she smiled and moved with rapid steps to pull shortening from the cupboard and berries from her freezer. Daddy was wrong. Taylor smiled at her discovery. Grandma's cooking and caring helped her as much as it did all the people she served.

"You know, dear," her grandmother eyed her critically as she set the ingredients for her tarts on the counter. "You're going to need a few more clothes. You could probably find enough to get by for a few days at King's in Hailey, or you could go on to Gooding. There's a small department store there."

"I'm not leaving you alone," Taylor rejected her grandmother's suggestion.

"I'll be fine," the older woman dismissed her objection. "Those burglars are long gone by now. Besides, I won't really be alone. Stewart is here, and his grandson is coming to mow the lawn this morning."

"I don't like to leave you anyway." Taylor filled the sink with soapy water and began washing the breakfast dishes.

"Wendy will be here any minute as well, so don't you worry," her grandmother continued to urge her to go shopping.

When Stewart's fifteen-year-old grandson, Levi, arrived a few minutes later, Taylor took one look at the lanky, broad-shouldered youth mowing Grandma Lilly's lawn and decided she would go shopping after all.

Returning from collecting her purse, she discovered Wendy had arrived and took a few minutes to stop in Clay's office to say hello to her. Peeking through the door, she found Wendy standing next to Rambo's cage, whispering nonsense to the bird.

Rambo cocked her head and moved closer. "What a good girl," Wendy crooned as she stroked the side of the bird's head with two fingers. Wendy was so absorbed in her feathered friend, she hadn't heard Taylor's approach.

Tapping lightly on the door, Taylor got the other girl's attention. "I left a list of Clay's appointments on his desk."

"Oh hi, Taylor. I'm sorry you had such a bad time yesterday. You didn't catch cold or anything from jumping in the river did you?" Wendy asked, her eyes wide. "I think you were really brave."

"I wasn't so brave," Taylor brushed off the compliment. "There wasn't time to worry about being scared."

"Well, I think you were wonderful. The whole town is talking about how brave you were. But why didn't you tell us last night?"

"I guess I didn't want to think about it," she excused her silence on the subject. "I've got to replace a few clothes though now," Taylor told her. "Yesterday's burglar wiped out my wardrobe."

"That's just so mean!" Wendy showed her indignation. "Sister

Jordan told me how they tore up both your clothes and Clay's and that they even ruined your shoes."

"Clay's in worse shape than I am," she grimaced. "I had a couple pairs of pants in the laundry room, but he doesn't have anything but what he has on. My dad is sending me some clothes from home, but I thought I'd better get a few things to tide me over until he remembers to send them." She turned toward the door and noticed the two bags on the floor where Clay had dropped them the night before. Obviously Clay had forgotten the purchase he'd made in Twin Falls. She scooped up the bags to carry them upstairs.

Feeling reluctant to leave her grandmother alone for long, Taylor decided to try the small variety store in Hailey. It wasn't hard to find, and the variety of merchandise in the store certainly explained its name. The selection of shirts and blouses surprised her, and it wasn't difficult to find replacements for most of the items she'd lost, though they weren't the brand names she would have selected at home or on the occasional trips she made to Salt Lake.

On her way to the checkout counter she passed a rack of shirts in men's sizes. She thought of the lone white shirt she'd hung in Clay's closet and remembered the size. Impulsively she pulled three shirts from the rack and went looking for men's work socks to add to the stack of articles she carried in her arms. Clay would need pants, too, but the little store didn't stock much of a selection of jeans.

On the way back to Fairfield she found herself drawn to the spot where Peggy's car had gone into the river the day before. Pulling to the side of the road, she sat still, looking over the water and thinking of how frightened she'd been when she saw the car disappear over the embankment. Instead of pulling back onto the road, she turned off the engine and opened the car door. In minutes she was standing beside the river. Deep gouges showed in the bank and across the grass, revealing the path the car had taken as the tow truck dragged it from the river.

Gazing down at the water, she could see it was much shallower today than it had been yesterday. Many more large rocks could be seen and the current didn't appear nearly as swift. She could pick out the narrow channel of faster water where she had tumbled and struggled to find her way to the surface and felt her breath quicken as she remembered how desperately she'd longed for a single gulp of air.

Everyone seemed in awe of her attempt to rescue Cindy and she was the only one who knew that saving herself had been far more difficult. The thoughts that had swirled through her mind in those black moments when she thought she was going to die bothered her still. She'd thought many times as a girl growing up without her mother that seeing her for even a few seconds would bring her the greatest joy she could ever know, but if that glimpse had truly been her mother and not the frightened imagining of her stressed mind, it wasn't joy she'd felt. It had been more like the time she'd hidden a doll-size china teacup belonging to another little girl and brought it home in her pocket. She'd disappointed her mother then, and somehow she was a disappointment to her now.

"Why, Mommy? Was it because I stopped trying to get out of the water, or is it something more?" She whispered the words aloud, and they drifted away on a small breeze which brought her no answers. Her thoughts turned to the sadness she'd seen on her father's face when she'd been tempted to give up her struggle to reach the water's surface. She knew he loved her and that he would have been inconsolable if she had drowned, but honesty forced her to admit it wasn't even his sorrow that had caused her to resume her fight for life. It had been Clay. She couldn't begin to fathom why Clay's mocking appraisal had motivated her, when the hurt and despair of the two people who loved her most hadn't been enough.

And the child she'd clung to, refusing to give up? It wasn't Cindy. The brief illusion had been an infant. Her own child? She'd never wanted a child, but she'd wanted that child desperately. Something splashed in the water below, and she felt a sudden chill. It was time to get back in her car and return to check on her grandmother.

Glancing toward the sky, she saw that clouds now obliterated the sun. For just a moment she longed for the feel of a thick quilt and Clay's reassuring arms. Dismissing the sudden longing as a carryover from the previous emotion-packed day, she hurried back to her car. She didn't need Clay or any other man.

A smattering of rain drops landed on her windshield as she put the car in motion and left the river behind. As she drove away, she wondered if she would ever truly leave that river behind. Much more than the emotion-packed trauma of rescuing a family had occurred there, and she needed time to sort out the events of that afternoon in her mind.

CHAPTER 14

The rich, fruity aroma of blackberry tarts greeted her when she entered her grandmother's house. Grandma, Stewart, and Stewart's grandson were seated at the table with a plate of the little pies and a jug of milk. They looked up when she entered the room, and Grandma jumped up to fetch another glass.

"Just let me take these bags upstairs," she told them. "I'll be right back."

"You better hurry," the boy laughed as his hand closed around one of the tarts, "or there'll be nothing left but the smell."

"There'd better be some left!" she attempted to sound threatening. Nonetheless, she hurried and within minutes joined the others at the table.

"Ah-h." She closed her eyes, savoring the first bite. "Food for the gods," she murmured.

"Not likely," Levi mumbled around a mouthful of hot blackberries. "This stuff is too good for the likes of Zeus and his crowd."

"You're an authority on Greek mythology?" She couldn't help teasing the kid who seemed to have acquired a taste for her grandmother's tarts.

"Sure," he grinned. "You didn't think us Fairfield kids were just hicks who spend all our time studying cows, did you? I read all about Mount Olympus, home of the original keg party. That Zeus guy had all the babes convinced he was a god so they would feed him grapes while he laid around lapping up booze."

"We must have had different textbooks," she said with a laugh. "But all kidding aside, Grandma, these are delicious."

"They were always your favorite." Grandma beamed her pleasure at the praise.

From the corner of her eye, Taylor saw Levi reach for the last tart on the plate. "No fair!" She swiftly reached past him to claim the treat.

"Hey!" he protested.

"Sorry." She smirked unrepentantly. "That's what you get for starting without me." She slowly sank her teeth into the tender crust.

Stewart's warm chuckle caught her attention. He spoke to his grandson. "That's just what your aunts did to your dad. I used to tell him big sisters were part of God's plan to keep boys humble."

"That explains why I didn't get any sisters," Levi quipped with a teasing glance at Taylor.

Taylor started to laugh, then fell silent. She had been treating Levi Darnell like a little brother; more than that, the four of them sitting at the table felt like family. Only Clay had been missing. But Clay and the Darnells weren't family, only Grandma Lilly. And she didn't like it one little bit the way her mind had automatically included Clay in that little tableau.

"Did Wendy get a tart?" Taylor asked as she licked the last of the sweet juice from her fingers.

"She left a long time ago," Levi volunteered. "The tarts weren't done yet."

"It was so late when she got here, I was surprised to see her leave just an hour later," Grandma said with a hint of disapproval in her voice. "She took that silly bird with her, too, so I thought she would come right back."

"She took Rambo?" Taylor couldn't imagine why Wendy would have taken the ornery bird.

"Cage and all," Levi informed her.

Taylor knew Wendy was attached to the bird, but she thought Wendy should have asked permission before taking Rambo, and she must not be planning to come right back if she took that monstrous cage with her.

"Taylor," Grandma Lilly turned to her, interrupting a train of thought Taylor didn't want to pursue anyway. "Would you mind taking a plate of tarts out to Peggy?"

"I'd love to," she agreed to the errand. She'd like to see for herself that Peggy and her little girls were safely back home. "I'll just go get my car keys and do it right now."

"I'd be happy to help," Levi volunteered.

"'Fraid not, son." Stewart placed a hand on the boy's shoulder. "I promised your dad I'd have you back in time to do your chores."

"Besides it wouldn't be safe to take you along," Taylor teased. "I want to get to the Friedrickson ranch without losing a few tarts along the way."

"All the more reason for me to go. You know, to keep you honest." They all laughed and Taylor ran upstairs to get her keys again. On an impulse she changed into one of her new blouses and grabbed the sweater she'd purchased to go with it. It only took a moment to clip off the tags before hurrying back down the stairs.

She was pleased she remembered the way to the Friedrickson ranch. In a way it was hard to believe that only yesterday morning she'd played with the girls and their new colt without any premonition of what the day would bring.

She exited the highway to make her way to the ranch. The gravel road was in serious need of a little more gravel, she thought as she dodged potholes. At last she reached the gate and bumped up a dusty lane. Seeing several cars parked in the drive, she hesitated, realizing Peggy already had company.

"I've come this far, I might as well go to the door and deliver Grandma's tarts," she convinced herself as she pulled in behind a car with out-of-state license plates. She wouldn't stay long. Before she could knock on the door, it was flung open and Gina catapulted into her arms.

"Taylor! Taylor! Mama is home and Grandma came!" the little girl shouted as she hugged Taylor. "Mama didn't get drownded."

"I'm glad." She hugged the child back and found speaking taxed her throat.

"Hello," a voice came from behind her. She straightened and turned to see an older version of Peggy coming toward her. The woman's cheeks were damp, and without saying a word she embraced Taylor as well. After a moment, the woman drew back and gave her a watery smile.

"There are no words that even begin to express my gratitude," she whispered in a husky voice. "If you hadn't been there . . ." She dabbed at her eyes with a soggy tissue she found in a pocket.

"Is Peggy really all right?" Taylor asked.

"Oh my, yes. And anxious to see you. Please come in." She gestured toward the open door. "Gina saw you get out of your car and I followed her to the door. I couldn't wait to meet you. Oh!" She suddenly stopped. "I'm sorry. I didn't introduce myself. I'm Janice Peterson, Peggy's mother."

"Nice to meet you." Taylor smiled back at the woman.

"Come," Gina tugged at her hand, and she let the child lead her into the house.

Peggy wasn't lying in bed as she had expected but was seated in a large recliner with an afghan across her lap and a low table beside her. An assortment of drinks and snacks covered the table. But what caught her attention was the man sitting on one corner of the sofa, nearest Peggy.

"Hi!" She tried to focus on Peggy, but she couldn't help noticing Clay. What was he doing here? She stepped closer and set the plate down where Peggy could reach it. "Grandma Lilly made these for you," she said.

"Mm-mm. Your grandma is the best cook in Fairfield." Peggy smiled and lifted one corner of the plastic wrap to pinch off a piece of a tart. "Be sure to thank her for me."

"I will." Taylor smiled back.

"I'm so glad you came," Peggy told her. "I've wanted to thank you for . . ." Her voice wavered and she paused to get her emotions under control. "Please sit down." She waved her good arm toward the sofa where Clay sat.

Taylor hesitated but decided it would be churlish to refuse to sit beside Clay. It wasn't that she had anything against the man. It was just that she felt awkward and self-conscious around him . . . though she hadn't felt awkward the day before, she remembered. They had been more like a team, anticipating the other's every move—at the river and on the dance floor, an impish voice in the back of her head reminded her.

"Anyway, I was trying to tell you, both of you," she included Clay, "how thankful I am that you saw what happened and got us out of the river. I was so afraid my girls . . . I don't remember . . ."

Clay placed his big hand over Peggy's smaller one. "We're glad we were there, too."

"You could have been killed . . . You risked your life for us," Peggy continued the attempt to express her gratitude.

"I was never in any danger," Clay protested. "I got lucky is all. When I couldn't open the door and couldn't squeeze through the broken window, I didn't know what to do. Then I managed to grab Gina, who had gotten her seat belt off, and Taylor was right there to take her from me, so I could pull you through the window next. I tried to get Cindy, too, but I barely managed to unbuckle her seat belt. She was my biggest worry, but fortunately Taylor was skinny enough to go right in after her. She's the real heroine of the day." Clay turned to her and she felt a wave of shock slide down her spine as he turned a smile loaded with respect and approval her way, leaving her somewhere between scorched and breathless.

Gina climbed on her lap and gave her another hug. Janice Peterson wiped her eyes and added a hug of her own.

She felt her face redden, and she found herself floundering for something to say. She had to remind herself it wasn't very flattering to hear Clay refer to her as "skinny," and she'd just as soon Peggy never knew how close she'd come to drowning herself after handing Cindy to Clay. She grasped for something to say to divert the attention from herself.

"Is Cindy all right?" she finally managed to ask.

"Yes," Peggy assured her. "I talked to her on the phone a little while ago. She woke up during the flight to Boise. Her doctor has run all kinds of tests, and Everett assures me he'll be able to bring her home tomorrow."

They talked for a few more minutes, then Clay stood. "I'd better get started on those chores," he told Peggy. "John Darnell planned to do them, but a few of his cows got in a hay field and I had to treat one for bloat, and he's running late now. I told him I had to come out this way anyway, so I'd take care of it."

"I can help." Gina slid from Taylor's lap.

"Not tonight, sweetie," her grandmother protested. "You can't go to the barn without someone to watch you, and your mommy needs me right now."

"I'll watch her," Taylor volunteered. The minute the words left her mouth, Taylor wondered if she'd lost her mind. She didn't need to spend any more time around Clay. The tug on her hand told her she couldn't back out.

While Clay forked hay to the mare in one of the stalls and carried grain to a couple of heifers at the opposite end of the barn, Gina showed Taylor where a nest of kittens slept. While they played with the kittens, Clay milked Everett's few milch cows.

"You want to feed the calves?" Clay called a little later, and Gina jumped up immediately.

"I do. I do." The little girl set the kitten she'd been holding back beside its mother and scrambled to her feet. Taylor followed her down the aisle to where Clay stood holding a large bucket in one hand and three smaller buckets in the other.

He led the way to a pen where half a dozen calves jostled each other aside in an attempt to stick their heads through the fence slats.

"They're almost big enough to be weaned," he warned Taylor as he poured equal amounts of milk in each of the three buckets, "so they might be a little rough. You feed those two." He pointed to two curly-haired black calves on the end.

"How?" Taylor looked helplessly at the bucket at her feet and back to the calves.

"Climb over the fence, and I'll hand you a bucket. Let one of the calves stick his head in the formula, and he'll take care of the rest. When he's through, I'll give you another bucket for the other one." He grinned like he was enjoying a joke at her expense. Her back straightened and she reached for the top pole of the small pen. Feeling clumsy, she climbed the poles and slid her leg over the top. As she stepped back to the ground she found herself surrounded by the calves, each one jostling and butting his way to get closer to her. Holding the bucket high, she wondered how she was supposed to make sure the right calf got the milk when she could barely stand upright and the calves all looked the same.

Suddenly the crowd around her diminished, and she noticed two calves were drinking from the buckets Clay held in his hands. Beside him stood Gina, helping him hold one of the buckets. Slowly Taylor lowered her bucket and a calf thrust his nose inside. She had no idea whether it was the right calf or not, but she didn't have time to worry about it as the calf butted and thrust against the bucket, nearly tearing it from her hands as it drank.

Feeding the second round of calves wasn't any easier and it was only the dripping mustaches the first round sported that gave her a clue to which calves had already eaten. Gina's laughter rang out and a little ache formed in Taylor's heart. She looked up to see the child petting a calf that looked as though it were trying to eat her shirt. The girl's face shone with delight for the young animal. Gina sparkled with life, and Taylor felt something deep in her soul that told her she'd never valued life enough before.

A picture formed in her mind of her mother pushing her in a swing. She remembered the sparkling eyes, the mouth tilted in laughter. The picture slipped away, and in its place came memories of her mother's still face as she'd kissed her good-bye one last time. Taylor was glad Peggy and Gina could go on making memories filled with love and laughter. She almost envied the other woman as she thought of how many opportunities Peggy would have to see that vital light in her daughter's face.

"Okay, we're through." Clay picked up Gina and swung her over the fence. "Next!" he called and held out his arms toward Taylor. For a just a moment she was tempted. Laughing, as surely he'd intended, she climbed the fence and swung herself to the ground.

After returning Gina to the house, Clay walked Taylor to her car. The sun was setting to the west, filling the sky with pink and gold and giving every cloud a rosy glow. The scent of roses filled the air, and the distant trill of birds settling for the night carried to them with the faint stirring of the air as daylight faded. They paused beside her car to watch the last of the glow fade away and the first star twinkle on the horizon.

"I'd better go," Taylor sighed. "It's so peaceful here, but after all that happened yesterday, I don't feel comfortable leaving Grandma alone very long."

"Yes, I suppose we should go." He sounded as reluctant as she felt and he didn't immediately make a move toward his truck. Instead he lifted his face and seemed to be watching the sky. She turned her face upward, too.

She was surprised when Clay gave voice to his thoughts a few minutes later. "When I was a little boy, my friend's dad took us on a camping trip in the Adirondacks. We slept on the ground without a tent, and I think I stayed awake all night just looking at the stars. I'd only seen stars like that in books. It was just so grand. I felt like I was looking right into heaven. Even now, I always feel closer to God when I look up at a star-filled sky."

"Didn't you camp with your father?" Taylor asked softly, not wanting to break the spell the night seemed to cast over the two of them.

"No, we always planned to go camping someday, but someday never came." He paused for several minutes then went on speaking as though he were thinking or remembering out loud. "Dad stood up for me when he could, but most of the time he was no match for my mother. He was a good man, but I don't think he was happy. I don't know what he wanted in life; he always seemed to defer to Mother's wishes. Once he said he'd always wanted to see the Grand Canyon and Old Faithful. Instead he visited Paris and London because that's where Mother wanted to go. I think he only stayed with my mother because he didn't want to leave me, and because he was too kind to take me away from her. Somehow that always made me feel guilty."

"Children aren't responsible for the success or failure of their parents' marriage," Taylor reminded him.

"Knowing something intellectually and feeling it inside are two different things," Clay retorted.

"With an example like your parents' marriage, I'm surprised you want to get married." Taylor shook her head, remembering Clay's claim that he was looking for a wife.

"I don't think marriage has to be like theirs," Clay surprised her with his serious tone. "All the while I was growing up, I thought I was missing out on something important and that I was responsible for Dad's unhappiness."

"Do you still feel that way?" she asked.

"Not completely. I understand now that Dad brought a lot of his unhappiness on himself because he never told Mother what really mattered to him. He never took charge of his own life but just drifted in whichever direction she set. After I joined the Church, I saw some really good marriages and learned the Church has a lot of good advice for building strong marriages and families. I know now what I missed, and I want the kind of marriage and home I believe God intended for his children. I want the kind of happiness the

Friedricksons have, and Blaine and Andrea, the kind I believe your grandparents shared for fifty years and will have again for all eternity."

"According to my dad," Taylor spoke wryly, as though she suspected her father had romanticized his memories, "his marriage to my mother was nearly perfect. I don't remember her very well, and I don't know whether she was happy or not. I just remember all the years of hurt and loneliness he has had to endure without her. I don't want to love someone so much that if either of us should die, the one left behind has to go through all he has suffered." Taylor's voice was low and intense. Clay didn't say anything, but he quietly reached for her hand and she knew he was offering her comfort, but she wasn't ready to drop the subject yet.

"Intellectually I know my mother couldn't help leaving Daddy, but in my heart I think I've always blamed her for his unhappiness," Taylor said aloud what she hadn't ever voiced before. "You say your dad wasn't blameless for his poor marriage, but I suspect he blamed your mother for both his and your unhappiness during those years and that deep down you hold her responsible, too. No one should allow anyone else to have that kind of power over them," she concluded.

He didn't speak for what seemed a long time. She probably shouldn't have expressed her opinion so bluntly.

"Actually I don't blame my mother," Clay finally broke the silence. "Dad let her down by not being an equal partner in their marriage. When he didn't carry an equal load, she picked up the slack. I love my mother a great deal, and I have no doubt she loves me, but shouldering the responsibility for our family alone for so many years has turned her into a bit of a tyrant. After so many years of taking charge, I'm sure she finds it frustrating that I don't share her views of what is important."

"And what do you consider important?" There was more than idle curiosity behind her question. For some reason she really needed to know what he thought mattered.

"The gospel is important to me. So is my career and the life I've chosen to live, though Mother dismisses my choices as mere whims." Clay sounded more sad than bitter. "She says my position in the community, family, and money are what really matter, and that it's time for me to grow up and accept my responsibilities to her and to Jessica.

"It's our perspective on what is important that differs. Position only matters to me as far as being a respected, contributing member of society. To my mother 'family' is a sort of snobbish designation that excludes others; to me it's a unit that loves each other so much that others—including God—are always welcome." There was a wistfulness to his voice.

"And money? Can you truthfully say money doesn't matter to you?" she asked.

"No, I can't say that," he conceded. "I like the comforts money can buy as well as the next guy. And like most men, I can't help seeing financial success as a measure of my success in my career, but I don't think about money all the time. Designer labels, luxury cars, and the jet set scene mean nothing to me. Like most people, I sometimes think about what I'd do if I had a lot of money. I hope I'd do something good to help people or animals."

Taylor thought about his words as the dark deepened and more stars took their place in the night sky. She didn't need him to say aloud that his mother was disappointed in him. His decision to live in the West, his failure to choose a career that would bring him fame and fortune, his rejection of a wealthy woman with a name his mother considered important, and probably his choice of religion in his mother's mind were considered a rejection of her.

"Clay . . ." She tentatively placed a hand on his arm. "It's not easy being the only child of a single parent. Sometimes I feel smothered and that Daddy has so many plans and expectations for me, there are no choices left for me to make. I know he's lonely and fearful of losing me. Do you think your mother feels the same way?"

"I'm sure she does, but knowing that doesn't make it easier," he admitted. His free hand covered hers, holding it against his arm.

"I was watching Gina as we were feeding the calves, and I remembered my mother pushing me in a swing when I was about her age." Taylor wasn't sure why she was telling Clay this. She never talked about her mother. It had been an unwritten rule in her home that neither she nor her father ever talked about her mother. She'd understood from the start that mentioning "Mommy" made Daddy sad. Something compelled her to continue trying to explain the brief memory to Clay. "Seeing Gina laugh and look happy tonight, I was thankful that Gina won't have to grow up without her mother. Then it struck me that I was remembering my mother as laughing and happy. There seemed to be something profound in seeing that she had been happy, and I wish I had remembered it a long time ago."

"Your father was wrong to discourage your memories of your mother," Clay whispered. "Every child needs two parents, and memories could have sustained you through the trials of growing up without her. In some respects, my father was just as absent as your mother. Though he was physically present, he was so emotionally distant from my mother, that she, too, was a single parent in most ways."

She felt Clay gently brush his fingers against her cheek. She hadn't known she was crying. Now she sobbed in earnest. His arms came around her and he held her until the tears stopped.

"I'm sorry," she said, feeling embarrassed for her display of emotion.

"Don't be," he murmured against her ear. She pulled back, knowing she should put some distance between them, but he didn't release her. Instead he smiled down at her. Her breath caught when she saw his gaze drift from her eyes to her mouth, which suddenly felt swollen and dry. She could feel the rapid tempo of his heart through his shirt as his arms tightened around her and his mouth descended toward hers. Then she forgot to think; she could only feel.

CHAPTER 15

A persistent ringing in her ears invaded the private world where she floated in some vague dreamworld big enough for only two. Clay released her mouth with a groan that sounded as though he were in actual pain. It was a good thing he continued to hold her, or she would have collapsed at his feet.

"Clay Curtis here." Clay's voice penetrated the thick wool that seemed to encompass her. The ringing wasn't in her ears; it was Clay's cell phone! His body stiffened and his arm dropped from around her waist.

"No, she's not with me. I haven't seen her all day." Obviously he wasn't talking about her, Taylor surmised. Besides the only person who might be looking for her was Grandma Lilly, and she knew Taylor had gone to the Friedrickson ranch.

"All right, we're on our way." He clicked the off button and turned to Taylor with a puzzled frown on his face. "Wendy is missing. Lilly said her parents have called twice looking for her, and Tommy Beredsford also came by the house. When he discovered she and I were both gone, he became agitated and insisted we'd run off together. He refuses to leave until I come back. Paul and Joyce Carlson also seem to think I've eloped with their daughter."

"Oh dear," Taylor couldn't resist a bit of teasing. "I guess that makes me your alibi. Don't worry. I'll confess you were with me."

"Thanks." Clay pulled a face. "I guess."

"I wonder where she is?" Taylor mused aloud. "Grandma said she didn't stay long when she came this morning and that when she left she took Rambo with her."

"What?" Clay sounded shocked. "Why did she take Rambo?"

"I don't know, but she took the cage, too," she said, repeating the little Grandma Lilly had told her.

"This is weird!" He reached for her car door. "Come on, let's go. I have a bad feeling about this."

Following Clay's taillights, Taylor drove faster than she ordinarily would have on the bumpy county road. Her mind swirled with questions, but she had few answers. At unexpected moments and in spite of her attempts to avoid remembering, her thoughts returned to those few minutes when Clay had held her. It was just a kiss, she reminded herself as she tried to focus on Wendy, but it resisted being relegated to the back of her mind.

She hadn't meant to kiss Clay. He wasn't her type at all. Actually she wasn't too sure what her type was. She just knew Clay wasn't it. She'd never had a serious boyfriend, and she certainly didn't recall any kiss like that one before. That wasn't to say she thought of Clay as a boyfriend. He was strictly small town and looking for marriage and kids, while she wanted a career and city excitement. Still she felt a tingle of excitement recalling the way he—

No, she wasn't going to think about Clay. She'd concentrate on Wendy. Where could the silly girl have gone? And why take Rambo with her? It didn't make sense, but then Taylor had noticed Wendy frequently didn't make sense. No, she didn't mean that. Wendy was a sweet girl—just a bit impractical—and Taylor really was worried about her. Something about Wendy's disappearance troubled her, and she didn't think the girl would suddenly show up with some silly but simple excuse for worrying everyone. And all right, she'd admit it, she didn't like the way Wendy's parents and Tommy assumed Clay was involved with Wendy. The way he had kissed Taylor didn't seem to leave room for an interest in Wendy.

Enough! So there was an element of physical attraction there. She'd ignore it. Better yet, she'd help him find the wife he claimed to be seeking. But she wouldn't pick someone like Wendy. A busy man like the vet needed a wife who could handle the business end of his practice, who had a firm commitment to the gospel, possessed enough interests of her own not to resent his long hours, and who would be happy living in a wide-spot-in-the-road town. There was something terribly familiar about the woman she'd just described.

Who? Uh oh, she'd just described Grandma Lilly! A giggle escaped her throat. Too bad Grandma already fancied herself in love with Stewart Darnell!

Clay settled his foot a little more firmly against the gas pedal when he reached the highway. He didn't doubt the Carlsons would be delighted to have their suspicions concerning him and their daughter confirmed. Paul and Joyce had been matchmaking from the first day they'd met. Well, it wasn't going to happen. Wendy didn't interest him at all. He hoped nothing bad had happened to the girl and that she wasn't in some kind of trouble, but he didn't have a clue where she might be—or why she'd taken Rambo with her.

Rambo! That was the part that worried him. That bird seemed to be in the middle of everything that had gone wrong all summer. He suspected the bird was somehow involved in the break-ins in Fairfield and possibly the one in New York. Even Wendy's mugging and the Friedricksons' accident might even be linked to Rambo if the key to his office was what the muggers were after when they stole Wendy's keys, and if the burglars who broke into Lilly's house were fleeing the scene of the crime when they cut Peggy off, causing her to lose control of her car.

Getting off to a bad start with Taylor was Rambo's fault, too. The woman couldn't stand him. Well, maybe she liked him a little bit. She hadn't protested when he'd kissed her. And that kiss! How did that happen? He certainly hadn't planned to kiss Lilly's prickly grand-daughter! He wasn't exactly sorry he'd kissed her, but getting it out of his mind wasn't going to be easy, and it was bound to make living in the same house with her more difficult.

Kissing Taylor had been a big mistake, even if it hadn't felt like a mistake at the time. It was definitely further evidence that he lacked good sense when it came to women. She was beautiful and she fit much too well in his arms, but she had her sights set on bigger things than becoming a small-town vet's wife, and he had no intention of ever moving back to the city. That thought made him a little sad, then he wondered why he was even thinking of Taylor and "wife" in the same sentence. For a brief moment he wondered if he might possibly be able to change her mind about small-town life. Failing that, he wished he were the kind of man who could enjoy a brief summer fling, then at the end of summer go on with his life and his practice while she went on to her big-city dreams. It would never work. He wasn't that kind of man and she wasn't that kind of woman.

His thoughts surprised him. What did he really know about Taylor? Not the things he thought he knew about her, he concluded. She wasn't empty-headed or lazy. There was more beneath that beautiful exterior than he had guessed. He suspected her faith ran deep, and he'd seen her courage firsthand. And if she could manage a state-wide political campaign, what else might she be able to manage? A picture of his office came to mind, but he pushed that thought aside. Wendy was his office manager . . . wasn't she? A suspicion began to rise in his mind. It was Taylor who had cleaned up his office after the burglary, and she had seemed to know where everything belonged. Wendy had been nowhere around when the agenda for today's appointments had mysteriously appeared. Wendy's maturity and capability in his office had seemed out of character and too good to be true. Perhaps they really had been.

Taylor had probably been laughing behind his back the whole time! His hands tightened on the wheel and he increased his speed. No way would he let a woman manipulate him again the way Jessica had, lead him on, let him hope, then expect him to drop all his dreams and plans for her. A deep ache began in his chest and he suddenly knew Taylor could hurt him far more than Jessica had. Jessica's rejection had nearly killed him. If he let himself care for Taylor, he doubted he would survive when she walked out on him and his way of life.

Taylor was less than a minute behind Clay when he pulled into the driveway, but he didn't wait for her. He was already through the door when she rushed inside.

"Where is she?" Tommy was demanding to know.

Clay brushed him off to question Lilly. "Has anyone heard from Wendy?"

"No one has heard a thing," Grandma Lilly told him. "When I finally managed to convince Paul and Joyce that Wendy wasn't with you, they called a deputy. After talking to them, he'll come here. He should be here any minute." The deputy arrived before Taylor managed to close the door behind her.

"Hello, Miss Jordan." The officer smiled as he touched his cap and she recognized the same young man who had turned up to investigate Peggy Friedrickson's accident and with whom she'd danced the night before. She smiled back at him and ushered him ahead of her into the living room.

At once, Deputy Donaldson became all business, turning his attention to the other occupants of the room. He questioned Lilly about Wendy's short visit to the office that morning, jotting down notes as she responded. Next he turned to Clay, who insisted he hadn't seen his office manager or talked to her all day. To Clay's obvious annoyance, the deputy left the impression he didn't quite believe his assertion.

"Now I need to see the office where Ms. Carlson was last seen." The officer turned to Lilly. She looked toward Clay as though seeking his permission. When he gave a slight nod of his head, she led the way to the sunporch-turned-office.

As the deputy followed Lilly to the office, he matched his steps to Taylor's, and the others trailed behind. She could see at once that nothing seemed to be disturbed, with the glaring exception of the large birdcage, which no longer sat in the corner. Taylor edged her way toward the desk, hoping to find some message from Wendy, but it appeared to be empty save for a couple of sunflower seeds, a paperclip holder, a pink message pad, and a cup holding some pens and pencils. The message pad was smooth and unwrinkled without a message of any kind on it, not even the usual hearts and flowers Wendy usually doodled while talking on the phone. The notes taped to the side of the file cabinet were all familiar and related to Clay's veterinary practice.

The deputy checked the few items on the desk and opened the drawers one by one. He raised his eyebrows at the selection of nail polish filling one drawer but refrained from commenting. When he finished examining the office, he made a notation in a small black notebook while Tommy watched anxiously.

"Do you think Wendy has been kidnapped?" the young man blurted out.

"No motive," the deputy responded with a frown of annoyance.

"Where could she be?" Lilly questioned. "She isn't here and she isn't at home."

"Probable runaway." The deputy closed his notebook and thrust it back in his pocket.

"Wendy wouldn't run away!" Tommy protested. "Not by herself." He glanced darkly toward Clay.

"A lot of teenagers run away." The deputy sounded bored. "They want to be on their own and escape parents who want to control their lives, or they're just looking for excitement."

"Are her clothes missing from her house?" Tommy thought to ask.

"Hard to tell," the officer answered reluctantly. "Her mother is still checking to see if a few things might be missing."

"A few things! Wendy wouldn't take a few things. She wouldn't go anywhere without a truck full of clothes! And what about makeup—did she take that?"

"She has her own car and her handbag with her," the officer answered stiffly.

"She couldn't have much money in her purse. I don't pay her much and her father doesn't have a lot," Clay pointed out, and Taylor could tell he, too, was skeptical of the runaway theory.

"She has access to your business account. Perhaps you should check that as soon as the bank opens in the morning." The officer hitched his tool belt higher and moved toward the door.

"Wendy wouldn't steal!" Tommy was aghast at the suggestion.

"Seems she helped herself to Dr. Curtis's pet bird." The deputy paused to turn to Clay. "You want to file charges?"

"No, of course not," Clay scowled as he spoke. "You're not giving up, are you? You're still looking for her?"

"No reason." The deputy hitched his belt again. "The girl is of age. No one is filing any charges against her. If she wants to take off, that's her right."

"Wendy wouldn't just . . ." The words trailed off as Tommy followed the officer to the door.

Once more Deputy Donaldson touched his cap and smiled at Taylor. "I'll be in touch, ma'am," he said before exiting the door. Taylor stood staring after the deputy, forgetting to close the door. For some reason that set off Clay's temper, and he was tempted to tell the officious man what he could do with his "getting in touch with Taylor." He could just stay away from Taylor! Reaching for the door, he gave it a shove that slammed it shut with a resounding thud.

The sharp sound of the closing door aroused Taylor from her

thoughts. Clay's office had looked normal, but she couldn't shake the feeling something was different. She was going to look again. Her grandmother was voicing her disapproval of the deputy's assumption as Taylor hurried toward Clay's office.

Clicking on the light once more, she let her eyes rove from one end of the room to the other. The gerbils huddled in one corner of their cage, gazing fearfully out. Her attention focused on the desk. Something about the desk . . .

"What is it?" a voice behind her asked and she turned to see Clay standing in the doorway.

"I don't know," she mused aloud. "The desk doesn't look right."

"The desk?" His voice sounded puzzled. "It looks the same to me except for the calendar. That was ruined by the burglars yesterday."

"I made a new one . . ." Her voice trailed off as she grabbed the wastebasket and began searching through it. Her absentminded admission confirmed in Clay's mind that his earlier suspicion regarding Taylor's familiarity with his office had been correct. This knowledge left him feeling foolish and sparked a flare of anger. He'd get to the bottom of the two young women's deception and tell them what he thought of their childish prank! They'd played him for a fool! He glared at Taylor, a glare that went right over her head. While he'd been caught up in his thoughts, she'd been searching the wastebasket. With a little exclamation of triumph, she pulled a wrinkled, wet, oversized sheet of paper from the bin. Clay joined her at the desk as she smoothed it across the wooden surface. He stared at the paper, seeing nothing particularly significant.

"It looks to me like Wendy set the birdcage on the desk before leaving the office and a little water spilled from Rambo's water dish," Clay noted as he checked the piece of paper.

"Yes, and there's a couple of new appointments, too," Taylor pointed out. "But nothing that indicates where she planned to go today." Discouraged, she sank back in the big office chair.

"The appointments should tell us who she talked to last." Clay scrutinized the calendar more closely and shook his head as though dismissing hope that either of the callers could be of any help.

"You could call them," Tommy spoke from the doorway. It was the first Taylor was aware that he'd followed her and Clay to the office. His face revealed both hope and fear.

"If either caller was someone Wendy knew well, she might have chatted with them about her plans." Taylor tried to let Tommy down easy. "But one appointment is with Amanda Benson. Wendy doesn't like her at all because Amanda boasts about shooting stray dogs and cats that wander onto her place and upset her precious Flopsy. Wendy makes any conversation with her extremely brief. The other appointment is for a consultation with Amy Morrow's foreman, Joe Terrence."

"She'd talk to Miss Morrow. She really admires her," Tommy put in eagerly.

"Miss Morrow doesn't call here personally," Taylor told him. "Mr. Terrence would have been the one to call. He's pretty gruff and impatient. He wouldn't have encouraged any conversation."

"Someone has to know where she is!" There was a note of desperation in the young man's voice.

"You know her better than any of us," Clay spoke impatiently. "Don't you have any idea why she'd leave so abruptly or where she might have gone?"

"I thought she was with you." Tommy clenched his fists at his sides.

"Well, now that you know I haven't seen her all day, can't you come up with another idea?" Clay paced across the floor, stopping only to straighten the gerbils' cage before continuing his agitated pace.

"If I knew where she was, I'd go get her," Tommy defended himself.

"Tom!" Clay snarled. His hip struck the corner of the desk, and he staggered to a sitting position on its shiny surface. "Get out of here!" He looked like he'd say a lot more if he didn't have his mouth clamped shut in a tight line.

"Sorry, I . . . ," Tommy stared aghast at Clay's stormy features as he took a hesitant step backward.

"That's no way to talk to Tommy." Taylor turned on Clay. "There's no reason for being rude. He's as worried as we are, and I think he really cares about Wendy!"

"I do care about her." The boy looked as though it wouldn't take much to cause him to burst into tears.

"The cat! I stumbled over the dumb cat!" Clay rubbed the spot where his hip had struck the desk and glared at the offending animal who cheerfully ignored him. With Rambo missing, no one had bothered to close the door separating the office from the kitchen.

Taylor felt a sudden urge to giggle which she barely managed to stifle. The cat appeared totally oblivious to the people in the room, having reverted to his long-ago kitten days. Crouching low, he batted a pink ball of paper across the room with one paw, then mimicking a jungle relative, he stealthily launched an attack on it. Leaping high in the air, he pounced. The wily prey zipped across the room, finding refuge under the desk. Tom flew after it.

The three people in the room watched the cat, totally fascinated by his antics as he delicately poked one paw under the desk. When that paw failed to free the paper, the big yellow cat tried the other paw.

Taylor found herself watching the cat as though mesmerized when she, in fact, felt like screaming. What was wrong with them all? They were watching a cat who was caught up in his second childhood as though he were the most fascinating thing on earth when Wendy was missing and no one seemed to have a clue where she had gone. The police thought she was just another runaway, and her parents were convinced, in spite of a call from Grandma Lilly, that their daughter had eloped with Clay. She just hoped the deputy would disabuse them of that notion! Personally, she couldn't shake the feeling Wendy was in some kind of danger.

Thinking of Deputy Donaldson frustrated her even more. How dare he assume Wendy had run away!

As she watched with reluctant fascination, Tom hooked a claw in his pink adversary and gently pulled it from its hiding place. He shook his paw. The paper remained stuck to his claw. He shook it again, but the paper tenaciously hung on. He batted at it with his other paw. When that didn't work, he growled then leaped to the top of the bookcase. The paper was now the pursuer! Tom yowled loudly as he leaped from the bookcase to the desk, then catapulted to the top of the file cabinet. Papers slid to the floor along with an open bottle of nail polish.

"That cat!" Clay exploded as he lunged toward it. "He's going to destroy what's left of my office!"

"Don't grab his tail!" Taylor shouted as she joined the chase.

"I got him!" Tommy yelled, then added, "He got away."

"Pink!" Clay's voice erupted like a howl.

"What's going on?" Lilly had to shout to make herself heard over the noise in the office. Tom streaked between her legs and she staggered against the doorsill.

"Catch Tom!" Clay roared and nearly finished toppling her over as he dashed after the cat.

Catch Tom? Taylor thought he only wanted to stop Tom from leaping all over his office. Of course, the paper needed to be removed from the cat's claws before the poor thing had a nervous breakdown. Maybe they were too late for that! That paper . . . She froze, then tore past her grandmother, leaving the older woman reeling once more. *The paper was pink! It had come from the message pad on the desk. The much-too-neat message pad! Wendy was a doodler. She always made scribbles as she talked on the phone. That pink paper could be a clue!*

She stopped abruptly when she ran into Clay's back. She might have fallen if he hadn't reacted quickly to catch her. His arms came around her, and for just a moment she forgot all about Tom and Wendy.

"You all right?" Clay asked.

"Just a little winded," she gasped back, feeling more than a little breathless. It was all that running, then plowing into Clay's back. Her shortness of breath had nothing to do with Clay's arms wrapped snugly about her.

"Where's the cat?" Tommy charged into the living room, and Taylor took a step away from Clay. She tried to ignore the sense of loss she felt as he dropped his arms, setting her free.

"Behind the couch." Clay was all business again. "Help me pull it out." He turned to Taylor. "When Tommy and I move the couch, see if you can catch Tom. That paper could be important!"

"You think it's a clue?" Tommy's face lit up and he dashed to the far end of the sofa.

"Will someone tell me what's going on?" Grandma Lilly demanded as she puffed into the room.

"Tom has a paper stuck on his claw, and we think it might help us find Wendy," Tommy offered a quick explanation. "The doc and I are going to move the couch and Taylor will grab Tom!"

"Nonsense!" Lilly scolded. "That's no way to catch Tom!"

"What would you suggest, Grandma?" Taylor asked. "We really

have to get that paper."

"All three of you sit down," Lilly ordered. Reluctantly they did as she instructed. Taylor nervously eyed her grandmother. She couldn't see how this was going to work. They couldn't just sit around waiting for Tom to emerge from his hiding place.

Grandma left the room and Taylor fidgeted. From the corner of her eye, she could see Clay had his doubts, too. Tommy clearly thought her grandmother had crossed some mental line.

A whirring noise came from the kitchen, and to the astonishment of all three of the skeptical waiting occupants of the front room, Tom streaked from his hiding place and dashed toward the kitchen. Leaping to their feet, they followed in time to see Lilly tug the scrap of paper from the cat's paw. Wordlessly she handed it to Clay while Tom greedily devoured the can of cat food Lilly had dumped into his bowl.

"What does it say?" Tommy's voice was high from nervous strain. He attempted to peer over Clay's shoulder. Taylor eyed the paper eagerly as well.

Clay picked at the edges of the paper, smoothing and unraveling it. Several tears and puncture marks made the task difficult. At last he had it open. Flattening the paper on the kitchen table, he frowned then turned the paper to a different angle. "It's Wendy's handwriting," he verified. "But she only wrote three words and drew some pictures. It doesn't make any sense."

"Wendy sketches hearts and flowers and things that pop into her mind while she talks on the phone," Taylor explained. "The pictures don't always mean anything, but the words are usually key words from the conversation."

"You should have seen her school notebooks!" Tommy grinned in remembrance.

"These pictures aren't hearts and flowers." Clay scowled at the paper. "They're kind of gruesome. One looks like an ax and this one looks like a tombstone."

"Good grief! That doesn't sound like Wendy." Taylor moved closer to see the paper better.

"What are the words?" Lilly asked from behind her.

"*Diamonds. Crop. Dead,*" Clay read. "That doesn't make sense," he added.

"What's this?" Tommy peered around Clay's shoulder. He pointed at an odd sketch that appeared to have been hastily drawn by a child or by a shaky hand.

"Looks like a bird to me," Taylor answered. "Do you suppose she meant it to be Rambo?"

"It looks like a plain old barnyard rooster to me," Lilly contributed to the discussion.

"This one down in the corner is obviously a house." Clay pointed to the last wobbly sketch.

"The pictures probably don't mean anything," Taylor mused. "But the words must have come up in one of the calls. I can't imagine Wendy discussing diamonds or crops with Joe Terrence, and he wouldn't have called a vet about an animal that was already dead."

"The word 'dead' could have come up in a conversation with Amanda Benson," Lilly spoke up. "Wendy blames Amanda for every dog or cat that disappears around here."

"Do you think 'diamonds' might refer to the ones in your ring that was stolen?" Taylor asked Clay.

"I'm not sure she even knew about the ring," he answered. "I never told her, so unless you did . . . ?"

"No, I never mentioned it to anyone except Grandma. I thought her homeowner's insurance might compensate you."

"That isn't necessary. It's covered in a policy my mother has on all of her jewelry," he told them.

"I don't think there's anything unusual about Wendy talking about diamonds," Tommy spoke up. "She thinks about getting married a lot and makes no bones about wanting a big diamond. If someone told her they had an animal that was nearly dead and they wanted Clay to come right away, she might have written it down, but she never talks about crops. Plants and farming don't interest her at all."

"People living in a farming and ranching community today think of crops as grain and hay, but crop does have other meanings," Lilly frowned as she stared at the word.

"You mean like 'to cut'?" Taylor asked. "Maybe that's why she drew the ax."

"There's another definition, too." Clay stared grimly at the rooster Wendy had drawn beside the ax. Tommy picked up on his meaning immediately.

"Roosters have crops! When I was a little kid, my sister Gwen broke her favorite necklace while she was gathering eggs, and even though we all looked we couldn't find all of the beads. Weeks later when Mom was getting a rooster ready to fry, she found the missing beads in the rooster's crop. Do you think . . . ?" Tommy's voice rose in excitement.

"No, that isn't possible," Clay interrupted.

"What are you talking about?" Taylor turned to Clay, feeling as though she'd missed something.

"Many birds have pouched enlargements in their throats or gullets where food is stored to be masticated later. Small stones or gravel in this pouch help the process. Roosters and chickens have been known to spot shiny stones lost from rings and swallow them. Once swallowed, the stones have lodged in the birds' crops for quite a long time," Clay explained.

"If some lady noticed the diamond was gone from her engagement ring and she thought a rooster ate it, she might have called here to see if you could get it back for her without killing the rooster," Tommy theorized.

Clay smiled. "I suppose it's possible, but Wendy didn't make an appointment for me with anyone who might have a rooster."

"Wendy took Rambo to the beauty parlor with her the other day. What if someone who was there that day is missing a stone from her ring and called here to accuse Rambo of eating it?" Lilly asked.

"Birds in the parrot family don't swallow stones. They have powerful beaks that can crush seeds and insects that a rooster couldn't begin to handle with its smaller beak. If a cockatoo saw a diamond, it might try to crush it, but it wouldn't swallow it," Clay explained. "Of course, it couldn't actually crush it either."

"Neither Grandma's hypothetical lady nor Wendy would know that." Taylor felt her excitement growing. "If Wendy thought someone was threatening to kill Rambo to retrieve a lost diamond, she'd hide her somewhere. She's pretty attached to that bird!"

"You could be right," Clay conceded. "But where would she go? Where would she hide Rambo?"

"Maybe . . ." Tommy paused. "I'm not sure, but that last picture doesn't look like a house—I mean an ordinary house. It looks more like a cabin to me. The more I look at it, the more it looks like my family's Soldier Mountain cabin."

CHAPTER 16

The truck lurched toward the side of the road and Clay wrestled with the steering wheel to bring it back to the narrow ruts. A quick gasp from both of his passengers told him they were acutely aware of how close they'd come to the steep drop-off mere feet away.

"Dad probably isn't aware of how much damage that storm a couple of days ago did to the road," Tommy said apologetically as a tire hit another deep pothole.

"It's not all the road," Clay said. "It's the darkness. I don't think this road was meant to be driven at night. Chuckholes and ruts can't be seen soon enough to dodge." Thick brush and trees bordered the road, which twisted and turned sharply up a narrow canyon. The main canyon road had been bad enough, but this seldom-used trail leading to the half dozen cabins situated in the side canyon was intensely dark and lonely. On the other road, they'd passed a few vehicles, belonging to fishermen or campers, but they had this road all to themselves. A half-glimpsed flash of distant light in Clay's rearview mirror gave him pause. There couldn't be another person dumb enough to travel this road at night. He dismissed the vague uneasiness the glimpse of light had given him.

They probably should have waited until morning to check out the Beredsford cabin. Wendy might not even be there, and here they were risking their lives on this treacherous road without anything more to go on than a scribble on a piece of paper that might or might not represent Tommy's family cabin. Besides, leaving Lilly alone might not be the wisest thing to have done. Clay was glad he'd at least taken the time to call Stewart and his grandson to come stay until he and Taylor got back.

At last they rounded a curve, and Tommy drew his attention to a large fir tree a short distance ahead. "Turn to the left, just past that tree."

Clay swung the wheel to the left and the truck crept up an incline. From the top he could pick out the outline of a cabin nestled in the trees, well-hidden from the road.

"She's here!" Taylor pointed ahead, excitement and relief in her voice. "There's her car!"

Clay scanned the small clearing in front of the cabin and breathed his own sigh of relief when he, too, spotted the small four-wheel drive Tracker he recognized as Wendy's car. He pulled up beside it, set the brake, and turned off the engine. The engine noise seemed to resonate in his ears as the canyon walls echoed the sound back to the clearing. Taylor and Tommy were out the passenger door before he could exit his own side. Together they scrambled up the cabin steps.

"Wendy!" Tommy called, pausing at the door which stood open. There was no answer. "Wendy!" he shouted again before plunging into the darkness. Clay followed with the heavy-duty flashlight he'd pulled from behind the seat of his truck. A prickling at the back of his neck prompted him to turn and search the blackness behind them. With his flashlight he swept the clearing, but all was still.

Taylor turned toward Clay, and his flashlight caught an anxious expression on her face, causing him to wonder if she felt the same uneasy sensation of being watched that he did or if it was simply a trick of light and shadows. He didn't know what to say—perhaps he was afraid to say anything. A single light in the center of the room blinked on, and he realized Tommy had flipped the switch on a battery-operated lamp. Clay took in the main area of the cabin in one quick glance. It was empty, except for the usual furniture and Rambo's cage.

"She's here somewhere. I'll check the loft." Tommy started up a ladder along the far wall, his voice trailing behind him.

"Be careful," Taylor called back to him as she followed Clay into the room. She stood looking around while Clay opened a door leading to a small bedroom with barely enough room for a double bed and a dresser.

"She's not in here," Clay announced the obvious.

"She's not in the sleeping loft either," Tommy informed them as he rejoined them.

"Is there a bathroom?" Taylor asked. She looked about the larger combination living and cooking area in a way that revealed she was far from comfortable with finding the cabin empty. The memory of the flash of light he thought he'd glimpsed in the mirror increased his own uneasiness.

"Uh, it's outside," Tommy informed her. "You think she's out there?"

"We'll have to check," Clay said. "But I don't have a good feeling about this."

"She has to be here somewhere," Taylor pointed out. "Rambo's cage is over there by the fireplace, and her car is outside."

"I assume that's her purse, there on the dresser." Clay pointed to the bag.

"Yes, it's Wendy's," Taylor identified it.

"All right, let's walk all the way around the cabin and check the outhouse," Clay suggested.

"Okay," Tommy said. "But I don't see why Wendy would take your bird out there."

Clay silently agreed. It didn't make sense to take the cockatoo along to answer nature's call after dark. It would make a lot more sense to leave Rambo in her cage and take a flashlight.

Fifteen minutes later they reassembled in the cabin. Tommy looked pale and Taylor didn't even try to hide her concern.

Clay took charge. "All right, let's think this through. Wendy and Rambo are not in this cabin or anywhere close, but they've been here. Since Wendy's car and purse, as well as the birdcage, are still here, she must intend to return. There's no place within walking distance she could have gone for something to eat. She might have gone for a walk and gotten lost. Are there any hiking trails around here?" He turned to Tommy.

"Quite a few," Tommy answered. "They're not the formal kind of trails like you find in parks or around forest area picnic grounds. They're just animal trails and paths the people who own these cabins have made over the years."

"Is there one she would be more likely to follow than any of the others? Does she have a favorite?" Clay pursued the question.

"She doesn't hike much, and she hasn't accepted my invitations to come here since we were little kids, but sometimes the ward youth groups come up here for wiener roasts, and she's come with them.

There's a fire pit and some logs we use for benches a short distance up one trail. She might remember it." He sounded doubtful, obviously unconvinced Wendy would have ventured far from the cabin.

"We have to consider she might be hurt," Taylor brought up the unpleasant possibility. "Wendy isn't the sort of girl who would stay out in the woods after dark."

"You're right," Tommy agreed. "Wendy isn't the outdoors type. She's either hurt or lost, or she'd be right here with every light on. I just can't believe she came here alone!"

"Could there be someone else with her?" Clay asked.

"I don't think so," Tommy responded as though he'd been wondering the same thing. "Her friends have all gone away to school or for summer jobs. She likes the Beal twins, but they're gone, too. They left on missions early last month."

"We'd better check out the area around the fire pit." Clay sighed as he directed another question to Tommy. "Do you happen to have another flashlight or two around here? This is the only one I've got." He indicated the long black utility light he held in one hand. "It would be better if we each had one."

"Sure." Tommy hurried to one of the kitchen cabinets for the flashlights. He handed one to Taylor before turning off the lantern, plunging them into the dark. In the sudden blackness, a squeak came from the front porch, sounding to Clay's ears like a footstep.

Tommy's light clicked on. "I'd better remember to close the door or squirrels and raccoons will wreck the cabin while we're gone." He moved toward the entrance. Taylor's flashlight came on and she followed. Feeling foolish, Clay turned his big mag light on, too, before stepping onto the porch. His imagination didn't usually play tricks on him, but he sure hoped his companions didn't figure out he'd been convinced seconds ago that a two-legged predator rather than some forest creature was spying on them from the porch.

With their flashlights aimed toward the ground, Clay and Taylor followed Tommy from the porch, past Clay's truck, and a short distance down the road.

"We're just about to where the trail starts," Tommy turned to inform them. "It's that wide spot we passed on our way to the cabin just before this little hill."

They topped the hill and Tommy continued to lead the way to where a path left the road. Taylor fell in behind him and Clay brought up the rear. Before ducking onto the brush-lined trail, Clay flashed his light back the way they'd come, then down the road. The light didn't penetrate as far as he would have liked into the deep blackness, where heavy tree limbs almost met across the road, and dense shadow provided his imagination with impossible-to-fathom hiding places. Shaking off the sensation he was being watched from a hidden vantage point within the shadows, he hurried to catch up to Taylor.

"Are there any bears or mountain lions around here?" Taylor whispered after a few minutes on the trail, and while Clay debated reassuring her or admitting he was nervous, too, Tommy chuckled. "It's always possible, though we've never seen any in this canyon. You're not scared, are you?"

"I'm not scared exactly," Taylor whispered back. "But I think we're being followed."

"If a cat were following us, we wouldn't hear it," Tommy scoffed. "And bears are so fat and well fed this time of year, they're no threat unless we practically trip over one, come between a mama and her cubs, or carry food around with us."

"I heard something," Taylor persisted.

"The canyon magnifies sound, especially at night." Tommy dismissed her concern.

Clay wished he were as confident as Tommy that there was nothing to worry about. He too had heard sounds like a large animal attempting to move stealthily through the brush, but unlike Taylor, he'd immediately suspected human pursuit. He moved closer to Taylor in a protective gesture she clearly didn't appreciate. It wasn't too dark to see the scowl she directed his way before she hurried forward to walk beside Tommy.

They walked for several more minutes, and twice Clay heard sounds off to their right that didn't sound like normal forest sounds to him. He didn't say anything, but when he lengthened his steps to move closer to Taylor and Tommy, Taylor didn't shy away, and several times he noticed her taking surreptitious peeks into the darkness beside the trail.

Suddenly Tommy's light went off. Taylor's followed suit. Not understanding why, Clay pressed the button on his light, plunging the three of them into darkness.

"What's wrong?" he whispered as soon as his eyes adjusted enough to allow him to make out Taylor's and Tommy's shapes in the dark.

"I just got thinking," Tommy whispered. "If Wendy sees our flashlights she won't know it's us, and she might hide. I think that's why she left the cabin; she saw the truck's headlights."

"Of course," Taylor latched onto the simple explanation. "If she thought Rambo was in danger, she'd try to hide her!"

"We could just call her name. I'm sure she'd recognize any of our voices," Clay suggested.

"I don't know . . ." Tommy's voice trailed off and Clay recognized a reluctance Tommy obviously didn't want to admit to.

"Why don't you two macho guys just admit there's something or *someone* out here that might mean Rambo, or possibly Wendy, some kind of harm?" Taylor snapped.

Clay moved closer to the other two and lowered his voice even more. "There's definitely something moving parallel to us, but like Tommy, I doubt it's an animal of some kind. If someone is following us, we have no way of knowing if it's some friend of Wendy's playing a prank or if it's the burglars who ransacked Lilly's house, and I think we should be as cautious as possible."

"Yeah, I didn't want to scare you guys, but I've got a creepy feeling we're not the only ones looking for Wendy." Tommy's voice was a barely audible whisper.

"What are we going to do?" Taylor asked. "I don't want to lead whoever Wendy is hiding from right to her."

"I've got an idea." Tommy placed a hand on each of their shoulders, drawing their ears close to his mouth. "About ten yards from here the path passes close to a massive boulder. At that point, thick brush grows close to the path. Several years ago, my brothers and I found a hidden route through the brush to a shortcut that leads to the fire pit. When we get to that spot, I'll go that way and you two keep following this trail. If someone is following us, they won't know I've gone ahead and I can keep Wendy out of sight."

"How will we meet up again?" Clay asked.

"If Wendy is there, we'll take another trail I know back to your truck. If she isn't, I'll wait for you at the fire pit," Tommy whispered as he began to move ahead. "I'll leave a handful of pebbles and pine twigs on the rim of the fire pit to let you know I've been there and gone on."

"Just a minute," Taylor placed her hand on Tommy's sleeve. "I think we'll all feel better if we take time to ask God to lead us to Wendy and to protect us."

"Taylor's right," Clay whispered. "But I think He'll understand if we make it short."

"All right, go ahead," Tommy paused. "Clay will you . . ."

When Clay finished the quietly whispered prayer, he and Taylor fell in behind Tommy on the trail. Movement was necessarily slower without flashlights, but as his eyes adjusted, Clay felt more secure. Still when the shadow that was Tommy disappeared, it was difficult not to call him back.

By unspoken consent, neither he nor Taylor spoke as they continued to follow the trail, though Clay noticed Taylor slowing her steps to walk beside him. Without consciously planning the gesture, he shifted his flashlight to his left hand and reached out with his right to Taylor. Her fingers threaded through his and they walked on together.

Taylor didn't want to admit she was scared. It had been many years since she'd camped overnight and there was something about walking through this forested terrain in the dark that left her uneasy. Knowing that both Clay and Tommy shared her suspicion they were being followed didn't comfort her any. She was glad for the reassuring feel of Clay's hand, but she couldn't shake the feeling something was wrong.

The trail widened at last and they found themselves facing a clearing just as a sliver of moonlight shone between the clouds. Logs formed a semicircle around a rock-lined hole in the ground, and it was easy to visualize a dozen or more teenagers and their leaders gathered around a fire, roasting hot dogs and dropping burnt marshmallows into the flames. In a setting much like this, Taylor had first discovered the courage to stand and bear her testimony to a group of girls much like herself at the end of her stake's Young Women rough camp almost ten years ago. A moment's nostalgia for that long-ago camping trip and the spiritual closeness she'd felt to her Heavenly Father held her motionless until Clay's whisper broke the spell.

"They're not here."

Abruptly returning to the moment, Taylor searched the dark

shadows for Wendy and Tommy. She couldn't help being conscious of how easily the shadows could hide someone.

"You wait here," Clay continued to whisper. "I've got to check the fire pit."

"I'm not staying here alone," Taylor whispered back.

"If someone's watching . . ."

"I don't care. I'm not staying here alone." She took a step into the clearing. His hand gave hers a quick squeeze and he stepped out beside her.

Without speaking they moved to the center of the clearing. Taylor unconsciously stiffened her spine as they moved away from the deep shadows the tall trees provided, feeling as though eyes bore into her back. A rustling of branches and the crack of a twig snapping as though a careless shoe had landed on it, left her wanting to scurry back into the shadows. Clay didn't alter his slow, steady steps. She wouldn't show her fear either! Matching her steps to his, she kept walking.

It seemed to take forever, but at last Clay stopped beside the circle of rocks.

"Don't look down," Clay hissed in her ear. "Keep your eyes on the trees while I check."

Resisting the urge to look for Tommy's signal, she struggled to appear casual as she looked around. It might be her imagination but the shadows appeared especially thick not far from where she and Clay had emerged from the trees. Was someone watching them from the thick shadows?

"They've been here!" Even using a barely audible whisper, Clay couldn't hide his excitement. "Let's get back to the cabin."

Taylor didn't have to be told twice; she couldn't leave the clearing fast enough. Only Clay's grip on her hand kept her from dashing as fast as the darkness would permit back into the relative security of the trees. She wanted to shout her relief that Wendy had been found. At the same time she wanted to shake the girl for giving them such a scare.

Halfway across the clearing, she blinked her eyes. Had a shadow moved? Surely not! Something about the dark night, the remote canyon, and the recent events was sending her imagination into over-drive. But what if she hadn't imagined the movement? Clay's quick-ened pace made her suspect he felt some ominous presence, too.

In seconds they were on the trail, but Clay didn't slow his steps, leaving her struggling to keep pace. Her pulse pounded in her ears and she felt her breath coming in gasps. They came to the narrow spot beside a big boulder where Tommy had left them. Instead of pausing to catch their breaths, Clay urged her to move faster and she did her best to comply. The pounding in her ears sounded eerily like someone was following in hot pursuit, and it fueled her determination to keep moving.

She rounded a curve in the trail, and her toe struck a protruding root, catapulting her forward. But for Clay's quick reaction, she would have fallen. His arms came around her, dragging her upright, and steadying her against his chest as she regained her balance. Together they breathed deep, ragged breaths, and beneath her ear she heard the rapid thump of his heart. It took only seconds to realize she was hearing more than the beat of Clay's heart. Footsteps were pounding down the trail behind them!

She straightened just as Clay jerked her toward the trees. Scraping through the thick brush, he pulled her behind the wide trunk of a sagging conifer. Sticky sap stuck to her arms as she hugged the tree trunk and the rough bark attacked her skin and hair. Ignoring her discomfort, she huddled beside Clay, only peeking out enough to watch the trail. In minutes their vigilance was rewarded as two black shapes bounded into sight, passed their hiding spot, and continued down the trail. The bulky figures definitely were not Tommy and Wendy!

Taylor rocked back on her heels. Even with all the ominous sounds and the sensation of being watched, she hadn't really believed someone was following them. Seeing the two hurrying figures made their predicament too real.

"Come on," Clay urged her to her feet. "Let's see if we can find a shortcut through the trees. We've got to reach the cabin and warn Tommy and Wendy before those two get there."

He was right! They had to warn the others, but if they left the trail how would they find their way back? She didn't have any idea which way to go.

As though reading her thoughts, Clay took her hand. "We can't stay on the trail. As soon as they realize they've passed us in the dark, they'll stop and wait to ambush us. If we cut a straight diagonal toward the cabin, we might beat them there." Wiping her sweating palms on her jeans before taking the hand he offered, she hoped he had a better sense of direction than she did in the dark.

In a few minutes it occurred to her that they were skirting a small hill, and she hoped it was that last rise before the clearing where the cabin sat. Once past the hill a meadow separated them from the line of trees that hid the road from their view. They seemed to be following a trail of some sort, though it wasn't as delineated as the wide trail they'd recently left, but at least, they could move faster along it with only deep grass and a few low shrubs on either side to slow their movement.

"The road should be just ahead of us." Twenty yards or so from where the thicker growth began, Clay paused to breathe the warning in her ear. She searched the darkness for the lighter ribbon that would indicate the road. Instead she detected a familiar dark shape.

"Clay, I think that's . . ." She lifted her arm to point, heedless of the fact that he would only vaguely be able to determine the direction she was pointing.

Clapping a hand over her mouth, he tugged her to a crouching position behind a clump of brush. Seconds later and a short distance ahead, a light came on, revealing the interior of a car and two figures scrambling to get inside it. The light was quickly extinguished, indicating the closing of the doors though no sound reached where they hid and there was no sound of a car engine starting.

"They're waiting for us," Clay whispered. "They expect us to walk up that road." She understood now why the car doors hadn't slammed shut and why there was no sound from the car's engine.

"We've got to reach the cabin and warn the others," she whispered back.

"Right," Clay concurred. "Since they're watching the road, hopefully, they won't look this way." His words reminded her of their open position in the small meadow and made her glad the sky was overcast. Even so they would have to move further back to the protection of the trees until they were well past the car where the two men waited to make certain they weren't seen.

"Do you think they know Tommy isn't with us?" She hesitated before leaving the scanty protection of the shrub they'd hid behind.

"They likely think he stayed in the trees while we checked the fire pit clearing. If they knew we had split up, I'm sure they'd be hurrying to get to our cars instead of waiting for us here," he pointed out before crouching low to make his way to the next concealing bush. Taking a deep breath, she followed him.

Moving with infinite care, they crawled through the grass and hid behind clumps of brush when they could. Her ears strained to hear the sound of pursuit, and she felt only relief when clouds blacked out the sliver of moon. A cold breeze rippled through the grass, and when an icy raindrop struck the back of her neck, she jumped, thinking she'd been shot. A scream begged for release as for one crazy second she thought the trickle of moisture on her neck was blood. There was no pain and blood was warm, wasn't it? Realizing her folly, she determined to control her fear better. She was glad the dark and the rain hid her overreaction from Clay.

When they reached the trees and Clay helped her to her feet, she looked around nervously, trying to get her bearings. Straight ahead she could barely make out through the falling rain the shape of the cabin and the two vehicles parked in front of it. There was no sign of Tommy and Wendy, but they were probably staying out of sight, waiting for her and Clay to arrive.

Staying in the trees, both to stay out of sight and to shelter from the rain, they worked their way around the clearing to approach the cabin from the rear. A soft whimper of sound halted their footsteps. Listening intently, they heard a faint murmur above the drip of water making its way through the overhead tree branches.

Motioning for Taylor to stay behind a tree, Clay worked his way closer to the sound. In seconds he was back. "It's Tommy and Wendy," he whispered. Elated, she followed him through the damp underbrush until she spotted the teenagers sitting together on a large rock, partially hidden by the trees surrounding the cabin. Wendy seemed to be crying while Tommy attempted to comfort her.

Soon they were all hugging each other and whispering questions. Fearful their greeting might be overheard, Clay asked for silence. "We need to talk, but not here," he whispered. Tommy jumped to his feet and supporting Wendy led them deeper into the trees. When Clay stopped, he explained about the car and its occupants waiting further down the road. "We need to leave here as quickly as possible." He doubted they needed his grim warning.

"We can't take your truck or Wendy's car." Tommy kept his voice low. "The tires have been slashed on both vehicles." Wendy began to cry again, and Taylor placed her arms around her.

"What about the other cabins? Could we hike to one of them?" Clay asked.

"Sure. But those guys will get tired of waiting pretty soon. They'll come here, then the next step will be the other cabins." Tommy's argument made sense.

Wendy gasped, then asked, "What if they have guns?"

"We've got to find shelter and figure out a way to notify the police," Taylor said as she held Wendy closer. She wasn't sure the girl was shivering from fear or cold. Between the high altitude and the rain, they were all wet and cold.

"There's a cave near the top of the canyon. The climb is kind of steep, but I think we can make it." Clay heard a sharply indrawn breath come from Taylor at Tommy's suggestion, but she didn't voice any fear.

"Are there snakes in it?" Wendy asked suspiciously and Clay wondered if the same concern had caused Taylor's reaction to Tommy's plan.

"No snakes," Tommy promised, but the tone of his voice told Clay the boy wasn't certain there wouldn't be any other wildlife making themselves at home in the cave, and he remembered the mountain lion marks on the young horse he'd recently treated at the Morrow ranch.

"How far are we from the Morrow ranch?" he asked.

"About four miles if we go up the side of the canyon," Tommy reported. "The Morrow ranch is our closest neighbor. I thought we could go as far as the cave, and if we're not too tired and the rain doesn't become worse, we might go on to the ranch."

"I think we'd better start." Clay looked around as he spoke. "The rain might keep our pursuers in their car for a little while and give us a head start. You lead the way, Tommy."

Tommy picked up a backpack lying on the ground, slipped the straps over his shoulders, and reached for Wendy's hand. Clay ushered Taylor ahead of him, and he brought up the rear.

CHAPTER 17

The trail Tommy followed was fairly easy until they came to where the canyon began to slope sharply upward, then Taylor wasn't certain they were even following a trail as they zigzagged up the steep incline. Several times Tommy stopped beneath a rocky overhang to allow the others to catch their breaths. Each time they began to move again, Clay stayed behind to watch and listen for pursuit, then he would hurry to catch up with them again.

Taylor's hands were cold and slippery with mud, making it difficult for her to grasp rocks and brush as she struggled to keep from sliding back down the way they'd come. The thick mud clung to her shoes, making movement awkward. Several times Wendy slid backward into her, nearly sending them both crashing to the bottom of the canyon. Sometimes only Clay's steadying hand prevented disaster from occurring.

At long last Tommy led the way beneath a canopy of thick fir trees. There he paused. "I think we're safe for now. The cave is just on the other side of these trees. Anyone climbing the way we came won't be able to see it."

"Good." Clay leaned forward, resting his hands on his knees while he took deep breaths.

"Uh, I'd like to check it out first—make sure nothing has moved in since I last came up here." He looked hesitantly toward the two women.

"I'll come with you," Clay offered, and Taylor noticed he pulled his heavy mag light from his belt where he'd tucked it earlier to leave his hands free. She wasn't sure she wanted to know what Tommy feared he might find in the cave. Forcing herself inside a cave would be hard enough.

"Wait here," Tommy told Wendy as he slipped the backpack from his shoulders and handed it to her. Wendy didn't argue with her friend, so Taylor decided she might as well stay with the younger girl rather than point out to the men that they were being a tad chauvinistic.

Along with the cold that left her shaking came an intense sense of loneliness as the faint sounds of the men's careful movements turned to silence. Turning her head, she listened for any sound coming from the canyon. All was still except for the soft patter of rain. Finally she turned to see Wendy looking bedraggled, with her wet hair clinging to her face; she was hugging the pack Tommy had handed her. She didn't remember him carrying the pack earlier when they left the cabin to search for Wendy. Had the girl had it with her?

"What's in the backpack?" she asked softly.

"Rambo." Wendy uttered the single word, then looked around fearfully as though she expected danger to suddenly leap from the trees.

"Rambo!" Taylor had forgotten all about the bothersome bird. "Why did you bring that bird up here?" she exclaimed.

"Those men said they were going to cut her up to get the diamonds," Wendy's teeth audibly chattered as she tried to explain. "I couldn't let them kill her."

"No, of course not," Taylor put her arms around the shaking girl. "But she's a tropical bird. Isn't it too cold for her here?"

"Yes, but I didn't know where else to go, and I don't have any money. I didn't know it was going to be so cold; it's still supposed to be summer. I found a baby blanket at the cabin, and I wrapped her in that so I could start a fire, but I couldn't get it started, and then I saw headlights coming. One of Tommy's little brothers left a backpack on the floor beside the sofa, so I put Rambo in it and ran," Wendy tried to explain.

Taylor had more questions, but they would have to wait. She hoped the bird hadn't succumbed to the cold or suffocated in the blanket Wendy had used to keep her warm. For now she was just glad the bird wasn't squawking. Her major concern at the moment was getting warm and dry.

Her eyes had adjusted to the dark, and she could see that Wendy was trembling with cold. She and the two men were dressed in jeans and wore cotton knit shirts, but Wendy's thin capri pants and waist-skimming, sleeveless top didn't offer much protection from cold or scrapes. She'd wished for a pair of hiking boots as she struggled up the mountain such as the two men wore, but she suspected Wendy's sandals had been much worse than her own canvas deck shoes.

A faint rustle caught her ear, and she looked up in the direction where the men had disappeared. In a moment Clay materialized out of the darkness to stand beside her. Wordlessly, he took her hand and she moved closer to him.

"The cave is a good hiding place," he assured her as he led her toward it. Taylor shuddered at the mere mention of the word "cave." Caves were small and dark, and didn't they house bats and bears, maybe even spiders?

But it wasn't a true cave, Taylor realized as she let Clay lead her into a narrow fissure in the steep side of the canyon. It was more like the two halves of a huge rock that had split down the middle. The crack was wider at the base than at the top, allowing rain to penetrate the center of the cavelike opening, but still providing enough overhang on either side for two people to huddle out of the rain. She couldn't see how far the crack extended, but Tommy answered her unasked question.

"This crack runs about forty yards," he volunteered. "It twists some, and sometimes it's wider; some places, it's pretty narrow. From the other side you can see the Morrow place. The climb is steeper on that side than on the side we came up, so if it's all right with all of you, I think maybe we ought to stay here until morning."

Taylor's heart fell. She doubted she'd survive the night if she had to sit around in wet clothes as the temperature continued to fall. One look at Wendy told her the girl was in worse shape than she was. They couldn't stay here all night! Besides she knew Grandma Lilly must be terribly worried by now over their long absence.

"We're all pretty cold. It might be safer to keep moving," Clay cautioned. He'd seen the disappointment on Taylor's face, and it was quite obvious to him that Wendy was shaking with cold and her movements were becoming lethargic.

"If we had a fire . . . ," Taylor began.

"There's plenty of firewood in here, and there's even a spot wide enough to build a fire a little further along, but I don't know if there are any matches," Tommy explained. "My brother and I hid some up here a long time ago, but I don't know if I can find them."

"We don't need matches," Wendy spoke up. "I was trying to start a fire when I saw your headlights coming up the canyon. The fireplace starter is in the pack with Rambo. I was going to build a fire at the wiener roast place."

Clay stared at Wendy, wondering how the girl's head worked. If she was scared enough to run from the cabin, how had she even considered building a fire that might be seen through the trees?

"Good girl," Tommy practically crooned, and Clay wondered if he didn't see the incongruity of Wendy's words or if he was so in love with the girl, he didn't care if she didn't always make sense.

They were soon deep enough inside the fissure that Clay deemed it safe to turn on his flashlight, and in minutes Tommy had a small fire burning at a spot where the overhang provided eight or ten feet of protected space. Huddling as close as they dared to the flames, they wished for a few hot dogs to roast and complained that as soon as one side of their frozen bodies began to warm the other side turned to ice.

Finally Clay felt warm enough to ask Wendy what had prompted her to flee to the Beredsford cabin. For an ordinarily talkative girl she was slow to answer his question, but then Tommy placed an arm around her shoulder, and she began to speak.

"The phone kept ringing," she began. "I wrote down some appointments, and I was just getting ready to turn on the computer when he called."

"Who called?" Clay asked, soft encouragement in his voice. He hoped to get her talking and to interrupt as little as possible.

"He didn't say his name, but he was the same man who called that other time." Wendy looked down at her dirty, chipped nails.

"Do you mean the man who was rude to you and accused Clay of stealing Rambo?" Taylor, too, tried for clarification.

"Yeah, that one." Wendy nodded her head. "He was really mad and he said he was going to cut up Rambo to get his diamonds back."

"Did he say anything more about the diamonds?" Clay asked.

"No." She chewed on a broken fingernail for a moment and muttered something about wishing she had a nail file. Suddenly she looked up, a smile on her face. "His name must be Winslow! He said Rambo stole the Winslow diamonds."

"Winslow diamonds? You're sure he said Winslow?" Clay sat back in stunned disbelief.

"Doesn't Rambo belong to Jessica Winslow?" Taylor asked, turning to him.

"That's right, Jessica Winslow was Clay's snooty New York girl-friend." Wendy blinked as she made the connection, and at once turned to glare at Clay. "Why did you let poor Rambo eat Jessica's diamonds?"

"Hey, wait a minute," Clay tried to defend himself. "I didn't let Rambo do anything. Cockatoos don't eat rocks, not even stones as pretty as diamonds—which reminds me, where is that blasted bird?"

Wendy patted the pack resting in her lap and continued to scowl at Clay. "Then why does that man want to cut out her crop if she didn't eat the diamonds?"

"I don't know," Clay conceded. "Maybe he doesn't know much about birds in the parrot family, and he just thinks Rambo swallowed the diamonds."

"But you know something about some diamonds called the Winslow diamonds, don't you?" Taylor interjected.

"Yes," he admitted. "I've seen them a few times. They belonged to Jessica's grandfather, and now to her. They're worth an awful lot of money. They're extremely valuable diamonds, smuggled out of Europe by the old man when he was young. He was a diamond cutter in Berlin, and when he came under suspicion during the early days of World War II because a pretty young Jewish woman worked for him, he sewed as many gems into his and the woman's clothing as he could, and they attempted to make their way out of Germany. He had papers, but the Jewish girl did not. When she was stopped at the border, he pretended that one diamond was all he had and he traded it to a guard for her freedom. When they finally reached America they were married, and he used part of the diamonds he brought to New York to set up his business, but he kept the four best stones as a good luck talisman. His two sons followed him into the business, but they and their wives were killed in an airline disaster fifteen years ago, leaving him with four young grandchildren to raise. He promised the diamonds to his only granddaughter, Jessica, on her wedding day. Since the old man died, I expect the stones are hers now."

"Sounds to me like someone stole them," Tommy announced the conclusion he'd drawn.

"As soon as we get out of here, I'll call Jessica and ask her if the diamonds are missing," Clay promised on a stifled yawn.

"I don't understand why, even if the Winslow diamonds are missing, anyone would connect them to Rambo or know where to find her," Taylor puzzled aloud.

"Rambo didn't steal them," Wendy's voice wobbled, and her eyes glistened with unshed tears.

"No, Rambo didn't steal the diamonds," Clay agreed. "But someone broke into Jessica's apartment just before all this trouble started. He may have known Jessica and her cousin Jacob had argued over the diamonds and that she refused to leave them in Winslow Enterprises' vault. The thief could have assumed she had them in her apartment. The thief didn't find the stones but instead found an address and date book with my address and a notation to ship Rambo to me. He likely made some assumptions about the whereabouts of the diamonds."

Silence followed the explanation of his theory, and although no one said anything, he knew they accepted his logic. As his gaze landed on Wendy, he noticed the way she clutched the bag, holding Rambo in obvious fear.

"Here, let me check Rambo," he said gently as he reached for the backpack. For a moment he thought she wouldn't let him have the bag. Her grip revealed her concern for the bird, but because he hadn't seen her peek inside even once, he guessed she was afraid the bird was already dead. As much as the bird annoyed him, he hoped it had survived the recent traumatic events. There was only one way to find out.

Opening the pack, he ran his fingers down the feathers covering the bird's softly fluttering throat, then stifled a laugh. "That darn bird's cozier than we are. That's some nest you built." He smiled at Wendy and she smiled back in obvious relief. The heavy canvas had kept Rambo dry, and the baby blanket had provided an insulated nest, protecting Rambo from both bumps and cold. Gently Clay folded the flap back over the pack and drew the zipper almost closed.

"I think you should all try to sleep now. I'll wake you if it looks like we might have company," he offered.

"We can take turns watching," Tommy made clear his intention to share guard duty with Clay. "I got up late this morning, so I can take first watch. I'll call you in two hours."

"I slept late, too," Wendy spoke up. "I'll watch with Tommy."

Before Clay could object, Taylor turned to Tommy. "Wake me in two hours also. If we watch in pairs, we can help each other stay awake."

She held her breath waiting for a macho protest from Clay. Instead he said, "Before Taylor and I fall asleep, I think we should take time to thank Heavenly Father that we've made it this far and ask for His continued help and protection."

"Good idea," Tommy seconded the proposal, and the four of them knelt around their small fire while Clay expressed the feelings they all shared. Warmth filled Taylor's being that reached far beyond that of the small blaze around which they knelt.

Taylor found sleeping on the hard ground difficult, and even though she fell asleep repeatedly it was only to wake up again. The narrow slit of sky overhead helped, but she couldn't entirely shake the sensation that the cave walls were about to collapse inward, burying them alive. She was actually glad when it was time to join Clay for a couple of hours of guard duty.

Sitting side by side next to the fire, they didn't speak at first. Taylor noticed Wendy wasn't shy about leaning against Tommy's shoulder, and he didn't seem to mind serving as her pillow while he only had the rock wall behind him to lean against. Both seemed to fall asleep immediately.

"I think it's finally stopped raining," Clay broke the silence. Looking up at the narrow slice of sky above them, she decided he was right. She could see several specks of light that looked like stars.

"Do you think the men we saw will come after us now?" she wondered aloud.

"They might," Clay said. "But I've been thinking. Lilly knows where we were going, and she'll be worried that we didn't return when we should have. I suspect our deputy friend has been called to check the cabin by now."

"Do you think Rick will catch those men?" she asked hopefully and Clay frowned, not liking her casual use of the deputy's first name.

"I don't know," he answered, more calmly than he felt. "Their car is pretty well hidden, but I'm sure that as soon as they see a sheriff's car go by, they'll head the other way."

"Are the Winslow diamonds so valuable that someone would pursue Rambo this far to steal them?" Taylor wondered aloud as she stared past the fire, trying to avoid looking directly at the flames.

"They're worth a lot," Clay agreed. "I don't know exactly how much, but each stone is approximately four karats. They're probably worth enough that, if sold, a person could live on the proceeds quite comfortably for a good long time. It's not only their size that makes them unique but their color and flawless perfection. One is a rare yellow diamond, one a rose, and the other two are brilliantly clear. Jessica wanted one of the clear stones set in an engagement ring, but her grandfather wouldn't consent."

"Why not?" Taylor puzzled. "If he planned to give them to her for a wedding present anyway, why didn't he want her to use one for a ring?"

"I don't know, perhaps it was a holdover from his flight from Nazi Germany. He considered the jewels a kind of insurance policy; they're lightweight, easy to conceal, and negotiable in any monetary system. If he ever had to run for his life again, the diamonds meant security, and he wasn't in a hurry to part with them," Clay theorized.

From talk of the diamonds, their muted conversation drifted to other topics until Taylor noticed the sliver of sky above them had turned to gray. A peek at her watch told her it was almost morning. With the lightening of the sky, she found she could breathe a little easier and surprised herself by admitting her battle with claustrophobia to Clay. His sympathy went a long way toward making her feel less of a coward.

"We'd better wake Wendy and Tommy," Clay stood and extended his hand to help Taylor to her feet. "It's light now and we should be on our way."

Tommy grumbled about not being awakened for a second round of guard duty, but agreed they should go on. Wendy stretched and yawned, then as though suddenly remembering Rambo, she opened the backpack. Taking a handful of sunflower seeds from her pocket, she tried to feed Rambo. The bird immediately struggled to escape her confined space and protested vehemently when Wendy pushed her head back down and threw the seeds inside the bag. When she drew the zipper almost closed, Rambo continued to protest for several minutes, scratching and clawing against her canvas cage. Wendy merely straightened, nodding to the others that she was ready, and Tommy led the way through the narrow chasm to the opening that overlooked the Morrow ranch.

The sun was casting its first rays over the mountain when they emerged from their shelter. Taylor noticed but said nothing when Tommy took Wendy's hand to lead her down the steep mountainside. She couldn't help remembering how Clay had held her hand through much of their flight and felt a strange bereavement at its absence now.

On the pretext of tying her shoe, Taylor braced her foot against a rock and glanced back. Clay stood a few feet in front of the hidden exit point with the sun highlighting his form. His dark curls were more pronounced, and thick stubble on his unshaved face lent him a rakish air. A muddy, wrinkled shirt and pants caked with mud didn't detract from his appearance in her eyes. Most women would find him devastatingly handsome, she conceded. Realizing where her thoughts were going, Taylor chastised herself. Clay was unarguably attractive, and his levelheaded good sense had certainly been instrumental in their escape last night, and yes, she'd enjoyed their long, rambling talk through the night, but she mustn't fancy she cared about him. He was bent on being a country vet, and she had dreams and goals that would carry her to the bright lights of San Francisco or New York, perhaps even to Paris or London. Straightening, she followed the others down the mountainside until Tommy found a trail that meandered toward the pristine white board fence of the ranch.

Joe Terrence saw them coming and came to meet them, riding on the back of a showy black gelding. Recognizing Clay, he swung to the ground and shook his hand. Clay introduced Tommy and the two women to him, and after a brief summary of the night's events, Joe insisted the two women ride the horse back to the stable. Wendy accepted the offer with alacrity, but Taylor was noticeably reluctant to ride. Clay wondered briefly if she didn't like horses or if she didn't know how to ride when she insisted on continuing to walk.

Stumbling with fatigue, Taylor struggled to match her steps to those of the men. It had been tempting to ride the horse, but she suspected if she stopped moving on her own power she'd fall asleep. Besides since childhood she'd fantasized about racing across a meadow on the back of a beautiful black horse. She didn't want her first experience riding a horse to be when she was so tired and muddy she couldn't enjoy the experience.

She was only vaguely aware of entering a large timber-and-stone house and of being greeted by a slender woman with fantastic auburn hair. She heard Clay ask to use a phone to call Lilly and the sheriff's office, then the woman was leading her down a hall and suggesting she take a quick shower and lie down. Taylor barely managed to remain standing while she washed off the thick mud, pulled on borrowed sweats, then stumbled toward the bed. Softness touched her head, and her eyes closed.

* * *

Taylor yawned and stretched, then her eyes popped open in alarm as the events of the night came rushing back to her. After only second or two she remembered being ushered into one of the bedrooms in Amy Morrow's house to rest until someone came for them. She moved her arm so she could see her watch, then scrambled off the bed. She'd been asleep for hours! Her bare feet sank into a luxurious carpet, and she looked around for her shoes. She had to find her friends and get back to her grandmother's house.

Her shoes were beside the bed with her freshly laundered clothes. She quickly changed, dashed water on her face, and using a brush she found lying on the vanity, brushed out the worst of the tangles in her hair. The rain had turned her hair into a mass of snarls, and as she brushed it, it took on the bushy characteristics of a perm gone bad. She wished she had an elastic band to hold it back, and for a moment she envied Wendy, whose hair had flattened and hung in strings about her face as the rain pelted them.

Anxious to join the others, Taylor stepped into the hall and made her way through the silent house. Even in her hurry, she was impressed by the beauty of the rooms she passed. Though not ostentatious, each one was beautifully furnished, and the ample windows showcased breathtaking mountain vistas. Eventually she found the kitchen and was surprised by the homey warmth of the room. Sunflowers dotted the valances at the top of the windows, and a matching tablecloth covered a table tucked into a windowed alcove. A basket of rolls on the table reminded her she was starving. She paused briefly to read a note beside the basket, urging her to help herself. Eagerly she reached for a roll and was surprised to find it was slightly warm.

Hearing a sound behind her, she turned to see two small dogs, their toenails scuttling against the tile floor, hurrying toward her. They appeared excited by her presence, and she stooped to give them each a pat. With perky pink bows adorning their fluffy white fur, they looked like a child's toys, but since Ms. Morrow didn't have children, Taylor assumed the tiny poodles were the actress's pets.

She had the vaguest memory of arriving at the house and being offered food and something to drink before being shown to a bedroom. She had only meant to rest, not actually sleep, until the sheriff's department sent someone for them. She couldn't believe she'd fallen asleep and the others had let her sleep away most of the day. Where were they anyway? Surely they hadn't left her!

Stuffing the last bite of her roll in her mouth, she found a door and stepped outside, taking care that the little dogs didn't follow her. She could see the stables and a group of people gathered around a palomino horse with ribbons braided in its mane and tail. As she started toward them, Amy Morrow mounted the golden horse and began a leisurely canter around the corral. Taylor couldn't see Wendy or Tommy, but a sudden spurt of happiness filled her when she spotted Clay. She wasn't sure whether it was the reassurance that she hadn't been left behind or the man himself who brought a smile to her lips.

She didn't want it to be the man, but deep inside she knew she was going to have to examine her feelings for Clay soon. She didn't want to do it now though. Now she only wanted to enjoy this beautiful day and be grateful she was no longer stumbling through the dark with someone chasing her. Clay lifted his head and his eyes met hers, sending a message that left her breathless. The man beside him said something, and it seemed to her that Clay showed a measure of reluctance to turn his attention back to the older man. Feeling self-conscious, she slowed her steps. But unable to direct her gaze elsewhere, she watched Clay coil a rope in his hands as he talked to the shorter, slightly rotund man beside him.

"Good morning," Joe Terrence greeted her first and the group of men all turned to say hello. Joe offered introductions to the men, and she learned that the man she'd noted earlier was Miss Morrow's regular veterinarian, Charles leClerc. Miss Morrow dismounted and held out her hand to her. Taylor took the opportunity to thank the other woman for her kindness in taking them in.

"It was my pleasure," Miss Morrow smiled before continuing in a mock whisper, "It's not often I get to be part of a real-life drama. If your adventure had been a movie, I would be jealous because it seems you got both the greatest role and the most handsome leading man."

Before she could respond, a tall, young man thrust out a hand saying, "Hey, you're worth the trip out here." He grinned as he informed her he was leClerc's pilot and suggested they go sit on the patio in the shade while the others "talked horses."

"We've got to be leaving," Clay interrupted, possessively touching her elbow as though staking his claim. Once Taylor might have laughed at the gesture, but now she felt a moment's elation, quickly followed by a touch of annoyance. Not that she wanted to spend time with the handsome young pilot; she just didn't want Clay assuming a relationship that could never be.

Stepping away from Clay's hand, she schooled her features to hide the sense of loss the gesture brought. *Get used to it,* she scolded herself. *Falling in love with Clay is just plain stupid. If you let yourself do it, you'll never be free.*

But if you don't, you'll never be happy, a second voice inside her head warned.

CHAPTER 18

In spite of all his own warnings, he'd done it again. Clay frowned at the road, wondering how this could have happened. He'd sworn he'd never love another woman who didn't share his values. He'd known from the start that Taylor was only spending the summer in Fairfield because her father had coerced her into staying a few months with her grandmother to break the news to her that he had a cozy senior citizen apartment all picked out for her.

Next month both Lilly and Taylor would pack up and leave. Lilly wouldn't go willingly, but Taylor could hardly wait to start her new life in San Francisco. Now that he knew she had been the one to organize and set up his office, and knew as well of the work she'd done for the senator, and the MBA she'd earned, he suspected she'd do just fine. Probably much better than fine. The left front tire dipped into a spine-rattling rut he should have missed, giving him an excuse to scowl at the rough road.

He'd been wrong to assume Taylor was empty-headed and greedy just because she was beautiful. All his life he'd resented the assumptions people made about him because of his appearance, but that hadn't stopped him from making the same assumptions about Taylor. She wasn't lazy and she didn't place worldly possessions at the top of her priority list. She hadn't expected her grandmother to wait on her or entertain her lavishly as he had at first expected. She was someone he'd come to admire for a great deal more than the lovely exterior he'd resented being attracted to. Though she wasn't the calculating, socially ambitious woman he'd expected her to be, he thought sadly, she was still like Jessica in one way. She wanted to live her life in a faster lane than the one he'd chosen.

Jessica had faked an interest in the Church, but Taylor's testimony was real. He'd sensed her sincerity when Peggy Friedrickson had her accident, and he had learned the gospel was important to her as he'd gotten to know her better and had listened to her comments in church and around Lilly's table. Last night she hadn't faked her faith in the Lord either. There had been a oneness between them as they'd sat before the fire discussing their individual beliefs and dreams. Though he suspected there were some aspects of the gospel that caused her to struggle, he knew she allowed her faith to guide her.

That's why her attitude toward marriage didn't make sense to him. It took real restraint to avoid pounding the steering wheel with his fist. She'd told him marriage and children didn't figure into her plans. Her lack of enthusiasm for pursuing a family of her own confused him. From the time he'd joined the Church, he'd been taught that the family was the basic unit of the Church and that women should aspire to be mothers. Didn't she believe that, too? Didn't normal Latter-day Saint women want husbands and babies? But then most Latter-day Saint women probably hadn't been raised by control-freak fathers who made even talking about their mothers taboo!

Gloom settled over him as he contemplated his feelings for Taylor. He'd known for weeks that she was becoming increasingly important to him. In so many ways she was everything he wanted in an eternal companion. He admired her courage and compassion; she was smart, cared about spiritual matters, had a wide range of interests, and their conversations left him feeling challenged and exhilarated. And yes, she was a joy to look at. He knew physical perfection didn't matter, and in fact, was highly overrated by society as a whole, but he knew now it wasn't Taylor's stunning appearance alone that attracted him. It was the whole woman. He wished they could at least be friends. But he didn't have to be a rocket scientist to figure out he couldn't handle being "just friends" with her.

"It's beautiful up here." Taylor peered out the open window of his truck and gave a little sigh of appreciation. His heart accelerated— Taylor even shared his love for the mountains! Maybe, just maybe, he could convince her to stay. His hopes flared, then died. He couldn't do that to her, even if she loved him, and he was by no means certain she did.

He thought about how much he'd always resented Jessica and his mother for ignoring his dreams and goals, and now compared their tactics to Taylor and her father's determination to ignore Lilly's desires and shuttle her off to a retirement complex. Of all the gospel concepts he'd learned since joining the Church, the one members referred to as "agency" was probably the one that stirred him the most deeply. He truly believed the Lord wanted all of His children to make those choices that determined the direction of their life freely and without physical or emotional coercion. Forcing or manipulating someone to live a certain way, even if it was the right way, was wrong. He groaned inwardly. His mother and Jessica were wrong, and so were Taylor and her father. Clay would be as wrong as they were if he tried to manipulate Taylor to be part of his life; he couldn't steal her agency to choose to live her life the way she wanted.

* * *

It was mid-afternoon when they pulled into Clay's parking spot next to Grandma Lilly's fence, and Taylor was stiff as she climbed out of the cab of his truck. The trip had taken almost an hour, mostly over unpaved roads, but it had seemed longer, mostly because she was so tired and because Clay hadn't been inclined to talk. He'd seemed preoccupied the entire way. She'd used the time to do some thinking herself. She was beginning to care altogether too much for the country vet, but she couldn't be in love with him. That would never do! She'd been under the thumb of one well-meaning, controlling man all her life, and she certainly wasn't going to trade a father for a husband! Stifling a yawn, she headed for the gate that separated the two properties.

"I don't believe it!" Clay's exclamation brought her to a halt.

"Don't believe what?" She glanced around, feeling confused.

"Look at that!" He pointed toward his clinic. "Jones and his crew are actually working!" She followed the direction he pointed. Two men knelt on the roof, hammering shingles in place. Bib Jones stepped from the front door with an electrician's belt strapped around his waist. He waved and she waved back.

"How long has it been since you checked on their progress?" Taylor turned back to Clay and couldn't quite keep the amusement out of her voice. She knew Clay usually left for his first appointment while it was still dark and often didn't return until after sunset.

"Too long." He started toward the structure.

Taylor reached out to catch his arm. "It will wait," she told him. "Right now you need sleep more than anything."

"I've got appointments . . . ," he protested.

"First check on poor old Rambo." She steered him toward her grandmother's house.

"I checked Rambo this morning. She's fine—ornery as ever." Reluctantly he matched his steps to hers. They were still arguing when they entered the house through the back door.

"Hi!" Wendy greeted them with a broad smile. Taylor was surprised to see her. She'd assumed the girl would have used their overnight adventure as an excuse to take the day off. Was it just her imagination or was there something different about the girl?

"Are you all right?" Clay asked. "No one's been around or made any more threatening calls?"

"I'm great." Wendy laughed, looking none the worse for her experience. "Tommy's in the front room asleep on Lilly's couch, and Stewart Darnell's in the kitchen with Lilly, and his grandson is hanging out in the tree house so Rambo and I are well protected."

Taylor and Clay joined her laughter. Yes, something was definitely different. There was something about Wendy that made her appear older, more mature.

"If you don't mind, I'm going to take Rambo back to New York," Wendy told Clay. "I don't think she's safe here anymore."

"You're probably right," Clay agreed. "I think taking her back to Jessica is the best thing to do. Let me know when you want to go, and you can charge your expenses to my credit card and stay at my mother's condo while you're there."

"Actually Sister Jordan and I have already started making plans." Wendy smiled a secret smile and changed the subject. "Did you see Ms. Morrow's dogs?" she asked Taylor, her bubbling manner returning.

Taylor nodded her head and Wendy went on, excitement sparkling in her eyes, "Aren't they cute? Dr. leClerc groomed Marie and he let me trim Renee. He showed me how to clip the ends of

Rambo's wing feathers, too, so she can't fly away, but she can still fly enough to stay out of Tom's reach."

"It sounds like you were busy while I was sleeping," Taylor smiled back.

"I groomed one of Ms. Morrow's horses, too, and I've decided that's what I'm going to do with my life," Wendy announced with a happy smile. "I'm going to learn all there is to know about grooming pets. I don't really want to be a secretary, and it was much more fun cutting Renee's hair and putting little pink bows in it."

"Are you telling me I'm about to lose my office manager?" Clay asked.

Wendy hung her head. "I really haven't done much. Taylor—"

Clay cut her off. "We can talk about it later. For now I'd better find a list of my appointments for today and get to work."

"I canceled your appointments," Wendy told him a bit smugly. Taylor was surprised that Wendy had taken the initiative to do so.

"Canceled them?" Clay sounded equally astonished.

"Well, I didn't actually cancel any of them, but none were emergencies, so I postponed them until tomorrow or the day after. Everyone already knew about our adventure and thought it was a good idea for you to take the day off," she went on to explain.

"An excellent idea," Taylor beamed at Wendy, then turned to Clay, "Now there's no excuse not to get some sleep."

"That's not exactly true," Clay grinned back. "I don't have a bed anymore, and it seems young Tommy has already staked a claim to the couch. But to be perfectly honest, I'm sure a shower will do me as much good as a nap. That is, if I can beat a certain young lady to the hot water."

"Be my guest," Taylor gestured grandly toward the door leading to the interior of the house.

Wendy giggled. "You'll find a bed in your room, Dr. Clay. Lilly had the guys move an old one down from the attic and put it together. I helped her put fresh bedding on it. There's a chest of drawers, too, and Lilly put your clothes in it."

"What clothes?" Clay asked with a rueful glance down at his filthy, torn, and rumpled pants and shirt.

"The ones Taylor bought you. And some blue packages of," she hesitated, her eyes wide and innocent, "uh, unmentionables that

Blaine Gardner said would fit you." Taylor suspected Wendy was struggling to hold back another giggle. The girl was incorrigible, but she had to admit she seemed to have everything well under control.

As Taylor entered the kitchen, she could see through into the living room. Tommy's stockinged feet hung over the end of the sofa, and Stewart's mouth hung open slightly as he snoozed in the recliner.

"Some watchmen!" Clay motioned toward the sleeping pair, then his eyes met hers, and they shared a moment's amusement. Placing a finger to his lips to signal silence, he tiptoed toward the stairs.

Stopping to hug her grandmother who sat at the kitchen table, Taylor assured the older woman she was fine, while her eyes followed Clay as he climbed the stairs. He was exhausted whether he'd admit it or not. She hoped he'd be able to sleep the rest of the afternoon and right on through the night without any emergency interruptions. Turning back to her grandmother, she noticed the shadows under the older woman's eyes. The night had been hard on her, too.

"You're going to have to make your mind up about him." Lilly nodded her head toward Clay as he disappeared from sight.

"What do you mean?" Taylor was surprised by her grandmother's awareness of her confusion.

"He's been badly hurt by one woman who couldn't accept him as he is. I wouldn't want him hurt again," her grandmother warned.

"I won't be here long enough to hurt him." She tried for a breezy tone. Anyway, if someone got hurt, she suspected it wouldn't be Clay but herself. "He knows all I want is a career in the biggest city I can find."

"Just be sure, dear," Lilly took Taylor's hand, "that really is what you want."

"I've wanted a business career as long as I can remember, you know that," she told her grandmother as she stooped to give her a hug. "If Daddy hadn't . . ." She stopped, not wanting to tell her grandmother she would already be in San Francisco starting that dream if her father hadn't insisted she spend the summer in Fairfield first.

"If Andrew hadn't sent you up here," her grandmother finished for her. "Which reminds me, your father has called six times since you left here last night. He's really upset and insists he's coming to get both of us." She sighed and shook her head. "That man should have remarried years ago."

Taylor slid into the chair opposite Grandma Lilly. "I used to wish he'd get married again, but Daddy won't ever remarry. When I was a little girl, I once asked him to find a new mommy for me, and he got terribly angry. He said he loved my mother so much he could never marry anyone else and that I was being disloyal to her to suggest such a thing."

The older woman reached across the table and covered her grand-daughter's hand with her own. "He was wrong. There would have been no disloyalty in finding a good woman to care for you. I can't help believing he would have been happier, too, with a companion who might have tempered his insecurities."

"Insecurities!" Taylor couldn't believe she'd heard right. "Daddy is the least insecure person I know!"

"There's more than one way to express insecurity." Lilly spoke softly and there was pain in her voice. "Don't think I'm unaware of the bold way he meets every challenge in his business life or the way he tends to take over or take charge of every group with which he becomes involved. As a little boy, he never wanted to play with other children, he needed a night light, was afraid of shadows, and dragged around a plush puppy for years. He was terribly afraid of changes or surprises. Eventually he discovered he could prevent changes by always being in charge, and he set out to control everyone and every-thing around him. I don't know what made him need so much control. Sometimes I've blamed myself for giving in to him too much. I've wondered if I didn't take some childhood trauma seriously enough or maybe his little sister arrived too soon, before he was ready to stop being my baby.

"Your Aunt Linda never let him get away with running her life, though he certainly tried, but unfortunately your mother wasn't like that. She adored him and seemed happy to let him make all the deci-sions. The more she leaned on him, the more desperate he became to control everything around him. Perhaps if she'd lived, she would have learned to stand up for herself, or perhaps her love alone would have been enough to temper his insecurity, but I do know that without her, he has grown worse."

"What do you mean, he's gotten worse?" she asked, though she suspected she knew what her grandmother referred to.

"It's this notion he's gotten into his head that I'm some helpless old lady who ought to be in a care facility." She pressed her lips together and huffed in annoyance.

"Oh, Grandma, I'm sorry. I guess you know that's why he sent me here this summer, to convince you to move into a little apartment in a senior citizen complex being built near our house in Pocatello. He paid the deposit months ago."

"Yes, I knew." There was a spark of anger in Lilly's eyes that gradually turned to pity.

Taylor felt guilty for her part in her father's plan and ashamed that she had agreed to the plan for less than noble reasons of her own. "I've been so selfish." She began to cry. "I thought that if you were living close to Daddy, he wouldn't keep finding excuses to keep me from leaving home. I kept telling myself you're too old to really be in love with Stewart, and Daddy was just thinking of what's best for you, that he wants to make your life easier, and you'd be happier close to your son and without so much work to do. I was wrong and so is he. I know how much you care for Stewart and that he cares for you, too, and that there is no reason for you to give up your home or your ward. You have friends here you've known all your life, and you deserve to be with them, not with a bunch of strangers. And you don't need Daddy interfering in your life every day!" It all came out in a rush of noisy tears.

"Oh, honey." Lilly came around the table to take her weeping granddaughter in her arms. "I've been selfish, too. All summer I've put off having this talk with you because I was enjoying having you here. It was almost like when you were a little girl, and I would insist that Andrew send you to me for the summer."

"I loved those summers." Taylor wiped her eyes and attempted to smile.

There was pity in her grandmother's voice as she went on, "Now certainly doesn't seem like the best time to tell you this, with you tired and needing a shower and some sleep. I wouldn't have chosen to speak to you now if your father weren't on his way, leaving me no other choice."

"Daddy's on his way here? Now?" Taylor gulped.

"I don't want to cause trouble between you and my son," Lilly continued in a severe voice, "but you need to look beyond his plan to stick me in that little apartment and face the fact that he sent you here this summer to keep you from pursuing your own life. He didn't need you to break the news to me; he already told me his plans months ago, and I told him no and will keep telling him no. It's you I'm worried about. I don't think you've ever learned to tell him no. Somehow you've always seemed to believe Andrew's happiness was your responsibility."

Taylor hung her head. Grandma Lilly was right. Somewhere deep inside she'd known her father was using concern for his mother as an excuse to keep his daughter from leaving home to establish a life of her own. And maybe she was more like the mother she scarcely remembered than she wanted to admit.

She'd always had a hard time refusing her father anything. He loved her and she loved him, but she'd always deferred to his wishes rather than face a confrontation with him—just as her mother had. A faint memory from the past surfaced in her mind. It was of her mother telling her to eat the broccoli on her plate because it would make Daddy happy. Another memory crowded that one out. She was sitting on the floor, her toys scattered about the room, and her mother was kneeling beside her. In soft tones, Mommy was cajoling her to pick up her toys before her father came home, reminding her that Daddy wouldn't be pleased if the house was messy when he got home.

Was that when she'd begun assuming responsibility for her father's happiness? Or had it been when her mother died and she'd sensed not only her father's loneliness, but that somehow her mother had done something wrong. She hadn't minded Daddy, she'd gone away, and then she couldn't ever come back.

"Daddy needs me," she whispered around the thick lump in her throat. "He doesn't have anyone else. But sometimes I feel like I'm being smothered. I didn't want to come here this summer; I wanted to go to San Francisco, but I really didn't protest very hard. I think I was afraid to go so far."

"Afraid you wouldn't measure up to your dreams?" Grandma asked softly.

"No," she hesitated. "In a way I've always been afraid that if I went away, I could never come back. I think that's why I didn't protest too much either when Daddy decided I should give up my scholarship to Stanford and attend the University of Idaho instead."

"That's why you need to leave. Right now." The shock her grandmother's words brought must have shown on her face because Grandma went on, "Unless you leave before he gets here, you can be sure he'll have some other plan to keep you near him. You'll try to placate him and delay your own plans again to appease him. That won't be good for either of you. I love you both, but allowing him to run your life won't make either of you happy. He's become a bully and you've become afraid to try your wings. There's a narrow line between honoring your father and your God-given charge to exercise your own agency. Unless you choose to act for yourself now, your fears will increase and leaving will become harder, not easier."

"I don't understand. How can I leave?" Her voice wobbled as she recognized the truth of her grandmother's words. She'd struggled all of her life to please her father. She saw now that his approval had only come when she followed his plans. His disapproval of her friends, the classes she chose, and her career plans had never been matters of a lack of trust in her judgment, but an attempt to discourage her from leaving him.

She should be angry, but instead a wave of sadness swept over her. Her father loved her and he probably had no understanding of what he was doing to her or to his mother. In his misguided way he was doing what he believed was in their best interests. He'd deny it if she even suggested he was usurping his mother's and his daughter's agency. A glimmer of understanding convinced her that her grandmother was right. Her father *was* insecure. He was terribly afraid of losing those he loved, just as he'd lost his wife. He was as afraid of being on his own as Taylor was. As long as he could keep those he loved close to him and control where they went and what they did, he felt more secure, more able to protect them, and could thus protect himself from hurt and loss.

"Genna was your father's anchor," Lilly spoke of Taylor's mother. "She was a great deal stronger than your father ever suspected, but her dependent nature made him feel strong and needed. When she died, your father felt lost and betrayed. You were a helpless child who did need him, and for years your dependency kept him going, but it has also provided him with an excuse not to take chances or explore his own potential. You were his excuse not to take risks. I don't want either of you wasting your lives with the mistaken notion that you must protect each other from life. You need to get on with yours, so that he'll have to do the same."

"He'll be so hurt if I just leave," Taylor protested. "I want to go, but it seems cruel to go without telling him good-bye. And where would I go?"

"If you were eighteen, I would agree, but you're almost twenty-four and haven't gotten up the courage yet to make one choice independent of your father. I don't think you're ready to risk a confrontation with him." Lilly drummed her fingers on the table and looked worried. Finally she sighed and went on, "I have no right to decide for you any more than your father does. It's your choice, but Wendy and I have worked out a plan so you can take care of the Rambo problem at the same time."

Her grandmother went on with a sly twinkle in her eye, "I've made reservations for the two of you on a flight to New York this evening. You can take Rambo back to Jessica, and while you're in New York you can look around and see if you really want to spend the rest of your life in a big city. If you make a clean break without even a telephone call, you'll have a chance to think about what you really want without his opinions influencing your decisions. Now go shower and think about it."

Ten minutes later Taylor stood in the shower, letting the hot water drum against her aching body and feeling grateful Clay hadn't hogged all of the hot water as she had once done to him. She tried to view her situation objectively, although objectivity didn't come easily when her emotions were at stake. It had been just her and Daddy for so long. Did she really want that to change? A glimpse of herself as a fifty-year-old woman still sleeping every night in a frilly, pink and white bedroom in her French white twin bed and eating every meal across the table from her aging father brought tears to her eyes.

She remembered the arguments they'd had over her choice of schools and her frustration each time a young man had come to pick her up for a date, and she'd watched as her father subjected him to a humiliating interrogation. Daddy had jokingly made fun of all her friends, she realized now, and it hadn't just been the boys. She'd never had a "best friend." She had many "friends," but there had never been one special girlfriend. Wendy was the girlfriend she should have had in her early teens. With someone like Wendy she would have experimented with clothes and nail polish, flirted with boys, and giggled together between classes.

She looked down at her hands, seeing a little heart decal on her pinky nail that Wendy had put there a few days ago, and smiled. It was so incongruous to think of Taylor Jordan—serious, dependable, class valedictorian, senator's campaign business manager, MBA—and Wendy Carlson—flighty, boy crazy, manicurist extraordinaire, and would-be pet groomer—as friends. Yet over the past couple of months they had become close. She'd set out to help Wendy learn to run Clay's office efficiently, and in the process the girl had matured a great deal. She had changed, too, Taylor thought. She'd learned every minute didn't need to be filled with serious pursuits, and perhaps they had each learned a valuable lesson about taking responsibility for their own lives.

Taylor reached for her shampoo and worked a rich lather into her matted hair. As her fingers massaged her scalp, she thought about her grandmother's advice. She didn't want to leave home this way. It seemed so cruel. On the other hand, returning Rambo to Jessica as quickly as possible seemed the best solution to ending the break-ins and threatening telephone calls. She didn't know what those men would have done if they'd caught them last night.

She was pretty sure their pursuers were the same men who forced Peggy Friedrickson off the road, then hadn't stopped to make sure she and her children were all right. Last night, that memory—along with the attempted ambush of her and her friends—had been enough to convince her that the threats were genuine and that none of them would be safe until Rambo returned to New York. If she waited for her father's arrival, she and Wendy would miss their flight. Besides her grandmother was right; she had some thinking to do and she needed to do it alone.

Making up her mind, she turned off the water and reached for a towel. She would go to New York. But even as she rushed to dress, she wondered if she was rationalizing or if she was really afraid her father would prevent her from leaving if she waited. Daddy would understand. Well, maybe not. She didn't want to believe her father had manipulated her all these years. Yet, she couldn't think of one time she'd had a problem that he hadn't solved it for her. He wasn't really some kind of control freak—was he? She couldn't think. It was all too confusing. The thought of being alone frightened her. She didn't want to leave Daddy—or was it Clay she didn't want to leave? How did Clay suddenly get into this dilemma? She didn't want to think about him. Thoughts of Clay simply confused her more.

She only knew she had to make this trip. If she couldn't handle a trip to New York City by herself, she'd never manage the career she'd dreamed of for so long. And this wasn't a permanent break anyway, she told herself. She'd be back for the rest of her things before going on to San Francisco. She could tell Daddy good-bye then, and she'd come home to visit him as often as she could.

When she stepped out of the bathroom, she stepped right into Clay's arms. Startled, she pulled back a step but he didn't let her move far.

"Lilly just filled me in on her plan for you to accompany Wendy to New York to take Rambo back where she belongs. I've called my mother. She'll meet your plane and you can stay with her as long as you like, both you and Wendy. Jessica is already staying there, but Mother has plenty of room, and the security in her building is the best in the city. You'll both be safe there, and Jessica can take over protection for Rambo, which she can easily afford. I've asked Mother to show you the city and get tickets for some of the better shows for you while you're there."

"I can't afford . . . I don't have the right clothes . . . How did you know I'd agree . . . ? Oh!" She felt like screaming—or crying. She couldn't go to a Broadway show in her jeans and a dime-store shirt! But worrying about clothes felt so petty in light of all that had happened. And how could Clay be so sure she would actually go? *She* hadn't even been completely sure herself that she would actually choose to go.

"Go, Taylor." Clay's voice softened to a persuasive tone, and instinctively she wanted to protest. She didn't want to be told what to do, and she certainly didn't want Clay to want her to leave, but neither would she let him think she was a coward.

"It's for the best," he continued in that soft tone. "I didn't get a chance to find out whether the Winslow diamonds are actually missing or not, but someone believes they are. Those people are becoming progressively more dangerous. Once Rambo is no longer in this house, you and your grandmother and Wendy will be safe again here. I told Lilly I would take Rambo back myself, but she convinced me you and Wendy would be able to leave without being followed more easily than I could."

"But they followed Wendy before," Taylor argued.

"No, they followed me. I led them to Wendy and endangered all of you," Clay pointed out.

"Won't they follow us again when we leave the house? Especially if Rambo is with us?" Taylor continued to argue.

"I don't think so. Lilly and Wendy have quite a plan." A grin lit up his face and without allowing her to argue anymore, he picked up a small suitcase she recognized as her own, took her arm, and headed for the stairs.

CHAPTER 19

As they started toward the stairs, a rumble she'd been too engrossed in conversation to hear sooner vibrated through the house. She recognized the sound of a helicopter.

"Charles leClerc," Clay explained with a wry twist to his mouth, and Taylor remembered that though Clay seemed to like Ms. Morrow's long-time veterinarian friend, he hadn't appeared quite so fond of his fellow vet's young pilot. "Wendy arranged for him to pick up the two of you and discreetly drop you in Boise before continuing on to Los Angeles. Deputy Donaldson has informed us two men in a black Sunbird are aiming field glasses this direction from the hill behind Glendowski's feed store right now. They're too far away to be any threat when you board but close enough to see both of you and our feathered troublemaker depart. They'll have to decide whether to follow you or continue to watch me.

"Donaldson will make certain you get a comfortable head start before he allows them to leave town. He can stop them to check the car's registration or something, but he can't arrest them without concrete evidence. Once Donaldson lets them go, it will take them some time to track down the helicopter's destination. Hopefully, once they do, they'll think you've gone to Los Angeles, too."

They'd reached the bottom of the stairs, and Taylor could see both Wendy and Lilly peering through the curtains. Tommy and Stewart were close behind them, and a spirit of excitement crackled through the room. The sound of pulsating rotors sent Grandma's knickknacks skittering toward the edges of tables and shelves. Lilly rushed about the room, moving the fragile china figures to safer positions, and Tom dived for safety behind the sofa.

Stewart opened the door, looking back expectantly toward the occupants of the room. Tommy quickly bent his head toward Wendy. When he straightened, he was carrying a small pet carrier, an overnight case, and a satisfied grin. Wendy's smile appeared a little smug, too, as she hurried to keep step with him. Lilly kissed Taylor's cheek and told her not to worry.

"I'll have a talk with Andy when he gets here," she promised. "Once he calms down, I'll make certain he understands this is something you have to do. Have a good time," she added.

"You'd better hurry," Stewart called to her and squeezed her shoulder as she brushed past him.

Clay walked beside her until they reached the point where the helicopter blades spun over their heads. He tossed the bag he carried into the open door, then turned back to her. Thinking he only meant to assist her with the long step into the chopper, she held out her arms. Clay's arms wrapped around her and his mouth met hers. She may have been startled for just a moment, but she soon forgot everything except Clay.

There was no guessing how long the kiss might have lasted if it hadn't been for the voices both behind her and aboard the helicopter urging her to hurry. Clay lifted her aboard the chopper, and almost immediately the door closed between them. She was still fastening her seat belt when she felt the craft begin to move upward. Turning to the window, she saw Clay, Tommy, and Stewart surrounding her grandmother. Their hands were lifted in a farewell gesture, and tears sprang to her eyes. Blinking them back with a reminder that she'd given in to the urge to cry a little too much lately, she continued to watch the figures grow smaller until they disappeared from sight.

She continued to stare out the window long after Clay, the house, and even Fairfield had disappeared from view. She knew she was off on the adventure of her dreams, and soon she would be in New York with all its bustle and excitement. Still, she couldn't help feeling she'd left what mattered most behind. Softly she touched her bottom lip with the tip of one finger.

Rambo squawked, voicing her disapproval of the helicopter ride, and Wendy removed her from her carrier. Charles attached a small tether to her leg so she couldn't fly around and disturb the pilot. He also substituted a solid-sided bird carrier for the one Wendy had carried aboard. The new carrier looked like a large handbag with a shoulder strap.

"Once we get to Boise, keep her in the carrier with the flap closed over the side," he told her. "You'll have to keep her confined while flying on commercial planes. It's probably best not to draw attention to her in Boise or Seattle, but when you have brief layovers in other cities, you can let her out on the tether for short bouts of exercise."

It wasn't until they boarded the plane in Boise that Taylor discovered how complicated their flight arrangements were. From Boise they flew to Seattle. In Seattle they changed airlines and flew to Dallas, where they would change planes again, then on to St. Louis and Chicago. Once they reached Chicago, however, they were on a through flight to New York. Her grandmother had even gone so far as to book their passage under her mother's maiden name. Grandma Lilly obviously watched too much TV.

They were over Texas before it occurred to Taylor to wonder how Wendy had managed to convince her parents to let her make the trip. When she asked, Wendy giggled then explained, "It wasn't too hard. At first they said no, then I told them if they didn't let me go, I was going to run off and marry Tommy."

"You didn't mean it, did you?" Taylor gasped in shock.

"About marrying Tommy?" Wendy's voice was a mite defensive.

"No, about running off," Taylor clarified. "I like Tommy, and I think he'll be a great husband for you someday, but you're both a little young for marriage now."

Wendy giggled again, then spoke seriously. "He was so brave and always thinking about the rest of us when we were trying to escape those robbers and save Rambo. After his dad came to get us, he insisted he take us back to the cabin to fix my tire and get Clay's truck for him. We talked a lot while we were keeping watch last night and again on the ride back to town. He thinks I was really brave, too. He said most people don't have the courage to act on their convictions, but I proved I did when I ran away with Rambo so no one would kill her to get those diamonds. He said that's how he feels about the gospel and why he has to go on a mission, because when someone really cares about something, they have to act on it even if its dangerous and scary."

Taylor took Wendy's hand and gave it a quick squeeze. "I thought you planned to marry quickly so you wouldn't have to live at home much longer. If you marry Tommy, you'll have to wait until he finishes high school and goes on a mission for two years."

"I know," Wendy sighed. "It seems like such a long time. But when I get back from New York, I'm going to go to school. My parents don't know it yet, but I'm going to learn how to groom pets and show animals. Dr. leClerc said he could get me into a school in Salt Lake that specializes in animal grooming, and that when I finish school, if I decide I don't want to keep working for Clay, he'll hire me."

"You're serious about this, aren't you?" Taylor asked Wendy, wondering how the girl had changed so much.

"My parents wanted me to marry Clay. They think his wife will be the richest, most important woman in Fairfield," Wendy confided. "I thought I wanted that, too, because he's so good-looking and he's kind to animals. I thought it was perfect that he's already gone to school and has a good job with plans to build a big, new house. But I never know what to talk to him about, and he knows all those big words that make me feel stupid. And, well—he's just not Tommy."

"No, he's definitely not Tommy." Taylor smiled back at her friend, feeling a mixture of pride and amusement at the sudden foray into adulthood Wendy was exhibiting. She couldn't help wondering if it would last. "Do you really think you can wait three years for Tommy?" she asked.

"Yes, I do." Wendy spoke with confidence. "Tommy says leaving isn't as important as arriving, and I have to think about where I want to be, not what I want to leave. Going to school and doing something I really like will help the time go faster, and if I have a good job when Tommy comes back from his mission, we'll be able to get married right away instead of waiting until after he goes to college. He wants me to take institute classes while I'm going to school, and you know what? I'm going to do it. I don't have a strong testimony like Tommy does, but I want to have one. I want to be able to look at things the way he does, and like you do. I really admire you, and I would have made a really big mess this summer if you hadn't helped me."

"You helped me, too," Taylor whispered back. Wendy looked surprised, and Taylor hurried on. "You've been a wonderful friend."

Wendy smiled mischievously. "I think that honor goes to Clay. You care about him the same way I do about Tommy."

Taylor couldn't deny Wendy's words, but neither could she accept them. Clay certainly meant more to her than she wanted him to. She'd never been so comfortable talking to anyone else, and she'd never wanted to touch or be with anyone else the way she did with him. Even dangling from a tree, she hadn't been immune to his extraordinary good looks, but she'd since discovered he wasn't comfortable with his appearance and didn't believe anyone had ever really loved him for himself. Her attraction to him went way beyond his looks or even the keen mind she admired. His commitment to the gospel lent him an aura of authority she found essential. She'd always admired people who worked hard, were confident, and still gave of themselves to those less fortunate or in trouble. Clay was all those things, but she didn't love him. She couldn't allow herself to love him. She wouldn't spend her life in some man's shadow in a small backwater town.

Wendy curled in a ball and slept between Dallas and Chicago, woke up to change planes, then went right back to sleep. Taylor slept little and when she did fall asleep, she found herself reliving Clay's good-bye kiss over and over. Each time he held her close, she felt surrounded by light and joy. Then he would disappear and her father would tell her it was all her fault and that she should have listened to him. Then she'd awaken, feeling lonely and afraid. Occasionally Rambo made a soft chirring sound and Taylor suspected she was feeling lonely and afraid, too.

When the plane finally landed, her back ached, her head throbbed, and her legs felt like wet spaghetti. She knew she looked a mess in her limp cotton shirt and faded jeans. Her makeup was long gone and her hair frizzed more on one side than the other. She'd say she was too tired to care, but she did care enough to not want to meet Clay's mother looking like a war refugee. But at this point, what could she do?

Wendy ran her fingers through her hair and searched for her shoes, first with one foot, then the other. When she found them, she slipped them on, then quickly pulled a tube of lip gloss from her bag. After a couple of quick swipes at her mouth, she eyed Taylor critically.

"Here!" She thrust the lip gloss in Taylor's hand and reached to fluff her hair for her. Her actions told Taylor she looked even worse than she'd thought.

Slowly they made their way to the front of the plane, gave each other tentative smiles, and stepped into the tunnel leading to the air terminal. A swirl of people and noise assaulted their eyes and ears as they looked around for a woman who might be Clay's mother. Her eyes skipped past two fashionably dressed women and continued to search the crowd.

"I think that's her," Wendy clutched Taylor's arm and whispered in a hushed voice. "I'm almost positive I recognize Jessica Winslow, Clay's fiancée."

"Former fiancée," Taylor automatically corrected without questioning why the distinction mattered. She followed the direction Wendy indicated to the women she'd dismissed seconds ago. The glamorous redhead definitely wasn't Clay's mother, which left the model-slim blond. At first she appeared to be a contemporary of the redhead, but a closer look indicated she was older. Clay hadn't led her to expect matronly, but this woman was Hollywood chic! No, not Hollywood, she amended her thoughts. This woman had class and money and undoubtedly a pedigree chart that shouted blue blood. She might look young and glamorous but definitely not Hollywood slick.

"Let's get this over with," Taylor muttered under her breath, gripping her small carry-on bag tighter and squaring her shoulders.

"Okay," Wendy agreed, sounding as though she, too, was having misgivings about approaching the pair. She shrugged the strap of Rambo's carrier higher on her shoulder and tightened her hold on her overnight case.

"Excuse me," Taylor spoke to the blond, ignoring the younger redhead. "Are you Mrs. Curtis?"

The woman looked startled, and her eyes swept over Taylor's disheveled figure with a disapproving frown before speaking. "Yes, are you . . . ?"

"Taylor Jordan. And this is Wendy Carlson," Taylor finished.

Samantha Curtis introduced Jessica, who was too well bred to hold her nose, but she certainly gave the impression she wanted to. She barely acknowledged the introduction with a nod of her head, and Taylor felt an instant dislike for the young woman. She and Wendy might not look like candidates for the country club after seventeen hours of planes and airports, but they were still human! Actually,

Taylor thought that Wendy and Jessica looked a great deal alike, except for the color of their hair and the condition of their clothes—even though Jessica had doubtless paid many times more for her curly hair and skimpy skirt than Wendy had. The four women stood awkwardly for a few seconds, then Rambo emitted a loud squawk.

"Rambo!" Jessica forgot her feigned boredom and reached for the carrier Wendy held. For a moment Taylor wasn't certain Wendy would relinquish her grip on it. Only she saw the hint of sadness in the young woman's eyes as she surrendered the carrier to the bird's owner.

"I've missed you, baby," Jessica cooed to the bird when she lifted the side flap. Rambo ruffled her feathers and arched her back, sending the crest of feathers on her head into a peak resembling a war bonnet. She studiously ignored her owner.

"I'm sorry," Jessica whispered to the bird as if she believed Rambo could understand. "I didn't mean to hurt your feelings. I was afraid . . ." She trailed off with a wary glance around the waiting room. "We'd better go." She thrust the carrier back at Wendy and turned sharply toward the exit.

"We can arrange to have your luggage delivered," Samantha spoke up as Jessica led the group toward the exit.

"This is all there is." Wendy hefted her bag a little higher. "We didn't want to risk baggage transfers, and Clay said we could buy whatever clothes we needed after we got here." Taylor hid a smile. She'd wondered why Wendy had agreed to the trip without bringing a dozen suitcases.

The expression on Samantha's face would be cause enough for a good laugh, Taylor thought, if she didn't somewhat share the woman's chagrin. She was surprised Wendy was handling the situation so well, but then, at the moment Wendy was much better dressed than she was and looking forward to a New York shopping excursion. But why was she spending so much time worrying about her own appearance? True, she was accustomed to dressing well, but she'd never been obsessed over fashion or style or been particularly concerned about what other people chose to wear. So why did it bother her so much to meet these two women in her faded jeans and a dime-store shirt? Surely it didn't matter one way or the other what Clay's mother and former fiancée thought of her.

It was absurd to feel at a disadvantage beside them. She was still the same person she'd be even if she had been wearing the most distinguished and expensive suit hanging in her closet back in Pocatello. Come to think of it, her best Worth suit wouldn't measure up next to Samantha Curtis's elegant attire.

Wendy was uncharacteristically quiet during the cab ride from the airport to the Curtis condo. Perhaps she felt intimidated by the towering buildings, the traffic, and noise. She'd confided during their flight that she'd never traveled further than Boise before, and Taylor had little more experience. There had been a number of visits to Salt Lake, one to Los Angeles and Disneyland, and a hurried overnight trip to the nation's capitol once. She'd visited her aunt once in Phoenix, too. Her father could have traveled more if he'd wanted to and taken her to the exciting cities she'd dreamed of, but he hadn't been interested and had found excuses why she shouldn't travel without him. She'd never disputed his judgment—until now.

But now was not the time to think about her father and her ambivalent feelings toward him. She was in New York City! She should be pinching herself to make certain she wasn't dreaming. As heavy as her eyes felt at the moment, she'd rather be dreaming. Where was the excitement? New York City was the ultimate big city; she should be bursting with enthusiasm and plans. But instead of seeing the magical city of her dreams, she kept remembering all the years she'd thought herself independent and a little superior to other girls, when in fact she'd been manipulated and isolated from those who might have been her friends. Instead of excitement, she felt depression. Of course, she hadn't had much sleep in the past forty-eight hours, but she should still feel more enthusiasm than this!

* * *

To say Clay awoke feeling vaguely dissatisfied was an understatement. Taylor was gone and he had no idea whether or not she would return to Fairfield. He seldom saw her in the mornings before he began work anyway, so to be so conscious of the emptiness of the room down the hall didn't make sense. The empty basket on the bathroom counter only deepened his own sense of emptiness. He didn't try to kid himself. He knew perfectly well Taylor was the reason for the strange mood he found himself in this morning. He missed her and he wasn't quite sure how she'd come to occupy such a large part of his life.

Letting himself out of the house quietly, he walked toward his truck. When he reached it, he paused to let his eyes sweep over his clinic. The exterior appeared to be almost completed. Keeping the contractor working on his clinic was one more thing he'd discovered Taylor had accomplished to make his life run more smoothly. Changing his direction, he detoured toward the new building. Trying the front door, he found it unlocked.

The sun was just coming up, providing enough light through the large waiting room windows to encourage him inside. He looked around appreciatively, knowing that with the addition of furniture, the room would be warm and welcoming. Slowly he made his way across the reception area to a hall that led to four examination rooms, a surgery, a storage room, and his own soon-to-be office. He stood before his office window and gazed across an overgrown pasture to the rise where his home would one day stand before a background of trees. In his mind he could see his children playing in the open meadow. On the wide porch of the two-story stone house he could see their mother call to them, and he knew the woman was Taylor.

He shook his head, chasing away the image. Taylor wouldn't be part of his dream; she had dreams of her own, and they didn't include a country vet and a town too small to even boast a single stoplight.

Returning to the hall, he found the staircase leading to the apartment above. The apartment wasn't as close to completion as the rooms below, but he could see it wouldn't be long until it was ready for occupancy. He didn't remember choosing the carpet or tile, but he liked the blended shades of green that someone, probably Taylor, had chosen. He'd once visualized Jessica living here with him until the house was completed, but he could see now it wouldn't have worked. Looking around, he couldn't begin to imagine Jessica here. Though the great room was light and inviting, it wouldn't have been grand enough for Jessica, and Jessica would have never chosen restful shades of green. It was odd that color should be the one thing that finally made him see how fortunate he was that Jessica had broken their engagement. He couldn't bear to live his life amid the off-whites, creams, and pale tans with which Jessica surrounded herself.

He should be excited and proud, knowing he was close to realizing the goal he'd set himself to establish a clinic and to be completely self-sufficient. In a matter of weeks he could move into his own place. He didn't need his mother's money or Jessica's. But the prospect wasn't nearly as thrilling as he had expected. He would miss the coziness of Lilly's kitchen; he'd even miss the ongoing battle between Rambo and Tom. Most of all he'd miss Taylor. He wondered how long he'd even have Wendy's help. He had the impression that she was more than a little excited by Dr. leClerc's offer to help her learn pet grooming. How strange that during the months she'd worked for him and he'd avoided her, he'd never realized they really did share a love for animals.

They had more than concern for animals in common. They were both in love, though not with each other.

He didn't doubt Wendy and Tommy would make it. Their flight across the mountain in the rain that night had given them both some kind of insight into their relationship, and at least for Wendy, had bolstered her sense of self-worth. Something about their feelings for each other seemed to bring out the best in both of them. The challenges facing them wouldn't be easy, yet he envied them.

He wished his own challenges were half so simple. Tommy and Wendy openly cared about each other, while he feared Taylor still considered him the enemy. In a way, he supposed he was just that, the enemy to all her plans. She was attracted to him, maybe even liked him, but she was too smart to allow herself to love someone like him who was fleeing from the very life she dreamed of.

After a last look around, he started toward the stairs. He had appointments to keep, and if he didn't hurry he would likely run into Taylor's father and become embroiled in another argument. He winced thinking of Andrew Jordan's noisy explosion when he'd arrived two hours after Taylor and Wendy's departure. The man had truly expected Lilly and Taylor to be packed and ready to follow him back to Pocatello when he'd arrived that night. He didn't know the two feisty women in his family as well as he thought he did, Clay thought with a smile of satisfaction.

His smile faded and he amended the thought. Andrew Jordan had underestimated his mother, but he might be right about Taylor, although not for the reason the man believed. Taylor would have gone with her father because she loved and pitied him, not because she agreed he had some right to order her life for her. And for that reason Clay knew he could never tell Taylor how he felt about her. He couldn't bear to turn the love she might feel for him into a snare the way her father's love had.

Lilly had told her son some plain truths about his domination and manipulation of his daughter's life, but the man stubbornly refused to admit he was guilty of any wrongdoing. To his way of thinking, he had exercised his priesthood responsibility as head of the family to decide what was best for both his mother and his daughter. It was his duty, he had proclaimed, both because of his God-given role and because of the love he held for them both, to keep them safe.

Clay had meant to leave the room and stay out of what was a family matter, but he found he couldn't. When Andrew had ordered him to pack up his things and move out so that he could close up the house, Clay had turned to face the man, and speaking through almost clenched teeth, he had reminded the older man, "My contract is with Lilly, not you. I've done nothing to break my end of the bargain, and I'm not leaving."

"I speak for my mother!" Andrew had roared.

"No, you don't, Andy," Lilly had reminded him. "There is no need for Clay to leave. He's a model tenant. Besides, I'm not going anywhere."

"You stay out of this," Andrew spoke to his mother in a sharp voice. "I'll handle this."

"No, Mr. Jordan," Clay injected. "If you try to break my contract, it's my attorney who will be handling you."

"Are you threatening me?" Andrew drew himself up to his full height, which he realized too late still placed him several inches shorter than Clay.

"It seems to me you're the one doing all the threatening," Clay attempted to speak reasonably. The confrontation made him feel ill. The last thing he wanted to do was fight with Taylor's father.

"Andy, stop this. Right this minute." Lilly shook her finger at her son. "Taylor and I have tiptoed around you so long so as not to hurt your feelings and because we felt sorry for you. But no more. You've become a bully."

"I'm not a bully," Andrew protested, sounding to Clay like a sulky little boy.

"You are," Lilly went on, oblivious to her son's protest. "I'm happy right here in Fairfield, and I've made up my mind—I'm going to marry Stewart, and it's time for Taylor to try her wings and build a life of her own. It's time you did the same."

"You don't know what you're talking about." Andrew gave his mother an intimidating glare. "Now stop all this chatter and tell me where my daughter is, then get in there and get packed, or I'll do it for you."

"Mr. Jordan," Clay found himself speaking more sharply than he intended, "if you intend to remove Mrs. Jordan from this house forcibly, you'd better have a court order declaring her incompetent to control her own affairs. Otherwise, I'll call the police and have you removed. I know a deputy who would do almost anything for your mother and daughter."

"For heaven's sake!" Lilly glared at both of them. "I'm not going anywhere. I told you that. And no one is calling that nice deputy back to this house tonight. Andy, you can sleep on the daybed in your sister's old room tonight. And, Clay, I know you're exhausted. There's a bed waiting for you in your room. Now both of you better get some rest."

To Clay's surprise, Andy turned obediently toward the stairs, though not without a few grumbles about the daybed being too short.

"Andy," Lilly spoke again, and when her son turned his head, she lowered her voice to an almost conspiratorial whisper. "How long has it been since you read the one hundred twenty-first section of the Doctrine and Covenants? Perhaps you should take a close look at verses thirty-nine and forty-one."

When Clay reached his room, he quickly undressed and slipped into the bed awaiting him. There was a little table with a lamp beside the bed. He turned to shut off the light and recognized his scriptures sitting beside the lamp and wondered how they had managed to survive the vandals who had destroyed his room. Then he remembered discussing a doctrinal point with Stewart a few days earlier. He must have left them on the end table beside the sofa in the front room where Lilly would have found them and returned them to his room.

Impulsively he turned to the scriptures Lilly had advised her son to read. *"Unrighteous dominion . . . no power . . . maintained by virtue of the priesthood . . . only by persuasion, by long-suffering, by gentleness and meekness . . . love unfeigned."* He closed the book, turned off the light, and smiled in the dark.

He thought again of the verses he'd read. They fit in well with his own strong views on agency. Like Andrew Jordan, his mother had dominated and controlled both him and his father for years. He could easily see how she, like Taylor's father, had used his love for her to make him feel guilty when his choices hadn't been the same as hers. She'd used her family's social standing like Andrew used his priesthood, as a badge of authority for her actions. And again, like Taylor's father, she'd dismissed as unimportant the plans and goals of her offspring, assuming she knew what was best for him. A sudden picture of Taylor escaping a lion only to fall into the jaws of a tiger assailed him.

He was being ridiculous. His mother placed too much emphasis on good manners to treat Taylor badly. But there were all kinds of ways to inflict pain politely, a part of his mind argued. He wished he'd gone to New York with Taylor. It was his responsibility, not Taylor's, to get Rambo back to Jessica, and his mother wouldn't mistreat Taylor if he were there to protect her. And what if the men trying to steal the Winslow diamonds had somehow followed her?

Perhaps he should go to New York and bring Taylor safely back, but even he could see the arrogance behind that thought. Taylor could handle the task as well as he could, and she didn't need a baby-sitter. Honesty forced him to admit his real concern was that Taylor wouldn't want to come back, no matter how much he wanted her to . . . And that made him as bad as her father.

He found himself kneeling beside the bed as words began to pour from his heart. He asked God to protect Taylor from the evil men who sought to steal the diamonds by stealing Rambo. He asked that his mother would treat Taylor with warmth and kindness. He paused for several minutes, then made one more request, "Father, I love Taylor Jordan. She is the woman I want beside me for all eternity. Even so, I want her happiness above all else. Please protect her from me. Please grant me the strength to avoid using the love I suspect she feels for me to trap her into a life she doesn't wish. Please grant me the strength to honor her agency." He closed the prayer and wondered if he was being arrogant to think he had any chance of persuading Taylor to choose him over the life she'd planned for herself if he tried.

CHAPTER 20

Taylor sank down on the park bench beside Wendy, but she didn't release her grip on the bag she held. This was the first time she and Wendy had ventured out shopping alone, and she was determined not to tempt a thief to grab what she had purchased, even though she hadn't bought much, just a green silk shirt. Wendy had bought half a dozen pairs of cotton and denim pants, an equal number of shirts, and a gorgeous dress to wear tomorrow night when they accompanied Samantha and Jessica to dinner and a Broadway play. Wendy tossed her bags beside her and reached for the roll she'd bought to feed the pigeons and squirrels in the park.

Taylor still didn't have a dress to wear to the play, she thought wearily. Perhaps she should have purchased the dress Samantha had encouraged her to buy the day before, but she'd never paid that much for a dress before in her life. It didn't measure up to her standards of modesty either. She wasn't a prude, but she couldn't get enthused about a dress that covered less than her bathing suit did. She'd always shopped for quality, and she knew quality carried a price tag, but that dress was ridiculously overpriced, and no matter how well made it was, she'd never wear it enough times to justify the price. And even if price weren't a consideration, she wouldn't be comfortable in it. She'd simply have to wear the long black skirt she'd bought on their first shopping excursion with the silk blouse she'd bought this morning. It wouldn't be as elegant as the gowns her hostess and Jessica were bound to wear, but she would be comfortable with the understated class of the more simple outfit.

She watched Wendy break off small chunks of bread and toss them to a noisy crowd of birds. Wendy seemed to be enjoying herself in New York, though she was quieter and more subdued than she'd been all summer. She seemed to enjoy the daily shopping excursions, and she called Tommy every night to tell him about the sights she'd seen and the adventures she'd had visiting the fashionable stores she'd only heard about before now. Taylor personally felt she'd done enough shopping in the last few days to last her a lifetime.

It wasn't shopping, sightseeing, fancy restaurants, or even Broadway shows that made up her dream of city life. The only glimpse she'd caught of that dream was when Jessica had shown her the towering building that was home to Winslow Enterprises. Taylor had learned that Jessica, although a major shareholder, had nothing to do with the operation of the vast conglomerate. She was content with her grandfather's choice of her cousin Jacob to serve as CEO and happy to let him make the decisions that controlled their grandfather's empire, even though she'd made it clear she didn't much like the young man or either of his brothers. She was satisfied to have Jacob inherit control of the company while she inherited the bulk of her grandfather's fortune. Taylor wondered briefly how the arrangement suited Jacob's younger brothers.

Jessica didn't seem to have many interests beyond shopping and parties, she mused. No, she had one other interest. Clay. Clay might consider their engagement at an end, but Jessica didn't. She and Clay's mother were still planning a wedding. Frankly Taylor couldn't see what had ever drawn the two together. Jessica was beautiful and she had gobs of money, but she couldn't imagine the Clay she knew in Jessica's world of slinky evening gowns, tuxedos, and all-night parties. And there was no way she could imagine Jessica helping Clay feed calves or diving into a storm-swollen river to rescue an unconscious woman and her children. She was doing it again, she thought. No matter what she started out thinking, her thoughts always turned to Clay.

"Taylor," Wendy interrupted. "Do you remember when you asked me why I wanted to leave Fairfield?"

"Yes, you said you wanted to get away from your parents." Taylor had wondered a number of times, as Wendy had talked of Tommy's and her plans to marry, how her desire to escape her parents' dictatorial control meshed with Tommy's plans to take over his father's ranch, which was less than ten miles from Wendy's father's farm.

"Yes, well, I expect we'll fight a lot, and I'll get angry when they try to tell me what to do, but I'm sure it will work out. They don't bother me as much as they did," Wendy admitted.

"Perhaps they recognize you've become an adult," Taylor suggested.

"Maybe that's it." Wendy didn't sound convinced. "But I think it's more than that. I think it's me. Before, I just wanted to escape, and I thought getting married was the only way I could take control of my life. When I ran away with Rambo, I kept thinking I was going to die before I got to do anything, and I thought of so many things I wanted to do. But I didn't ask if you remembered because I wanted to talk about me. I just wondered why you want to leave. Are you running away, too?"

"I don't live in Fairfield. There was never a question of my staying there," she reminded Wendy, but as the words left her mouth, she wondered if they were the truth. She'd never expected any profound analysis to come from Wendy, but in a way the girl had been more honest in her examination of her motives than Taylor had been. Taylor knew she was just as guilty of wanting to run away. Just as she'd come to New York to escape her father, her dreams of corporate success were a kind of escapism, too. There—she'd admitted what she'd carefully avoided examining too closely in the past.

For years her dreams had centered around creating a life for herself in a faraway city, of burying herself in a career beyond her father's control. She loved her father but she resented the strictures and narrowness of a relationship that plunged her into guilt whenever she strayed from his careful agenda. The duties and responsibilities of loving and being loved were like an overgrown vine that strangled and blocked the view, leaving her feeling caged. Was it any wonder she didn't wish to add any more family to her life in the form of husband and children?

Why did the mention of husband and children bring to mind first Clay, then the little Friedrickson girls? Were the feelings she had for Clay love? If so, was she running from him, too? She didn't like to think of herself as a coward.

She'd been in New York almost two weeks now, and in that time she hadn't talked to her father once. It was the longest she had ever gone without any contact with her father, so was it any wonder she felt a bit shaky, a lot like when she'd been eight and her father had removed the training wheels from her bike. He hadn't wanted to take them off, but she'd insisted. No other child on their street over six still used training wheels. She remembered her father running along beside her bike, fearful she would fall, and how he'd locked up her bicycle so she could only ride it when he was there to steady her if she wobbled. She hadn't ridden a bicycle once since that summer.

Anger engulfed her. She hadn't done a lot of things because she feared failure if her father wasn't beside her or because his constant help eliminated the challenge.

"You don't seem to be having a good time." Wendy tossed the last of the bread to her feathered friends and brushed off her hands. "New York was one of the cities you talked about all summer, and I thought you'd be really excited to be here."

"I am excited to be here," Taylor insisted. "It's just that I haven't seen anything but stores and restaurants yet."

"New York *is* stores and restaurants!" Wendy laughed. "Tomorrow night we'll see a Broadway show."

"I'm looking forward to it, but do you know what I really think of when I think of New York?" She went on without waiting for an answer. "The New York Stock Exchange, Chase Manhattan, the United Nations, the publishing district, the corporate headquarters of hundreds of business giants."

Wendy laughed again. "We're quite a pair. We both dreamed of escaping to the city, but neither one of us is happy here. You dreamed of becoming the chairwoman of the board, and I wanted candlelight dinners with a penthouse view. You saw yourself in a power suit, and I envisioned slinky evening gowns. Well, you know what? I adore the things we've seen in all the fabulous stores we've visited, but I didn't buy anything I couldn't have bought just as easily in Twin Falls or Boise. Tommy and I won't have much money to spend on clothes after we're married, so I don't want a closet full of slinky evening gowns I can't wear after I go to the temple. I don't have any place to wear them anyway, and I need to save my money for school!"

"I can't believe you said that!" Taylor burst into laughter.

"See what I mean? I'm a changed woman!" Wendy joined her laughter. "Candlelight dinners and all the glittering lights in the world are no fun if Tommy isn't the man across the table from me."

Taylor stopped laughing. "Don't give up," she told her friend.

"Someday you and Tommy can leave your eight kids and fourteen pets with your parents and come back here for that romantic dinner. You'll have a ball, and your parents will wonder why they were so anxious for you to get married!"

Wendy laughed harder, then she sobered. "If not here, then perhaps an occasional night out in Sun Valley or a weekend in Salt Lake. What really matters is being together forever. You were right about keeping the promises I'll make in the temple. Until I discovered how much Tommy means to me, I really didn't understand how important keeping all the promises we make can be. I was so scared when I was hiding all alone in the mountains, and I kept thinking everything would be all right if Tommy were with me. I prayed the hardest I've ever prayed in my life that he would come, and he did. And both times that Clay prayed, something happened inside me. I want that feeling and Tommy with me forever."

Taylor envied Wendy. Even though she and Tommy would be apart for most of the next three years, and they might grow apart during the long separation, she glowed with hope and dreams. Even her faith in God was new and exciting. She would also be spending her days at Clay's clinic brushing and trimming every dog in town and sticking little pink bows in their hair. If she ran out of dogs, Tommy's cows would likely sport pink bows as well. A wave of melancholy swept over her. She wouldn't be there to see it. Even worse, she wouldn't be part of it.

"Uh, Taylor, I think there's something you should know." Wendy spoke tentatively, and the hesitancy in her voice warned Taylor that Wendy had news she might not like. "Remember it was Sunday a few days after we got here? Last night Tommy said your father went to church that day with your grandmother, and Betty Glendowski came right over and sat beside him. And last night he took her to dinner in Sun Valley."

"You're kidding!" Taylor gasped before dissolving in laughter. Wendy joined her and both girls giggled until tears came to their eyes.

"You're not upset?" Wendy wiped her eyes to ask.

"Serves him right," Taylor sputtered between bursts of laughter.

"Betty really is a nice person," Wendy finally offered. "She's always been kind to me."

"I'm sure you're right," Taylor continued to chuckle. "And my dad really is a good person, too. It's just the idea of Bossy Betty making a play for the Control King!"

"Come on." Wendy reached for her packages. "Let's haul this stuff back to Mrs. Curtis's apartment, then go check out those places you want to see. If we're lucky we'll miss 'dear Jessica.'"

Taylor winced at the tone of Wendy's voice. Wendy and Jessica hadn't exactly hit it off. Rising to her feet, Taylor reached for a couple of Wendy's bags, recalling how hurt Wendy had been by the way Jessica had kept Rambo in her bedroom, making it clear the bird was off-limits to the younger girl. Jessica also made a point of looking down her nose at Wendy's colorful clothes and wildly painted finger-nails, even though the two women actually had quite similar hair-styles and taste in clothes. The only real difference was that Jessica bought her clothes abroad and Wendy bought hers at discount stores.

Jessica never missed an opportunity to point out Wendy's lack of taste and her extreme youth, and she flounced to her room whenever poor Wendy called Tommy. If she didn't know better, she'd think Jessica was jealous of Wendy. But Jessica didn't even know Tommy, and according to her and her would-be mother-in-law, Clay was the only man for her.

A wicked thought occurred to Taylor. Jessica knew Wendy worked for Clay—did she think Clay was the man Wendy was head-over-heels in love with? Taylor couldn't recall Wendy actually mentioning Tommy by name, only as her fiancé or by some endearment. The thought brought a grin to Taylor's face.

They let themselves into the apartment with the key Samantha had given them. Everything looked pristine and lovely, which meant the maid had come and gone. Not a sound met them.

"I guess no one's here," Wendy said.

"Samantha! Jessica!" Taylor called, feeling they should announce themselves. Something about the silence felt heavy, almost ominous. They listened a moment, then made their way to the guest rooms they'd been assigned. Taylor dropped Wendy's purchases on her bed, then started toward her own room. A faint metallic sound brought her to a halt.

"Did you hear something?" Wendy paused, tilting her head to one side as though listening for the sound to repeat itself.

"It was probably just Rambo," Taylor responded, then realizing she was whispering, spoke in a more normal voice. "She probably heard us come in and wants a little attention."

"I'm going to check on her," Wendy stated her intention firmly.

Taylor hesitated, listening for the sound, then said, "You shouldn't enter Jessica's room without an invitation."

"There! I heard it again." Wendy started toward the door. The sound had been louder this time. "Rambo might be sick or her cage could have fallen over."

Reluctantly Taylor followed Wendy down the hall. The other girl paused long enough to knock, then opened the door to Jessica's room without waiting for an answer. Taylor saw only a blur that was Wendy stumbling backward, propelled by a figure pushing her. Before she could move or scream, a heavy body shoved her aside, sending a sharp pain through her shoulder as the man knocked her to the floor. Her head hit the wooden frame of a doorway, leaving her with a sensation of creeping darkness hovering over her.

Resisting the momentary blackness, she struggled to sit up. Her first thought was for Wendy. Panic filled her when she didn't immediately see her friend, and when she would have screamed, she remembered their attacker. He could be nearby and might return if she called Wendy's name.

Dazed and shaken, she pulled herself upright. From the other end of the apartment came the sound of a door closing, followed by the firm click of the latch falling into place. Hopefully that meant the intruder was gone.

"Wendy?" she ventured a whispered call, and when there was no answer, she raised her voice to call louder. "Wendy, are you hurt?"

"I'm all right, but she isn't." Wendy's voice sounded faint and scared. Taylor's eyes focused at last on the other girl, who was sitting with her back propped against the hallway wall, looking straight ahead into Jessica's room.

By the time Taylor reached Wendy, she could see that Wendy was shaking, her eyes still transfixed on something she could see in the bedroom. Taylor turned toward Jessica's bedroom and saw Clay's former fiancée sprawled motionless on the floor beside her unmade bed. Taylor shoved back the dizziness that threatened to send her spiraling toward the floor again and moved unsteadily toward the body. She noted the pale taupe silk pajamas and the bare soles of the woman's feet. Gingerly she knelt, staring at Jessica's thick mane of silky curls.

"Is she dead?" Wendy whispered from the doorway. Taylor didn't immediately answer. She couldn't. For one thing she didn't know the answer to the question, and for another, her vocal chords seemed to be malfunctioning. Overcoming a reluctance to touch the unnaturally still figure, Taylor brushed the deep red curls aside and pressed her fingers against Jessica's carotid artery. She nearly wept with joy when a slight flutter met her touch.

"She's alive!" She shared the good news with Wendy but kept her attention focused on Jessica. She examined the unconscious woman as carefully as she could, without moving her, for any sign of an injury. She was relieved to see no blood or wound other than a lump the size of a small egg on Jessica's temple. She'd been struck, and struck hard, by something.

"Should I call an ambulance?" Wendy asked. Taylor looked up to see Wendy standing beside a large, draped birdcage resting on the floor. From the squawks emanating from behind the black cover, she assumed Rambo was fine but not too happy.

"Yes. Use the phone in the den. I don't think we should touch anything in here," she answered Wendy's question. She heard Wendy leave, then pulled the bedspread from the bed to cover Jessica. She'd read somewhere that a person who was unconscious should be kept warm.

Wondering what she should do while waiting for the ambulance, she nervously looked around and was startled to find that the room was nothing like she'd expected. Instead of the pale colors and whites Jessica seemed to prefer, the room was decorated in decidedly masculine shades of navy and maroon. Wildlife posters and equestrian prints hung on one wall, and a sturdy bookcase, stuffed to overflowing with books, was topped with sports trophies. A man's silver hairbrushes mingled with feminine toiletries on a nearby bureau. Closet doors stood open, revealing ladies' apparel hanging beside trousers and jackets that definitely didn't belong to Jessica. A small table beside the bed held a hinged picture frame. On one side was a group shot of an elderly white-haired man and four smiling young people. Jessica was the only female in the group. The other half of the frame held a photo of Jessica and Clay, and they certainly looked happy.

Comprehension came slowly, leaving Taylor stunned. The room was Clay's! With two empty guest rooms, Samantha had given Jessica Clay's bedroom. All the implications of the gesture swirled through Taylor's head, and she felt herself growing angry, whether for Clay's sake or her own, she didn't know. She just knew Jessica had no business touching Clay's things, sitting at his desk, or sleeping in his bed. If Samantha thought she could . . . A chill slid down Taylor's neck. Where was Samantha?

"Wendy!" she called in a half-scream. "Mrs. Curtis! Samantha! Where is she?" She jumped to her feet and peered fearfully toward the door.

"She's not here," Wendy spoke before hurrying into the room. "When I called for an ambulance, I saw a note for Jessica beside the phone from Samantha. She said she was meeting a friend for lunch. The ambulance should be here in a few minutes."

Kneeling once more, Taylor checked Jessica's pulse. Jessica groaned and shifted as though she might be about to awake. In the distance Taylor picked out the wail of a siren and sought to reassure the injured woman. "The paramedics are coming," she whispered. "They'll take you to a hospital and help you."

Jessica moaned and attempted to sit up. "Don't move," Taylor encouraged her to lie still until help arrived. The buzz of the intercom sent Wendy scrambling to let the paramedics in.

"Don't let anyone in," Jessica suddenly spoke in a faint, tearful voice.

"It's the paramedics. They'll help you," Taylor attempted to offer reassurance.

"I don't want anyone to see me." A tear slid down Jessica's pale cheek. "My head hurts," she added with a moan.

"It's all right." Taylor attempted to sooth the distraught woman. "You've been hurt, and the paramedics will give you something to stop the pain."

"Where's Clay? He can't marry that silly girl!" Jessica sounded hysterical. "I won't let him! He's mine!"

"Clay isn't going to marry Wendy," Taylor attempted to quiet the upset young woman. "She's engaged to Tommy Beredsford."

"Engaged? Tommy? But Clay said . . ." She didn't finish whatever Clay had told her but seemed to slip back into unconsciousness.

Taylor visually searched the room as though looking for something to cling to. *Please, Heavenly Father . . . ,* she mouthed, not even certain what she prayed for. Her eyes lit on the picture frame, and she realized the elderly man must have been Jessica's grandfather. She looked like him, in a more feminine way. The other three men must be her cousins, she decided. They didn't look much like her, but two of them looked vaguely familiar. Peering closer, Taylor stifled a gasp. The one standing beside Jessica looked remarkably like the driver of the car that forced Peggy Friedrickson off the road!

"I didn't tell him . . ." Jessica's voice sounded faint as she tried to speak again.

"What?" Taylor tried to make sense of Jessica's words while her mind still struggled with the possibility that one of Jessica's cousins was responsible for the near tragedy that occurred two thousand miles away.

"About the diamonds . . . I told him Clay . . . you have to warn him . . ." Jessica mumbled a few words, then her voice trailed off.

Taylor's attention focused sharply on Jessica's words at the mention of Clay's name. "What about Clay?" she questioned.

"The diamonds," Jessica answered in a dazed voice. "I told him Clay kept the diamonds when he sent Rambo back."

"You what?" Taylor practically shouted, but Jessica didn't answer. She was still as two young men carrying black bags followed Wendy into the room.

Samantha arrived before the paramedics left the apartment with Jessica. She insisted on accompanying them to the hospital to be with the woman she claimed was "practically her daughter-in-law."

"I think Clay would disagree," Wendy muttered as she closed the door firmly behind the trio surrounding the stretcher carrying Jessica toward the elevator.

"About what?" Taylor asked, her mind still on the conversation she'd had with Jessica. The young woman had sounded almost like she knew her attacker. Could her suspicions be correct? She chewed her bottom lip. And what was that business about telling her attacker that Clay had the diamonds?

"Clay isn't going to make Jessica Samantha's daughter-in-law, no matter how much she wants him to," Wendy expressed her opinion emphatically. "I think he has someone else in mind for that role."

Taylor ignored the innuendo she knew was aimed at her. "Wendy, come with me. I want to show you a picture, then I think we should go home." When Wendy looked startled, she told her what Jessica had said while waiting for the ambulance. She hesitated, then decided to let Wendy see the photograph without first sharing her suspicions.

"It's him! The man at the bank!" Wendy pointed to the same man Taylor suspected of being the hit-and-run driver. "And that's the man I saw bending over Jessica when I opened her door!" She pointed to another face in the photo.

"We probably should call the police, but something tells me those two are already on their way to Fairfield. We should go home, too, to warn Clay," Taylor said.

"You're right," Wendy agreed and the wide smile that lit her face told Taylor that Wendy wasn't at all sorry to cut short their visit to the city. "I'll start packing."

"And I'll call the airline to see how soon we can get a flight." Taylor was suddenly all business. It wasn't until after reservations were made and she was closing her suitcase that she realized she'd called Fairfield "home."

CHAPTER 21

Clay pulled into his usual parking space and cut the motor of his truck. It wasn't dark yet, though the heavy thunder clouds gave an illusion of approaching night. It seemed strange to return to his office so early, but things had gone well all day, and several calls had taken less time than expected. Truly a rare day! He considered grabbing some bait and heading for a fishing stream for a few hours but decided against it. From the look of the sky, it would soon be raining. Besides without an office manager, there were a few things he needed to check on to be ready for tomorrow.

As he climbed out of his truck, he paused a moment to look over his soon-to-be clinic. A feeling of pride swept over him as he admired its straight, clean lines and envisioned the improvements in the service he could provides for his patients when he moved his practice into the new clinic. He'd made daily inspections for two weeks, with each visit increasing his anticipation of moving into the building. It was the fulfillment of a dream. He considered making a quick tour of the building, then decided against it. He really did need to look at his schedule for tomorrow and order some antibiotics.

As he walked toward Lilly's house, he noticed in an abstract way that the workmen had already left for the day. Then he remembered it was Friday, and Bib had told him his men would be leaving early on Friday since two of them had a wedding to attend in another town, and the third one had asked for a day off to take his kids camping. Clay glanced at the threatening clouds and hoped the campers weren't tent-camping. At the door a sound behind him caught his attention. He turned to see Bib Jones's old truck clattering up the drive.

Thinking the contractor had forgotten something, he waved to the other man before stepping into his office.

Seating himself at the computer, he noticed right away that he had mail. As he checked the messages, he felt a grin spread across his face. Until Taylor and Wendy had left for New York, he'd had no idea how organized his office really was. His clients could e-mail their concerns, and make appointments electronically anytime, night or day, which meant no more missed messages from the supply store or animal pharmacy in Twin Falls, and he could find his bank balance with a couple of clicks. He was impressed, too, with the medical and veterinarian sites, including a pharmaceutical dictionary Taylor had bookmarked for him. Scanning his field notes into a waiting file took mere seconds. His telephone calls were all neatly recorded, and a fax machine added to the ease with which he could send and receive communications. The office could almost run itself, he thought, and with that, his smile faded.

He didn't want his office to run by itself. He wanted Taylor back in the chair he presently occupied. She'd done a great job of arranging his office so that even someone with practically no office skills, namely Wendy, could handle the day-to-day operation. But it wasn't an office manager he wanted back. As much as he appreciated the efficient way his office operated, it was the woman, not the secretary, he missed. Well, to be truthful, he did miss having an office manager. There were some things only a real person could handle, and the efficiency of the programs Taylor had set up would gradually disappear without her there to keep them updated.

He missed Taylor, not only in his office, but everywhere he went. Her image already haunted him each time he stepped into the small bathroom upstairs or seated himself at Lilly's breakfast table. He couldn't look out the window without seeing the tree where she'd flung her shoes at him as she dangled from a high branch at the beginning of the summer. She was everywhere—the highway leading to Twin Falls, in the river, at the Friedrickson ranch, and in the mountains and canyons. Even finding himself seated behind Betty Glendowski and Taylor's father at church a few days ago had left him feeling lonely and empty because Taylor wasn't beside him.

How had he let this happen? How could he have allowed himself to fall in love with Taylor? Perhaps a more pertinent question would be, why had it taken him so long to realize he was in love with her? A voice in the back of his head kept demanding to know what he was going to do about it. What *could* he do about it? His life was here and when Taylor returned from New York, she would go to her father's house in Pocatello to pack up the remainder of her things before moving to San Francisco to begin her career.

Idly, he clicked a few more sites Taylor had marked as favorites and nearly fell off his chair when pictures of his clinic filled the screen. He'd already figured out that she hadn't heeded his orders to stay away from his plans for his clinic. As he perused a virtual tour of the construction site, he understood better why Bib had suddenly become so industrious.

"Doc! Doc Curtis!"

He looked up to see the contractor lumbering across Lilly's back lawn toward the sunporch. Hurriedly he rose to his feet and met Bib Jones at the door.

"You better come quick!" Bib panted. "Vandals have near wrecked the place."

Quick steps carried Clay across the lawn. He vaulted the hedge while Bib took the longer route through the gate. His mind churned with questions. Had the thieves who had broken into Lilly's house returned? Surely they didn't think he'd hidden Rambo in an unfinished building?

"Clay!"

He paused, thinking he had to be hallucinating. For a moment he'd imagined he heard Taylor calling his name.

"Clay!" He heard his name again. Slowly he turned around. He hadn't imagined anything! Taylor, in gray slacks and a white blouse, was hurrying toward him along the gravel lane on his side of the hedge. A bright red cardigan sweater fluttered from her shoulders, held in place by a single button. He took a step toward her, and it was the most natural thing in the world to wrap his arms around her. Forgetting his clinic and the vandals, he hugged her tight, reveling in the feel of her in his arms. She'd come back!

At the same time he became conscious she was pulling away from him, he heard labored breathing behind him and remembered the contractor. Slowly he dropped his arms to his sides.

"'Evening, Taylor," Bib greeted her. "You'll want to see this, too," he went on indignantly. "Someone wrote all over them walls I just got painted. Made a devil of a mess, dumping paint, breaking windows, and all that!"

"Then I'm too late," Taylor cried.

"Too late?" Clay questioned.

"Yes, Wendy and I flew back to warn you," Taylor began her explanation. "Jessica told him you have the diamonds."

Perplexed, Clay stared at her. "She told him . . . ? Taylor, you're not making a lot of sense."

"I know. It's a long story and it's starting to rain. Do you think we could go inside?" Taylor asked, casting a fearful glance toward the trees and shrubs surrounding the new clinic.

Seeing her hesitation to continue their conversation until they were alone, Clay ushered her toward the front door. Bib followed as far as the doorway, where all three paused to look at the trashed room.

"This is awful!" Taylor exploded. "They won't get away with it," she assured the unhappy contractor. "This time I know who is responsible. Have either of you called the sheriff's office?"

Both men shook their heads. "I wanted to see the damage first," Clay explained. "As soon as I finish looking around I'll call, but what do you mean you know who is responsible?"

"When I get my hands on those kids . . ." Bib started.

"It wasn't anyone from around here, and you don't know them," Taylor quickly assured him. "And they aren't kids."

"Are you sure?" Clay asked. Taylor nodded her head emphatically. He looked a little doubtful, but she didn't say anything more. He suspected she wouldn't until they were alone.

He turned to the older man. "Bib, I appreciate your coming to get me so promptly, but I don't want to keep you any later. I can call the sheriff, and if he needs to speak with you, I'll give him your phone number."

"Well, in that case, I'll leave you folks now and get on home to dinner. I'll be back in the morning to clean up and see what needs fixin'." Bib shook his head once more before saying good night and making his way back to his parked truck.

Clay paid scant attention to the departing vehicle or the rain that had begun to fall. Even the vandalism of his clinic faded in importance. His whole attention focused on Taylor, and he had to struggle to keep from taking her in his arms again, and telling her how much he'd missed her. Instead he spoke gruffly in an effort to camouflage his feelings. "All right," he began, "what are you doing back here so soon? And what makes you think you know who is responsible for this mess?" He waved his arm around the paint-spattered room. He might fool her into thinking his only concern was for his clinic, but he couldn't fool himself.

It didn't take long to fill him in on the attack on Jessica and to tell him she'd recognized Jessica's cousin as the man driving the speeding Sunfire earlier in the summer.

"Is Jessica going to be all right?" Clay asked, shock evident in his voice. Taylor had to remind herself that Clay and Jessica had been friends for years, long before they became romantically involved, and that it was only natural for him to be concerned about a woman he'd known most of his life. It also made her feel small to recognize a flash of jealousy.

"You're sure it was one of the men with Jessica in that picture who was driving the car?" Clay asked. "The glimpse you caught of the driver of that car was awfully brief."

"I know," Taylor conceded. "But I know I'm right. Besides Wendy confirmed it. He and one of the other cousins were the same men who attacked her."

"I know all three of Jessica's cousins were pretty upset when they discovered how much their grandfather had favored Jessica in the disposition of his estate. Jacob seemed particularly concerned that the old man had tied his hands by eliminating a financial cushion he could draw on if the company faced a cash-flow problem. Jacob had some expansion plans that had to be put on hold, but the company's stock is holding steady, and frankly, I just can't see him involving himself in something like this. On the other hand, when he learned his grandfather had promised all four of the Winslow diamonds to Jessica, he did become pretty angry. He argued that each of the cousins should have one of the gems. Seth and Ben were particularly livid since they only received small stock portions and no cash. They both hold positions in the company, but they don't share their brother's commitment to the firm. They would rather play and party than work."

"I take it Jessica refused to share," Taylor speculated.

"She was quite adamant about that." Clay's response was on the dry side, but after meeting Jessica, Taylor had a pretty good idea of how explosive Jessica's response to the suggestion had been.

Clay ushered her forward to take a better look at the rest of the clinic, and they slowly made their way through the debris littering the floor. Even in the waning light, they could see broken construction materials, shattered glass, and the crude obscenities painted on the walls. Clay felt sick at the wasted material and the inevitable delay in completing the clinic that would follow the wanton destruction.

After viewing the office and several examination rooms, Clay held open one of the two doors leading to a room designed for small animal surgery. When a flip of the light switch brought no results, he continued to hold the door to allow the fading light to filter inside. Stepping past him into the surgery, Taylor looked around and shuddered. Foul words covered the walls, and a bucket of paint had been dashed against the surgical cabinets.

"Clay, look at this," she called when she managed to make out the words written across one wall.

"Just a minute." Clay reached for an unopened paint can lying nearby to prop against the door before picking his way across the room to stand beside her.

"DIAMONDS OR DEATH!" he read aloud, ending with a snort of derision. "A little melodramatic, wouldn't you say?"

"You don't think they mean it?" she asked, remembering Jessica. She wasn't too sure Jessica would have survived if she and Wendy hadn't returned to the condo when they did. If Jessica's cousins were responsible for the attack on her, what might they do to Clay and herself?

"No, I don't think that threat is anything more than an attempt to scare us," Clay theorized with confidence. "Even Seth is smart enough to figure out that if I have the diamonds and he kills me, I won't be able to tell him where they're hidden."

The sound of a slamming door met their ears. Startled they turned toward the sound and saw only blackness. Claustrophobic panic had Taylor grasping for Clay's shirt.

"It's all right," Clay assured her and she was grateful for the arm he slipped around her shoulders. "It's storming pretty hard now and with windows broken out, a gust of wind blew the door shut. It's nothing to worry about."

But she did worry, especially when a sound much like running footsteps reached her ears. Clay didn't say anything, so she tried to dismiss the sound as runaway imagination, but she found she had to ask.

"Clay, did you . . . ?" A loud crash came from above them, and she didn't finish the question.

"We'd better get out of here," Clay warned softly. He reached for her hand and slowly they felt their way along the wall to the closed door. Several times the smooth wall turned slippery to her touch and she knew she'd run her fingers over the still-wet graffiti.

At last Clay recognized the change in texture as his hand swept across the door, and he quickly found the door knob. Nothing happened when he twisted it.

"It's stuck," he grunted as he shoved his shoulder against the door. Taylor added her weight to his but even their combined efforts didn't move the door.

"There's another door on the other side of the room; let's find it," he tried to speak confidently, but some premonition was making him uneasy. He tried to attribute the feeling to the intense blackness of the room. Being designed as a surgery, there were no windows in the room. With no power in the building, the lateness of the hour, and a storm blotting out any light that might have been provided by the moon or stars, no light seeped under the doors.

It didn't take long to work their way to the other door, and he wasn't surprised to find it wouldn't open either. After several futile attempts to force the door open, Taylor asked, "What are we going to do?"

He had no idea, but he didn't want to scare Taylor further by admitting that. "I guess we just wait. Your grandmother will miss you pretty soon and come looking for you."

"She doesn't know I'm back," Taylor told him, and he was glad to note her voice sounded steady. She'd admitted her claustrophobia to him when they'd kept watch that night in Tommy's cave. "Tommy met us in Boise, and he and Wendy dropped me off here. I didn't even take my bag inside the house. When I saw you and Bib hurrying toward the clinic, I set both my bag and my purse on the front porch and came after you. By now the rain has probably ruined them both."

Clay was quiet for several minutes, worrying how the forced confinement in the dark would affect Taylor. She'd had a few unpleasant moments in the cave, and this was far worse. Finally he warned, "We may be trapped here all night until Bib returns to clean up."

"I know," she spoke without panic. "I'll be all right. You're with me and that helps."

Her simple statement of faith touched him deeply. He reached for her hand once more and led her to where they could sit with their backs to the cabinets. It wasn't the most comfortable spot in the world, but it wasn't too bad either. They were together, and he knew he would cherish this night for the rest of his life. Only an hour ago he'd feared that he might never see her again except for those rare times when she might briefly visit her grandmother. Now he had the whole night before him.

Hoping physical contact and conversation would keep Taylor distracted, he placed an arm around her. When she leaned her head against his shoulder, he decided the physical contact part was working—for him anyway. He certainly felt distracted. But he figured he'd better work a little harder at distracting her.

"What did you think of New York?" he asked, trying to get the conversation part of his plan going.

"It's interesting." She paused before going on. "New York is a fascinating city, but unfortunately I saw little of the part of the city I wanted to see. We visited Bergdorf Goodman when I really wanted to see the New York Stock Exchange. I wanted to see the Winslow corporate offices, instead I saw a glittering showroom. The UN head-quarters was on my must-see list, but your mother had reservations for Elizabeth Arden and tea at the Plaza Hotel."

Clay chuckled. "I should have known Mother would have her own ideas about the important sights to see."

"Your mother was kind to me, but I don't feel I really got to know her. She's was always busy with luncheons and various committees where the conversation was so polite and trivial, no one ever really said anything. At home she fussed over Jessica, and though I wouldn't say she ignored me, she made it quite clear she didn't approve of Wendy and had little time for either of us," Taylor told him.

"Poor Wendy," Clay laughed. "She doesn't exactly make a great first impression."

"That's not true," Taylor defended her friend. "She was on her best behavior this whole trip. No bare midriffs, only one pair of earrings at a time, not one miniskirt the whole trip, and she only took four colors of nail polish to New York with us. She loved the shopping trips your mother planned. The problem was you!"

"Me?" Clay was incredulous. "But I've never given Mother any reason to dislike Wendy. I've only ever said nice things about her. When I thought she was the magician managing my office, I praised her endlessly, and come to think of it, I haven't mentioned to my mother yet that you were the real miracle worker."

"That was doubtless part of the problem," Taylor told him. "She and Jessica heard all the praise you heaped on Wendy, but since neither one has any interest in your business, they interpreted everything you said as interest in Wendy herself. Then when Wendy made no secret of being in love and called Tommy every night, they both assumed you are the man in her life," Taylor informed him.

Clay groaned. "Mother still hasn't given up hope that I'll marry Jessica."

"Neither has Jessica," Taylor reminded him.

"They're both wrong," Clay spoke with certainty in his voice. The only woman he wanted to marry was the one in his arms right now. He pulled her a bit closer. He wished he could tell her his feelings. For several minutes he said nothing. He couldn't tell Taylor how the initial attraction he'd felt for her at the beginning of the summer, and which he'd fought so rigorously, had grown to so much more. His mind drifted pleasantly over all the pictures it had stored of Taylor over the summer.

"What is that sound?" Taylor's voice jarred him and he realized he'd nearly fallen asleep. He blinked his eyes in the darkness and shrugged off the sleepiness that was making him feel a bit too relaxed if he was going to keep Taylor distracted from her fear of close places. He leaned his head to the side and attempted to hear whatever Taylor had heard.

The sound of rain striking against the building reached his ears, and he could hear some kind of vehicle not too far away. He heard Taylor yawn. If she was half as tired as he was, perhaps she'd fall asleep and they could both rest until Bib returned in the morning.

No, he didn't want to fall asleep so soon. This would be the only night he'd have with her; he didn't want to spend it sleeping. He wanted to savor this one time he'd be able to hold Taylor close and pretend it was forever.

"How long will the oxygen last in this room?" Taylor suddenly asked, and this time there was a nervous edge to her voice.

"We don't have to worry about running out of air," Clay attempted to reassure her. Evidently he wasn't doing a good enough job keeping her claustrophobia at bay. "Enough air will come under the doors to prevent that from happening."

"Then why do I feel lightheaded? I can hardly stay awake!" Taylor protested.

"You're tired," Clay tried to convince her of the normality of her fatigue. "You just finished a long flight, following a harrowing experience." He ended with a yawn of his own.

"You're tired, too." It sounded like an accusation.

"Yes, I am tired." His voice sounded slurred and his head hurt. He had a right to be tired, but he didn't often get headaches. He worked long hours . . . yes, but today he'd quit early. He never felt this tired when he worked a hard day and tumbled into bed around midnight or got called out in the middle of the night.

"Clay, do you think Jessica's cousins are still here?" Taylor's voice sounded groggy and far away like that car. No, the engine was bigger than a car engine. It was a truck.

He struggled to pull his thoughts together and answer Taylor's question. "Ben and Seth? Why would they be here?"

"They want Jessica's diamonds and she told them you have them, remember? I think they locked us in here to scare you into giving them the diamonds." Taylor sounded like a frightened child. Something in her voice pushed him to struggle against the overwhelming urge to sleep. Taylor admitted to having a fear of enclosed spaces, but she wasn't a fearful child; she was brave and intelligent. Could she be right? Had Ben and Seth locked them in here?

Alarm bells began going off in his head. Something was wrong. The drone of an engine suddenly sounded like a threat. Either he was becoming paranoid, or they had to get out of their accidental prison. Or was it accidental?

"Taylor!" he spoke sharply and the way she jerked told him she had been nearly asleep. "We've got to get out of here. Let's go back over by the door."

"Okay," she mumbled, but he had to nudge her to get her to start moving. The crawl back to the door was torturous. His lungs ached and he longed to stop and rest. Perhaps if he'd been alone, he would have given up, but he couldn't stop when he knew that stopping might cost Taylor her life. He had no doubt now that they were breathing carbon monoxide fumes and that sleep would be death.

CHAPTER 22

"Why do they want to kill us?" Taylor gasped, and he knew she was just as aware of what was happening as he was. She was smart and had probably figured it out even sooner than he had.

"Don't talk," he whispered. He wasn't concerned with being overheard, but speech would only accelerate the loss of breathable air and exhaust them faster.

At last he found the door. Dropping flat, he attempted to run his fingers beneath it. They would only go far enough to convince him some obstruction was lodged in the space under the door. He poked and pushed, skinning his knuckles, but he couldn't move his fingers far enough to push whatever it was away. He felt Taylor's hand next to his on the floor and knew she'd had the same idea.

"Carpet . . . rags . . . something wedged tight," she muttered.

"Can you move it?" he asked with his mouth pressed against her ear. He hoped her smaller hands could accomplish what his larger ones could not.

"There!" Her voice was triumphant. "I moved it a little."

Sweet, rain-washed air filled his nostrils where he lay with his face against the floor. Taylor lay beside him, and the hiccuping breaths she took told him she was scared. Her fear filled him with anger. Somehow he had to get her out of here and find whoever had done this terrible thing. Taking deep gulps of the clean air, he felt his mind clear slightly, enough to let him know they still weren't out of danger. The small amount of clean air coming under the door wouldn't save them.

"We have to get out of here," Taylor said. "Seth and Ben might be here, and they could have heard me tell you I could identify them.

Even if they think we're dead, they won't leave without trying once more to get the diamonds. They've searched here. What if they've gone back to Grandma Lilly's house to search again. This time they might hurt her!"

Her words galvanized him. They needed more air, and they needed a way out. Lying flat on the floor his belt buckle scraped against the floor, giving him an idea. Stripping off the belt, he pushed the stiff leather against the rags stuffed under the door. It was tedious work, and he wondered as he jabbed the stiff point under the door repeatedly if it was worth the effort he was expending. When he felt the obstruction shift at last, he lay still for several minutes gulping in the widened trickle of clean air before struggling to his knees.

"Stay here," he whispered to Taylor in a grim voice, etched with worry. "I'll clear the other door." He didn't doubt he would find the space under the other door blocked as well.

"No, I'm coming with you," she said.

"You'll be safer here where there's a little breathable air." He gathered his feet beneath him to stand and touched her shoulder, encouraging her to remain near the pocket of air. Taking a couple of deep breaths of the air flowing under the door, she arose to her feet and he gave up arguing. She was too claustrophobic to stay alone. He reached for her hand and felt it tremble in his. Holding on to each other, they began the trip across the room to the other door.

"Wait!" She stopped short.

His heart took a dive. If she was already so weak she couldn't make it across the room, what chance did they have? He reached for her, knowing he'd do anything to get her safely back to the stream of air flowing under the door. To his surprise he found she was removing her cardigan.

"The pipe!" she said, breathing as little as possible, but her words galvanized him. He'd given no thought to the source of the exhaust fumes, only to ventilating the room. He should have considered finding a way to stop the deadly gas from entering their prison. Why hadn't he thought of locating the source of the threat?

The opening through the block wall, intended to carry electrical wires to the outside horse grooming area, was the logical conduit since electrical wiring hadn't been run through it yet. The exhaust from the engine they could hear running had to be pumping the fumes through that pipe. If the pipe was blocked, the gas couldn't reach them and the engine might even stall.

With a couple of sweeps of his hands along the wall, he located the pipe he'd noticed in his earlier surveys of the construction area. Taking Taylor's sweater, he worked feverishly to stuff it into the small opening Bib had left for the electric wires. He mustn't cough, he admonished himself in a vain effort to resist breathing the foul gas. His head reeled and his hands shook.

A wave of dizziness sent him staggering to his knees. He could do no more. Taylor tugged at his sleeve and he roused himself, aware he needed to get back to the door. His lungs were screaming for air and his head felt too heavy for his neck to support. Whether it was Taylor's persistent tug on his arm or something deep in his soul that urged him on, he found the strength to struggle toward the door.

Confused and disoriented, he fought the urge to lie still and sleep. Taylor's hand constantly reminded him he wasn't alone. If he gave up, she would waste her tenuous strength trying to rouse him and she would die, too. He couldn't let that happen.

A whimper of sound reached his ears and he realized Taylor was crying. His brave, strong Taylor was crying! The sound brought all of his protective instincts forward. He'd get her out of here somehow! Shaking off the heavy fog that surrounded him, he placed an arm around Taylor and willed his tired legs to carry him the remaining distance.

It seemed to take an interminable length of time to locate the door, but when his fingers finally stubbed against the frame, he sank to his knees, pulling Taylor with him. Pressing themselves to the floor, he discovered they weren't out of danger yet. No cool air flowed beneath the heavy door. Had he gotten confused and found the wrong door or had their captors replaced the rags he and Taylor had laboriously pushed aside?

Reaching for his belt, he discovered it wasn't around his waist. He'd had it when they started toward the second door, but he must have dropped it when they stopped to stuff Taylor's sweater in the pipe. Futilely he jabbed his fingers against the bottom of the door. His fingertips touched the rags, but he couldn't push them far enough to dislodge them. Taylor wiggled closer and he slid away a few inches to allow her better access. They needed a tool—almost anything would do—a screwdriver, a wire, even a . . . nail file. "Do you have a nail file?" he coughed as he attempted to speak.

"No . . . left purse . . . porch." Taylor's voice was thin and bordering on panic.

There had to be something he could do. It was so hard to think. At least if they died, they would do so together. No, they weren't going to die. He wouldn't even consider that possibility. But they would, if they didn't get out of here in the next few minutes. If only he weren't so sleepy . . .

Slowly he became aware that Taylor's arm was still. She was no longer trying to push the rags away. "Taylor!" It should have been a scream, but only a hoarse croak came from his throat. Evidently it was enough to partially rouse her, because a low moan that might have been his name reached his ears.

"Please, God, help us," he found himself praying. "Please don't let Taylor die." Fervently he poured out his heart until warmth and peace entered his soul. Whatever happened, it would be all right.

Taylor made a low sound like a child whimpering in her sleep, and he reached for her, pulling her close. His thoughts swirled in his brain like a kaleidoscope gone mad, but one thought emerged. He didn't want to die together; he wanted them to live together until they were old, then continue on together forever. It didn't matter where they lived, so long as they were together. If God would give them another chance, he would sell his practice and move back to New York, go to San Francisco, anywhere she wanted to go, just so he could come home to her at the end of every day and hold her through every night.

"Taylor, I love you," he whispered into the silky hair covering her ear. She didn't respond and his eyes closed. He shifted to hold her closer and felt a sharp jab to his knee. With one hand he reached to brush aside the round, flat object, but instead of brushing it aside, he grasped it. His befuddled brain told him there was some significance to the object, but he couldn't think why it mattered.

Slowly, as though a parent were explaining to a child, the prompting came. He held the round lid of a paint can in his hand, knowing it would fit under the door.

"Hold on," he whispered to Taylor as he gently released his hold on her. "Don't give up."

With clumsy hands he thrust the metal lid under the door and withdrew it to push it under again. Air, laden with the wonderful sweet aroma of rain, flowed beneath the door. Quickly he ran the stiff piece of metal the width of the door before dropping it to move Taylor closer to the stream of air flowing in its wake. Lying flat beside her, he reveled in the small cross-current of air moving across the floor, telling him the other door was still unobstructed.

"Taylor," he whispered with his last remaining strength. She coughed and he felt a shudder run through her. His hand covered hers as he lay beside her greedily gulping the rain-scented air, praying it would be enough.

"Clay! Dr. Curtis!" The sound of his name came faintly to his ears. He might be imagining the old man's voice. Or it might be the answer to his prayer. If Stewart Darnell was here in this unfinished building, he had to draw his attention and let him know he and Taylor needed help.

"Some . . . one here," Taylor murmured and he felt a wave of hope. Taylor wasn't unconscious, and Brother Darnell was really searching for them. Drawing on all the strength he could muster, he kicked his boot against the door, hoping the old man would hear the sound.

The air seeping under the door was reviving her senses, and Taylor became aware of the sounds Stewart was making on the other side of the thick wood panel. A sliver of light danced across the narrow line where she pressed her face. Squeezing her eyes tightly shut, she whispered a prayer of thanksgiving. She'd been so afraid of dying in this small, dark space.

"Hurry, Stewart! Push!" Her grandmother's voice reached her ears and her relief intensified. Despite their obsession to gain the diamonds, the Winslow brothers hadn't injured her grandmother.

"Grandma!" Taylor choked out the single word.

"Hush, don't try to talk," Clay cautioned and the concern in his voice revived her further. Remembrance of his whispered declaration of love filled her heart to overflowing for a moment until doubt flooded into her mind. She'd been more asleep than awake; she might have imagined the words. She was still so groggy, perhaps she was only imagining right now the tender concern in his voice.

The door flew open, sending a wave of fresh air to bathe her face and hands. With it came a circle of light and the sharp gasp of Grandma Lilly as she discovered not only Clay, but her grand-daughter lying on the floor.

"Taylor! I thought you were safe in New York!" The elderly woman knelt beside her.

"Don't dawdle, dear," Stewart's voice commanded. "We've got to get these two out of here, and it won't do any of us any good to keep breathing exhaust fumes either."

As the older couple helped them to their feet and led them, stumbling outside, she heard Clay ask, "How did you know we were here . . . that we needed help?"

"We didn't at first," Stewart answered. "We had dinner at my son's home, and I was just bringing Lilly home when we passed a car parked in the bushes where it don't belong about a block from here. Then when we got to the house, we saw all the lights were on, and there were shadows moving around inside, both upstairs and downstairs."

"We knew it wasn't Andrew because he took Betty to a movie, so we sneaked up to a window and peaked in," Grandma Lilly's voice turned indignant. "A stranger was snooping through your files, and since we knew there was more than one intruder, we backed off and decided we'd better find a telephone."

"That's when we noticed your truck parked where you always park it," Stewart added. "We thought you'd just arrived and that you were inspecting your clinic like you do most nights. So we hurried over here to warn you. When we passed your truck, I remembered your cell phone and looked inside, thinking we could use it to call the deputy. I didn't see the phone, but something told me to pick up that big flashlight I saw sitting on the seat and come here after you."

"We had no idea you were here, too." Lilly hugged Taylor. "It was that generator of Bib's running on and on and the mess we found the minute we walked through the door that told us something was wrong."

"I'll be forever grateful you showed up when you did," Clay wheezed and bent forward with his hands resting on his knees while he breathed deeply. After a moment he straightened and spoke again. "You'd better turn the light off. I don't think I want those guys to look out the window, see the light, and know we've escaped."

The light clicked off. For just a second the panic of being enclosed in darkness returned to her, but gradually Taylor's eyes adjusted. Her stomach still felt queasy, but that was probably due to breathing the carbon monoxide-laden air. Her legs felt wobbly, too, she realized when she tried to take a few steps on her own.

She would have fallen, but for both Clay and Lilly reaching out to steady her. Clay's hand trembled almost as much as her own.

"Taylor needs to sit down and rest," her grandmother spoke over her head to the two men. "She ought to be in a hospital."

"Clay, too," Stewart agreed.

"I'm all right, but we can't rest here. Ben and Seth might come back to check on us," Clay pointed out.

"I don't think either one of them can make it to your car, Stewart," Lilly worried. "Maybe we should take Clay's truck, even though those awful men will probably hear the engine start. We can be a long way from here before they get to their car and try to follow us."

"I left my keys along with my phone in the office," Clay told the older couple. "You two go ahead. The rain has stopped and we can hide in the trees until you bring help."

"You'll get wet," Lilly objected.

"I don't mind," Taylor agreed with Clay's suggestion and Grandma Lilly finally capitulated.

Taylor leaned on her grandmother as they moved slowly toward the row of trees and shrubs separating the two properties. She felt guilty placing so much of her weight on the older woman. She was young and strong; she should be helping her grandmother, not the other way around. A glance at Clay told her he was having the same trouble accepting Stewart's help.

A trickle of rain water made its way down the back of her collar as she wedged her way into the thick shrubs. The ground was reasonably dry where she sank to sit with her back against a tree trunk, breathing hard. Thankfully the thick canopy of leaves had protected the ground somewhat. She felt Clay take his place beside her and heard him whisper a warning to her grandmother and Stewart to be careful and to stay well away from the house.

After the older couple disappeared from sight, Clay leaned back against the tree trunk, too. She welcomed the warmth of his big body beside her, and it seemed the most natural thing in the world when he wrapped an arm around her shoulders and slid a little closer.

It may have been a few minutes or half an hour before she noticed that a gap in the hedge they cowered behind provided her with an excellent view of the back of Grandma Lilly's house. Through it she could see two figures moving with frantic haste inside the house, picking up and discarding items as they rushed around. She straightened, leaning slightly forward, when she spotted two more figures slipping around the side of the house and moving surreptitiously toward the tree supporting the old tree house. It took a moment longer for it to register that the pair sneaking across the grass was her father and Betty Glendowski, and that they were heading toward the deep shadows under the old tree. They paused beneath the limb where she'd once dangled, and to Taylor's astonishment, the two figures melded into one!

Clay stared at the couple standing no more than twenty feet away. When he'd first spotted them moving almost stealthily around the side of the house, he'd thought Stewart and Lilly had returned with some dangerous scheme to attempt to thwart the robbers. It didn't take long to recognize the pair as both younger and heavier than his elderly friends. His fingers tightened on Taylor's shoulder as he worried whether they were friend or foe.

He was still debating whether to warn the couple or to keep his and Taylor's position secret when the larger of the two looked up, his attention caught by the two men ransacking Clay's office. He released his partner and began a determined march toward the back door. Something about the way he moved denoted anger, and Clay knew he wasn't a friend of the two searchers inside the house. The slightly smaller figure appeared to make some hasty conclusions as well, and detoured toward the nearby woodpile, then raced after the first figure with two large chunks of firewood, one under each arm.

"That's Daddy!" Taylor recognized the figure that was almost to the back door and rose to her feet.

"And Betty Glendowski," Clay added in disbelief, staring after the large woman packing two lengths of firewood in Andrew Jordan's wake.

"We've got to help them!" Taylor stumbled from their hiding place. For a fraction of a second, Clay's sluggish mind wondered which pair needed his help and which needed his pity—the two miscreants inside the house or the formidable team of Betty and Andrew.

"Stay here," Clay warned Taylor, but she ignored his warning. Trying to stop her would be useless. He'd have to get there first. Welcoming the adrenalin surge that wiped away the lingering grogginess in his mind, he charged across the lawn.

"Whither thou goest, I will go," the old scripture repeated itself in Taylor's head and in a strange way comforted her. Her heart had known long before her head that she was ready to follow Clay anywhere.

"We're in this together," she told his back and stumbled after him toward the house. Even as she worried for their safety, she felt a surge of pride. Clay was the man she wanted to be her partner forever, and when this was over, she was going to tell him so!

As her father flung open the back door, the first sound that reached Taylor's ears was the enraged howl of a cat, and she watched in awe as Tom flung himself from the top of Rambo's abandoned cage toward Seth's head. Seth screamed and beat ineffectually at the cat as Daddy and Betty exploded into the room, swinging their chunks of firewood and yelling like warriors from the Middle Ages. A shot sounded in the night, and both she and Clay picked up speed. While she ran, Taylor prayed neither Daddy nor Betty had been hit.

Reaching the door, Clay grasped both sides of the door frame to steady himself. She ducked beneath his braced arms and stared in confusion. Seth sat in the chair behind the desk, cowering in fright from the large woman threatening him with a length of stove wood. A trickle of blood seeped from a long scratch on the side of his head. He looked terrified.

Daddy sat astride the prone, sobbing body of Ben Winslow. He held aloft a small log in a threatening gesture. Taylor had no idea when her father had acquired his weapon, but she was glad he had. A film of plaster dust covered everyone and everything from the hole in the ceiling left by a bullet gone wildly astray. To Taylor's surprise, her dad was smiling. He seemed to be enjoying himself! This was certainly a side of her sedate father she'd never imagined.

Clay leaned over to pick up the small gun that had dropped from one of the brothers' hands, emptied it, and set it on his desk out of reach of the two men, then he picked up the telephone. He nodded his head at something the dispatcher said before announcing to everyone in the room that Deputy Donaldson was already en route to the house and that other officers would arrive shortly.

CHAPTER 23

Well, this had certainly been a night of surprises, Taylor thought as she let the hot water beat against her tired body. It hadn't taken Rick Donaldson long to take charge of the two prisoners and hustle them away in his car. Corralling two New York jewel thieves had the deputy practically bursting the seams of his shirt with pride. The door had barely closed behind them when Stewart stood up to Taylor's father and announced that he was marrying Lilly, and they weren't wasting any more time. The wedding would be next week! Taylor had hugged her grandmother and turned to take her part against her father when, to her surprise, Daddy had placed an arm around Betty and informed them that he might soon have an announcement to make, too.

Taylor couldn't stop the laughter that bubbled to the surface. Stewart was already her grandfather as far as she was concerned; their wedding would only make it official. Until she'd heard his voice beyond the thick door holding her prisoner earlier tonight, she hadn't realized how deeply he'd entrenched himself in her heart. Grandma would be foolish not to marry him. But Betty and her father? Somehow she couldn't see the older girl as her stepmother.

Letting the water sluice through her thick hair, she luxuriated in just being alive, in being able to breathe and think. She'd been prepared to stand up to her father on her grandmother's behalf and to assert her right to live her own life, but her father had surprised her by muttering something about getting his deposit back on the apartment and that Senator Maxwell had called to ask if she would be interested in managing his home office in Boise. He sounded almost anxious to get his mother and daughter off his hands!

Her thoughts returned to Betty Glendowski and again she chuckled. She might not see Betty as stepmother material, but she had a hunch the girl would be good for her father. It just might be that what he needed was someone he didn't feel he had to protect. She'd probably cure him of being so bossy and controlling; on the other hand, his authoritative style might make Betty more feminine and demure. At any rate, they'd certainly proved they made a great team tonight. Their success in subduing Jessica's cousins might also help Daddy overcome the insecurity Grandma Lilly said plagued him. And wouldn't it be funny if Taylor wound up finally getting the brothers and sisters she'd always wanted?

A touch of melancholy replaced the laughter as she thought of the young siblings she might one day have. Would she have children someday the same ages to play with their "aunts" and "uncles?" She'd never wanted children before, but since she'd held the Friedrickson girls in her arms and carried them to safety, she'd found herself longing to once again feel a small warm body in her arms. She'd been unable to forget the imagined child she'd struggled to protect as her own life had nearly ended in the swirling water. That child had seemed so real, and she'd found herself wondering if the experience had occurred to remind her to fight for her life because her child couldn't live if she didn't. Feeling her own mother beside her that day had brought a return of memories that had somehow helped to wipe away her reluctance to become a mother herself.

She knew Clay wanted marriage, children, and all of the trappings, but what did she want? Since early in her teens she'd dreamed of a prestigious job, independence, and an apartment in a tall, modern skyscraper. Now that dream felt cold and lonely. She'd made up her mind as they'd charged toward the house earlier to tell Clay of her feelings if they survived the confrontation, but as soon as Deputy Donaldson drove away with the Winslow brothers, Clay had reached for the telephone to call Jessica. He'd still been talking to her when Taylor had climbed the stairs seeking a hot shower and her bed. She'd finally faced her feelings for him, but could it be that it was already too late?

Shivering, she turned off the water and reached for a towel before dressing in thick flannel pajamas. She brushed her teeth and considered blowing her hair dry, then remembered her blower was in her room and wrapped a second towel around her hair. Covering her pajamas with her terry bathrobe, she fastened the belt, opened the door, and walked into Clay.

"Save any hot water for me?" he drawled as he steadied her with a hand on each of her shoulders. She flushed guiltily and he grinned as though he knew the answer to his question.

"I'm sorry," she managed to say. "I took both towels, too, but I'll get you another one." She attempted to move toward the linen closet, but he stopped her.

"Since I have to wait for the hot water to replenish itself anyway, perhaps we could talk," he suggested.

"Okay," she agreed hesitantly, suddenly conscious that she was wearing a ratty old bathrobe over flannel pajamas and a long curl of wet hair was escaping from beneath the towel she wore like a turban on her head. And she was barefoot. At least she'd left off the freckle cream this time!

Clay led her to the stairs and tugged her down beside him on the top step. He laced the fingers of her right hand through his fingers and appeared to be absorbed in the contrast their two hands made for several long minutes.

"I talked to Jessica," he finally spoke and Taylor felt a heavy sadness. He was going to tell her the two had made up and he still planned to marry the other woman!

"I was right in thinking she had lied to me," he went on. "She hadn't told me everything about her grandfather's will either, it seems. Though Mr. Winslow had originally intended to give all four of the stones to her, he changed his mind when we broke our engagement. He added a codicil to his will, leaving one stone to each of his four grand-children. When Seth and Ben demanded theirs, Jacob removed them from the company safe and took them to Jessica's apartment. He spread them on a piece of black velvet on a table in Jessica's living room, and the four of them examined the stones. Later, over dinner in another room, they discussed who would take possession of each of the stones.

"Rambo was alone in the room with the diamonds for almost an hour. When the four cousins returned to each claim a diamond, the stones were gone. Jessica's apartment was on the sixteenth floor, and all four of them had been where they could clearly see the door leading to the hall the whole time. No one had entered or left the apartment, but the diamonds were gone. It was almost a month later when Ben read something about someone finding a ruby inside a turkey's crop at a poultry processing plant. That was when he and Seth broke into Jessica's apartment looking for Rambo and found a shipping receipt and my address instead."

"But how did the diamonds disappear?" Taylor wondered aloud.

"They didn't." Clay's voice conveyed a wealth of disgust. "Jessica guessed at once that Rambo had seen the stones and when she couldn't crush them, the cockatoo dropped them in her water dish. Jessica knew Rambo had attempted to hide glittering trinkets there before. They were in plain sight the whole time and Jessica knew it. After her cousins and the police left, she recovered the diamonds and hid them in her safety deposit box at her bank."

"I'm sorry, Clay," Taylor whispered, imagining how much it must hurt him to know his fiancée's lie had caused so much trouble.

"You don't need to apologize," Clay answered a little sharply. "You're not the one who needs to say you're sorry. Jessica and her vicious, harebrained cousins owe you and everyone else an apology, but it's not likely you'll ever receive it. How I could have ever been so stupid as to think I loved that greedy, conniving woman is beyond me!" His statement was all the apology Taylor needed. Her heart began to beat faster and she felt the corners of her mouth turn up.

"That's okay. It didn't all turn out badly." She snuggled closer to the man beside her. "Stewart and Grandma are getting married, and it looks like Daddy is going to be so busy trying to keep up with Betty, he won't have time to run either of our lives."

"You're okay with that?" Clay asked with real concern in his voice.

"You bet I am," she answered cheerfully. "By the way, where is everyone?"

"Stewart was concerned that the night's excitement might have tired Lilly, so he insisted she go to bed. He promised he'll be back tomorrow to help her straighten up and start planning their wedding. Andrew took Betty home, and since he's not back yet, I assume they decided to take the scenic route," Clay answered.

"Oh, and what do you suppose the scenic route might be?" Taylor bent her head in an attempt to peep up at him a bit provocatively.

"I think it goes a little like this," Clay whispered as he brought his other arm around her and bent to kiss her. When he pulled back to catch his breath, she tightened her arms around his neck and whispered, "And this?" before she kissed him again.

"Oh, yes, definitely that," he whispered back several minutes later.

She smiled, and words tumbled from her mouth without any preamble, "Will you marry me?"

He froze, and a look somewhere between shock and delight covered his face. "I thought you didn't believe in marriage," he finally gasped.

"I've changed my mind about a lot of things," she said, feeling suddenly shy. "I've discovered love matters more than anything else and that I love you."

"I love you, too, Taylor Jordan." His lips brushed the top of her hair, and she realized her towel turban had come undone.

"Is that a yes, then?" She turned eyes full of love toward him.

"A very definite yes." He kissed her eyelids and hugged her to him. "I'll sell my practice and go anywhere you want."

"No!" Her eyes popped open. "I don't want you to give up your practice. It's your dream."

"You're my dream," he told her. "With you as my eternal companion, I can be happy anywhere you are."

"That goes two ways, Clay," she pointed out. "I like the bustle and excitement of a big city, but this summer has reminded me I also like the quiet murmur of a mountain stream, star-filled nights, and feeling surrounded by caring friends. I'm fascinated by the complexities of running a business, but in today's world I can do that from anywhere. I can run Senator Maxwell's next campaign from right here and commute to Boise as needed, and there's a rumor going around that a certain up-and-coming veterinarian is going to need a new office manager."

"The job is yours, honey." Clay breathed the words, before covering her mouth with his own to seal the deal.

About the Author

Jennie Hansen attended Ricks College and graduated from Westminster College in Salt Lake City, Utah. She has been a newspaper reporter, editor, and librarian, and has worked for the Salt Lake City library system for nearly twenty years.

Her church service has included teaching in all auxiliaries and serving in stake and ward Primary presidencies. She has also served as a den mother, stake public affairs coordinator, ward chorister, education counselor in her ward Relief Society, and teacher improvement coordinator.

Jennie and her husband, Boyd, live in Salt Lake County. All five of their children and their spouses live nearby, which means that she gets to see her six grandchildren often.

Beyond Summer Dreams is Jennie's tenth book for the LDS market.

Jennie enjoys hearing from her readers, who can write to her in care of Covenant Communications, P.O. Box 416, American Fork, UT 84003-0416 or e-mail her at jhansen22@qwest.net.

An excerpt from the romance novel

The HEART Only KNOWS

Andi Reynolds didn't believe in harbingers, omens, or foreboding. It was difficult, then, for her to explain the flutter of her heart and sudden clamminess of her palms as she gazed up at the solitary crow perched in the rotted pine.

One crow for sorrow, two crows for joy . . .

Despite herself, Andi gripped her book as she glanced around. These woods were full of crows; there must be another one somewhere in sight. She knew from working at a zoo that crows are sociable creatures. It was only reasonable to suppose that this one was part of a flock.

Murder, she reminded herself. *A company of crows is called a murder.*

Her emerald eyes scanned the wide Arizona sky above the Mogollion Rim, but there was only the one crow to be seen. *One crow for sorrow.* Andi's heart went from a flutter to a steady thump, and her breath came a little faster. At the bird's sudden, raucous cry, she pressed the book to her chest, then closed her eyes and drew a deliberate, calming breath. This was ridiculous. She wasn't afraid of a *crow,* for heaven sakes.

Let my heart be still a moment and this mystery explore.

A dimple winked into Andi's cheek as she opened her eyes and smiled, remembering. Last night her brother had held a flashlight under his chin and recited "The Raven" for his part in the family reunion talent show. Apparently, pieces of Poe's classic were still caught in her subconscious, but that was just silly. It was almost noon on a bright and beautiful day in early September, not "once upon a midnight dreary," and she had to stop all this "wondering, fearing, doubting, dreaming."

Well, she thought as her dimples deepened, *perhaps not the dreaming.* All the dreaming she had done of late was of her fiancé, Greg Howland, and their still-too-distant wedding day. She pulled a cell phone from the pocket of her jeans to consult the time. Greg should be calling any minute now, which was why she had left the campground—to have a measure of privacy when he called to tell her about his visit to the District Attorney's office in Mesa.

A sudden realization came tapping at the door of Andi's conscious mind. While all the lovely wondering and dreaming she had done lately was of Greg, all the odd doubting and fearing of the last few days was for him as well. It wasn't foreboding she felt now as much as it was certainty of things unseen: Greg was in trouble. She knew it. She had known it for some time in fact—despite his denials—but she hadn't known the cure for his cares and could only guess at the cause.

But in an hour or so, she thought, as she continued to scan the sky for the black birds, she would finally see him again and hold him close and know that he was safe—if only for the moment—in her arms. But the sky was empty and the nagging fear returned. Shouldn't he have finished with the District Attorney by now? Greg had said he would call to tell her when he was on the way. Where was he?

One crow for sorrow, she recited, looking up at the majestic, ebony bird, *but only because one is such a lonely number.* Checking her phone to make certain it was on and that she was still within the cell area, Andi slipped it back into her pocket. The crow cawed out mournfully.

"Keep calling," she counseled it softly. "Your love will come."

Nevermore.

Andi frowned, then tried to shake off this final flight of her fancy by reminding herself that Poe had placed his raven on a bust of Pallas, the Greek goddess of wisdom, to show the folly of allowing superstition to overcome reason.

Thank goodness I've always been a reasonable sort of person, she thought as she turned away from the withered pine toward a more verdant part of the forest. *And thank goodness I'm studying Shakespeare this semester instead of Poe.*

She dropped the thin volume of *Romeo and Juliet* onto the soft carpet of pine needles and removed the phone from her pocket before sitting down. *If Romeo and Juliet had each had a cell phone,* she thought, *their romance would have turned out better.* She opened the book and turned to the part of the play where she'd left off earlier. *True, Romeo might still have been exiled to Mantua, and Juliet might have had to stay behind on that balcony in Verona, but at least they could have talked about it.*

Certainly Andi couldn't imagine asking, "Wherefore art thou?" of Greg and receiving no response. And there was no telling on any given day wherefore art he *was*, although it was never, unfortunately, in the bushes below her window. Being engaged to a professional athlete was not without its drawbacks. For one, it meant that she saw Greg more often on television and in newspapers than she did in person. But she was fortunate, she knew, to live in a time when she could at least talk to him. Without a doubt, hearing her love's voice every day helped stave off the fatal combination of melancholy and miscommunication which had sent Juliet to the apothecary in the first place.

Andi opened her book and tried to concentrate on Juliet's concerns rather than her own but found her attention wandering back to Greg. What was taking him so long? She fingered her phone and watched a squirrel gathering piñon nuts. When the rodent paused with full cheeks and seemed to regard her quizzically, she held up the phone. "I'm expecting a call," she told it. "Cell phones are the greatest invention of the twentieth century."

"Absolutely," a voice agreed.

As a part-time keeper at the Phoenix Zoo, Andi was used to talking to animals—but not to hearing them respond.

"If it's a choice between antibiotics and cellular communication," the voice continued, "give me a telephone any day." Andi's cousin leaned around the wide trunk of a nearby tree, where she had apparently been sitting—no doubt communing with nature, Andi thought.

"Oh, hi, Zona," she said, doing her best to muster a weak smile. If she had made a list of people she hoped to avoid by leaving the campground, Zona May Reynolds would have been at the very top. Andi tried not to stare at her cousin's boysenberry-hued hair and quadruple-pierced ears, but the only alternative was to gape at her outlandish outfit. Who but Zona wore a Speedo tank top with Bermuda shorts and combat boots? She looked like she had tumbled out of one of Andi's little sister's books—the one where you turned the tri-cut pages tomake a picture of something comic—in this case, a mermaid/tourist/fireman. Andi regretted the involuntary note of dismay in her voice as she asked, "What are you doing all the way out here?"

Zona lifted her own wonder of modern technology—a 35mm camera. "Photographing the wildlife," she said, "before somebody captures it all to put in zoos." Her crazily plucked brows rose in challenge.

If Andi had learned anything in the last day and a half of the reunion, it was that Zona May was not only anti-zoo, she was anti-Church and anti-everything-else right now. Unless you were prepared for a debate you couldn't win, it was prudent to defer to her on relatively minor issues like animal rights, and to avoid major issues like women and the priesthood at all costs. "Well, I came out to talk to—"

"The squirrels?" Zona interrupted.

"No," Andi said. "To Greg."

"Oh, right," Zona said. "The Jock. AKA Poster Boy for the Decline of Western Civilization." She got to her feet, making no effort to brush the forest floor from her baggy shorts before reaching for her camera bag. "I predict you'll get more intelligent responses from the squirrels."

Andi's eyes flashed, but Zona's departure and the digital melody of the phone saved her the necessity of a retort. She tossed her mane of auburn curls over her shoulder and pressed the button to turn on the phone. "Greg!" she said without waiting for a confirmation. "Where are you?"

"Just leaving town," he responded. His voice was deep and quiet and unbelievably dear. Andi's fingers curled around the phone as he added, "The deposition took a little longer than I expected."

"What did they say?" she asked. "Do they have enough on Zeke to convict him?" Greg's former publicist, Zeke Martoni, had attempted to blackmail the ballplayer, using his relationship with Greg's older brother to gain information for gambling on the World Series. Jim Howland had been ill, and Zeke had not only taken advantage of him, he soon had Jim addicted to drugs that dulled both his senses and his pain. Now Jim was dead, and Zeke had been indicted for extortion. Knowing this, Andi was even more concerned by Greg's reticence. She gripped the phone tighter. "Greg?"

He cleared his throat. "The DA said my testimony ought to guarantee Zeke fifty years behind bars."

Andi listened for elation—or at least satisfaction—in his voice, but it wasn't there. Instead, he sounded weary, and she prayed for words of encouragement. "Martoni will be almost a hundred years old if he gets out," she said finally. "At least we can be pleased about that."

"I guess fifty years in prison is going to have to do," Greg said. "At least until a better punishment can be arranged for eternity."

"Eternity?" Andi repeated as she looked up at the tips of the gently swaying trees. "Isn't that how long it's been since I've seen you?" As top pitcher for the Arizona Diamondbacks, Greg had been on the road with them for more than a week, but to Andi it had seemed more like a lifetime. "I've missed you," she whispered, surprised and pleased to find that her worries about Martoni were quickly overshadowed by the dappled sunshine on her face and the joy of knowing she and Greg would be together soon. "When will you be here?"

"About an hour and a half," he guessed. "Better tell the Board of Inquiry to assemble."

She smiled up into the sky—a sky as deep and blue as Greg's incredible eyes. "My family will love you as much as I do," she promised.

"Uh, huh," he said. "Tell me that one again. It's my favorite fairy tale."

He wasn't as serious now, Andi thought in relief. *Probably.* She could almost see his lopsided grin when he added, "I'll tell it to you then. Once upon a time there was a beautiful princess who lived in a tall ivory tower. Everybody in her kingdom was a scholar or an attorney or a physicist." He paused when she giggled then concluded ruefully, "And they all prayed each and every day for a hick ballplayer to come along to dumb down their bloodlines and—"

"You're the smartest man I know," Andi interrupted.

"Smart enough to marry you." His voice was rich and low and full of longing.

Andi was about to remind him that fairy tales always ended in "happily ever after" when the crow above her spread its blue-black wings and sailed from its perch on the pine to a fallen log not eight feet from Andi's knees. There it sat perfectly still, seeming to read her mind with its knowing yellow eyes. The blissful words she might have said died on her lips, and goosebumps rose on her bare arms.

'Tis the wind and nothing more.

"Hurry, Greg," she whispered.

"Andi? Is something wrong?"

"No," she said and the crow cocked its feathered head.

One crow for sorrow.

"Hurry and finish the story, Greg," she urged.

"Huh?"

"The fairy tale." Her voice sounded strained even to her ears, and she tried to lighten it by teasing. "Don't you know how to end a fairy tale?"

"You mean 'and they lived happily ever after'?"

"Yes," she said. Andi turned her back to the bird. "Promise me that we'll live happily ever after." She longed to be held in Greg's strong arms, but for now she would settle for just a note of reassurance in his voice. "Greg?" But there was only silence.

Slowly she removed the now quiet phone from her ear. He must have entered the first of the many canyons between Phoenix and the Rim. Their connection had been lost.